Coronado Beach

Coronado Beach

A Flower Fields Novel

Andrea Hershey

Published by
Artesian Well Publishing
www.ArtWellPub.com

Learn more about Andrea's books at AndreaHershey.com

This book is a work of fiction. All names, characters, locations, and incidents are the products of the author's imagination or are used fictitiously. Any resemblance to actual events, locales, organizations, or persons, living or dead, is entirely coincidental.

Published in the United States of America
First edition, May 2016

Table of Contents

1 Back to December

2008

TARA FIELDS SLEEPWALKED INTO THE KITCHEN AND started the coffee, although the darkness persisted. Her lambskin slippers padded noiselessly on the stone floor. The best thing about this time of day was the silence.

The dim light over the sink reflected off the granite countertop, warm tones of tan, black, and garnet. The mineral textures of the shimmering stone were as beautiful as any work of art. Absently, she eyed the shadows painting the walls. When she was a little girl, she had imagined they were pixies to protect her. The memory was bittersweet.

She closed her eyes against a now-throbbing headache. No point going back to bed. Experience had taught that sleep wouldn't come. The voices in her mind demanded attention.

Pulling her terrycloth robe tight, she got the newspaper from the front porch. The air was cool and pleasant, a typical southern California morning. No light streaked the horizon, just the streetlamps of an urban neighborhood that felt like a small town. Tara welcomed the black night that enveloped her like a blanket.

She knelt and picked up *The Observer*. She couldn't look at the headlines, not yet. The thought of writing the hard news stories had filled her with dread after she *became* one. But she wouldn't let fear stop her from analyzing every word.

Back in the kitchen, the aroma of coffee nudged up her spirits. She dropped the paper on the table in the breakfast nook and poured a tall mug, smoothing the bitterness with milk. She sipped, and warmth permeated her. A semblance of life seeped into her limbs, driving away the dull ache.

A helpless sigh escaped her lips. She missed the painkillers. While she was on opiates, she had fallen asleep the instant her eyes closed. Or at least went to a soothing place that felt like sleep, where the demons quieted for a while. But she'd stopped because Alex said the drugs messed with her head.

Alex. The pain writhed like a snake in her gut. She wouldn't give in. She had made the choice her sanity demanded.

Alex couldn't be part of her life anymore.

Karina Fields balanced on spiked heels as she glided down the back stairs to the kitchen of the house she shared with her sister. Yellow light spilled in through the windows. Tara was in the breakfast nook as expected, kneeling on a chair with the newspaper spread out on the table, neon green Post-It notes dotting the articles. That was her morning routine: scout the paper for ideas for her column.

But it hadn't been a routine morning. Tara's footsteps in the hallway had sounded way too early.

"Anything interesting?"

Tara greeted her with a soft smile, then smoothed her golden-brown hair. "Some economist says the housing market is contracting, and we're headed for a recession."

Karina shrugged. "People don't get their name in the paper by spreading *good* news."

"That doesn't make it less true."

"But it makes life more depressing."

Tara eyed her, lips pursed. "Kare, that suit looks great on you, but peach is not a power color."

She looked down at the narrow-waisted jacket and pleated skirt. The way the suit shaped to her curves was hellasexy. It might not scream kick-ass lawyer, but the color complemented her strawberry-blond hair. "I don't have to be in court today."

"Pastels say you're not serious. Is that what you want your colleagues at the public defender's office to think?"

"I've been there less than a year, and I've already gotten a promotion and a walled office."

"If you ask me," Tara teased, "they only gave you a walled office because you talk so much that you drive people in the cubes crazy."

"Well, I didn't ask you," she shot back, though she'd sometimes wondered the same thing.

She poured coffee and got out the skim milk, then sat at the table and took her sister's hand. "How'd you sleep last night?"

"I'm fine." Tara straightened. "You don't have to worry about me."

"You know, if you had epilepsy, you wouldn't think you could control your seizures without drugs. Insomnia is a medical condition."

"I don't have insomnia. I've just had trouble sleeping for a couple of weeks."

Karina sipped her coffee, the hint of cinnamon awakening her senses. "What triggered it? What happened a couple of weeks ago?"

Tara's eyes widened, then shuttered. "Nothing."

"Mm-hmm." Karina knew better than to push, but she couldn't simply let it go. "Just because I love to talk, that doesn't mean I don't know how to listen."

Tara sidled her chair over and rested her head on her sister's shoulder. Karina wrapped her arms around her and kissed her forehead. She'd always admired Tara's strength and self-reliance. Combing her fingers through Tara's straight, soft hair, the weight of her sister's grief reached in and squeezed her heart. She wished that just this once, Tara would find the strength to ask for help.

2 Blue on Black

ALEX KENT STRODE TOWARD THE PUBLIC DEFENDER'S
office of San Diego County to reclaim his life.
His Italian shoes hit the sidewalk like the boots
of a Prussian soldier. This final interview was a
formality—none of his competitors had a U.S. senator on
speed-dial. His credentials might get him an offer on the
spot.

They had to. This job was his ticket home.

His fingers brushed his silk tie, laying it flat. The
morning sunlight glinted off his gold band. He had let
Tara go, hoping she would find her way back once the
edges of grief had smoothed. Impossible while he
worked for a law firm in DC. Returning to California was
his Hail Mary, his last chance with the only woman who
made him feel like a good man.

The memories hit him like sleet on bare skin,
penetrating the walls of his chest and trickling into the
hollows of his belly. This wasn't the time for

distractions. Down, down, down he pushed the ache that had become his most faithful companion.

He entered the building and scanned the once-familiar surroundings. The lobby's tall curving archways and gold leaf seemed out of place in an office building that served the indigent.

But then, so did his Gucci briefcase.

He bit back a grin. In Washington, his wealth was a tool to intimidate people. That wouldn't do here, at least not after the interview. Too much flash would turn off a jury.

The elevator chimed his floor, and he headed down the dim hallway. With a compulsive glance at his watch, he rounded the final corner. A gasp caught his ear. Stopping short, he barely avoided colliding with Karina.

She teetered on leopard-print pumps, and he grabbed her with a steadying arm. Meeting his eyes, she paled and jerked away. The tight pull of her lips warned she hadn't forgiven him. She tilted her head to one side. "Is that you, Voldemort? I thought J. K. Rowling killed you."

Apparently, a year's absence hadn't improved Karina's opinion of him. Her resemblance to his ex-wife reawakened the biting pain in his gut. The heart-shaped face and high cheekbones were traits the sisters shared. But where Tara's eyes were almond shaped, Karina's were wide, giving her an innocent look—one she played to her advantage. Right now, her eyes danced.

He reined back the urge to hug her. "It's good to see you, Kare."

A sharp laugh escaped before dying in her chest. She straightened her nutmeg hair, worn tucked behind her ears as if she were always listening. "Are you lost?"

"I've got a job interview."

"You must be on the wrong floor. Brennan and Yost are on sixteen."

"The interview is at the P.D.'s office."

Beneath her raised brows, her eyes surveyed him. He didn't mind. He knew he looked good.

"Shall I call a doctor?" she teased. "Did you hit your head?"

"Seriously, Kare, I've got an interview in five minutes, and you're making me late."

She poked a forefinger into the lapel of his Armani suit. "*You* want to be a public defender."

"Why not?"

Her lips quirked into a smile. "You wouldn't be happy here. This job requires humility and compassion."

She was the same Karina, a kitten eager for play. But he didn't have time to get into it with her. He continued down the hall.

She called after him, the pitch of her voice rising, "This is a joke, right?"

Ignoring her, he pushed open the glass door to the office area. Stares of former adversaries didn't slow his pace. The clacking of the copy machine and the smell of coffee filled the air. Through the windows, a distant sliver of the bay glistened in the sunlight. *Home.*

Karina stared into the empty hallway, a white haze crowding her brain. Her family had barely recovered from the trauma of the shooting and the divorce—now, after a year of silence, Alex was back in San Diego?

He could only have one motive: Tara. Karina had to stop him. He didn't deserve Tara—not after skipping town instead of fighting for their marriage.

She headed to her cramped office, shutting the door and flopping into the chair. Her thoughts churned. A Beanie Baby perching on the desk stared at her, a penguin with a silly face. She picked it up and squeezed its midsection until its neck threatened to burst.

It was bad enough her only two felony cases would go to the new hire. She deserved those cases—had proven she could handle them. But turning them over to Alex? Having to work with him on a daily basis?

Plunking the penguin back down in the corner, she scanned the family photographs on top of her desk. Alex was in none of them, eradicated after he bailed. She massaged her neck until the muscles softened.

Her gaze rested on a picture taken at her law school graduation. She picked up the photo. Dressed in a black cap and gown, her purple collar edged in red, she stood flanked by her sisters, a giddy smile lighting her face.

Tara beamed in a halter dress with diamond cutouts at the waist. Lauren, the oldest, slightly taller, wore a navy suit and a sphinx-like grin, her dark hair long and straight. With their arms intertwined, the three sisters pressed together in front of a broad sandstone column and a waving palmetto.

Karina had been full of dreams that day—for herself, starting a career, and for Alex and Tara, starting a family. But the upheaval of the next year had buried her hope and shaken her foundation.

She set down the photo. *Stay focused.* Otherwise Alex would prey on her emotions.

He had never been Karina's favorite person. His sharp gaze and rigid posture oozed arrogance and cynicism. Yet his love for Tara had filled the room whenever they were together. When Tara married him, Karina accepted him into the family.

But family was supposed to last forever.

Karina grabbed the phone. It was almost lunchtime, so her sister Lauren, a sociology professor, was between classes. Lauren would know what to do.

Karina explained the situation, and Lauren said, "I don't understand the problem. Aren't there a hundred people at that location? You'll never see Alex."

"The job opening is on my team—his office will be next to mine." Tension wound through her gut. "He built a national reputation defending Senator Hartley. Why would a man with *that* on his resume want to work at the P.D.'s office?"

"To piss you off?"

Typical Lauren. They were in the middle of a family crisis, and she was flippant. Karina said, "Alex is only moving home to San Diego because he wants Tara back."

"She's seeing Perry now."

Karina cringed. "Ew."

"Perry's a nice guy."

"He's not her type."

"But Alex was exactly her type," Lauren said. "Nice is what she needs."

Karina flicked a paperclip across the room. Perry was personality *minus*, while Alex, with his self-possession and startling looks, changed the chemistry of every room he entered. How could Perry help Tara forget a man like that?

"We have to let her make her own choices." Lauren emphasized each syllable. "Even if we don't agree with them."

"She's grieving—she's not capable of making good choices."

"Try convincing her of that."

Heat shot through Karina like a starburst. "Why aren't you more upset about this?"

"Because I have a life?"

Karina jumped out of her chair, blood pulsing. Of course she had no life. Since the shooting, she'd been too busy taking care of Tara to go on a date.

"I don't mean to be dismissive," Lauren said in a soothing tone. "We can be her safety net, but we can't stop her from falling."

"So I should let Alex break her heart again?"

"If her heart is broken over Alex, it's because *she* broke it. As much as you and I love her, this is not our problem to fix."

"She can't handle any more stress right now."

Lauren's sigh was audible through the phone. "You called for my advice, so here goes. You're riding your high horse at a full gallop. Time to dismount, walk it to the stable, and let it chew on a bucket of oats for a while."

Karina strummed the pages of a legal pad with her thumb. "Is that a metaphor for minding my own business?"

"It's a metaphor for gaining perspective," Lauren said with a hint of a smile in her voice. "Look, you'll keep obsessing until you talk to Tara. It's your lunch hour, right? Go to the newspaper. Tell her Alex is back. See how she reacts."

Hmm. Maybe Lauren had a point.

Karina ended the call, then rubbed her temples to fight the beginnings of a headache. A hint of orange-ginger perfume rose from her wrists. The last thing she wanted was to meddle in Tara's relationship with her ex.

Yet Tara deserved to know he was in San Diego, and to hear it from someone who would break the news gently.

Karina walked the few blocks to *The Observer*. Tall buildings in an eclectic mix of glass, stucco, and gray brick gleamed in the sunlight that drenched the city streets. Sparrows flitted through the redbud trees, branches alive with pink blooms.

She entered the revolving doors of the newspaper building and headed up the open staircase. She peered into her sister's office. Tara sat typing intently, her hair brushed over one shoulder. The room was small, with books arranged on their shelves and the blinds open to let in the light. The desk was empty except for a MacBook and a set of *Wizard of Oz* figurines.

Karina tapped her fingernails against the open door. Tara looked up from the computer.

"Working through lunch again?" Karina asked.

"Blame it on my Muse."

Karina entered and closed the door. Tara wore a sweet smile, her body still. She seemed calm—content, even. Yet since the shooting, Tara's feelings had buried themselves so deeply, she was impossible to read.

Karina hesitated, bracing for her sister's reaction. "Guess who's back in town?"

Tara arched her brows. "Alex?"

Karina stiffened, unsure whether to feel relief or disappointment. "You *know?*"

"He called a few weeks ago."

The earth seemed to stop in its orbit while Karina's brain caught up. No wonder Tara wasn't sleeping. "And you didn't *say* anything?"

"It wasn't a sure thing." Tara shrugged. "Besides, I only wanted to divorce the man, not run him out of town. San Diego's his home—his family's here."

"You don't think he came back for that Arctic queen of a mother."

Tara scowled, a shadow crossing her features.

Bees buzzed in Karina's stomach. She wanted to commiserate with her sister, not upset her. "Too harsh?"

"You don't understand Holly. She grew up in an old Boston family where the only standards that mattered were good breeding and an Ivy League education. It's hard for her to open up to people."

"She's a fake."

"She's a philanthropist."

"She can afford to be," Karina said. Alex's mother seemed disingenuous, hiding her true feelings behind her wealth. No wonder Alex was emotionally defective. Yet badmouthing him and his family wouldn't help Karina's cause. The key was to keep Tara focused on the future instead of looking back. It was the only way she could heal.

Karina's glance fell to the grouping of photos atop her sister's credenza. Tara hadn't been as scrupulous in removing Alex from the mix. There he stood with his incisive gaze and uneven smile. Karina closed her eyes to stave off the memories. She couldn't understand why her sister welcomed them.

Tara rose. "He was my husband, Kare. Despite how things ended, I'm not sorry I married him."

Karina fought the rage swirling in her gut. Of course Tara wasn't sorry. Deep in denial, she hadn't felt anything since filing for divorce. She'd turned off her emotions—and Alex had let her.

He came from one of the most powerful families in the city. Yet, instead of contesting the divorce, he got on a plane—leaving Karina to glue together the broken pieces of Tara's life.

A cleansing breath helped her shake off the sense of injustice and despair. She couldn't risk upsetting Tara and shattering the exoskeleton of calm that protected her. Why could no one else in their family see how brittle she was?

Karina picked up a picture of the family taken two Christmases earlier, Tara wearing a green maternity dress, Alex beaming with his cheek pressed to hers. Karina winced at the joyful ignorance in their eyes. She wanted to jump inside the photo and warn them of what was to come, so they could stop it. So she could get her happy family back.

Tara pushed the door closed behind her sister. A deep breath slowed the thrumming in her veins. *Alex is home.*

For months, she'd worried about him living so far away. When the job in Washington first came up, she hated the idea of him leaving his family and friends behind while grieving. But he seemed so upbeat, she didn't stand in his way. Too late, she realized it was a ruse—he wanted her to ask him to stay.

She should have asked him.

She rose and picked up the Christmas photo from the credenza. Her forefinger traced the lines of his face. A yearning washed over her, followed by searing pain. Her heart closed like a metal door clanking shut—the way it always did when thoughts of Alex disturbed her calm.

Setting down the photo, she walked to the window. Cars crawled through the city street below. Her life was good now. Working as a columnist instead of an investigative reporter gave her perspective, and Perry chased away the nightmares.

Perry had no expectations, made no demands. He didn't talk about tomorrow or next year. When she went to bed at night exhausted from keeping it together, from the simple act of breathing a dozen times a minute even though everything hurt, when she could barely get out of bed the next morning and do it all again, Perry was happy just to hold her, to love her, with his version of love. It was as much as she could handle.

Alex, with his adoration and his aching heart and his need for control—she couldn't endure that when it took all her energy just to function. She was empty, with nothing to give.

The weight of her memories dragged her toward the abyss, fingers bleeding, clawing on bare rock to hold on. Alex loomed, reminding her of the tragic mistake that had changed both their lives. That wild, haunted look in his eyes when she had wakened from the coma. He would never cast blame. But how could he not feel it?

They were soul mates, but together, they were toxic. She was Cathy to his Heathcliff. Staying with him would have destroyed them both.

But Washington was no place for him. His life would get easier in San Diego. He needed the ocean, the sunshine, to feel whole.

This doesn't affect you. They would maintain separate lives. She couldn't risk that blinding, all-encompassing love that stripped her of identity. She wanted Alex to be happy, that was all. With everything they'd been through, he deserved some peace.

⁓❦⁓

Alex peered into his mother's office at the Matthew Kent Foundation. Holly Carter-Kent sat at her desk, absorbed in paperwork. At the sound of his knock on the open door, her gaze turned toward him, and his heart lightened at her smile—though he would never admit missing her.

She rose and hugged him, her perfume the scent of Madonna lilies. They were her favorite flower, stems tall, petals soft white. She adjusted his collar. "You look pale, darling."

His neck tensed, but he pushed on with the façade, knowing she could see through it. "I don't live on the beach in Washington."

His glance rose to the painting on the wall behind her desk, an original Kandinsky. Its reds and oranges swirled against blues and purples like lava spilling into the ocean—the sole flash of color in an office decorated in a spare, sophisticated style.

He drew back and mirrored her upright posture. He told her about the interview.

"You got the job!" Her eyes brightened. "Not that I had any doubt. Which firm?"

"It's with the public defender's office."

Her head tilted, auburn hair flowing to one side.

He held steady under her mystified gaze. "They represent people who can't afford lawyers."

"I know what a public defender does." She pursed her apricot lips. "I don't understand why you want to do it."

"Because I don't feel useful defending billionaires accused of securities fraud."

Her eyes widened. "You'd rather defend rapists and murderers? Crack addicts, wife beaters, prostitutes?"

The fear in her voice clawed at his stomach, but she had raised him to think independently. Perhaps she had overshot her mark. In her crisp Boston accent, she pronounced, "Sometimes I think you're determined to make yourself unhappy."

"Like when I married Tara?"

His mother stiffened. "Not at all. You know I love Tara. But if you'd married someone who shared your background..."

"You mean like you and Father? The man couldn't be in a room with you without a drink in his hand."

Her lips parted. She turned from him and walked to the picture windows.

Alex sucked in his cheeks, unsure where his anger had come from. The difference between his background and Tara's hadn't led to the failure of their marriage. His mother was soothing his guilt, blaming the divorce on things outside his control. Despite giving everything inside him, he hadn't been the husband Tara needed to support her through the loss.

That was no excuse for taking out his anger on his mother, an easy target. Harsh words wouldn't drive her away. She loved him unconditionally, the way he had thought Tara would. "I'm sorry. That was cruel."

She stood facing the horizon. He walked up behind her. The ocean rippled through the top-story view. On the low bookshelves sat pots of fragrant white orchids, perfectly arranged—by her assistant, a young man who managed her physical world so she could focus on art projects and research grants.

Alex touched his mother's shoulder. Without looking at him, she asked in an even tone, "Why do the people I love feel at liberty to say cruel things to me?"

"You cultivate the illusion that nothing bothers you."

"Because I don't whine like...the people on that Jeffrey Springer show?"

"It's Jerry Springer."

She spun to face him. "I also cultivate the illusion I know little of such things." Her cunning half-smile turned to a frown. "The thought of you associating with that sort of people—uneducated, undignified, unwashed—it makes my skin crawl."

"I associated with them when I was a prosecutor."

"But you represented the state. Not John Q. Heroin Dealer."

"I appreciate your concern, Mother..."

She fingered her necklace. "You think I'm meddling."

"I have to follow my conscience."

Her brows arched. "Of course." Heels clicked on the stone floor as she crossed to the center of the room. "I hope you'll be happy."

He had given up thoughts of happiness the day the divorce was final. But helping the indigent instead of the entitled might make his life worthwhile again. It was a start.

3 I Knew You Were Trouble

MONDAY MORNING, KARINA GAZED AT A KITTEN crouching underneath a shiny black Mercedes in the parking garage at work. She was determined to save him, like the other strays she had rescued, whether he cooperated or not. It would only take a minute to feed him, even though it might make her late for work. Even though her boss had just lectured her on The Importance of Punctuality.

She was never late when it counted, like when she was due in court. But to a seasoned bureaucrat like Victoria, that didn't matter. Rules were rules.

To Karina, rules kept people from finding a better way.

Her hand meandered toward a zip-top sandwich bag in the pocket of her business suit. "It's okay, kitty. I brought you a snack."

Squatting and balancing on three-inch designer pumps, she tossed a handful of kibble toward the suspicious feline. He watched her, green eyes glowing against golden fur, then turned away with regal aplomb. Amazing a starving two-pound kitten could cop that much attitude.

She gripped the car's door handle to steady herself, then chucked the remaining cat food toward the kitten. She started to rise, but her foot slipped back and her stomach jumped. Her knee hit the concrete and sharp pain spread. Her cry echoed through the parking garage. The kitten scurried away.

Karina swore under her breath, not wanting to frighten the cat any more. Its life depended on her befriending it and getting it to a no-kill shelter before someone called Animal Control.

She stood and rubbed the sore spot on her knee. Her pantyhose were shredded, but a spare pair was tucked into her briefcase. Worse, her shoes were scuffed—or rather, Tara's shoes, borrowed without permission. Seven hundred dollar Dior. No way Karina could afford to pay her back for them on a public defender's salary. She squeezed her eyes shut, praying the mark would come out with toothpaste.

She brushed the grit from her hands and her suit. *What a mess.* Fortunately, she didn't have court duty. Everything would be fine as long as she managed to avoid her boss. If Victoria saw her looking disheveled like this, it wouldn't help Karina's image.

She walked gingerly toward the exit, her knee stiff. Outside the parking garage, light filtered through the trees and cast shadows on the sidewalk. Cars rumbled through the narrow city streets.

She set her briefcase on her desk. Slipping the spare pantyhose into her pocket, she went into the ladies' room and washed her hands. A stall door clacked open, and Victoria emerged. Karina's chest deflated.

Victoria grinned and turned on the water at the sink next to her. "What happened to you?"

"I was feeding a stray kitten in the parking garage—"

"Fields, you're wasting your time caring for strays. You rescue this one, and another will take its place." Victoria dried her hands. "I admire your big heart. It's important to judge which battles are worth fighting."

Karina bit her cheeks. Victoria meant to be kind, but Karina didn't need a mother.

Victoria looked into the mirror and smoothed her shoulder-length ash-blond hair. Nearing fifty, she was tall and slender with the complexion of a woman ten years younger. "Tell me about the Santos case. Everything okay there?"

"No more trouble since he missed that anger management class last month."

"Remember to give the files for that case to Alex this morning. You'll continue to assist, of course, but I want him taking the lead." She shook her head. "Santos could go either way. One more felony would be his third strike."

"He seems sincere about staying clean and finishing that metal-working program."

Victoria smirked. "They always seem sincere." She strolled out the door.

Karina tromped into a stall to change her pantyhose. Her face warmed and tears rimmed her eyes. She wouldn't give up on Miguel Santos, any more than on the kitten in the parking garage. Her law degree gave her the power to make a difference, and that's what she intended to do.

Back at her desk, Karina anticipated her workday without enthusiasm. Alex had been a closed chapter, but now, five days a week, he would impose on her life.

The last time she and Alex had worked together—*her* clerking for Judge Walenski, *him* serving as deputy D.A.—the bright spot of her days had been indulging in opportunities to harass him.

A smile crept over her face.

She peered into Alex's office and watched him arrange personal items on his desktop: his grandfather's antique clock, a leather-bound copy of Machiavelli's *Discourses*, a photo of himself and his parents on the campus of UC Berkeley.

A frontal assault wouldn't work against him. He would respond to aggression with aggression, and she couldn't beat him that way. An indirect route was a more viable choice.

Standing in his doorway, she stroked the base of her throat and gave him a smile. "Bet this place is a box compared to what you had in Washington."

"It's fine."

"Why the P.D.'s office? You could've had your pick of private firms."

He gave her a quick half-shrug. "My family has a history of public service."

"Seriously? You mean because your mother was on city council?" Not very persuasive. More was going on with him. She approached and sat on his desk. "I can't picture you as an advocate for the indigent. It doesn't suit you."

"Maybe you don't know me as well as you think."

She ignored his gleaming eyes and faint boyish smile, and stared instead at the bump on the bridge of his nose. "If you insist on working here, I *will* make your life miserable."

He hung a framed diploma on the wall. "I'd be disappointed if you didn't."

His mechanical clock ticked like a metronome. She had seen him wind it many times, even though he could have replaced it with a battery-operated one. The clock was a family heirloom, and probably worth money. Everything he owned was worth money.

"You can't get to Tara through me."

"You weren't a factor in my decision to take this job."

Karina's ears pounded. "I won't let you hurt her again. You abandoned her when she needed you."

"She divorced me."

"She was crazy with grief over the baby."

"And I wasn't?" He rooted through his desk, then slammed the drawer shut. "You're out of line, Karina—this isn't your business."

"You made it my business when you left your mess with Tara for me to clean up."

"She'd stopped listening to me. If I'd kept pushing her, I'd have pushed her away."

Warmth bloomed in Karina's chest. "You can't come back a year later and pick up where you left off."

"This isn't a conspiracy." The muscles in his jaw twitched. "Washington didn't work out—end of story."

He glared at her with gray-blue eyes that changed with his surroundings, from a sea reflecting a summer sky to somber clouds before a storm. The expression in them was haunted. But Alex had a plan—he always had a plan. She wouldn't rest until she figured out what it was.

At lunchtime Alex strolled down Third Avenue, passing the opera house. Wagner heroines had nothing on Karina when it came to the drama queen act. How had he ended up the villain in her narrative? Didn't matter—he knew how to handle her.

The tree canopy broke as he approached Broadway and moved from shadow into light. In this bustling downtown, the air was clean, the breeze cool off the ocean—nothing like the gloomy skies and diesel fumes of Washington.

He headed to the Hall of Justice, a modern pyramid with thick columns at the entrance rising three stories above the sidewalk. The blue and green windows of the massive stone structure glinted in the sunlight.

Inside, he sauntered up to the desk of the district attorney's assistant—a blonde in her mid-thirties, maybe. She would have been prettier with less makeup.

"Alex Kent for Dayne Emery." A surge of excitement shot through him at the prospect of seeing his best friend again. Even from three thousand miles away, Dayne had been there for Alex through the bleakest days of the divorce.

"Yes, Mr. Kent, he's expecting you." The assistant picked up the phone and announced him.

The door opened and Dayne filled the entrance, six-five and built like a prize fighter. He smiled, teeth gleaming against blue-black skin. "Loser!" he said to Alex in his fake combative way. They clapped each other on the back. "You come crawling back with your tail between your legs?"

"I'm back to kick your ass in the courtroom."

Dayne shook his head. "You, a public defender. Never thought I'd see the day."

The two friends strode toward the exit. Dayne grinned as the elevator doors closed behind them. "What happened to that law firm job—you sleep with a senior partner's wife?"

"I'm not that guy anymore." Alex didn't mind Dayne's joking, but heaviness gripped his chest. When he was in his twenties, his reputation as a womanizer had served as a shield. Women pursued him for his wealth, and sometimes he succumbed. Now, that reputation felt like a weight around his neck. The only woman who had ever loved him for himself was Tara.

Alex and Dayne stepped outside. Alex felt the warmth of the April sun on his shoulders, but it couldn't melt the winter in his heart.

They walked to a restaurant on Harbor Drive and sat at a table on the patio. Alex stared at the menu, not reading the words. Getting the job at the P.D.'s office was one hurdle crossed. But it was nothing more than a distraction to keep his mind off the monotony of grief his life had become.

"You made the right decision," Dayne said in a smooth bass, as if reading Alex's thoughts. "You've got friends here."

"Not in the P.D.'s office."

Dayne nodded, drumming his fingers on the tabletop. "While you were a prosecutor, you pissed off every public defender in San Diego County."

"It's a gift." As a deputy D.A., Alex had been a tough competitor. His goal was not to make friends with defense attorneys but to annihilate them.

The waitress brought their iced teas. The sway in her hips as she walked away stirred no feeling in him. Random pretty women didn't claim his interest anymore, as if that part of him had disconnected.

He turned back to Dayne. "How's the D.A.'s office?"

Dayne unrolled his napkin and set out his silverware. "Hectic, but I like being busy. I started the gang-violence task force I promised during the campaign. It's a long road, though. Boys growing up without fathers...it's destroying our society."

The word *father* pressed on Alex. The last time they had lunched on this terrace, Tara had shown off her baby bump to Dayne's wife, Chantel. The memory of the women's laughter wafted on the breeze.

"You okay?"

Alex cast his eyes over the bay toward the isthmus of Coronado. The haze of stucco houses and terra cotta roofs glowed in the sunlight that bounced off the blue water. The view excited a familiar longing, the feel of home. Yet now, home carried the memories of an empty nursery, a crib unslept in, a marriage unable to endure the strain. He had worked with enough victims of violent crime to know that recovery could be slow. But it seemed he was taking too long. "I want to feel normal again. To sleep without waking to the sound of gunfire in my head."

Dayne twisted his napkin. "Give it time."

Alex stared at the tabletop, a mosaic of yellow and green tiles. The passionate colors of San Diego, the curves of its Spanish architecture seeped into his system, crowding out the cold white marble and rigid columns of Washington. He leaned back, his excitement at moving home returning. Above him, the sky was an uninterrupted canvas of blue waiting to be painted.

At the courthouse, Karina sat at a wood veneer table under fluorescent lights, her foot tapping the linoleum. The public defender on duty, she waited while the accused were arraigned and the indigent ones assigned an attorney. Listening to the charges, she made up stories in her head, wondering what sequence of events had led these people to this place.

A slender man no more than twenty was led in, shackled and wearing a blue-black jumpsuit. His dreadlocks contrasted with the delicate features of his face. His head was high, his chin forward, saying *you can chain me but you can't take my dignity*. Charged with armed robbery—his second strike. A boy with no sense of his future, he was on the brink of losing it.

Karina jotted some notes, considering the social programs that could help him. In his dark, narrow eyes shone fire and light. Her heart would not accept that this striking young man could be beyond the reach of compassion.

The defendants passed in and out in quick succession. Judge Rodriguez allowed no time for untidy emotion. Karina knew that the judge had grown up on the same streets as some of these defendants. His courage to dream had made the difference. If she could instill dreams in her clients, maybe they could break out of the patterns that brought them here.

During her drive home, she tried not to think about it, but the young man with the dreadlocks would not leave her mind. His determination could raise him from his situation or drag him further down.

A prickling feeling built in her stomach. Had anyone tried to save the man who shot Tara when he was young enough to choose a better life? Had his character alone led him to the violence that had fractured her family?

His death at the hands of police had not been enough to quiet Karina's mind. The evil in him haunted her: the randomness of his crime, his disdain for human life. Though she knew such people existed, the world she saw blended into the harmonious world she envisioned. Her perceptions moved fluidly between them.

Tara heard Karina's Miata pull into their garage. She looked up from the stove when her sister entered through the kitchen door. The house they shared was a rambling Victorian: Karina had fallen in love with its carved wood, its hidden recesses, and its fairytale colors. For Tara, the attraction was the modern kitchen, with its six-burner gas stovetop and conveniences ranging from a bread warmer to a wine refrigerator. She had inherited her mother's love of cooking, and the kitchen was where she felt her mother's spirit most.

As Karina put away her handbag, Tara slowly stirred the sauce. She had started to call her sister three times that day but had thought better of it. Why should Tara care how things had gone with Alex? He wasn't part of her life anymore. Yet somehow, now that he was back in San Diego, his gravitational pull was stronger.

Forcing a casual tone, she asked, "How was work?"

Karina drew in her shoulders. "There's a stray cat hanging around the parking garage..."

"No more strays, Kare. You bring one home, I get attached, and six months later it dies of leukemia. I can't handle it, okay?"

"Okay." Karina sighed.

Tara rattled the wooden spoon in the saucepan. "So did you have a good day?"

"I haven't saved the world yet, if that's what you're asking."

"Maybe you should aim lower."

Karina checked her reflection in the toaster. "Being a lawyer is hard. I should become a fashion consultant."

"Dad wouldn't be happy about that."

"Neither would my creditors."

Tara tapped her foot, then tried one more time. "Did anything happen at work?"

Karina grinned. "Oh, you mean with Alex? We chatted this morning. I can't figure out his agenda. If he's not trying to ingratiate himself with me to win you back, then why take a job as a public defender?"

Tara knitted her brow. Alex was the most generous person she knew. Why *wouldn't* he take a job as a public defender? "He got tired of working someplace where money mattered more than justice."

Karina's lips parted. "Wait. You talked to him?"

"When he called from Washington." Tara's heart fluttered at the memory of his voice. "Not since he came back to San Diego."

Karina took a lime from the fruit basket and rolled it back and forth across the countertop. "Then maybe he isn't scheming to disrupt your life."

"Alex wouldn't do that to me." Tara tried to smile, but her chest tightened. He had promised to stay away and would honor that promise. "He saves his powers of manipulation for the courtroom."

"You hope."

"I *know*." But Tara didn't know anything anymore. Her certainty had left when Alex had.

Later that week, Alex sat at his desk preparing for court. As he read, he doodled in the margin of his legal pad, straight lines intersecting and building on one another.

A shadow crossed his desk, and he looked up. Karina stood in his doorway. As annoying as she could be, he admired her persistence.

Her head tilted to one side. "Why are you here?"

"I work here."

Entering, she closed the door. "Why did you take this job? How does that fit into your master plan?"

"It's not complicated. Moving to Washington was a mistake—"

"I could have told you that a year ago. Oh wait, I did tell you, repeatedly, and you ignored me." She smoothed her hair behind her ears. "Why aren't you at some law firm, billing six hundred an hour, instead of working here for less than you pay your chauffeur? "

"It's not less than—" He hid a smile. "I won't have this conversation with you. Get out of my office."

Instead, she sat on the edge of his desk next to his chair, close enough for him to breathe the orange-ginger scent of her perfume. She crossed her legs, and her eyes challenged him. "I don't understand why you feel threatened by me."

"Is that why you keep bothering me? Because I'm threatened by you?"

"You made a choice. Tara's built a life without you. If you think you can use me to get to her—"

"I would never use you, Karina. I only want what's best for her." He steepled his hands. "That's why I moved to Washington in the first place. My motives haven't changed."

She shook her head. "Why the P.D.'s office? You don't have an ounce of empathy. As a prosecutor, you were ruthless."

"That's part of the game. My obligation was to represent the State of California, even if I disagreed with the law."

He stood, the memories needling him. "The last case I prosecuted was a woman with fibromyalgia who was growing pot for medical use. She started selling it without a license, because her condition kept her from holding down a job. The felony charge was her third strike. And even though she'd never been accused of a violent crime, my job was to send her to prison for twenty-five to life. Believe me, Kare, I was done with the D.A.'s office, even before—"

The memory hit him hard in the chest. He gripped the back of his chair, pain stealing his breath. He could feel Tara's blood warm on his skin, soaking through his shirt while his body shielded hers on the ground, bullets whizzing over their heads.

He looked up at Karina, her skin pale, her lips thin and expressionless.

Those days when Tara was in intensive care, her survival uncertain, Karina had been the one thing that stood between him and despair. When even his mother was too lost in grief to see Alex, Karina force-fed him hope. Relentlessly, she pushed him back from the brink, enveloping him when he lost control of his emotions, her love as big as the sea. Yet when he said goodbye before leaving for Washington, she wouldn't speak to him.

His breaths came sharp and deep. The color rose again in Karina's cheek. He'd have to work to rebuild her trust. After all, he'd abandoned her, too. Her response had been to leave his calls and texts unanswered. She expressed her surface emotions easily, even carelessly, but kept her deepest wounds hidden.

"What happened to Tara and the baby..." He grasped Karina's hand, but she pulled it away.

He clenched and unclenched his fist. "It hurt us all. I'm not the enemy."

"No, you're a deserter." She stared into her lap. "You left without thinking how it would affect your family. I thought you were a better man than that."

"I didn't leave out of selfishness. I gave Tara what she wanted."

"It's not what she wanted."

He lowered his head. Tara had been unlike herself in the months after the shooting, as if some frantic fear had overtaken her. He couldn't break through her stony determination. "It's what she asked for. I had to respect that, even if she was wrong. I loved her enough to leave, and I love her enough to stay away."

Karina looked up at him, the pain in her eyes waning. "I wish I could believe that."

"I haven't contacted her once since I moved back."

She pursed her lips. "Maybe that's part of your strategy."

"My only plan was to come home and do something useful with my life."

Her eyes grew pensive.

He weighed his next move. He had learned during his marriage that Tara's silence wasn't a sign of weakening resolve but of emotional overload. The same was true of Karina. Pushing her would spark anger. She needed time.

Her natural affection would work in his favor. She wanted to believe the best about people, even when she shouldn't. He had warned her more than once about giving an undeserving boyfriend a second chance. But she wasn't naïve. She didn't give third chances.

He looked into her wan face. Her large eyes gave her a childlike expression. Maybe that explained his impulse to protect her. He reached out and squeezed her arm.

"Don't touch me." She squirmed, her voice placid. "I still don't like you."

"Then why are you sitting on my desk?"

She hopped down and headed for the door. With a backward glance, she said, "I'm not as naïve as you think. I *will* figure out what you're up to."

He watched her walk away, glad she worked on his side and not the prosecution's. Her passion and tenacity were persuasive. Yet despite her protests, Karina was starting to thaw.

A short time later, Karina was back. She leaned against Alex's door jamb like a model against a sports car. "I need you to do me a favor."

Alex grinned. "Now why would I do that?"

Gazing at him—eyes large, lips pouting—she looked adorable. Another man might have thought she was making a play for him. He knew better. She flirted with everyone: men, women, babies, dogs, even shoes. Especially shoes.

"All the copiers on this floor are out of paper," she said. "I'm going to scout around the building to find some."

"You're stealing copier paper?"

"I'm confiscating some in the name of the citizens of San Diego County."

"Why are we out of paper?"

"Because it's the end of the month." Her brows arched. "I see you haven't met Stella the office supply

Nazi yet. She's the reason we all tape our names to our Bic pens."

"She hoards pens and paper?"

"Welcome to the public defender's office." Karina started to walk away, then came back. "Wait, I didn't tell you my favor. Lauren is meeting me here for lunch—"

"Lauren's coming?"

"Don't look so happy about it," Karina teased. "She doesn't like you, either. If she gets here before I get back, tell her I'll just be a minute."

His eyes followed as Karina ambled away. She could turn street-hardened judges to butter, but her charm wouldn't work on him. She was resourceful, though. To win Tara back, he'd need Karina as an ally. That was okay. He understood her vulnerabilities.

He half-watched through the doorway, eager to see Lauren. The oldest of the Fields sisters was quietly sensible, impervious to her siblings' drama, her ironic wit surfacing when least expected. When she approached. a baby on her hip, he stood in his doorway to greet her.

"Hey, loser." She wore her usual teasing expression, but her dark hair was shorter, barely reaching the tops of her shoulders. The warmth in her brown eyes softened the look of her tailored charcoal suit. She responded to his hug with a lingering squeeze.

"How've you been?" he asked.

"Busy. I made a person." She kissed her daughter's dark hair. "Alex, meet Nerissa."

He grasped the baby's hand and lost himself in her blue eyes. "A fine Shakespearean name."

"We call her Nissa. Do you want to hold her?"

An ache rose in his chest. The baby offered no resistance to his outstretched arms. He clutched her close to his heart, and her baby powder scent filled him with longing. "How old?"

"Eight months."

"She's a beauty. Like her mama."

"Please." Lauren rolled her eyes.

Nissa started to fuss. He blew a puff of air into her face and stopped her tears, then bounced her until she smiled.

"You're a natural with babies," Lauren said.

"While Tara was pregnant, I learned as much as I could so I wouldn't screw up." His throat closed, and his gaze stayed focused on Nissa.

Lauren's hand pressed his arm, her grip firm and steadying. "With so much love inside, you'll make a great dad someday."

He raised the baby's fingers to his lips, wallowing in her softness. "I'm not sure I'll get another chance."

"Don't say that."

"Tara was the only woman I ever wanted children with. I can't picture anything else."

"You've been through a trauma. It's not the sort of thing you just get over." Her brown eyes gazed at him with a soft, earnest expression. "If you need someone to talk to—"

"I'm fine."

"You're really not."

He ran his hand across Nissa's wispy hair, then spotted Karina heading toward them.

She quickened her step. "There's my girl!" Sidling next to him, she scooped Nissa from his arms.

Lauren looked at her watch. "So much for a nice restaurant."

"Sorry." Karina smothered Nissa's face with kisses.

Lauren turned to him. "Can you join us?"

His chest tightened. "I've got a hearing this afternoon. Great seeing you, though."

She squeezed his arm and gave him a wistful smile.

He didn't realize until that moment how much he'd missed her, missed being part of a family that expressed love so openly. Watching the sisters walk away, he listened to their muted laughter until silence once again filled his ears.

4 Hurt

SUNDAY, ON THE WAY HOME FROM CHURCH, TARA SAT in the passenger seat of Karina's car. The azaleas were in bloom, but the gaudiness of the colors annoyed her, and the muscles of her jaw tightened. She looked at Karina from the corner of her eye. "Why didn't you tell me Lauren talked to Alex last week?"

"I didn't think it mattered," Karina said.

"And he ran into Dad at the country club yesterday. Now, everyone in the family has seen Alex except me."

Karina slowed for a curve. "But that's good. Whatever his motives were in moving home, at least he's not pressuring you."

Tara tapped her foot on the floorboard. She had never suspected Alex's motives—she lacked her sister's flair for drama. Her glance fell to the clock in the dash. "We're running late. Perry will be waiting when we get home."

"Why do you keep dating a man who won't go to church with you?"

Heat bloomed in Tara's chest. "I'm still working on him."

"You've been working on him for three months."

"I'm more patient than you," Tara said.

"Patient...deluded..."

"At least I have a boyfriend."

Karina turned onto the interstate. "I'm enjoying my freedom."

Tara suspected that her sister's sudden disinterest in men signaled a larger problem, one Karina wouldn't admit. From the time she was a teenager, she had charmed young men into pattering after her like puppies. That had changed when Alex left town.

Tara looked over at her. "If something's bothering you, you can talk to me. I'm not as fragile as you think."

"What's bothering me is that Perry takes you for granted."

"The way your boyfriends have always taken you for granted?"

"Do not psychoanalyze me." Karina veered toward the exit.

Tara watched the shopping malls give way to the quiet streets of Mission Hills. Elegant Spanish-revival homes neighbored modest craftsman bungalows. The city sloped below, the downtown and the harbor visible in the distance.

The water called to her, as it always did. She missed living on the beach, the gentle swish of the waves like background music. Why hadn't Alex contacted her since moving home? They were on friendly terms. Maybe he was waiting for her to make the first move.

Karina pulled up to the house, its smoky violet clapboards trimmed with plum and lapis. On the porch swing sat Perry.

"There he is—always punctual," Tara said as she got out of the car. And predictable. No wonder Lauren liked him and Karina didn't.

Karina hadn't liked Alex, either, but that was never a problem. The night before the wedding, she said, "You're so lucky you found your Prince Charming."

Tara felt lucky then, too. Now, heading up the walkway toward Perry, she wondered whether her fairytale endings had run out.

∽≈⬥≈∾

Late that afternoon, Karina clambered up the steps to Lauren's front porch and rang the doorbell. Hugging herself, she stared at the tan painted floorboards. The situation with Alex had gotten out of control. If Tara wouldn't listen to Karina, maybe she would listen to Lauren.

Karina heard footsteps and looked through the stained glass sidelights. Lauren opened the front door. Its welcoming wreath of dried rosemary shook.

"Let me guess," Lauren said. "You're upset that Tara's gone to see Alex."

"She called you?"

Wearing a Mona Lisa smile, Lauren led Karina into the family room. Karina scanned the earth-toned furnishings, hoping the Zen-like décor would calm her frazzled nerves. The style ranged from the intricate patterns of the arts-and-crafts movement to the simple grace of the prairie school. How did Lauren keep the place so neat with a baby in the house?

Standing at the window, holding Nissa, was Lauren's husband, Sean Lindstrom, a grown-up California boy with sharp blue eyes. Denim shorts and an aquamarine tee-shirt clad his slim frame. He acknowledged Karina with a smile, but she was too upset to smile back.

"I don't see the problem." Lauren flopped onto the couch. "Tara wants a civil relationship with her ex. What's wrong with that?"

"Letting him back into her life will undo her progress. She could fall for him all over again."

"Alex is a good guy." Sean sat in a chair cattycorner to Lauren. "And he was crazy about Tara."

Karina's jaw tensed. "Three months after the shooting, while his wife's body was still healing, he moved to the other side of the country."

"She served him with divorce papers," Lauren said.

"She wasn't thinking clearly." Seriously, did no one else get that? "Just because Tara asked for a divorce, that doesn't mean she actually *wanted* one. If love conquers all, Alex didn't even dress for battle."

Lauren's eyes turned to Sean, who stroked his chin. "Kare," he said, "I think this has more to do with you than it does with Tara."

She glared at him. "If I want your services, I'll make an appointment, and you can bill me. In the meantime, stay out of my head."

Lauren smiled, then raised her brow. "Maybe Sean's got a point. Remember how Greg drifted out of your life while Tara was in the hospital—"

"This isn't about Greg." She paced, her blood pulsing. How could everyone be so blind? "Alex abandoned his family." *He abandoned all of us.*

Lauren stood. "If Tara's still got feelings for him, she can't move on without resolving them. And you know as well as I do that once she makes a decision, there's no point in trying to stop her."

An ache settled in her temples. "How can you be so calm about this?"

"Because I know I can't change the outcome. And because it's Tara's life."

"Is it wrong for me to want to protect her?"

Lauren took Karina's hands. "She doesn't need protection from Alex. He loves her as much as you do. Trust him to do the right thing."

Karina sank onto the couch and stared at the coffee table. Her eyes followed the grain of the burled walnut, the pattern swirling like an Impressionist painting. She wanted to trust Alex again. But one simple fact stood in the way.

"He left."

Lauren sat on the couch beside her. "What did you expect him to do?"

"To wait for Tara to change her mind."

"He'd have had a long wait. She hasn't changed her mind yet."

Karina squeezed the cushion beneath her, the sturdy fabric rough on her fingers. Was Lauren right? She looked at Sean. "What do you think?"

"My rate is one fifty an hour." He grinned.

She narrowed her eyes. "Seriously."

He set Nissa on the floor, and she crawled over to a set of soft fabric blocks in the corner. Sean's eyes followed a moment, then turned to Karina.

"I think Alex and Tara have both been through a lot, and we've got no right to judge them for their choices."

Karina stiffened. "I'm not judging them. I don't understand how Alex could give up so easily."

"He didn't give up," Lauren said. "He regrouped. Now he's back, and ready to fight."

"You think?" The knot in Karina's stomach loosened. She hadn't considered the situation from that angle. If that was true, then maybe Alex wasn't a danger. Maybe he was the key to repairing her broken family.

No, that couldn't be true. Could it?

Lauren shrugged. "I don't know what his intentions are. But the fact that Tara's gone to see him tonight means she still has feelings for him. Whatever happens between them, they deserve our support."

Karina rubbed her arms, her thoughts jumbled. She knew Tara wasn't ready to let Alex back into her life. But in time...

She squeezed her eyes shut to stop her thoughts. This was her fear when he first took a job at the P.D.'s office. She *had* to fight this urge to solve other people's problems. Whatever happened between him and Tara was their business. Karina couldn't let herself get drawn into the middle of it.

She leaned back against the couch and gazed out the window, spires of red hollyhocks swinging in the breeze. Seeing Alex would shock Tara's emotions out of their hiding place—that much was certain. Whether for better or for worse, she couldn't say. But she'd know soon enough.

~∘§∘~

Tara closed the door of her silver Mercedes. Her eyes scanned the house that had been her home, the lawn leading down to the ocean. Her lungs expanded in a long, deep breath. She could do this.

She approached the portico, the entrance flanked by Corinthian urns spilling with verbena and purple fountain grass. The beauty of the place filled her with yearning but also a sense of peace. She didn't want Alex to think he had to avoid her. She just wanted to set the record straight.

Her footsteps thudded on the granite steps. The massive mahogany door was curved at the top, the wood rich and warm. Her stomach fluttered, but that was just nerves. Once this first meeting was behind them, things could get back to normal. Her fingers found the bronze plate of the doorbell and pressed the button.

The butler opened the door and she hugged him. His temples had started to gray, but his manner was as calm and cheerful as ever. He motioned for her to wait in the front parlor.

She sat on the ivory couch, the chenille soft and inviting. A bowl of glass-beaded faux fruit sat on the end table. The mid-century look had been Alex's mother's choosing, but Tara had seen no reason to change it. It gave the house a feeling of continuity.

Tara heard Alex's footfall, recognizing the sound of his Sunday loafers. She rose and wrung her hands. But she couldn't stop her lips from curving into a smile.

Alex blinked when he entered the parlor. The butler had announced Mrs. Kent, and Alex had expected his mother. The error rumbled over him like a rockslide when he saw Tara.

His eyes turned to the portrait hanging over the stone fireplace. The stern face of his great-great-grandfather, the railroad baron, stared back. Alex breathed. When his thoughts settled, he looked back at his ex-wife.

Her hair was longer now, sleek and honey-gold, falling halfway to her waist. Her face was so lightly made up that only he would have known that the look wasn't natural. His heart thumped, and he swallowed twice to find his voice. "It's good to see you."

"I hope it's okay to drop by." A smile sweetened her expression. "I didn't want us to meet by chance. It would be awkward running into each other at a party or restaurant."

Her words were like a punch to the chest. His hands slid into the pockets of his pressed khaki shorts.

She broke the silence. "How's the P.D.'s office? It must be a big change for you."

He manipulated the pieces on an antique chess board. "I've worked as a defense lawyer for the past year."

"Representing senators and CEOs."

Was that pride in her voice? His scalp tightened, and he evaded her glance. "How are things at the newspaper?"

"Good! The digital version is attracting new readers, and my column is gaining a fan base."

"Do you like working as a columnist?"

She hugged herself, rocking forward and back. "It's quieter. In a good way."

He understood what those words meant. Safer than working as an investigative reporter. Less chance of getting shot.

Silence stretched between them. Apparently she was unwilling to talk about it, even with him.

Wandering to the French doors, he watched the sea wash over the jagged sand. What was she thinking, ambushing him like this, and expecting him to carry the conversation? He turned back to her. "How long do we need to make small talk before the awkwardness wears off?"

She flinched, her smile crumbling. "It's been a year, Alex. Why can't we move past this?"

The muscles clenched in his neck. She had no right to keep setting the terms. She had begged him not to fight the divorce because she wasn't strong enough to fight. But even that wasn't enough. She wanted to be in charge of his feelings, too.

He eyed her with a steady gaze, his throat taut. "Sorry it doesn't suit your timetable that I'm still in love with you."

Her body stilled. She looked away. Her coolness fueled his anger.

"Tara, you're the one who came here."

"That was a mistake." She headed toward the front door, then stopped, gazing at the marble floor. "I never wanted to hurt you."

"You weren't thinking about me. All you wanted was out."

Without a word, she twisted the doorknob and left.

His lungs filled with air chilled by her absence. He poured himself a scotch but set it undrunk on the coffee table. His head sank into his hands, the blackness of his self-loathing filling his vision. She had approached him with kindness, and he had chased her away.

The irony made him flinch. His strategy had worked. When he didn't contact her, she came to him. But blindsiding him like this, showing up unexpectedly, gave *her* all the power. So what had his plan accomplished? He'd exposed his weakness and gotten nothing in return.

She was right—he should be past this. But after everything he had done to make her happy, a drug smuggler's bullet had destroyed all they built. Alex thought their love was stronger than that. Had she changed along the way, or was some failing in himself to blame?

He massaged the bridge of his nose. His questions were fruitless. Only she knew the answers, and she wanted him at arm's length. Any closer would force her to feel the pain.

Maybe he'd made it too easy for her. In their grief, they'd both acted without thinking through their decisions. Was it too late to go back?

He rotated the glass on the coffee table. Pressuring her wasn't the answer. He would let her come to him when her emotions subsided, when she could be rational, when they could speak the same language. Any other tactic might backfire.

Of course, there was no guarantee. She might not be part of his future. Could he fall in love again? Did he want to?

His thumb massaged his wedding band. Wearing it felt natural. His marriage was still part of him, that circle of gold a life preserver. She had made a vow to God. No piece of paper from the government could change her heart. He took the glass of scotch into the kitchen and dumped it down the sink.

❦

Monday morning, Karina pulled open the glass door to the public defender's office. Her taupe designer suit had cost next to nothing at a church bazaar, but she felt like a million bucks—or at least full-price.

Karina wouldn't let Alex get to her. She was a lawyer—she could be objective. Heat rushed through her at the memory of Lauren and Sean's words, linking her feelings about Alex to her ex-boyfriends. Okay, so Greg had abandoned her while Tara was in the ICU. But

Karina hadn't been that serious about Greg. The sex was such a non-event, she was thinking of breaking up with him anyway. You'd think a man with a body like that would have some stamina.

Spotting Alex, she briefly made eye contact before moving on. Her leather computer bag thumped onto her desk.

He approached. "Are you free for lunch? I need someone to brainstorm with."

She checked her smartphone. "Sure." She powered up her computer and straightened the folders on her desk.

He eyed her, brow drawn. "Everything okay?"

A thin stream of air escaped her lips. "We need boundaries. We're colleagues, nothing more. My loyalty is to Tara."

"I'm not asking you to be disloyal to Tara."

He was kidding, right? "So it's a coincidence you took a job here."

"When Dayne told me about the opening, I didn't know I'd be working with you." He shrugged. "When I found out, I thought it might be fun."

She choked back a laugh. "Because we've always gotten along so well."

"You don't hate me as much as most people here do."

When Alex had worked as a prosecutor, she once saw him reduce a public defender to tears. That emotional outburst had shocked him, throwing him off his game, and he turned conciliatory—backtracking and softening his tone. Karina knew how to call his bluff.

"I won't be your go-between with Tara."

"If I have something to say to Tara, I'll say it." He set his jaw and looked away. The muscles in his face were taut, but his eyes were soft and distant.

"Did you and Tara fight last night?"

He turned toward her. "She didn't tell you?"

"She barely spoke after getting home," Karina said. Tara had been in one of her moods, one even Karina's persistence couldn't penetrate.

"She wanted me to say I was over her. I couldn't do that."

The ragged edge to his voice pierced Karina's heart. Alex never would have left, if Tara hadn't thrown away a perfectly good marriage instead of working through the pain. True, *he* was supposed to be the strong one. He was supposed to fight. Yet the twisted expression on his face reminded her that he had suffered, too. Family mattered to him. He shouldn't be alone.

"You're a desirable man, Alex. You could have any woman in this city."

"Except the one I want."

"Maybe if you got Tara drunk first..." she teased.

His lips flexed. "I'll take that under advisement."

She walked around her desk and drew him into a hug. He squeezed her as if his body was starved for touch. She remembered this feeling, the closeness they had shared during their darkest days, when Tara was in a coma teetering on the edge of life. If he had stayed, Karina could have helped him and Tara put their marriage back together. But he hadn't given her that chance.

Once alone, she pondered the situation. His leaving town had been a bad choice, but her job involved looking beyond bad choices and helping clients make the most of their lives. If she could do that for accused criminals, why not Alex?

Trying to patch up the hole Alex had left in her family hadn't worked. Maybe the solution was to stitch him back in.

Her heart would stay open as long as he didn't pressure her sister. Tara seemed to have it all together, but she was wound so tightly that the slightest stress could send her spinning out of control. Her sense of calm held her together, even if it was an illusion. Karina served as a buffer to make sure Tara unwound at her own pace. Right now, her pace was glacial. Karina wondered if she could speed it up.

That night, while setting a pair of purple earthenware plates on the kitchen table, Karina looked over at Tara taking the lasagna from the oven. To anyone else, Tara's silence might seem peaceful. Her sister knew better.

Tara had something on her mind, and Karina had a good idea what.

"When you saw Alex last night," Karina asked, "did you get what you wanted?"

Tara scowled, slamming the oven door shut.

Karina continued, "It drove you crazy he didn't call. So you went to his house."

"I didn't want him to think he had to stay away."

"Do you feel better, knowing he's still in love with you?"

Tara's lips parted. "I don't want him to be in love with me."

Karina rattled the silverware and thumped it into place. "Tara, you rushed the divorce through. You refused to get counseling. I wonder if you were trying to free yourself from the pain, and Alex represented pain to you. If a man loved me that much, I'd think twice before letting him go."

Tara dropped the bread knife onto the cutting board, then strode over and placed her hand on Karina's forehead. "You don't have a fever, yet you're delirious!"

"Sooner or later, he *will* move on. And if that's what you want, fine. But if you're dating Perry instead of a real man because you want another chance with Alex, then you need to act soon."

Tara's mouth tightened. "Perry's good to me."

"He leaves you numb." Karina breathed to calm her emotions. Tara needed support from her, not anger. "Maybe if I'd been through what you've been through,

I'd want to be numb, too. But one day, you'll want passion again. Perry can't give you that, and it's not fair stringing him along."

"Can't I have some peace in my life?"

"Of course. You deserve that. But denying who you are won't make you someone else."

"Stop it, okay? Just...stop it." Tara folded the paper napkins and set them next to the plates.

Knowing better than to push Tara too hard, Karina hugged her. "I want you to be happy."

"I *am* happy. You don't have to worry about me."

Karina pinched her lips together, picturing how big the crater would be when Tara finally crashed to earth.

⁓◦§◦⁓

Saturday morning, as the first light of dawn stretched through the window, Alex lay in bed on the edge of wakefulness. Paralyzed from sleep, he couldn't fight the memory that played again like a dream.

"Alex, what the hell are you doing here?" Lieutenant Chantel Emery eyed him hotly, her petite frame clenched like a fist.

"Looking for Tara. She got a tip." This corner of Barrio Logan was no place for a pregnant woman alone, not with dusk closing in. Long shadows crept from the abandoned department store across the street, its boarded windows staring like sightless eyes, the mural on its face scarred black with obscenities.

Chantel tightened her jaw. "The officers let you through—even with the street cordoned off?"

"The street's not cordoned off."

Panic swept her features, and her sharp staccato voice spilled into her radio.

His senses alert, he scanned the dusty sidewalk, the smell of baking asphalt heavy in the air. Tara walked toward them, half a block away. Flooded with relief, he rushed toward her.

Her smile challenged him. "I thought you didn't know anything about this."

"I thought you weren't coming." He kissed her, placing his hand on her midsection, feeling the baby tumble. "Sweetheart, we need to get out of here. This street was supposed to be closed to pedestrians—"

A flurry of shouting shocked the air, then the pop of a single gunshot. Tara fell to the ground, and Alex dropped down beside her. A barrage of bullets thundered. He shielded her body, his gut undulating in horror. Blood pooled on her shirt and bathed the hand she held to her belly.

Muddled thoughts floated, incoherent in his mind. His body shook as if chilled. Smoke caught in his throat, and her whimpers echoed in his ear. Cheek pressed to hers, he barely heard her stuttering voice, "The baby, Alex."

His eyes burst open, and the gray surroundings wrenched him back to his waking life. The bed lay empty beside him. He rose and walked to the window, greeting a sky absent of color. The sea stretched to nothingness before him.

Hours later, Alex stood in the breakfast room, the aroma of coffee piercing the mist in his mind, helping him navigate the tightrope between grief and everyday life. The sky was blue now, a soft pastel, and the sea a brocade of turquoise and sapphire. The sun's rays bathed his shoulders as he stepped outside the sprawling Spanish-style mansion, its rough walls tempered by palmettos and the water gurgling in hidden fountains.

A figure on the beach caught his eye. The muscles of his neck and shoulders softened, easing the tension he hadn't realize was stored there.

Slowly, he approached Tara. The breeze tousled her hair and her white peasant blouse. Silhouetted against the broad swath of coast and the deep stretch of ocean, she looked small and vulnerable. But her strength and determination rivaled that of anyone he'd met in Washington.

She didn't react as he sat next to her. Her hand scooped up the Coronado sand, golden flecks shining before spilling like water through her fingers. "I hate how we left things last week." Closing her eyes, she breathed deeply. "And I've been trying to figure out how to tell you that, without getting into another fight."

He picked up a shell and caressed it between his fingers, polishing its iridescent surface. "I can't bear for us to act like strangers. You're my wife—" The words stopped in his throat. "At least in my heart you are."

She took his left hand. "Alex...this ring symbolizes something that doesn't exist anymore."

He pulled his hand away, and heaviness weighed on his heart. "A love with no beginning and no end. I guess that never existed in the first place."

"Part of me will always love you."

"I don't want part of you." He rose and walked along the beach, the earth sinking beneath his feet.

She followed. "I hate seeing you in pain."

"You can't divorce me, yet not cause me pain." He stopped and turned. "Is it absolution you want?"

"I want to know you're okay."

"I won't jump off a bridge, if that's what you're asking." He lifted her face toward his, brushing her cheek with his thumb. "You're not responsible for me. I gave you the divorce so you could be happy. So be happy. You owe me that."

5 Can't Fight the Moonlight

THE FOLLOWING SATURDAY, ALEX CLIMBED THE FINAL bank of the fairway leading to the eighteenth hole. He grinned at Enrico, his caddie. "It's on the green."

The golf ball glistened in the afternoon sun. Dayne Emery, the D.A., clenched and unclenched his fist, flexing his thick biceps. He loomed over Alex. "You can't make that shot."

Alex smirked at his friend, watching for the rest of the foursome to catch up. His partner for the round was Jack Fields, Tara's father, whom Alex still counted a good friend. Dayne had partnered with Sean Lindstrom, Lauren's husband, for the sake of Sean's ample handicap. But nothing had seemed to work in Dayne's favor that breezy May afternoon.

Topping the hill, Sean hung his head when he spotted the ball. He looked at Dayne with resignation in his gray-blue eyes. But Jack, walking two steps behind, gave Alex a smile.

Dayne glowered at Sean. "They're kicking our asses."

"I played the best game of my life," Sean said. "I can't help that you suck."

"Jack, tell him which one of us sucks."

An impish grin lighted Jack's features. "Today, Dayne, it's all you."

Alex chuckled, grateful to Jack for suggesting the round. Standing on the sculpted lawn beneath the wide California sky, he felt in his element. He eyed the distance to the hole. It was doable.

The caddie, a diminutive man in his late fifties with a modest mustache and shining eyes, handed him a putter. "You can do this, son of *El Jefe.*"

Alex squeezed the soft rubber grip, then tightened his jaw. "If I make this shot, am I *El Jefe*?"

"If you make this shot," Enrico said, "you are *El Jefe.*"

Alex stood over the ball while Dayne swore in the background. Alex, his eyes like slits, pointed his putter at Dayne, who fell silent. Alex lined up the shot, the muscles in his face softening as his mind focused. He tapped the ball. It glided over the grass...and plunked into the hole.

Dayne paced, pounding the turf with his club. "He did *not* shoot an eagle."

Alex savored the moment. The breeze rustled through the Torrey pines. He gave his putter to Enrico, who shook his hand and said, "Well done, my friend."

The four golfers headed to the clubhouse, following a wide brick path that curved past a pond edged with reeds. At a booth in the bar, the air conditioning cooled their flushed faces, while beer and sandwiches eased their tempers.

Alex recounted his dinner at the White House a few months earlier, after he had secured Senator Hartley's acquittal. "I don't think I'll be invited back," he said. "I gave my business card to the chief of staff, and told him to call if he needs a defense lawyer."

Dayne smiled. "And you gave that up for the P.D.'s office?"

The glitz of the ball gowns and paparazzi faded from his mind, replaced by back hall conversations and sniping against his client on CNN. "It got exhausting, watching those people wonder who their friends were. What's the point of having power if all you do is parrot the party buzzwords, instead of actually *leading*?"

His cell phone vibrated and he took it from his pocket. He excused himself, then stood and clicked the phone on while walking toward the terrace.

"Nick Spencer," Alex said, "how's it hanging, bud?"

"I'm not your *bud*. I would have deleted you from my phone the day you left the firm, but I knew something like this would happen."

Alex pushed through the French doors. "What's up?"

"My boss needs some files from your old laptop for an audit on Monday. My car is packed to drive Vanessa and the girls to Rehoboth Beach—"

"Rehoboth's not a real beach. You should come to California."

"You should kiss my ass. I'm supposed to leave for vacation first thing tomorrow, and I can't find your damn files to upload to the FTP site."

Alex tapped the toe of his shoe on the flagstone. "I deleted the sensitive stuff from my hard drive after I copied it to the secured server."

Nick turned silent.

Alex said, "Can't you check the server?"

"VPN is down. Shit! If I have to drive to the office tonight, Vanessa will kill me."

"My secretary knows how my files are organized. She can find what you're looking for."

"You're sure all your files are on the server?" Nick asked.

"You don't trust me? I'm hurt."

"Trust the guy who stole the Hartley case from me?"

Was he still on that kick? "I can't help it if Deb wanted me to take the lead."

"Deb. She ask you to call her that in bed?"

"No, in bed she wanted me to call her Senator," Alex said. "Len Hartley heads the IRS. You think I'm dumb enough to seduce his wife?"

"Yes. Listen, I'd love to chat, but not with you. If those files aren't on the server, I'll hunt you down and kill you."

The line went dead, and Alex clicked off the phone. He looked out at the landscape. Water splashed over the gray boulders of a manmade waterfall. Under different circumstances, he and Nick Spencer might have become friends. But Alex had no regrets.

He turned toward the French doors leading back to the bar. Beyond the glass, Dayne debated hotly with Sean. Jack intervened. The two younger men listened, then nodded.

Alex smiled, admiring Jack's easy way of bringing people together. Jack had fathered no sons, yet he had amassed them. His relationship with Alex and Sean was natural enough, but Jack and Dayne were an unlikely pair. Alex didn't know the details, but he'd learned that Dayne had met Jack as a teenager. The son of a Presbyterian minister, Dayne led a church program to distribute leftover food from restaurants to needy families. Jack became a strong supporter—first of the program, then of Dayne himself.

Jack had introduced Dayne to his family, and Dayne sometimes babysat the three little girls. Dayne had once embarrassed Tara by telling Alex the story of how, at age ten, she had baked Dayne a cake for his eighteenth birthday. Too impatient to wait for the cake to cool, she had frosted it while it was still hot, and it had crumbled. Lauren made the best of it, scooping it into bowls and serving it with spoons. Karina, her face smudged with chocolate, stood on a chair and declared that cake should always be served that way.

A waitress passed in front of the French door. Alex headed inside and slid back into the booth, listening to the conversation in progress.

"The mayor won't get that housing ordinance through city council." Jack's voice rasped like aspens in the breeze. "It's a short-term solution to a long-term problem."

"The mayor is a short-term thinker," Alex said. "How he got re-elected..."

"It was a close race," Dayne said, "but he's a smooth talker. His opponent couldn't make up for the recognition factor."

"When times are tough," Sean said, "change becomes one more thing to fear."

The waitress brought the check, and Jack signed the credit card receipt. Alex left the table alone, wanting time with his thoughts.

A photo hanging in the clubhouse gallery stopped him. There stood his father, Matthew Kent, after breaking the course record. Next to him, no taller than his golf bag, was Alex. Yet Alex remembered that day. A cap had shielded his eyes from the sun as he ran to keep up with his father and grandfather strolling along the fairway. His father, after eagling on the eighteenth hole, lifted him and asked, "Are you proud of me?" and Alex nodded, not knowing why he should be proud, but knowing he was.

Alex grew up understanding that his father was an important man. People called him *sir* and did what he said. But he always had time for his son. Some weekends they would camp in the mountains, building a fire under the stars. His father would teach him the names of the constellations and he would remember them. They'd tell each other stories of epic battles fought by the ancients whose names were recorded in the stars. Drifting into sleep, Alex would dream that his father was Orion, hero and mighty hunter.

Yet he couldn't think back on those happy times without recalling the day his relationship with his father had changed. When he was fifteen, Alex came home to the sound of his mother's sobs. On the couch, his father sat with shoulders bowed, submerging his guilt in a glass of scotch.

Alex stared, suddenly comprehending that the half-whispered rumors he'd overheard for months about his father were true. Burning with anger, he sat with his mother as she wept. He struggled for years but couldn't forgive his father—not until it was too late.

With a sick feeling in his stomach, Alex remembered the urgent call while he was working at the D.A.'s office that had summoned him to the E.R. His father lay on a gurney in a tiny room, machines hooked to his body. Tension gripped his mother's features, her hand clutching his father's. She eased when she saw

Alex. He pulled a chair beside the gurney, and serenity swept over Matt's expression.

"Alex." He forced out the words on a faint breath. "My son." His pale face showed deep lines around his eyes. The sprinkling of gray at his temples had turned solid white.

Before Alex could speak, the heart monitor squealed and the room filled with medical staff. Alex clutched his mother and dragged her shrieking into the hallway. It took all his strength to hold her back. It was the only time he ever saw his mother lose control. He still sometimes woke to the memory of her screams.

Alex startled when Jack patted his back, interrupting his thoughts. Jack's eyes were on the photo of Matt leaning on his club wearing a satisfied grin.

Jack smiled. "That could be you."

Alex's chest rose with pride, then shrank with shame. The feelings were inseparable when it came to his father, and how alike they were.

Jack walked with Alex to the parking lot, the towering live oaks casting them in dappled shade. They had made this trek together many times. Jack had been a surrogate father, and now, despite everything, his friendship endured.

Alex reached for words, but they were garbled in his head. He mentally recited the presidents: *Washington, Adams, Jefferson...*

"Thanks for inviting me today," he said. "It means a lot."

"You'll always be a son to me, Alex."

Madison, Monroe, Quincy Adams...

Eyes straight ahead, Jack said, "Come to the party tonight."

Alex laughed. "I'm not crashing my ex-wife's birthday party."

"You and Tara will fight, then you'll make up."

Alex admired Jack's uncomplicated view of the world. Jack believed that no problem was too large to solve with a good meal, a bottle of wine, and conversation. The challenge was getting people to the table.

Alex's mother's form became visible across the broad lawn, coming from the main hall and heading toward her car. She was dressed almost casually in a silk blouse, crepe pants, and her favorite Ferragamo flats. "How was the game?" she called.

"I am *El Jefe*." Alex smiled.

Her features brightened as she approached. "You shot twelve under par?"

"Four under."

"Then you're not *El Jefe*." She patted his arm.

"What would I do without you to remind me of my shortcomings?"

"You'd be insufferable, darling."

She turned to Jack and pressed his hand. "And how did you do?"

"Sean scored better than me."

She laughed. "Poor Jack."

"Were you here for lunch?" Alex asked her.

"I met with Brooke Genovese. The Kent Foundation is sponsoring a benefit for the Arts Council next month."

"Nice of you to come to Brooke's rescue."

His mother twisted her pearl earring. "The Arts Council shouldn't suffer because she got distracted managing the mayor's campaign." She smiled at him. "Can you join me for dinner?"

"I'd be honored—plus, everyone else I know will be at Tara's party."

"Is that tonight?" She looked toward a distant cloud.

Jack's gaze fell to the cracks spreading through the asphalt. She brushed her hand against his arm, adopting a cheerful air. "Kiss Tara for me."

He nodded and left them with a reluctant gait, his unspoken words disturbing the silence.

Alex walked his mother to her Jaguar, realizing she had lost Tara too, though she bore the hurt with her usual grace. When they reached her car, he opened her door. She looked at him with a smile that didn't reach her eyes.

"Mother…" he started, but couldn't form words.

"Four under par." She looked at him intently. "You make me so proud."

A lump formed in his throat. More was behind her words than a golf score. With a flicker of hope, he resolved once again to be a man who put his family above all else, the way his father had tried but failed to do.

That evening, with Karina at her side, Tara drove across the bay. She watched the Hotel del Coronado come into view, a fairytale castle rising from the sea. Lying between the sapphire waters of the marina and the silver sands of the Pacific, the resort was a masterpiece of Victorian architecture, its gables and turrets dripping with white gingerbread and crowned with red tile. Palm trees opened like parasols over the walkways.

The sisters wove through the garden and across the lawn to the cottage that Dayne and his wife, Chantel, had booked for the party. A concerto rose from the string quartet playing in the corner. The tables were cloaked with linen, the chairs slipcovered in lavender. Tara and Karina were the first guests to arrive.

Dayne kissed their cheeks, and Chantel beamed in a lava-colored dress that showed off her skin, brown with undertones of ochre. Rings adorned each finger, and her nails were long and painted. Tara liked seeing her dressed up. A police lieutenant, Chantel rarely had the chance to wear girly clothes. So when she did, she made the most of it.

Chantel eyed the sisters, then pressed her hand to her hip. "Where are your dates?"

"We're each other's dates," Karina said.

Chantel shook her head. "Now that's just sad."

Tara didn't argue, though she didn't think it was sad. Tonight was an opportunity to focus on herself.

The room began to fill. Tara mingled, collecting hugs and smiles from the guests. Their love filled her heart, and almost made her forget what she had lost.

Lauren arrived with Sean by her side and Nissa in her arms. For Lauren's benefit, Tara modeled her gold Givenchy sheath dress. Her eyes followed Sean's to the gift table, where Karina was assessing the packages. Tara said, "Kare seems confused over whose birthday it is."

Lauren smiled. "You knew when you moved in with her that it would be a joint property arrangement."

But Karina spotted Nissa, and the gift table surrendered her attention. She rushed over and appropriated her niece from Lauren, cooing over the little party dress, red satin trimmed with bows. "I found a new date."

"Sorry, my turn." Tara took the baby.

Seeing her father at the bar, she wandered over to him. She and Jack shared the same tawny hair and soft, open features, though Jack's face was more square and his hair pleasingly sugared with white.

"Dad, stop watching the wait staff," she said. "They're not your employees—you're a guest tonight."

He smiled. "How do you always know what I'm thinking?"

"I'm a journalist. I can read people."

Tara had been reading her father her whole life. From the time she could crawl, she followed him everywhere. During her preschool years, a little desk in his study offered a place for her to draw or color while he worked. The desk grew as she did, but it retained its place as long as her father owned the house.

Jack reached for Nissa. The raspberry he blew on her cheek made her giggle. "She's a good baby, like her mama was."

"Wasn't I a good baby?" asked Tara.

"Mostly." He rubbed Nissa's fingers. "But you were the most willful child I ever saw. At two years old, you insisted on dressing yourself. Your buttons would be crooked, but you wouldn't let your mom fix it."

"I was worse than Karina?"

"She wasn't willful. She just cried nonstop if you put her down. For the first six months of Karina's life, your mom always had a baby on her hip, like she'd grown a new appendage."

Tara smiled, warmed by the memories. But something was missing. Her gaze scanned the room, and her heart cracked: she missed Holly.

Excusing herself, Tara took out her cell phone. She wandered onto the terrace. In the darkness, beyond the expanse of sand, waves rumbled against the beach. She scrolled through her contacts for Holly's number, but then slipped the phone back into her purse. She didn't want Holly to feel her loyalties torn.

Tara's gaze turned toward the coastline. She couldn't make out which lights belonged to the home she had shared with Alex. Yet it was there, distant, but within the range of her sight. His presence enfolded her, as it always did, his spirit whispering in her ear.

A door closed behind her. Dayne approached, near enough that his spicy cologne teased her nostrils. She touched his arm and smiled. "Thanks for doing this."

"You need to know, the divorce doesn't change things between us. We've been friends a lot longer than I've known Alex."

"But if it's awkward for you..."

"Why would it be awkward for me? Not saying I understand, but I'm not taking sides."

The ocean pushed toward the shore. "Every time I looked at him, the pain in his eyes tore me apart. I failed him."

"He doesn't think that."

"Maybe not consciously." Her hands clutched the railing. "I couldn't live with it. I had to cut my losses to survive."

He laid his arm across her shoulder. "Give yourself time. Grief can mess you up. Remember that guy you dated after your mom passed away?"

Carlos. She hadn't thought of him in ages. They'd been friends for almost a year, and when her mom passed away, his kisses gave Tara comfort. But she soon realized her mistake. He had trouble accepting the breakup—until Dayne paid a visit to his dorm room and explained the situation.

She leaned against Dayne, feeling his warmth. Moonlight danced on the water. She couldn't dwell in the past. Focusing on the path before her, on things she could control, was the only way to reach the road to recovery. Accepting a life without Alex was the first step.

Back inside, Sean spotted Karina at a table by herself, her halter dress revealing silky shoulders that glistened in the candlelight. The string quartet was playing the second movement of *Eine Kleine Nachtmusik*, and it seemed written for her. But Sean worried at seeing her sitting alone.

In recent months, his sense of her vulnerability had grown. He tried to keep his training as a psychologist from interfering with his personal relationships, but a suspicion nagged at him that she was struggling with unresolved grief.

He walked up beside her, and her moist eyes turned to him. "It's not supposed to be like this."

Hand outstretched, he raised her to her feet and led her out onto the lawn.

She walked briskly, as if trying to escape her thoughts. Her voice broke. "Alex should be here. Why didn't he love Tara enough to stay?"

Sean plucked a hibiscus flower from the hedge and handed it to her. "Tara's not like you. When you're upset, you surround yourself with people. Tara needs solitude to sort through her emotions. Alex loved her enough to leave."

Her quick steps led them to the pool. She flopped into a chair, and he sat beside her. Above them, moonlight tore the clouds. The night breeze whispered through the palm trees.

"It's not your job to fix Tara's life," he said. "It's taking too much out of you—you're carrying around her pain *and* yours. Worse, you're projecting onto Tara what you would feel in her situation. But that's not what Tara feels."

The water cast ghostly reflections onto Karina's features. "I can't believe Perry blew off her party. He's a freelance photographer—he could have refused that job. His girlfriend's birthday is more important than a few extra bucks."

"Tara doesn't see it that way."

"Of *course* she does." Karina jumped from her chair. "Alex would never have missed her party."

She marched back to the cottage. Sean watched her go. Part of him worried her romantic ideas of love would leave her brokenhearted. Part of him worried she was right, and Tara was suffering more than she showed.

Rejoining the party, Karina got a glass of champagne. By pretending to have a good time, she often managed to have one. Maybe other people influenced her too easily. But no point in wasting champagne thinking about it.

Instead, she caught up with old friends and made new ones. She filed mental notes about promising young men for future reference. She thought about Alex, and told herself to stop.

It was Alex and Tara's screwed up life. Not like they listened to her, anyway. But if those two couldn't make it, there was no hope for Karina. Pursued by men who were really boys, she was tired of their expectations, sex in exchange for love. She'd thought Alex was different. But he had left, and men don't leave.

Eyes closed, she listened to the string quartet. Who had classical music at a party, anyway? She wanted to dance, to work off her pent-up emotions, to stand on a table and yell at everyone for celebrating when Tara's heart was torn in two. Couldn't anyone else see that?

But Karina couldn't blame them, really. Tara was smiling and talking with her usual animation, hugging the guests as they departed. She looked fine, even though her insides were locked up in a medieval torture device.

A waiter walked by with a tray of champagne, and Karina took another glass. Maybe Sean was right, and she was projecting her own feelings of loss onto Tara. Time to stop living through her sister. Time to enjoy her own damn life.

After the string quartet had gone, Jack and Sean loaded the gifts into Tara's car. Sinking into a chair, Tara suddenly felt exhausted. She'd drunk too much and eaten too little. Her sheath dress barely left room for her to breathe. Perry would have liked the way she looked in it, though.

A chill rushed through her. Perry hadn't crossed her mind all night.

She darted into the ladies' room, her throat thick but her eyes unable to form tears. Locking herself into a stall, she inhaled deep breaths of apple-scented air. Her whole life, her heart had never steered her wrong. Now her emotions seemed out of reach. Her fists unclenched to reveal the deep grooves her nails had left in the heels of her hands. She hadn't felt a thing.

Her heart raced as if from too much caffeine, though she'd had none. She unlocked the stall door with a metallic clack. At the sink, she let the water run hot and scrubbed her hands, then took a thick paper towel from the basket on the vanity and dried her fingers one by one.

Slipping out the door, she heard the clanging of the wait staff clearing the serving utensils. The gift table was empty now. Lauren sat in a chair, the baby sleeping on her lap.

Karina walked up and put her arm around Tara. "Ready to go home and open your birthday presents? We can change into pajamas and drink hot chocolate. I'll write down who got you what, while you unwrap that good loot."

Tara smiled. "Sounds like a plan."

Piped-in tango music punctuated the air. Karina grabbed Tara's hand and dragged her to the middle of the room. Neither of them could tango, but Karina made a good show of it, dipping Tara and spinning her until she grew dizzy. For the first time all evening, the band of tension squeezing her stomach loosened.

Giggling, the sisters stumbled out onto the terrace to catch their breath. The breeze off the ocean cooled their faces. Karina's voice was soft. "Perry's not a good boyfriend. You know that, right?"

Tara knew. Gazing into the crisp points of starlight, she recalled the lilt of his laugh, the gentleness of his touch, the intensity in his eyes when he watched her. Yet she wouldn't be sorry to lose him. She couldn't even feel sadness anymore.

6 Take a Chance on Me

THE FOLLOWING WEEK AT LUNCHTIME, ALEX ENTERED
Susanne's Bistro, a restaurant near the Gaslamp
Quarter overlooking the harbor. Sunlight
bounced off the water and bathed the dining room in
light, glittering through crystal chandeliers and casting
rainbows onto the fresh flowers and linen tablecloths.
The wait staff bustled by, carrying French-inspired
dishes, artful presentation enhancing the piquant
aromas.

Alex tugged the cuffs of his suit jacket,
straightening the sleeves. An hour earlier, he had been
looking forward to lunch with Dayne, when the text
came that Chantel was joining them. Alex loved Chantel,
but he knew her well enough to guess she had an ulterior
motive. Like fixing him up. He had been on enough bad
dates in Washington—he didn't need a repeat.

Approaching the hostess station, Alex spotted
Dayne and Chantel standing in the dining room dressed
in dark suits. They were chatting with his ex-father-in-

law, Jack Fields, the owner of the restaurant. The formality of Jack's starched shirt and olive-striped tie contrasted with his more casual personal style.

He greeted Alex with a cheerful handshake, seating his friends at a table in the middle of the room where they could be seen. Jack was a modest man, but when it came to business, he didn't miss an opportunity to flaunt his connections. Alex admired Jack's shrewdness. Everyone in the restaurant would know the D.A. was dining there—and the mayor, too, at a long table nearby.

Jack motioned for their waitress before heading off to assist his other customers. The threesome had just placed their orders when one of the mayor's pretty-boy flunkies approached, summoning Dayne. He rose and excused himself, his hand trailing across his wife's shoulder as he walked away.

Chantel leaned toward Alex, the narrow cut of her black business suit highlighting her curves. Her eyes focused on her husband. "Notice how the mayor didn't stand up when Dayne got to his table? Dayne has to bend toward him, as if the mayor has all the power."

"Image is everything," Alex said, "when you've got no substance." He watched the two men. The mayor was tall and athletic, his blond hair streaked with gray. But at six foot five, Dayne was taller still and broader.

Alex recalled meeting him for the first time, refusing to be intimidated by Dayne's stature and his position then as assistant D.A. When Dayne pushed,

Alex pushed back. That moment forged the beginnings of their friendship.

Chantel sat back in her chair. "If the mayor had any real power, he wouldn't surround himself with sycophants. See how bored Councilman Yusef looks? He doesn't think much of the mayor, either."

She shook her head, bouncing ringlets of bronze hair. "How much you think the mayor's suit cost? Not as much as yours, I guess. That cashmere?" She reached over and rubbed the fabric at his wrist between her fingertips. Then, a scowl crossed her face. She tapped Alex's wedding band. "How long you been divorced?"

He smirked and withdrew his hand.

Her smoky gray eyes gazed at him. "You wear that ring, Tara knows she's got you. Take it off, you'll show her what she could lose."

His jaw stiffened.

"Stop giving Tara what she wants," Chantel said. "Make her deal with you."

His eyes followed a waitress walking by. He didn't mind Chantel's teasing, but the last thing he needed from her was relationship advice.

He turned back to see her sliding her fingers along her gold necklace. "Tara dumped that guy Perry," she said. "You've got an opening."

The brief thrill in his stomach twisted into a knot. "It's too soon. If I upset her—"

"Upset would be good for her. She's too damn complacent."

Alex aligned the salt and pepper shakers with the little vase of Gerber daisies. *It's not that simple.* Pressure led Tara to retreat further. Was it presumptuous to think he had something to do with her breakup? His neck tightened when he remembered what Karina had said—how the guy had missed Tara's party, when it was all Alex could do to stay away.

Dayne walked back toward them, his lips a grim line. Retaking his seat, he grumbled, "I hate politics."

"Sugar, you're in the wrong line of work," Chantel said.

"The mayor wants me to make a deal in the Pauling case."

She nodded. "The trial of a serial killer won't bring in those tourism dollars."

Alex leaned toward him. "You don't answer to the mayor. You're the face of justice for San Diego County. He's a bureaucrat at the top of the food chain."

Dayne tapped his hands on the table. "A trail of blood leading from the crime scene to Pauling's bedroom...The only deal he'll get is lethal injection."

Alex sucked in his cheeks. Since the divorce, he couldn't make a decision without second-guessing himself. But Dayne was unplagued by doubt, even when a man's life rested in his hands. Alex wanted that self-assurance again.

The next morning, Karina swiveled in her chair. With a lab report in one hand, she massaged her temple with the other to ward off a headache. Alex appeared in her doorway. She tossed the file onto her desk.

"Not only was my client ID'ed by the three victims," she said, "his DNA was found at all three crime scenes." Her stomach twisted. "I was hoping this one was innocent."

"They're all innocent, Kare."

"Could the PVC test be wrong?"

Alex grinned. "You mean the PCR test."

"Isn't that what I said?"

He pushed the door shut, and his eyes gleamed. "How many professors did you sleep with to get a law degree from Stanford?"

"I didn't have to sleep with them. With an ass like mine, all I had to do was walk away."

Alex smirked and sat in the chair opposite her. "It *is* smokin' hot."

She narrowed her gaze. Only Alex could get away with saying those things to her at work. Still, she didn't mind when people underestimated her. It gave her a tactical advantage. "Did you want something?"

"Miguel Santos. His case file doesn't give much to go on. A string of misdemeanors, two felony convictions...What do you know about him?"

She sat back, still seething about handing that case to Alex. Something about Santos had touched her. Seeming hopeless, he had needed a champion in his corner. "Mild-mannered guy with a drinking problem. Whenever his ex-wife gets drunk or high, she goes to his place and berates him until he takes a swing at her. Then, she has him arrested."

"So that's why Santos took out a restraining order."

Karina rose, worry pulsing through her. She sat on the desk in front of Alex. "Is Santos in trouble again?"

"Missed his second anger management class. Judge wants to schedule a hearing. You know the history—would you mind working with me?"

"You want the help of someone who earned her law degree on her back?"

"I know you're secretly brilliant. Believe it or not, some men like smart women."

Her chest deflated. "I've sworn off men."

"You're a lesbian now?"

"I've stopped dating until I figure out why I get involved with the wrong guys."

He sat next to her on the edge of desk. "You date the wrong men to sabotage yourself."

Her blood rushed, warming her cheeks. "Now why would I do that?"

"You saw how devastated your father was when your mother died. You watched my marriage to Tara disintegrate. That would scare anyone."

Her vision darkened. "You don't know me." She hopped down from the desk and headed for the door. Then, she turned. "This is my office. Get out."

Across town, Lauren sat dressed in a prim gray business suit, Nissa squirming in her lap. The campus daycare center had closed after a water main break, leaving no time for Lauren to make child care arrangements before this meeting at the Kent Foundation. Holly had sounded understanding on the phone. But now, Lauren watched Holly's face uncertainly. Without this research grant, Lauren had little hope of getting tenure. Feeling small in this office with its austere lines and art deco furnishings, she answered endless questions about methodology and cultural bias, wondering whether she had made the biggest mistake of her life.

She understood how the Foundation worked: the board reviewed the grant applications, but the ultimate decision was Holly's. This final interview helped her judge the applicant's commitment and thoroughness.

And Lauren had turned it into a Mommy & Me class.

When Nissa began to wail, Lauren wanted to do the same. She held her daughter against her shoulder, rubbing her back. Silent, Holly stood and walked to the window.

Lauren stared into the vacated chair, its taupe cushions framed in polished chrome. She had spent hours preparing for this meeting, organizing her notes, rehearsing her answers—and it was a disaster. Rather than continuing the agony, she was about to apologize and attempt a graceful exit, when Holly said, "How's Tara?"

Lauren blinked, and her stomach sank. How could she have been so self-absorbed? Holly's lingering looks at the baby...they hadn't signaled disapproval. Nissa reminded Holly of the baby that Tara had lost— that they all had lost.

Swallowing her emotion, Lauren rose, rocking Nissa in her arms. "Lately, Tara's had more good days than bad."

"During her recovery, I worried she'd be left unable to bear children. Thank God that didn't happen."

Lauren approached Holly and followed her gaze. Beyond the window, the thin thread of the Coronado Bridge traversed the water and strung the isthmus to the city. From this distance, imperfection faded, and the world below them gleamed.

Holly looked at Lauren and smiled, then turned her eyes to Nissa. Her fingers brushed the baby's cheek. Lauren perceived in Holly's face the same studied reserve she saw in her own mirror—emotions too vibrant, too volatile to show the world.

Suddenly realizing what Holly was too polite to ask, Lauren said, "Would you like to hold the baby?"

Holly beamed. She reached for Nissa and clasped her to her heart, cooing into the baby's ear. Lauren envisioned Holly as a young mother, tickling her son, kissing his toes…and feeling his pain more heavily than her own.

Lauren looked out over a sea eerily serene beneath a pearly sky. The only sound was the soft breath of the ventilation system. "When I saw Alex, he seemed to be carrying a lot of guilt."

Holly bit her lip. "He blames himself for what happened. He couldn't protect his daughter, so he doesn't deserve children. He couldn't save his marriage, so he doesn't deserve love."

"I tried to get him to talk about it…"

Holly nodded. "Grief is a solitary thing. Moving three thousand miles away made it harder."

"Now that he's home, maybe things will get better." Lauren hated offering a hollow platitude, but her insight into his heart was too nebulous to verbalize. Despite his professional success, he seemed haunted by feelings of inadequacy in his personal life. She couldn't understand why.

Holly's glance wandered to the stack of papers in her outbox—donations to worthy causes, Lauren imagined. Holly surrounded herself with goodness but couldn't stop evil from reaching its fingers into her pristine world.

"Sometimes I wonder if my work here is pure vanity," Holly said. "Sadness and violence are all around us. Does education truly make a difference?"

Warmth filled Lauren's chest. "I think it's the only thing that can."

Holly's expression softened. She kissed the baby's cheek and handed her to Lauren. Then, she picked up a pen. Eyes glinting, jaw firm, she wrote another check.

At lunchtime, Karina rapped on the open door to Sean's office, the sound hollow in her ears. He looked up, eyes drooping. She could only imagine the heaviness of his emotions. A clinical psychologist for the county, he had spent the morning testifying at the competency hearing of accused serial killer Wes Pauling.

Her insides grew cold, thinking about Sean interviewing that monster.

"Glad you're back," she said. "Let's go to lunch."

"I have a ton of paperwork—"

"You have to eat," she said.

"I can eat at my desk."

"Not today. You need a break."

He raised his brows but argued no further.

They walked to a sandwich shop, and the air conditioning raised goosebumps on her arms. The smell of vinegar wrinkled her nose. As they waited in line, she asked, "Want to talk about it?"

"Nothing to talk about. Like I said on the witness stand, he was cogent, coherent, and showed no remorse."

"And how does that make you feel?"

Sean smiled. "You're analyzing *me* now?"

"I don't want you taking this home to my sister and my niece."

"I do this for a living. I can handle it."

She nodded, stomach tightening.

He asked, "Are *you* handling it okay?"

"I keep thinking about the man who shot Tara. Would he have felt remorse, if he'd lived? It would be easier to forgive him if I thought he'd be sorry."

"Forgiveness isn't about the other person," Sean said. "It's about letting go of your anger."

He was missing the point, as usual. "Ethically, if the man didn't repent, is it my Christian duty to forgive him? Would he even have cared about killing Tara's baby and destroying her marriage?"

"You need to come to terms with this. Eventually, you'll have to defend someone like him."

"I'm not wishing eternal damnation on the guy. I just wish, for one day, he could feel what I feel."

Sean touched her shoulder. "Maybe you should talk to someone."

"I thought I was."

"No, I mean..." He smiled. "Never mind."

Reaching the counter, Karina ordered a Greek salad, and Sean a tuna sub. With their lunches tucked into a white paper bag, they walked along Broadway toward the harbor, then sat on a shaded bench near the contemporary art museum.

His cell phone beeped. Checking the text message, he brightened. "Lauren got the grant."

Karina's stomach jumped. Though happy for Lauren, she hadn't expected Holly to be that generous.

He scowled. "You didn't think she would?"

"If Holly wanted to punish Tara for divorcing Alex, this was the perfect opportunity."

"Holly's not like that."

"She's incapable of showing human emotion, just like Alex." Karina's gaze fell on a sculpture shaped like a giant coin balanced on its rim, frozen in that moment before it should logically topple over. "Have you ever seen her smile? Have you seen her shed a tear?"

Sean sat back and the bench creaked. "The day of the baby's funeral—after you and Alex went to the hospital to sit with Tara—Holly broke down."

Karina stared at the bows of her shoes. The shooting had hurt Holly, but little else seemed to faze her. "She seemed relieved by the divorce. Like she never wanted Alex to marry Tara in the first place."

"She put on a good face to keep Alex's spirits up during the most difficult time of his life. That doesn't make her the enemy."

Karina nodded and pushed the painful thoughts from her mind.

Returning to the office, she entered the empty break room and got a bottle of water from the drink machine. She sank onto the couch, the tension in her neck rising to her scalp. Emotions flooded over her, jumbled images, the memory of Holly's ashen face when she had rushed into Jack's office at the restaurant—

where Karina had met her father for dinner—and said in a controlled voice, "I'm taking you to the hospital. Tara needs you."

Holly's summons was firm but gentle. As Karina and her father climbed into the back of the limousine, Karina vaguely imagined they would find Tara in the emergency room getting stitches. Slowly, the gravity of the situation spilled from Holly's lips. Yet it wasn't until Karina saw Alex, dressed in hospital scrubs, that she comprehended Tara's danger. Alex was translucent. Paralyzed with terror, he faded into the furniture. When the doctor told them the baby was lost, Alex murmured, "It's my fault," speaking with such conviction that Karina believed him.

Viewing those memories through the prism of time, she pressed her fingers to the cream-colored couch, outlining the stripes of olive and burgundy.

Alex, passing by, entered and sat beside her. The weight of his presence sent a tingle up her spine. She studied his features—the concern in his eyes, the lines in his forehead. In a soft voice, she asked, "Why are you nice to me, when I'm so mean to you?"

"You're one of my favorite people. Even when you're mad at me."

She gripped his hand. "Sometimes it's easier to be angry than to let the pain in."

"And it's especially easy to be angry with me."

Because Alex, for all his skill at argument, never made personal attacks. He defended himself without retaliating. Underneath that abrasive exterior was a kind and gentle heart.

She swallowed the pebble in her throat. "How could it take me so long to see that you're a good man?"

He lowered his eyes. "I cultivate the illusion I'm not."

"To keep people distant, like your mother does." She stroked the curve of his hairline above his ear. His body contracted at her touch.

"Women look at me and see money. Tara was the first one who loved me for *me*. I don't know how to find that again."

"Your heart isn't open. You're still healing." She searched his eyes. "I wish I could do something to make you happy."

The corner of his mouth quirked up. "You could get Tara drunk for me."

"Getting laid won't solve your problems."

"It'll solve one of my problems."

Karina didn't argue. She rose and approached the window. The sun was high, and the glare dazzling. The city was stark in the unforgiving light.

He walked up behind her and put his arms around her waist. The intimacy of the gesture surprised her, yet it felt natural, affectionate. After all, he had been her brother-in-law for three years.

She laid her hands on his, realizing how much she missed a man's touch. She wondered whether it was time to start dating again.

"You hug great," she said, "even from behind."

"I always thought it was better from behind," he murmured in her ear.

She turned. "Naughty boy!"

"You're right. I should go to my office and forget how good you smell—"

"Alex—"

"I'm going."

He left, but the sensation of him remained.

❦

That evening, Tara and Karina went to Monterey Jack's Dance Hall and Saloon, the lounge at their father's restaurant. The décor featured memorabilia from the days of wranglers and gold miners and railroad towns springing up on the plain. But the gleaming cherry bar would have looked at home in a five-star hotel. The atmosphere downplayed a martini menu as varied as any in San Diego and a wine list to delight the most discriminating oenophile.

Beyond the picture windows, a pair of pelicans swooped by, their acrobatics synchronized as they plunged into the harbor after their prey. The sisters found seats at the bar. Tara wriggled into place, her narrow dress clinging to her hips. Karina's diaphanous skirt flounced over the barstool.

Tara ordered a zinfandel, and Karina a cosmopolitan with two orange slices. Karina excused herself, and Tara watched her navigate through the crowd toward the ladies' room.

Tara turned as the bartender delivered their drinks. He smiled. "The gentleman at the other end of the bar asked me to put these on his tab."

She peered through the crowd and spotted Alex. She waved him over, but he lifted his hand to decline. Rolling her eyes, she motioned again. He relented. Though she offered him Karina's seat, he continued to stand.

"It's good to see you." Her cheeks warmed. "It's been a while."

He grinned. "When you asked for the divorce, you said you needed space."

"And you gave me a continent." She swirled her wine and watched him from the corner of her eye. "I'm glad you're back."

He nodded. "My Washington experiment failed."

"Senator Hartley would disagree."

Alex arranged swizzle sticks into a triangle.

"How do you like working as a public defender?" she asked.

"Haven't embarrassed myself too badly."

"Please." She crumpled her cocktail napkin into a tight ball. "Do you miss Washington?"

He picked up his scotch, the ice cubes rattling. "In Washington, I could immerse myself in my job. But living at the beach house, working with your sister—I'm forced to deal with my grief."

She met his eyes, but under his steady gaze, looked away. She couldn't talk about it—she just couldn't.

He laid some cash on the bar and pressed his lips to her forehead. With an ache, she watched him go.

Karina returned. Tapping her fingers on the bar in time with the music, she scowled. "What's wrong?"

Tara lowered her eyes. "Alex was here."

"You chased him off?"

"We had a nice chat." Tara flattened her napkin, smoothing out the wrinkles.

Karina scrunched her brow. "What's up with you two?"

"Nothing. We're divorced."

"Because when you see him, all you feel is pain." Karina massaged the stem of her glass, then met Tara's eyes. "Are you sure the pain you feel isn't because you still love him?"

Tara sank her head into her hands, but Karina persisted. "A desirable man like Alex won't stay alone long."

Tara sat up. "He's seeing someone?"

"He's looking. Why do you think he was here?"

The next morning, Alex walked along the beach with his mother, the damp air hanging between them. The sand was soft and cool between his toes, but his shoulders felt heavy. He slid his hands into his pockets and gazed into the distance.

His mother's voice rose as softly as the breeze. "I saw Lauren yesterday. We met about a grant proposal, then discussed...other things."

He furrowed his brow. "Meaning me?"

"Meaning you and Tara. And...Susannah."

He halted.

His mother touched his arm, and the puckers of his seersucker shirt felt rough on his skin beneath her fingertips. "You need to talk about it," she said. "The guilt is tearing you apart."

"I should have prevented it."

"You tried to prevent it."

The ocean heaved, and clouds gathered in the distance. He imagined his daughter running along the beach, her dark curls bouncing to the rhythm of her gait, while he and Tara followed a step behind. His eyes pointed toward the horizon but focused on nothing. "I don't understand how I lost control of my life. Tara gave up on us, and nothing I did could change that."

"The divorce was her way of forgetting."

"Like leaving town was for me."

"And now you're back." Sunlight turned his mother's hair to burnished copper.

"If you mean that now, maybe Tara's ready..."

"I'm just making an observation."

He kicked a pebble across the sand. His mind, adept at logic, felt ill-equipped to plumb the murky depths of emotion. He had tried to avoid intruding on Tara the night before, but she had invited him to intrude. What did that mean? Maybe it meant nothing, and his hope deceived him. But Alex trusted his mother's perceptions. She was not a careless woman.

"You think I should fight for Tara," he said.

"You should do what feels right."

"She says she wants me to move on."

"Do you believe her?"

Palm leaves sang in the breeze. He breathed to chase away the dark emotions weighing down his chest. "When I'm with her, I watch for a glimmer of what she used to feel. But the way she looks at me..." He swallowed hard, hating the sound of emotion in his voice. "I could be anyone."

Holly rubbed her arms against the chill. "It's the grief, Alex. Tara's not herself."

"If it were grief, she'd have come to me for comfort. She blames me for what happened."

"I don't believe that!"

His mother's certainty offered him no solace. He looked out over the waves until his eyes met the horizon, and the endless ocean dissolved into nothing.

At lunchtime on Monday, Tara scowled at her computer screen. Sunshine spilled through the window and onto the neat stack of reference books on her desk. Three times, she'd added and removed the same comma. She flopped back in her chair. She'd enjoyed her transition from reporter to columnist, but some days her words felt like abstractions separating her from the physical world.

With her fork, she tossed the wilting leaves of her salad. She tried to push down thoughts of Alex. It had felt good to talk to him Friday night. Why had she closed herself off when he spoke about his grief? She wanted to share those feelings with him. Yet like an injured lioness, she'd retreated into solitude, too vulnerable to let the pride see her wounds.

Tara looked up when her boss, Evan McCade, sashayed into her office. He was a man of thirty-three with delicate hands and thick biceps. Wearing a bright yellow shirt and teal slacks, he sank into a chair. "You know how my life sucks, right?"

She speared a mandarin orange in her salad. "Because you wanted to be a Vegas showgirl, but instead, your father made you editor-in-chief of his newspaper?"

"I'm driving this place into bankruptcy!" His shoulders slumped.

"What are you talking about? Ads are up, circulation's up..."

He rose, brushing his hand across his short black hair. "When I hired that new investigative reporter, I knew she was green. But she writes well. She's determined. She's got chutzpah."

"So what's the problem?"

"She doesn't know what she's doing!" He flung up his arms. "And I don't have time to train her. She needs a mentor."

Tara nodded. "You mean me."

"Could you do this for me? It won't involve any field work—just point her in the right direction."

Containing her excitement, Tara looked into his round, boyish face. "I'd be happy to."

His eyes brightened. "You're such a doll! What would I do without you?"

⁂

That afternoon, Tara met with the young reporter, Li Jing Wu, a petite woman with shoulder-length black hair and a childlike face. Her wire-rimmed glasses gave her a shy and unassuming look, but her eyes and ears missed nothing. She could eavesdrop in plain sight, and she ferreted out a story like a terrier hunting a rat.

Tara found that Li Jing had good instincts but little discipline. She didn't seem eager for help but didn't resist, either. She followed Tara's advice, and with gentle persuasion, became more respectful of deadlines and absolute accuracy.

One afternoon, Tara looked up from her computer to see Evan standing in her doorway, pressing his hands against the jamb. "The new girl needs help with a story."

"Her name is Li Jing."

He closed the door and gazed at Tara with eyes as blue as the noonday sky. "A source at city hall said...well, implied...there were some, you know, improprieties in the mayor's last campaign."

Tara lurched forward, grasping the arms of her chair. "You're giving a story like that to the new girl?"

"It's her source, it's her story. That's why she needs your help."

"This could be huge!"

His broad smile matched Tara's. "Remember, it'll be her name on the byline."

She didn't care about that. Here was a chance to stop living in her head, to deal more in facts than ideas. If the allegations were true... A cascade of possibilities flooded her mind.

He pawed at the air like a cat. "The source also said..."

She held her breath, watching his features.

He continued, "Someone in the D.A.'s office is protecting the mayor."

A shot of adrenaline forced her to her feet. She grabbed her desk to steady herself, thoughts racing. A chill raced through her, and her stomach twisted. "The D.A. is a friend of mine. I can't help Li Jing spy on him!"

Evan rocked from his heels to his toes. "She'll do the investigating, you just help with the process. Besides, there's no reason to think...I mean, the story isn't about Dayne Emery."

"No, it's about corruption in his office." Tara's heart clenched. "How can you tell me this, then ask me to keep it from him?"

"Because it's your job."

"I'm a columnist. I agreed to help Li Jing as a favor to you."

"You know, sometimes I think you forget I'm your boss."

"I thought you were also my friend."

He sidled up to her. "You could come to my place after work. I'll make mojitos and teach you Pink's latest dance moves."

Tara suppressed a laugh. Looking into his penitent eyes, she forgave her friend, but her anger at her boss persisted.

⁓⚜⁓

That evening, Karina stood in the church parking lot, leaning against her car. The sun radiated from behind the steeple, but the heat of the day was fading. The old stucco building glowed in the slanting light. A rabbit scooted across the lawn, stopping for a nibble before hiding among the white-flowered hawthorn. Traffic noise hummed in the distance.

Alex pulled up in his blue BMW, parking next to her cherry-red Miata. She smiled as he slammed his door. "You made it!"

He approached. "I can't believe you talked me in to this. I don't know anything about teenagers."

"It'll be fun. Besides, you'll be helping out the food bank."

"Can't I just send a check?"

"Don't be cynical. It feels good to help people."

His expression didn't soften.

"First order of business," she said, "what's our primary goal tonight?"

He crossed his arms. "Keep these kids in line."

"Sorry, the *correct* answer is, to inspire a love of volunteerism. These are good kids. We want them to feel a sense of accomplishment. So we do not give orders."

He scowled. "Then why did you ask *me* to do this?"

"Because everyone else was busy, while you have no life."

A breeze off the ocean cooled the air. The teens began to arrive, a giggling, boisterous bunch. Karina took out an orange plastic clipboard and wrote down each name as Alex loaded the kids into the van.

Karina drove to the food bank. The director, a reedy, umber-skinned woman with close-cropped gray hair and wearing a sarong of gold and fuchsia, greeted them outside. She and Karina spoke as they entered, while Alex herded the teens in behind them. With the director at her side, Karina assembled the kids in an open space near the warehouse entrance.

"Listen up, everyone," Karina said, pointing, "over on those pallets are crates of food. We'll be opening the crates and bringing the packages over here to put into boxes for individual families. To open the crates, we're using box cutters. If you mishandle a box cutter, I'll take it away from you.

"Also, you see that forklift? No one goes within ten feet of it. As usual, there will be no horseplay. We're here to have fun and help some families who are down on their luck, and to do it safely.

"Let's break into groups..." Karina looked into their faces. "Emily, honey, you're shivering. Remember when I said this was a warehouse, and you should dress warmly? Fortunately, I brought a couple of sweatshirts— this ugly pea green one, and this ugly puke brown one. Which do you want?"

Rubbing her gooseflesh arms, Emily sauntered over and took the green one. She put it on over her pale floral halter top.

"Remember," Karina said, "appropriate dress is the key to success."

The teens divided into workgroups, an adult overseeing each group. Once they developed a rhythm, the director retreated to her office, while Alex and Karina wandered among the kids. To Karina's surprise, Alex watched but didn't interfere, helping when needed, but otherwise staying out of the way. He seemed to enjoy watching the kids work things out for themselves. Karina, for her part, chatted with the girls, offering advice about clothes, makeup, and most importantly, boys.

Toward the end of the evening, Alex, his forehead creased, strolled toward her. "We've got a problem," he said in low tones. "That blond girl, dressed in black—I think her name is Sarah? I saw her putting packages of food into her tote bag."

Karina's stomach shrank. "Sarah's mom lost her job, and her dad's been delinquent with child support."

Alex scuffed his shoe on the floor. "I should have realized."

"Don't worry." She touched his arm. "I'll talk to Reverend Freeborn to see how the church can help."

Alex stroked his chin. "Think you can handle this without me for a few minutes? There's something I want to do. I'll need the van keys."

Karina shrugged. "Sure."

She handed him the keys, and he smiled.

Twenty minutes later, as the group was wrapping up, Alex returned and made an announcement. "An anonymous friend of the church," he said, "donated a door prize to give away tonight, as thanks for your hard work."

"An iPod?" Josh asked.

"Maybe next time," Alex said. "It's a gift card to Trader Joe's."

The group groaned.

Alex picked up Karina's clipboard from the crate where it sat next to her purse. "I'll select a name at random..." He closed his eyes and pointed to the clipboard. Opening his eyes, he said, "Sarah."

The girl's posture straightened and she blushed, her eyes widening. Alex walked over and handed her the card.

"Thanks," she replied in a small voice, turning her gaze toward the floor.

Karina's throat tightened, and warmth flowed into her fingertips. Kindness she expected from Alex, but sensitivity...She looked toward him. He wouldn't meet her eyes, but his cheeks flushed.

The teens gathered up their things. Karina saw Sarah disappear behind a pallet, then reappear with her tote bag noticeably lighter. Alex led the kids to the van, and Karina followed behind. She rested her hand on Sarah's shoulder. The girl turned to her, and they smiled.

Back at the church parking lot, after the teens had gone, Karina squeezed Alex's hand. "You were great tonight. You know teenagers better than you think."

"I remember being where they are." He kicked the gravel in the disintegrating asphalt. "It's important they learn confidence at that age. They can be disillusioned so easily."

He grew silent. Karina touched his arm until his emotion passed.

"I should head home," he said.

"Thanks for coming."

"It was fun," he said. "You were right."

"If you ever want to do it again...I plan activities for the youth group every month."

"Don't push your luck."

"Give it up," she said. "You can't fool me."

"Fine, next time the youth pastor comes down with bronchitis, give me a call. But only if it's an emergency."

She watched him drive away, and a sense of peace washed over her. She'd done a good thing, bringing people together who needed each other. She got into her car and drove home with renewed purpose. The headlights illuminated her path, and the cloaking darkness focused her vision. The open road was all she could see.

The following week Holly sat in her office at the Kent Foundation, waiting for a visit from Tara. The tension in Tara's voice over the phone had told Holly something was wrong. Tara tried to make light of it, but the swirling in Holly's stomach remained.

Since the divorce, Holly had barely seen Tara. Holly tried not to take it personally. She couldn't blame Tara for wanting to avoid anything that could remind her of Alex—and nothing could remind Tara of Alex more than his mother. They had the same rigid cheekbones, the same aristocratic nose, the same smile that danced in their eyes while the rest of their features frowned. Alex was unmistakably Holly's son.

Holly hoped this visit would thaw her relationship with Tara. There were few people in the world Holly loved, but Tara was one of them. Still, Holly wasn't optimistic. If Tara wanted to see her because she missed her, Tara would have said so. On the phone, she was vague, as if afraid someone would overhear.

Holly's dread worsened when Tara arrived. She looked drawn, as if some specter had inhabited her features.

She walked to the window of Holly's office, then stood hugging herself. "What I have to say can't leave this room. No one can know—not even Alex. Especially Alex."

"You have my word."

Tara kept silent, increasing Holly's alarm. But Holly didn't press her.

"How well do you know the mayor?" asked Tara.

Holly arched her eyebrows. "I worked with him on city council for six years, but I wouldn't call him a friend."

"The paper's investigating a report that his campaign violated financing laws, and now he's involved in a cover-up."

Holly drew her breath. "That's a serious charge."

"Is it plausible?"

She bit her cheeks. Scattered memories flitted through her mind. She hated to think ill of anyone, so sometimes avoided processing her observations. But she had no illusions about the mayor.

"If he were behaving unethically, it wouldn't show."

Tara stared into space. "I keep hoping it's not true. So many people will be hurt..."

Holly approached and gazed into Tara's face. "Darling, what aren't you saying? You're not this upset about the mayor."

"I can't put you in the middle of this. I wish I weren't in the middle of it."

"Why does Evan have you investigating this?"

"I'm not. He'd kill me if he knew I was talking to you." She pressed Holly's hand, then picked up her purse. "Thanks for your time."

Holly's chest tightened. "Before you go...Let's have lunch sometime."

Tara shrank and stared at the stone tile floor.

Holly stroked Tara's hair. "Running from the pain won't help you overcome it."

Tara began to shake, but she quickly recovered, wiping tears from her lashes. "I wish people wouldn't worry about me. I'm making you unhappy, Holly, and I don't want you to be unhappy."

"You mustn't think that way. You bring joy to every life you touch."

"I thought after the divorce, Alex would stop worrying about me. But he worries even more."

"Of course he does. He loves you."

"When I was pregnant...he constantly worried something bad would happen. But I can't blame him for being protective when he was right."

Holly clutched Tara's hand. "But that doesn't make you wrong. Pregnancy didn't deny you the privilege of living your life."

Tara's thin shoulders continued to droop. She kissed Holly's cheek before departing. Holly watched after her, wishing she could do more, but knowing that solace could only come from within.

⁕

Driving home, Tara tried not to think about it. She tried not to think how easy it would have been, the night she got shot, to go home after work instead of pursuing that tip. If she'd listened to Alex, his daughter would be alive.

That night, sleep offered no rest. A recurring dream haunted her. She was in the house where she had grown up, sitting in her father's study, coloring a picture with crayons of pink and blue. Her nimble fingers traced over each line, then filled in the shapes, using light pressure for wispy color, using heavy pressure for saturated color. She admired her creation, feeling pleased. Then Alex burst in.

"Where's the baby?"

Panic washed over her. What had she done with the baby?

She rushed around with Alex following, looking under the beds, into the closets, under the cushions of the couch. She ran outside, searching through the flowerbeds and peering under shrubs. Finally, she stood sobbing, and Alex shrieked, "How could you lose the baby?"

When morning came, Tara rose feeling spent. Her empty arms ached. She thought of Lauren with her perfect little girl and sank to the carpet. Eyes closed, she breathed deeply until the rage subsided.

At work, Tara shut her door and immersed herself in her column. By lunchtime, the dark mood had passed. Massaging her shoulder, she wondered why she had let the dream unsettle her. These days, thoughts of Alex always unsettled her.

His fears throughout her pregnancy had been irrational. Worse, he knew they were irrational, yet his only thought was safeguarding the baby. She did what she could to placate him—avoiding unnecessary driving, switching from weight training to yoga. But her job wasn't part of her life with Alex. She had spent too many years waiting for plum assignments to turn them down because she was pregnant. Alex vehemently disapproved, but after expressing his feelings, left it to her judgment. She followed her conscience—and the result was more horrific than Alex's worst fear.

Tara rubbed the back of her neck. She was tired of that dream and the dead-end road it led her down.

Reflecting on the past could only bring her pain. She needed to concentrate on the future.

Spurred by emotion, Tara finished her column early. She met with Li Jing that afternoon to review the file the young reporter had gathered on the mayor. To Tara's surprise, Li Jing had traced two sizeable contributions to donors in Mexico—conclusive evidence that the campaign had broken the law. "This is good work," Tara said. "This in itself is enough for a story."

Li Jing scrunched her nose. "But I've got nothing to link the D.A.'s office to the cover-up."

"Maybe your source was wrong about that."

"My source has been right about everything else."

Tara bristled inside at the dismissive tone but hid her annoyance. "Still, we should publish what we've got, before this gets out and we lose our chance. Let's talk to Evan—"

"I've already talked to him. He wants to wait, so we don't tip off whoever else is involved."

A chill rose from her gut to her chest. "That's a big risk, don't you think?"

"For a big payoff."

Tara rolled a red pen across her desktop. Why had Evan involved her in this, if he was going to make decisions without her?

"You know people in the D.A.'s office," Li Jing said. "Who has ties to the mayor?"

Tara shut her eyes against the din clanging in her head. She had hoped Li Jing would discover the truth herself. Instead, Tara was forced to say the words she had been dreading. Words that implicated two people she considered friends. "Maybe the link isn't political. The campaign manager, Brooke Genovese, used to date the A.D.A., Jerry Silverstein. They're still close."

Li Jing's eyes sparkled behind her wire-rimmed glasses. She rose and rushed from the room. The knot in Tara's chest tightened.

⁓⁓❦⁓⁓

Thursday after work, Alex and Karina went to Monterey Jack's. They found a table overlooking the bay, then ordered drinks and an appetizer. Alex took the folder on Miguel Santos from his briefcase, glad Karina had agreed to attend the hearing the next morning.

She flipped her hair. "Remind me again why you can't handle this case on your own?"

He squinted his displeasure. "Santos likes you. So does Judge Walenski."

"Don't tell me you're afraid of Fran Walenski."

"No, but you clerked for her," he said. "My client needs every advantage he can get."

"Despite his rap sheet, Santos is basically a good guy."

"With a penchant for beating his ex-wife."

"An ex-wife who bashed his head with a cast iron pan," Karina said, "sending him to the hospital with a subdural hematoma. Gail Santos is not the victim in that relationship."

He admired Karina's dancing eyes. She needed to believe that her clients could be rehabilitated—he understood that. But he worried at her downplaying Santos's history of violence.

The bartender delivered their drinks and a large plate of lime-glazed shrimp. Karina raised her glass of white zinfandel to Alex. "To dateless losers."

"We're not losers." He sipped his Sam Adams. "We choose not to date."

"How long has it been since you asked a woman out?"

He stared into his beer, the memories of his few dates since Tara shrouded in darkness. Women wanted the lifestyle he offered, and they were willing to use sex to get it. But without love, sex was a bodily function, and those women receptacles for his shame.

He eyed Karina, her expression open and eager. Apparently, she had adopted him as her latest project. For as long as he had known her, the men she dated were fixer-uppers: coming out of a disastrous relationship, or about to file for bankruptcy, or stuck in a dead-end job they hated. A ministering angel, Karina appeared in their time of need—but they didn't want to be saved. Fortunately, she had a short attention span. With nothing to attach her to these men, she moved on.

She squeezed his arm and looked at him with soft eyes. "You need to date. Think what you're denying the women of San Diego. You can't let that man-candy go to waste."

He scowled at her, his jaw firm, but the touch of her hand warmed him. His heart had been empty so long that even her careless teasing caused something inside him to stir.

7 Urgent

FRIDAY MORNING, HER STOMACH TENSE, KARINA entered the courtroom. It wasn't the sort of dignified space she had imagined when she was in law school. She strode through the gallery toward the podium, which was flanked by two tables so close together that the defense on the left side could shake hands with the prosecution on the right. Before them was the judge's bench, constructed of plain blond wood. Bookcases filled with heavy tomes covered three walls.

She slipped past Alex, who stood at the table reviewing his notes. He gave her a brief smile. Next to him sat Miguel Santos, a man in his mid-thirties with a stocky build and haphazard haircut. She was thankful she could smell no alcohol on him. She took a seat on his other side.

Santos's thick fists rested atop the table. His nails were dirty, and two of them showed bruised skin beneath. She pressed a comforting hand to his shoulder. Her gaze fell to a long, jagged cut on his forearm. He pulled down his shirt sleeve, trying to cover it, but his cuffs were too short.

The tension in her gut spread to her chest. Her glance wandered to the bailiff just to her left. The appearance of the husky young officer in the gray uniform did not fill her with confidence.

She told herself this hearing was routine. Alex would do the talking. She was there for moral support, for Miguel more than Alex. Miguel had seemed alone and hopeless when she first represented him—but she had gotten him into a metalworking training program that could lead to a good job. He had seemed excited about that. Why had he risked his probation? Was he drinking again? She hoped his ex-wife wasn't back in his life, criticizing him and undermining his confidence.

Karina looked again at the cut on his arm. It was pink and swollen. He needed to see a doctor. She wondered if she would have time after the hearing to get him to a clinic.

A door opened. The assembly rose at the entry of Judge Francine Walenski, a broadly built woman in her mid-fifties with gray streaking her short, black hair. Alex stood at the podium while Fran grilled him about the failure of his client to meet the terms of his probation.

Karina watched Miguel. His hands twitched, and he rocked in his chair. Karina glanced at the bailiff. He met her eyes.

The judge spoke. "Mr. Santos, domestic violence is a serious offense. The leniency I've shown in the past—"

Miguel jumped to his feet. "I won't go to jail for that bitch!"

Karina clutched the arms of the chair, anxiety rising in her stomach. But Fran knew how to handle these situations. Her unflappable manner had a calming effect.

Fran watched him over her glasses, then set her jaw firmly. "Another outburst like that—"

"I won't go to jail 'cause of her, you hear?" Miguel's face reddened.

Karina stood and squeezed Miguel's arm, whispering, "Please, Mr. Santos..."

Wide-eyed panic swept through his features. She turned to see the bailiff looming, Taser in hand.

Miguel yanked her in front of him. She pulled, but Miguel gripped harder, shielding his body with hers.

Adrenaline lit a fire low in her belly. The bailiff pushed forward, voice booming a warning.

She cringed, caught between them. Miguel slashed at the bailiff. A glint of light, and the bailiff jumped back, hand bleeding.

She gasped. Miguel's fist clutched a homemade knife of broken glass.

Terror closed her throat—a chaos of shouting and screeching chairs—a pang in her neck from the razor edge of the glass shank.

Her breath stopped and dread chilled her blood. She trained her eyes on the bailiff.

"Stay back," Miguel said. "Don't make me hurt the pretty lady." He panted hotly on her neck. The heel of his hand dug into her ribcage, cleaving her to his body.

Silence. The ticking of a clock. She prayed.

A shuffling behind her, and Miguel turned, angling her to the right. Officers now scattered through the courtroom couldn't use their guns in the confined space. She swallowed, heart hammering.

Alex stood close, his muscles poised to act. Her pulse slowed. He would protect her.

His face was stoic, but fire shone in his eyes. He stared at Miguel and said in a measured voice, "Think about what you're doing. You said Ms. Fields was the first person who believed in you—you don't want to hurt her."

"I don't want to hurt nobody." Miguel shifted his stance, turning to the judge. "But I won't go to jail 'cause of that bitch. She tricked me into marrying her, then destroyed my life!"

"You're not facing serious time," Alex said, stepping closer, "but you will be if you don't put that knife down."

"Back off!" Miguel glared at Alex.

Alex held up his palms and retreated. He stopped in the aisle in front of the gallery, standing between Miguel and the exit.

Miguel clutched Karina tighter, compressing her diaphragm. The knife pressed into her skin. Silently, she prayed. Images floated through her mind: her father sitting with Tara in the ICU, her mother wan from cancer telling her family she was going to a better place. Karina wished she could be brave, too. She thought of all the wasted moments in her life and wanted them back.

The judge spoke in an even tone. "Mr. Santos, I know how much trouble your ex-wife has caused you—"

"You don't know!" Miguel's tears dropped onto Karina's neck. "That bitch kept pushing me...I never meant to hurt her. She gave me no choice. She had a knife."

A chill swept over Karina. She understood. The clarity in Alex's eyes said he did, too.

Miguel's body straightened. "I won't go to jail over her. You'll have to kill me first."

A sob caught in her chest and her eyes burned. She wouldn't get out of this alive.

Alex clenched his jaw, determination in his features. "Mr. Santos, whatever you did was in self-defense. You won't go to jail for that."

A rustling behind her drew her eyes. The bailiff inched closer.

"What are you doin', man?" Miguel dragged Karina backward like a ragdoll, into the aisle. "You wanna make me hurt the pretty lady?"

Facing the bailiff, Miguel breathed hard. He held Karina tight against him, but her body was slumped sideways toward Alex.

Alex trained his eyes on the judge and clenched his fist, making a small tapping motion in the air. A sharp rap came from the judge's bench. Miguel spun toward the noise.

An impact from behind threw Karina forward, her head hitting the floor. The glass shank skittered toward the judge's bench.

The sharp ache of the fall spread from her forehead through her scalp. Miguel's weight lifted from her. She rolled away and saw Alex on the floor with his knee between Miguel's shoulder blades, while the bailiff cuffed Miguel.

She blinked, the silver spots before her eyes dissipating. Her mind tried to break through the fuzziness of fear. What had happened?

Miguel's arm had dropped when the judge pounded her gavel. Alex must have tackled him.

She pushed herself into a seated position, thankful that the floor was linoleum instead of stone. The bailiff led Miguel away.

Alex knelt beside her and helped her to her feet. She clutched her pounding forehead. Her legs felt unsure, and he held her arms to steady her.

She looked up at him, his eyes a calm harbor after a storm. The touch of his hands broke open the fear gripping her chest. Her body trembled, and a whimper rose from deep in her gut. With gentle fingers, he dried the tears dampening her cheek. She clutched his shirt and sank into the tender circle of his arms.

❧

Tara sat on a tan leather chair in her father's family room, waiting for a call from Evan. She stared at the opposite wall, into the fireplace. Its mouth was dark and empty.

Her gaze wandered to the couch, where Lauren sat stroking Karina's hair. Their father dabbed antiseptic onto a scrape on Karina's elbow. Her face twisted, and she sucked her breath through her teeth.

"Almost done, baby," their father assured her. He patted a bandage on. His eyes fell to the bump above her temple. "Sure you don't want to see a doctor?"

"I don't have a concussion. Just a little bump."

Lauren drew Karina close, and Karina laid her head on Lauren's shoulder.

Their father rose, then paced in front of the floor-to-ceiling windows. His right fist punched at his left palm. *Paper covers rock.* Tara knew the gesture well.

Silent, she clenched her jaw against the anger pulsing inside her. She didn't let herself think about how differently the day could have turned out.

The ringtone of her cell phone made her jump. Evan's voice brought the expected report. Tara clicked her phone shut and looked into Karina's anxious eyes.

"I'm sorry, Kare. Police found Gail Santos's body. Single gunshot wound and a bloody knife at her feet—probably how he got the cut on his arm."

"Then it was self-defense, like he said?" Karina asked.

"Looks that way."

Karina nodded, then sobbed on Lauren's shoulder.

Tara went to her father. His face contorted. She hugged him, sensing his rage. He had spent a lifetime protecting his daughters, and now they had jobs that exposed them to criminals.

Except Lauren, the sensible one. Tara wished she were sensible, too, so she wouldn't see her father's disappointment.

Most of her life, Tara's desire for his approval had guided her choices. After the shooting, while she stayed at his house during her recuperation, he sat with her for hours, caring for her physical needs. But he lectured her repeatedly about the divorce. Alex was a good man, and divorce was unchristian.

Tara was the only one who understood that the dynamic between her and Alex, their inability to communicate, had killed their daughter. Loving Alex was the problem, and leaving him the only solution.

Tears welled in her eyes, but she swallowed her sorrow. Karina was safe. That was what mattered.

Their father sat next to Karina. "Feel up to a family dinner at the restaurant tonight?"

Karina smiled. "That would be nice—except Tara's got plans with Steph."

Tara raised her brow. "I'll reschedule with Steph. I'm not leaving you home alone tonight." Stephanie was an old college friend, party girl *par excellence*, but family came first.

Karina flipped back her hair. "I don't need a babysitter. I'm fine."

"You're not fine," Tara said. "You're in shock."

"I've got a few bruises, that's all. Stop worrying."

Tara locked eyes with Lauren, who gave her a knowing smile. This was vintage Karina, creating drama over little things but downplaying the big ones.

"Kare, you don't need to protect us," Tara said. "Let us look after you."

Karina stood and hugged herself. "Please don't make so much of this. Santos was scared—but he wouldn't have hurt me."

Tara wanted to scream, *He killed his wife!* Yet she understood Karina's distress, how her family's fear magnified Karina's own. Maybe the best way to comfort her was to humor her.

"You could join Steph and me at the Saloon after dinner. Maybe some drinks and dancing would help you relax."

Karina smiled her assent.

Driving to the restaurant, Tara looked out over the city that sprawled below her, white stucco and clay roofs and blue ocean beneath a crystal sky. Tara was grateful to God—and to Alex. Alex had saved her sister, giving Tara one more reason to feel indebted to him.

She hated the resentment bubbling inside her. She knew that her own insecurities were to blame—not Alex. During their marriage, Alex had loved surprising Tara with little trinkets, like a gold bracelet or emerald earrings or a strand of natural black pearls. Tara loved his gifts, but over time, they made her feel like ornamentation, as useless as a peacock's tail.

She wasn't raised for a life of leisure. If she cooked a meal or did her own laundry, she risked offending the staff. So any lingerie that was too risqué for the maid to see, Tara stuffed unworn into the bottom of her drawer. She hated herself for being provincial. But in the end, her choice was to lose Alex or lose herself.

Tara drove into the parking lot of Susanne's Bistro. The family assembled in the waiting area. Jack greeted his daughters with a smile, more relief than happiness. Tara took Nissa from Lauren. The baby's softness soothed Tara's weary heart. She cooed to Nissa, "You've got your mama's dark hair and your daddy's blue eyes and your grampa's round belly…"

Jack patted his midsection. "This is all muscle, baby."

They entered the private dining room. The table was topped with blue linens and vases of yellow roses. Sean asked, "Why's the table set for seven?"

Jack grinned. "I asked a couple of people to join us."

Tara's breath stopped. She stared at her father, unwilling to believe he would go so far as to invite Alex.

Jack shrugged. "He saved your sister's life."

Her skin cooled, disbelief turning to dismay. "He's my ex-husband!"

Her throat closed as Alex and Holly entered. Alex's face flushed as he met Tara's eyes. She looked away, staring at the wall.

"You didn't talk to Tara before inviting us?" Holly's voice asked.

Tara retreated to a corner, still clutching Nissa. She breathed hard to prevent a rush of tears. Alex approached and murmured, "I'm sorry. If you're uncomfortable—"

"I'm not uncomfortable." Tara swung her necklace, and Nissa clutched at the gold cross.

"You're upset."

"Dad should have respected my boundaries. But he's right. You saved Karina's life. You deserve to be here."

"I won't stay if you don't want me to."

"I didn't say I don't want you to. I'm just surprised."

Alex scuffed his feet against the carpeting. "Look, I'm sorry about this..."

"It's not your fault. Dad can't accept that we're divorced. But I couldn't stay in an unhappy marriage just to please my father."

Alex's features froze. "We had an unhappy marriage?"

She turned her eyes back to the baby. "Toward the end."

A strange, hollow chuckle escaped Alex's throat. He withdrew. Tara watched him from the corner of her eye, her rage still burning. Lauren rushed over and led Tara into the ladies' room.

The door swung shut behind them. Lauren took Nissa, then said to Tara, "Go ahead. Let it out."

"My ex-husband?" Tara's cry reverberated against the tile. "What was Dad thinking?"

Lauren bounced the baby, looking into her eyes and smiling, calming Nissa's startled look. "Maybe he wasn't thinking about you."

"Please."

"Alex saved Karina's life."

"Proving to Dad, once again, how crazy I was to divorce Alex."

Lauren remained silent. Tara let her tears flow. Then, she dried her eyes and said, "I didn't need this, on top of everything else."

Lauren stroked Tara's back with her free hand. "What did you say that upset Alex?"

"Nothing he didn't already know." Tara stomped her foot. "It's not my job to worry about his feelings anymore. I don't have the energy."

"Honey, this has been a stressful day for all of us. Try not to take it out on Alex."

Tara closed her eyes. She breathed deeply, but her emotions continued to churn. "Maybe I should go home."

"Kare needs you here."

"So what do I do?"

"Order the most expensive bottle of wine in the house. Dad's paying."

⁓᭒᯽᭒⁓

In the private dining room, Alex stood quietly with no sense of his surroundings. The sound of his breath grew magnified, and the colors around him turned gray. His mother patted his arm, but she didn't speak. Alex was glad. He had no words.

He could not conceive where Tara's anger had come from. He'd poured his soul into their marriage. Now, she was rewriting history to justify her actions. He'd been a good husband. How dare she take that from him?

Tara re-entered the room with Lauren, but he couldn't look at her.

His mother led him to the table, where he sat between her and Karina. He stared at the tablecloth, the buzz of conversation playing in his ear but with no discernable words. Then, Karina touched his hand. He looked over at her, small and innocent, and suddenly knew that if he achieved nothing else in his lifetime, on that day he had done a worthwhile thing.

Warmth radiated from the candlelight, awakening the colors of the room. Alex knitted his fingers in Karina's. Her lips smiled, but her eyes were sad.

"You okay?" he asked.

"Thanks to you."

Alex looked away, but his heart opened. "Those years of college football paid off."

She squeezed his hand. He could sense the tension in her that she tried desperately to hide from her family. It reminded him, again, that the surface emotions she showed weren't the real Karina. Beneath the frail, vulnerable façade that drew men to her like bees to wild honeysuckle, she was the strong and determined woman who had graduated in the top one percent of her class from the best law school west of New England.

He got to see *that* Karina on occasion when they worked together. Her talents were still raw, but her memory of precedent helped her find connections between unrelated cases that opened up new strategies. And she had a surprising insight into human nature—when her compassion didn't blind her, as it had with Santos. But when Alex and Karina weren't discussing cases, the playful Karina dominated. He wished he could win her trust and break through her façade. The real woman interested him more.

Alex brushed aside her hair to look at the bruise on her forehead. "How's your headache?"

"The Advil is keeping the pain at bay."

"Sorry I hurt you."

"You saved my life, silly. I can handle a few bruises."

She spoke the words in a throwaway fashion. *You saved my life.* He knew she felt them more deeply. Yet Alex didn't see his actions in that light. Santos was a weak man who had to be stopped from hurting Karina. Alex had done what the situation required.

She stroked his fingers. He looked at her and smiled. The candlelight brought out the reddish tints in her hair.

When their salads arrived, Alex noticed that Karina tossed the romaine with her fork but didn't eat. He murmured in her ear, "No appetite?"

"Tired, I guess." She looked around the table with smiling eyes, then finally took a bite.

The waiter brought their entrées. Alex only half-listened as his mother spoke to Jack about the Arts Council fundraiser she had co-chaired the previous evening with Meg Silverstein.

Karina turned to Alex. "Meg Silverstein—isn't she Jerry's wife?"

"You know Jerry?" Alex asked.

Karina shrugged. "He tried to feel me up in the elevator yesterday."

Alex suppressed a grin. Karina was probably exaggerating for dramatic effect, but he wouldn't put anything past Jerry. "Marriage hasn't improved him."

Karina stole an oyster from Alex's plate. "Like *you* never felt up a co-worker on an elevator."

"Not without an invitation." Alex refilled Karina's wine glass. The stories of his dalliances during his single days were legend at the D.A.'s office, but there was little truth to them. He never initiated a relationship with a coworker, and he turned down more propositions than he accepted. Alex sipped his wine, but the tannins were bitter on his tongue. Some of the women had been sincere, but most were after his money. Just like the women since his divorce.

Alex leaned toward Karina and said, "Don't believe everything you hear."

"I don't." She laid her hand on his. "I don't have to. I know you."

Once their entrées were cleared away, Tara asked Karina, "Are you ready to go upstairs to meet Stephanie?"

Alex startled. The last time he remembered seeing Stephanie was Tara's birthday party three years earlier. Steph had bragged about sleeping with one of the Chargers.

"I think I'll pass," Karina said. "All I want is a hot bath and a warm bed."

Tara's head tilted. "I thought we agreed..."

"It's been a long day. I'm beat."

Conflict weighted the corners of Tara's lips. "You're sure you'll be okay at home alone?"

"I'm a big girl."

Tara knitted her brow, then glanced at her watch. "Steph will be here any minute. You'll call if you need anything, right?"

"Sure."

Tara shrugged. "Then I guess I'll go change."

"Can't you stay for dessert?" Jack tempted. "It's bananas Foster."

"Maybe I'll come back and have a bite of yours."

The gentlemen stood as Tara left the table. Alex sat back down, his shoulders heavy. He turned to Karina. "She still hangs out with Stephanie?"

Karina shrugged. "Steph's a lot of fun."

"Sure she is. Ask any guy in town."

Karina scowled, but he held his jaw rigid.

A few minutes later, Tara returned, hair down, makeup reapplied, wearing a short leather skirt and tight camisole. A chill sweep over Alex.

Jack offered Tara a spoonful of his dessert, but she declined. She rested her hands on Karina's shoulders. "If you need anything, call me."

"I'm fine."

"Denial," Lauren said. "It's a family trait."

When Tara left the room, Alex's eyes didn't follow. He exhaled until his empty chest ached.

Karina's hand clutched his. He squeezed it tight, fighting to contain his emotions.

"You're my hero," Karina said.

He turned and looked into her heart-shaped face. He understood what she was doing, yet he was grateful. A kiss to her temple warmed his lips. Seeing himself through Karina's eyes, for the first time in a long time he liked what he saw.

⁓⌇⁓

Later that night, Karina shot upright in bed, every sound amplified in the dark room. Seized with panic, she threw on some clothes and went down to the kitchen to check the security alarm. A glowing red light confirmed that the system was armed. But it offered little reassurance.

She slid a knife out of the wooden block on the countertop, the blade long and narrow. Keeping the knife close, she poured half a glass of wine and gulped it down. She stared at the clock. Tara wouldn't be home for hours.

She turned toward a noise. Her heart leapt to her throat, the outline of a face visible in the dim light—no, that was just a vase of flowers. Her muscles grew weak, and the knife clanged onto the floor. She grabbed her purse and jumped into her car.

On the highway, unsure where she was headed, her mind scrolled back to the tension in Lauren's face that afternoon, the terror in her father's eyes. She didn't want to worry them. She drove toward Monterey Jack's to join Tara, but no, she couldn't endure the crowd. At the exit for the Coronado Bridge, she turned.

Clouds crept along the face of the moon, casting inky shadows on the bay. Silence settled on the island. Beyond the reach of the city lights, the purple sky dissolved into black. The cloying scent of night jasmine hung in the air.

Karina navigated the tortuous driveway to Alex's beach house. When he answered the door, she rushed inside. Without a word, he laid his arm across her shoulders.

He led her into the dim front parlor. She stared at the wall, her gaze unfocused. Every time she closed her eyes, she felt Miguel's arm crushing her. She was afraid to blink.

Walking to the window, she surveyed the darkness, the waves rolling like serpents. The smell of blood haunted her memory—the blood oozing from the wound on Miguel's arm. She hugged herself and shuddered. Alex enveloped her, mooring her against the horror undulating in her gut. Wrenching in agony, she broke down.

He helped her to the couch. She slipped off her shoes and reclined against him. The chenille cushion caressed her bare feet.

His fingers slid beneath her hair. She curled into a ball and laid her head on his chest, feeling the hardness of his body beneath his cotton shirt. His scent was warm and mellow. Through the open window, the ocean murmured and pulsed with moonlight.

His arms cradled her, and her body rose and fell to the rhythm of his breath. She tucked her head under his chin, her heartbeat quick and tremulous, like a bird's. "You saved me," she said.

He lifted her face toward his, and his eyes scanned her features. His thumb brushed her cheek. "I couldn't let anything hurt you."

He kissed her chastely, and the softness of his lips surprised her. Her body rose toward him, yielding to his touch. He kissed her again.

Behind her closed eyes, light approached through the darkness. His fingertips awakened her senses. She heard the rushing of the waves, smelled the sweet salt air carried on the breeze.

She massaged his bicep beneath his shirt sleeve, craving his strength. His flesh was warm, muscles rippling beneath her touch. His lips kneaded her neck, sending shivers across her skin, his tongue warm and teasing. Her whispers urged him forward, and he fumbled with the buttons of her blouse.

With a sudden start, she pushed him away. "Oh no." She wriggled from his arms and jumped to her feet, struggling to fasten her blouse.

"Kare." Alex stood with a blank expression. "I'm sorry. I don't know how—"

"Save it." She slid on her shoes, grabbed her purse, and started out of the room.

He seized her arm. "Don't leave like this."

"I shouldn't have come." She jerked away. "I can't be your rebound girl. You're in love with my sister."

⚜

Karina stumbled to her car, her flesh still burning. With quick pants of breath, she fought to eradicate all memory of the previous five minutes.

The hum of the engine rumbled through her body. What the hell? Alex? She'd never been attracted to him, ever. Mostly, she hated his guts. Except...now, she had seen the soft side of him, the side Tara had fallen in love with.

Oh, shit.

She had kissed her sister's ex-husband, and it had been the hottest kiss of her life—a mix of tenderness and raw, hard need. Never had a man's arms offered that sense of safety and comfort before. Usually she overthought everything. But with Alex, she just *felt*—and it felt damn good.

Not that there could be anything between them, ever.

That would be insane.

She drove back to the mainland, radio blaring, and turned into the parking lot of Monterey Jack's. Inside, the bar was dark and crowded, the perfect place to disappear. She ordered a shot of tequila.

Tara was at a table near the dance floor, smiling. Pretending to be happy while she destroyed Alex's life. Karina looked away.

Her gaze remained fixed on the surface of the bar when Tara sat on the stool next to her. "I thought you were going to bed early."

"Couldn't sleep." Karina drank her shot. "You and Steph scope out any guys?"

"Steph did. She's over there dancing with him."

"At least one of us'll get lucky tonight." Karina drummed her hands on the bar to the penetrating rhythm of the music.

"I haven't given up hope yet," Tara joked, but Karina's tension didn't soften. "What's wrong?"

"Nothing another shot can't fix." Karina motioned to the bartender.

"Tequila won't get you over what happened today."

Dude, you don't know the half of it.

A comfortable buzz kicked in. The incident in the courtroom seemed a distant dream now, but Alex's hot, needy kisses were branded on her memory.

The bartender, muscle-bound and olive-skinned, hooked a lime slice onto the rim of her shot glass and set it in front of her.

"Thanks, Vinny. One more?"

"Not a chance, sweetheart. Your dad would kill me."

Tara stood and reached for her purse behind the bar. "Kare, you're exhausted. I'm taking you home."

Karina faced her. "I just got here, and I intend to have a good time." She sucked the lime and downed the shot.

"Let's dance, then."

"I don't want to dance with you." Karina glared. "I'm sick of you telling me what to do, when your life is a mess. You have a man utterly in love with you—who's rich and smart and gorgeous, and who treats you like a fucking queen! But instead of being with him tonight, you're here searching for some random guy to have mediocre sex with. God, you disgust me!"

Tara flinched. "I just want to have some fun. In case you haven't noticed, my life sucks right now." She flopped down her purse and sat next to Karina again.

"That's your choice. Instead of wrapping your legs around that barstool, you could wrap them around Alex. Tell me that wouldn't make you happier."

"For five minutes. Then I'd be stuck extricating myself from his life again."

"Why would you want to extricate yourself from his life? He's a catch, Tara. You won't meet another man like that."

Tara clutched her head. "He's wrong for me."

"You're full of shit—he's perfect for you! Yet you keep pushing him away." Karina stacked her shot glasses on top of each other. "One of these days, he's really gonna go. You're not the only hot piece of tail in San Diego."

"Karina, you're drunk. I'm taking you home."

"Get your hands off of me! I wish you weren't my sister!"

8 Disease

KARINA, WEARING LAUREN'S PAJAMAS, SHUFFLED into her sister's kitchen Saturday morning. She combed her fingers through her hair, working out the knots. Her mind was fuzzy, and her head throbbed. She squinted at the light streaming through the east-facing windows and bouncing off the white appliances.

Through half-open eyes, she spotted Lauren. "Why am I here?"

Lauren looked at her with arched brows. "Is that a philosophical question?"

Karina tried to scowl, but it made her head hurt even more.

Lauren poured Karina's coffee. "When Sean picked you up at the Saloon after your fight with Tara, you said you didn't want to sleep under the same roof as that slut."

Karina had hoped she'd dreamt that part of the evening. She sank into a chair in the breakfast nook, clutching her forehead. José Cuervo was not her friend.

Lauren placed a basket of store-bought blueberry muffins on the table. She squeezed Karina's shoulder, then sat across from her. "You and Tara have fought before. She'll get over it."

"It's deeper than that." Karina sat back and stirred her coffee. A cloud of milk softened the bitter liquid. The secret was pressing on her, threatening to escape. She needed Lauren's advice. Or maybe she needed for someone else to know and hold her accountable, so the madness from the night before wouldn't happen again.

Her stomach twisted into knots. If she said the words, her world would change forever. But Alex's kiss had already changed her world.

Karina breathed deeply. "Last night after dinner, I went to see Alex."

Lauren's eyes widened.

Karina drew in her shoulders. "I didn't want to be alone. Alex understood what I was feeling."

"And?"

Karina heard the accusation in her sister's tone. "We talked a little, and I cried a little, and then we"— Karina sucked in her breath—"kissed a little."

Lauren pressed her palms to her temples, then flopped her arms onto the tabletop with a thud. "I should have seen this coming. The way you flirted with him at dinner last night—"

"I didn't flirt with him! I cheered him up."

"You fed him off your plate."

"He wanted to try my scallops," Karina said.

"Apparently that's not all he wanted to try."

Karina shook her head. Maybe she *had* encouraged Alex's attention. But she never meant…

Her mind drifted back, her senses stirring with the taste of his kiss, the insistent way his lips had kneaded hers. The ache rose inside her again. Yet she knew the memory wasn't hers to keep.

Her fingers traced the grain of the wooden tabletop. She didn't meet Lauren's eye. "Alex and I shared a powerful experience in the courtroom yesterday. It awakened feelings that surprised us both."

"I get that, Kare. If he were anyone else…But Alex?"

"You mean because of Tara? She was awful to him last night. She doesn't deserve any consideration— from Alex *or* me."

Lauren glared. "You understand you can't date him, right?"

Karina scanned the pattern of lemons and creeping ivy on the wallpaper. The thought of dating him hadn't crossed her mind, but she didn't much like being told she couldn't.

Amid the silence, Sean entered the kitchen with Nissa. "Almost out of diapers." He kissed the top of Lauren's head. "I'll run to the store."

"I'll go." Lauren rose and grabbed her purse. "You explain to Karina why she can't sleep with her sister's ex-husband."

Karina clutched the arms of her chair. Sean stared as Lauren marched out the door.

His gaze turned to Karina. He stood unmoving for a moment, then paced to the window and back. Still clutching Nissa, he sank into a chair across from Karina but didn't meet her eye. His hand caressed the baby's hair, and the faint lines at the corners of his mouth deepened. Finally, he looked at Karina and said, "You know, Kare, I love Lauren, but if things don't work out between us, I'd be open to the idea..."

She kicked him under the table.

He grinned. "It's understandable, after what happened yesterday, that you might develop feelings for Alex—"

"He kissed me last night."

Sean whistled. He shifted Nissa to his other knee. "But it was just a kiss, right?"

"You mean, did I sleep with him?"

"No, but since you brought it up..."

"Of course not!"

"And you're not seriously considering—"

"I'm not considering anything. These emotions came out of nowhere." Tears rushed to her eyes. She grabbed a napkin and dried her face. She was so screwed.

Sean tapped his fingers on the tabletop. "Look at this objectively. Are you in love with Alex?"

"What? No!"

"Do you want to date him?"

She glanced at the table. Her hope grew cold. "Tara would never forgive me." Karina rose and poured herself another cup of coffee.

Sean put Nissa into the high chair. He walked up to Karina and rested his hand on her shoulder. "Yesterday, you were held at knifepoint. That's a lot to process. You need to find a healthy outlet for your emotions. Let your family take care of you—and stay away from Alex."

She shook her head. "I'm making too much of this. Alex and I got caught up in the moment, but it doesn't mean anything. It won't happen again."

She couldn't let it happen again.

Alex stood at his living room window, watching the waves ebb. A mug of coffee warmed his hands. In the daylight, listening to the ocean, he thought of Karina without the fever of the night before. His behavior had been foolish, but he felt no shame. He had expressed an honest emotion for the first time in months.

He could smooth over the awkwardness with Karina—*her* nature was pliant. But more was at stake than Karina's feelings.

The sound of the doorbell interrupted his thoughts, then Lauren's voice when the butler answered. *Fuck.* It was only a matter of time, but that was fast, even for Karina.

His gaze remained fixed on the receding ocean. Lauren's sensible shoes tromped into the living room, and she said, "Has some alien life form overtaken your body?"

"I assume you spoke to Karina." He turned to see Lauren's stance exactly as he expected it: hands planted on hips, right foot tapping, eyes narrow, lips taut, an angry strand of hair falling across her forehead.

She said, "If this is some twisted way of getting back at Tara—"

"The last thing I want is to hurt Tara."

"Then what were you thinking?"

Alex sipped his coffee, the question bouncing around his brain but finding no resting place. "I lost control."

"And what if Tara finds out?"

He slammed down his mug with a force that reverberated through his fingers. "I don't want that any more than you do. I'm the one in love with her, remember?"

"I remember—do you?"

His gazed rested on the black lacquer tabletop, then turned to the window. A seabird spiraled into the ocean.

Lauren approached. "I understand that losing Tara hurt you. But you can't involve Karina. You will break her heart."

He pinched the bridge of his nose. "I didn't plan it. It happened."

"It can't happen again."

The muscles in his jaw tightened.

She squeezed his arm. "Your loneliness is clouding your judgment."

He pulled away. "I'm okay."

"You're not okay. And now your behavior is hurting the people around you." Lauren tapped her foot. "You're an attractive man, Alex. Find yourself a woman and get this out of your system. Just stay away from Karina."

He opened his lips, but Lauren strode out. His chest deflated. Massaging his forehead, he sank onto the couch. Lauren was right.

Karina had made him feel alive in a way he hadn't since the shooting. Her soft body yielding to his touch had reminded him that he was a man.

He rose and walked to the window, annoyed he couldn't put her out of his mind. Picturing her wide eyes, her trembling lips, he wanted to offer her comfort...the comfort Tara had refused.

Opening the French doors, he stepped outside and the breeze touched his face. Distant sailboats cut the sea's glassy surface. He wouldn't let this attraction catch him off guard again.

His only fear now was Tara. Her anger the night before had been thick enough to slice—but that was stress. She had lost control before like that while they were married, and it hadn't been him she was really angry with. Her sister had been held hostage. Of course she was upset.

His neck tightened. What had he done? Had he blown any chance of being with Tara again?

Stroking his chin, he weighed the odds that she would find out. Who was he kidding? Those sisters didn't keep anything from each other. He had to prepare for the worst.

❧

That afternoon, Lauren sat on her bed folding laundry with Tara. Sunshine crept through the wooden blinds, casting alternating slats of light and shadow on their faces. The batik bedcover harmonized with the figures of ancient fertility gods arranged on a shelf running the length of one wall. The sleek lines in the rest of the house here relaxed into undulating curves and soothing shades of blue.

Lauren smoothed a pair of tiny, lace-trimmed socks with nimble fingers. Tara's hands were idle.

Lauren could see in her sister's face that Tara was processing the events of the previous evening—the tension with Alex, the fight with Karina. Tara sat cross-legged, her arms drawn close to her body.

Lauren had learned long ago that she couldn't protect Tara. As the middle sister, Tara felt every ripple in the family. She read looks and gestures, starts and silences, and intuited the truth.

Tara's voice rose small and childlike. "Do *you* know why Kare was angry with me last night?"

Lauren didn't look up. "It wasn't you, it was the tequila."

"Some of it was me."

Lauren bit the corners of her mouth, then snapped a miniature pair of blue jeans. "She was upset about how you treated Alex last night."

Tara's cheeks flushed. Her voice turned taut and hollow. "I know I was short with him."

"It's not just that, Tara. You told Alex you were meeting Stephanie, who's every man's idea of the perfect date—she can hail a cab while having an orgasm. And before you went to the bar, you made sure Alex saw that slinky outfit you wore."

Tara stared, her mouth gaping. "I came back to say good night."

"You made a point of showing him what he's missing."

Tara pounded the mattress with her palms. "Why would I do that?"

"To keep him interested. To drive him mad with desire. But you're really driving him into the arms of another woman."

Tara sat upright. "Is he seeing someone?"

Lauren stood and picked up the wicker laundry basket filled with baby clothes, placing it next to the door. She leaned back against the wall. Karina's judgment was gone. Alex's self-control was evaporating. Lauren trusted neither of them to contain their impulses. She met Tara's gaze. "Kare was upset about the way you treated Alex because...she has a crush on him."

Tara squinted, then let out a chuckle. "I thought you were serious. Karina can't stand Alex."

Lauren thrust her hands onto her hips. "Where have you been? She was all over him at dinner, and he did not push her away."

Tara rose. "Alex thinks of Karina as my little sister. Nothing could happen between them."

"If you don't wake up, something *will* happen."

"That's not possible." Tara pursed her lips. "Alex loves me."

"Alex isn't married to you anymore."

Karina was in her kitchen scrubbing the sink. Light flooded through the windows. The countertops were neat, the appliances sparkled, and a candle burned in the breakfast nook, scenting the air with ginger.

She rinsed the sink and looked around. Everything was just the way her sister liked it. The two hadn't spoken after Karina got home from Lauren's that morning, and Tara went out soon after. Karina didn't know where. She picked up a picture of the two of them from the windowsill over the sink, and held it to her heart. Something had changed between them, and it had nothing to do with the kiss.

Her impulse now wasn't to protect Tara from Alex. Instead, it was to protect Alex from Tara. She clenched her jaw at the memory of his face the night before at dinner, his devastation at Tara's anger. Yet Karina couldn't risk comforting him. Not anymore.

She'd have to approach the situation from the opposite direction. Tara needed a definite push out of the dark corner where she'd been hiding from her feelings. Since Alex's return, her blithe indifference had turned to moping irritability. The sort that Alex knew how to soothe, if Tara would let him.

Karina sighed and set the photo back into place. The sound of her sister's car drew her gaze toward the door. Tara entered the kitchen from the garage, her green eyes sparkling against a lavender polo shirt.

Karina swept her arm through the air like a game show hostess. "I cleaned."

"I see." Tara smiled.

Karina hugged her, breathing the almond fragrance of her hair. "I'm sorry!"

"Me too."

Karina couldn't let go, just *couldn't*, needing to strengthen the tenuous bond between them. She loved Tara more than anything and knew what it meant to almost lose her. The sob in Karina's throat escaped as a groan.

Tara kissed her cheek. "It's okay. We're okay."

She took Karina's hand and led her into the sunroom. They sat on the yellow cushion in the window seat. Outside, orange and gold daylilies swayed in the breeze. "Kare, I feel awful about the way I treated Alex last night. But that's between Alex and me. It has nothing to do with you."

Karina stared at the hardwood floor. "I know."

"You shouldn't have gone to see him last night."

Karina looked up, a zing of fear ricocheting around her stomach. Her fingers dug into the seat cushion. "Lauren told you?"

"Why didn't *you* tell me? Last night at the Saloon...You lashed out like I was a terrible sister, when it wasn't about me. It was about Alex."

"This is *not* about Alex." Karina jumped to her feet. "How do you think it made me feel, when you couldn't even thank him after he saved my life?"

Tara tapped her fingertips against her forehead. "You're right. I got caught up in my own emotions. I'm sorry."

She rose and approached Karina. "I should have been here last night. You didn't have to be brave, saying you'd be okay. Steph didn't need me. You did." Tara stroked her sister's hair. "That bruise on your forehead looks like it hurts."

"A little. The swelling's gone down."

"You're being brave again."

"No, really, I took a couple of ibuprofen. I'm fine."

Tara nodded, her eyes focused over Karina's shoulder. "Ever since the shooting, you've been here for me. If you hear me crying in the middle of the night, you come into my room and crawl into bed with me so I don't have to be alone. I should have taken care of you last night."

"It's okay."

"It's not okay." Her voice caught. "I *am* a terrible sister."

"No!" Karina squeezed Tara's arm. *I'm the terrible sister.* "I thought I would be okay. I should have just called you. It's not your fault."

"You went to Alex instead."

"I didn't want to worry you."

"Lauren thinks you have a crush on him."

Karina's shoulders clenched. She pulled away from Tara and rubbed the heel of her hand with her thumb. "Lauren should mind her own business."

"She's worried about you, sweetie, and so am I. You're vulnerable. Don't let gratitude blind you. Alex's charm can steal your breath, but he's not interested in you. You know that."

A faint chuckle escaped Karina's throat, and she sucked in her cheeks to keep from smiling. "If you say so."

"You don't seriously think—" Tara paled. Her lips parted.

Karina's cheeks burned. She'd said too much. Lightning shot through her, and a feeling like hot lead settled in her stomach. The walls of the sunroom pressed in, and the shadow of an arching palmetto outside the bay window darkened the floor.

Tara stared. "Did you and Alex...?"

Karina didn't move or even breathe. Every muscle in her body tensed. If she concentrated hard enough, maybe she could turn back time.

"What did you do?" Tara shrieked.

"It was nothing." Karina grabbed Tara's hands. Her ears rushed like water through a storm drain. She could barely force a sound from her throat. "Just a stupid kiss."

Tara shrank from her, fists tight, eyes dark. "You kissed Alex?"

"It was an impulse." Karina's voice pleaded. " It didn't mean anything."

Tara dashed from the room, the sound of her footsteps heading upstairs.

Karina swallowed the knot in her throat. Her body heaved with nascent sobs building in her chest, the weight on her lungs suffocating her. As panic streaked through her veins, chilling her with dread, a single thought crystallized in her brain.

Maybe this was the push Tara needed.

Karina stumbled into the kitchen and grabbed her cell phone from her purse. On the third try, she managed to select Alex's number.

"Hey, guess what," she said when he answered. "I did something stupid. No surprise there."

Silence followed, then a voice without emotion. "You told Tara."

"Uh-huh," Karina said with forced cheerfulness.

She waited for him to yell at her, but instead he said, "Tara helped create this situation, she can live with the consequences. You okay?"

"Me?" A searing pain in her stomach was quickly followed by a tightening in her shoulders. "I guess."

"You sleep last night?"

She brushed her hair behind her ears. "With the help of some tequila."

"You've had a rough couple of days. Stay away from the booze."

As she clicked off her phone, the front door banged shut. This time, Karina had a pretty good idea where Tara was going.

Tara wound her Mercedes up the gray stone driveway toward Alex's beach house. The familiar surroundings wrenched her chest. She parked in front of the six-car garage built in the style of a carriage house, the arched doors rough-hewn with a natural finish. Coming home to that sight had made her feel like a queen in a fairytale. She had never imagined that her happiness could turn to this. That Alex could betray her with Karina.

Flushed and trembling, Tara stepped out of the car. The warmth from the driveway penetrated her sandals. From behind the garage came the sound of a golf club striking its mark. She followed a brick path to the putting green and found Alex. The sea breeze ruffled his hair, but otherwise he looked unperturbed.

At the sight of him, a hot column of anger rose from her gut. "How could you do this to me?"

Still facing the ocean, he readjusted his grip on the club. "Do what?"

"You kissed my sister!"

Tilting his head toward the golf ball, he shifted his stance, then took a few practice strokes. "I have a divorce decree that says I can kiss whoever I want."

Her breath stopped in her throat. She clutched her white purse close to her body, fingers squeezing the supple leather. Why wouldn't he look at her? Her words from the night before crashed down on her. Her cruelty had hurt him more than she realized.

"I thought I meant more to you than that." Her strangled voice barely rose above the whooshing of the waves.

"You did. But you said yourself we had a bad marriage. Time to move on."

She bristled at the way he threw her words back at her. Her heel stomped into the sandy soil. "With my *sister*?"

He putted the ball into the cup. With a swagger, he retrieved it and set it on the green. He rose to full height. "Why not? She's convenient."

"Convenient? Is that what you told her while you were kissing her?"

"We didn't do much talking."

Pain balled in her solar plexus. She closed her eyes to shut out the vision of him touching Karina, but it didn't help. A deep intake of breath released the tightness in her diaphragm as she struggled to regain her composure.

The sun glimmered on the horizon, sinking toward the ocean. Gulls swooped over the water. Scrubby junipers clung to the earth, waves exposing their roots.

She had rarely seen Alex's vindictive side, but it was out in full force now. Karina wasn't dumb enough to believe he was in love with her, but she gave a piece of her heart to everyone she met. It wouldn't take much for him to break it.

"You're using her."

He dabbed his forehead with a towel, never lifting his gaze. "She came here crying, while you were out drinking with *Stephanie*. How am I the bad guy?"

His words pressed on her chest. She clasped and unclasped her purse. He was right. But Karina said she was going to bed, that she'd be fine. How could Tara have known she'd end up in Alex's arms?

Look at me, damn it. "You took advantage of her."

He shoved the towel into his back pocket. "That's the kind of guy I am. Women throw themselves at me, I give them what they want."

"Sarcasm doesn't become you."

"Self-righteousness doesn't become you."

"You kissed my *sister*."

He flexed his fingers and passed the putter into his other hand. Taking a fresh golf ball from his front pocket, he set it on the green. She stared at the back of him, stymied that he wouldn't face her. "Is this how you want things between us?"

He turned and stood erect. His lips were colorless but his features crisp. "I didn't want any of this. You wanted me out of your life—well, you win. I'm out of your life."

"And that means you're free to seduce Karina?"

His eyes narrowed, then widened again. He turned. Standing over the golf ball, arms straight, knees loose, he putted. The ball missed the cup by millimeters. He shook his head.

She gaped. "What about loyalty, Alex?"

His gaze locked with hers. "When you were released from the hospital, you moved into your father's house instead of coming home with me. When I begged you to see a marriage counselor, you filed for divorce. So don't talk to me about loyalty." Without looking away, he tapped his putter on the green. "We got divorced because you didn't want to fight anymore. So let's not do this. I'll stay out of your life, and you stay the hell out of mine."

Her throat tightened. "That's it? After everything we meant to each other?"

"You can't have it both ways. Either you want me or you don't."

She stood rocking, the trimmed cypress that separated the green from the sand contorting into alien shapes. "Please don't use Karina to punish me."

"I have no intention of hurting her. She's the one good thing in my life."

Tara's gut clenched. Could Alex really be falling for her sister? No, it wasn't possible. He was doing this to get back at her.

Damn it. Her sister was right. The best way to get to her was through Karina. Was that why he had taken the public defender job? Had he been planning to seduce Karina all these months?

Tara's spine lengthened. She strode toward him and pressed her finger into his chest. "You want to fight me for Karina? Fine—it's on. I promise, she'll choose me."

She rushed to her car without looking back. The engine purred like a panther licking its paws after a hunt, hiding in the heavy shade and waiting for the next opportunity to pounce.

⚜

Alex walked toward the house, ragged as a well-used dollar bill. How had he managed that charade with Tara? If he'd looked at her any sooner, he'd have been on the ground, begging her forgiveness. Not that he'd done anything to need forgiveness for.

Confusion and bitterness warred inside him. He'd never seen her so angry. This was good. When Tara expressed her feelings, she recovered quickly. But what would she feel once the anger was gone? Resentment? Loathing? Love?

Heading into the master bath, he tamped down his emotions. A quick shower washed away the sweat and grit of the summer day. Flannel shorts and a fresh T-shirt left him cool and comfortable.

He flopped onto the bed and rubbed his temples. It exhausted him, navigating the landmines of Tara's emotions. She had been angry at him even before the kiss, all because he'd shown up for a dinner that her father had invited him to. This, after he had disarmed a man threatening her sister. It made no sense.

He closed his eyes, hoping to sleep. Sometimes he dreamed of Tara, of her soft words and sweet caresses chasing away the madness.

He missed a woman's touch. Well, he knew where to find it.

A soft chuckle rumbled from his throat. If he wanted a woman in his bed, all he had to do was put on a suit and a Rolex and head to any bar in the city. Sex that easy was hardly worth having.

Karina was right—he needed to date.

A woman in the D.A.'s office—one he'd used to date—was single again, he'd heard. The two of them had had fun together. Maybe it was time to give her a call.

He picked up his cell phone and scrolled through the contacts, looking for Kimi's number. He scowled, let the phone weigh down his hand. Was this a bad idea? Dating someone in the D.A.'s office could be viewed as a conflict of interest now.

The phone beeped and slipped from his grasp onto the mattress. That tone—he hadn't heard it in months. The one signaling a text from Tara.

Was she trying to get the last word? His muscles braced, and he checked the message:

Thank you for saving my sister's life.

He sat forward and stared at the words. A gentle ache formed in his chest, and his lips pulled into a grin. It was a peace offering—that meant she wasn't angry anymore. Right?

His feet hit the floor and he walked to the French

doors. Call her? No, too pushy.

Think. Think like your future depends on it, because it does. She's receptive and vulnerable. This could be the moment. *Do something, damn it!* Do it now.

He hit Reply and sent the text before he could change his mind:

ur welcome <3

Shit, that was dumb. His hand covered his nose and mouth, cutting off his breath. Would she reply? Did the heart make him look pathetic?

Probably.

He had just given her all the power back.

Well, so what? Now wasn't the time for self-protection. He had shielded her body with his own while bullets flew over them. He wasn't afraid of an emoticon.

His eyes fixed on the screen. Nothing. Not that she had any reason to respond.

Stupid. She'd sent a text, and he'd replied. That was that.

He carried his phone into the study, hoping to get some work done. Before he could sit at the computer, his phone beeped. Another text from Tara.

Fat-fingering the keys, he finally managed to open the message:

<3

He sank into the chair, breathing to still the adrenaline coursing through him. Underneath her anger was love. Or at least a heart symbol.

He laughed, joy blossoming in his chest, but he reeled in the emotion. He didn't have her back.

Yet.

⁓⌾⁓

Karina stood at her kitchen counter over a tub of rainbow sherbet, wielding a spoon like an ice pick. She considered heating the container in the microwave but was afraid of making a gooey mess. So she waited, rattling the spoon against the dessert dishes, her eyes focused on the unnatural shades of lime and orange and raspberry.

Her father entered. "Everything okay?"

Karina laid the spoon on the granite, leaving an orangey-green ring. Tara would kill her if she saw it, but Tara was probably going to kill her anyway.

Karina closed her eyes, trying not to think of Alex. She missed men—the thickness of their biceps, the slant from their shoulders to their hips, the stubble of their beards after a long day.

With a pout, she looked up at her father. He hugged her, then scooped the sherbet into bowls. They sat at the kitchen table, and she sucked the dessert from her spoon. "You didn't have to come over tonight," she said.

"Tara said you got spooked here alone last night."

"I'm fine."

The imp in his eyes danced. "When you were little and got yourself into trouble, you'd announce to your mom and me that everything was fine. And we'd discover that the bathtub had overflowed, or your mom's nail polish was spilled on the furniture…Your mom always said if you didn't want attention, it was a sure sign you needed it."

Karina narrowed her eyes. "Shouldn't you be at the restaurant?"

"I'm entitled to a night off."

And so was Tara. She'd gone to Monterey Jack's to meet Stephanie again. This time, Karina wasn't invited. But Tara had told her, quite pointedly, to stay the fuck away from Alex.

Tilting her head, Karina puzzled over the situation. She didn't even like Alex—never had. So why, suddenly, did her knees quiver at the thought of him?

It wasn't because the man had saved her in the courtroom. Ironically, she felt like she was rescuing him. He needed her, and she loved to be needed. But she didn't love *him*, and if this attraction got out of hand, she would lose Tara's friendship and Lauren's respect— and if her father ever found out…

She looked up. Her dad's eyes hugged her like a quilt. She thought how nice it would be if he were around more often and didn't work so hard.

"Dad, why don't you date anymore?"

He grinned. "I have a full life."

She dug her spoon into the sherbet, scooping up a taste of each flavor. "Dating seems like a waste of time to me. Love should just happen." She sat back in her chair. "Do you think I try too hard?"

Her father looked at her acutely, his features soft. "I think you hope too hard."

Karina nodded. She thought back on her sad history with men and realized that all her relationships had been built on hope. She had never met a man who made her feel that he was The One. After the shooting, Karina had forgotten how to hope. Alex made her remember again.

Tara sat cross-legged on her bed at three a.m. thumbing through a photo album. Her eyes stopped at a picture of herself and her sisters gathered in front of a cornfield at their grandparents' farm. Thick green stalks rose above the girls' heads. Karina was tiny, perhaps four years old. Tara realized that even now—though she and Karina both stood five-foot-six and wore the same size clothes— she still thought of Karina as tiny.

Tara snapped the album shut and stuffed it among the volumes on the bottom bookshelf. She sat back against the headboard, resting her chin on her knees. Alex's words at the beach house rang through her memory. But she knew he'd spoken in anger when he ordered her out of his life.

She cringed at the thought of her coldness to him Friday night. *Had* they had a bad marriage toward the end? Tara couldn't remember. The last weeks of their marriage were a fog of hormones, grief, and pain killers.

She touched the scar on her belly. Outwardly, the damage to her body seemed small. But she'd spent two weeks in a drug-induced coma, slowly retreating from the edge of death. Susannah hadn't been so lucky.

Tara crept toward Karina's room, peering through the doorway at the moonlight on her sister's cheek. Karina slept. Tara was glad—she didn't want Karina haunted by guilt over a moment of carelessness born of gratitude and terror. Tara burned with rage thinking of Alex and Karina together. But at least she felt *something*.

Closing Karina's door, she went back to her own room. She turned off the lamp and stared into the black night. Swaddled in silence, her body stilled. Tara wasn't afraid of the dark.

❧

The following day after church, Tara sat on her porch swing caressing a gardenia blossom, the pressure of her fingers releasing its perfume. The brazen outer petals stretched to form a star, while the inner ones curled into a cup, protecting the delicate center.

She heard her sister push open the screen door. Karina sat next to her on the swing. Tara took her hand,

and Karina cried. Tara pulled her close. "We'll get through this."

Karina shook, her words escaping in short bursts. "I didn't...plan it. I stopped before it went too far... I could never betray you like that. Please forgive me."

Craving resolution, Tara said, "Of course I do."

She dried Karina's tears. "You've been through a trauma. Alex is good at taking the pain away—but you can't recover from the stress of the attack until you experience your emotions." She kissed Karina's temple, then rose and went inside the house.

In the kitchen, Tara trailed her fingertips across the granite countertop, listening for her mother's voice. She pictured her mother standing on a green hillside with Susannah in her arms, the baby smiling and cooing, the bright sunshine behind them. Amid the ache, Tara thought of Alex, and how simple things had been when they'd first fallen in love.

On the night he proposed, while they stood looking out over the ocean into infinity, he said, "I'll love you 'til I die." And she knew it was true, like the sunrise or the tides. The truth lived inside her along with her mother's love, pure and unalterable. But now she felt it starting to decay. Alex didn't belong to her anymore.

Tara's world unraveled. The tight cocoon that had held her since the shooting split into gossamer strands and floated on the wind. She stood exposed but free in a world of new possibilities woven of hope and not fear.

Alex reclined in a lounge chair beside his swimming pool, half dozing, an orange haze of sunlight penetrating his closed eyelids. The rustling of birds roused him, and he opened his eyes. Light glimmering off the water filled his vision. Through the whiteness, an angel approached, her hair a halo of gold. His eyes adjusted and he recognized Tara. Startled, he put aside the book that lay idle in his lap. He rose, conscious of being clad only in swim trunks.

Tara smiled. "Don't worry, I didn't come to yell at you again."

Alex met her eyes. Hope bloomed in his chest.

He led her to a cool grotto behind the waterfall that splashed into the swimming pool. Hidden from the house by a stone wall softened with cypress and bougainvillea, the pool had an irregular shape and an indigo bottom, creating the illusion of a deep lagoon.

Tara ran her hands down the edge of the rough stone bench where they sat. "I was out of line yesterday," she said. "I gave up any say over your life when I divorced you. But Kare agrees you're off limits to her. I hope you'll respect that."

"Of course."

Her eyes followed the cracks of the swept flagstone. "You're angry with me."

"No."

"Then why are you terse?"

He bit his cheek. "I don't want to say the wrong thing."

Her voice grew taut. "I'm sorry."

"I'm always glad to see you, though." He lifted her chin. "Even if you want to yell at me."

Amid the damp air, the diffuse light, the splashing sound of water, her eyes met his. She touched his chest, and his body rippled. Her features grew soft and pliant. Laying his hand on her arm, he caressed her rose-petal skin. Her face flushed and her breath quickened. He leaned in to kiss her, but she pulled away. He cringed, the spell broken. "I'm sorry."

"Don't be," she said. "I'm sending mixed signals, and that's not fair." A hummingbird hovered in the mist from the waterfall. "Sometimes...I miss how it feels to be in your arms."

He reached for her. She rested her head on his shoulder. He breathed the familiar scent of her, felt the familiar touch. Her body eased. She said, "Nothing can hurt me as long as I'm with you."

The cascading water could not drown the sound of a gun blast that vibrated through his memory. "I wish that were true."

Her fingertips glanced his cheek. "You have to forgive yourself, Alex. You did everything you could."

It hadn't been enough. He struggled against the whispers warning that he wasn't framed for love, that whatever success he achieved in his life, he'd failed at what mattered most.

Tara nestled her forehead against the curve of his neck. "I miss her."

He placed his hand on Tara's midsection, evoking soft memories of the nights he'd spent rubbing cocoa butter on her belly, feeling the baby tumble at his touch. Those had been the happiest moments of his life. They'd been the happiest of Tara's, too. She'd shared her joy with him, but she wouldn't share her grief. He wondered what deficiency in him had made his company unbearable when she should have wanted him most.

Tara stroked his fingers, then pulled away. "I should go."

He grasped her arms. "Do you have to?"

"If I stay, my feelings will get the better of me."

"And that would be disastrous."

"I don't know who I am anymore," she said. "I need to figure that out before I involve you."

"I'm already involved, Tara. I love you."

"All the more reason for me to be careful."

Wearing a bittersweet smile, she rose and walked away. He watched through the waterfall until she faded from sight.

9 Simply Irresistible

MONDAY MORNING, ALEX STEPPED ONTO HIS patio. The sea stretched to the horizon, the sun at his back. His conversation with Tara the day before still lingered in his mind. He had sensed an openness in her that wasn't there before. With determination in his chest, he took out his cell phone and dialed before he could change his mind.

She greeted him with a cheerful voice. "What's up?"

His excitement rose, but he kept his tone even. "I want you to know I'm thinking of you."

"Aww, you're sweet."

"I'm really not."

Silence a moment. "You are to me."

He swallowed hard to keep his emotions in check. "Hope you don't mind my calling like this."

"I like hearing your voice."

"I don't want you to think I'm pressuring you."

"I don't think that."

Seagulls arced over the ocean. Words rushed to his tongue, but he held them back. "Better let you get to work."

"'Kay. Call me anytime."

"Count on it."

He ended the call, unsure what had just happened, but feeling good about it. As eager as he was to get Tara back, he didn't need to make big strides. If he was careful and patient and kind, Tara would come to him.

Arriving at work with a big grin on his face, he spotted Karina sitting in her office, staring into space. His happy mood crashed. With a gnawing in his gut, he wondered if he had provoked her forlorn expression. She had accused him of planning to use her to get to Tara, and those words had turned into more of a prophecy than he cared to admit. Hurting her had never been his intention.

Entering, he closed the door. "You okay?"

"I've got a client accused of stealing a six-pack from a convenience store." Panic shone in her eyes. "It's his third strike."

Alex exhaled, stroking his chin.

"He's got two little kids," Karina said. "How do I tell a guy with no history of violence he's facing twenty-five-to-life for stealing beer?"

"When I was a prosecutor, I never sought twenty-five years for petty theft. It's not in the spirit of the law.

Talk to the deputy D.A. Plead the charge down to a misdemeanor."

"I already tried that. She laughed at me."

"Keep pushing. Your sister is a journalist. If this case plays out in the newspaper, it'll make the prosecutor look bad."

"If she'd show some humanity, I wouldn't have to resort to those tactics."

"It's your job to play hardball, Kare."

"I know." She picked up a chain of paperclips and passed them from one hand to another like a Slinky. "I just wish people weren't so mean."

He smiled. "I don't think I've ever heard a criminal lawyer say that before."

"Isn't that the point of becoming a criminal lawyer? To stop people from being mean to each other?"

Alex drew his brow. The way her mind worked continually surprised him. "Not for most of us."

"I guess it's just me." She reached across her desk and squeezed her stuffed penguin.

Alex walked up beside her, fighting the urge to touch her. "Are we okay?"

Sadness showed in the droop of her shoulders. "I'm okay. Are you okay?"

"Friday night—"

"It was a kiss." Her tone grew teasing. "It happens all the time—people kiss, then realize it was a mistake. Yet they go on to lead productive lives." She stood, her gaze locking with his. "If I weren't Tara's sister, we could play this thing out—sleep together, then end up hating each other, like a normal office romance. But with us, that can't happen."

He looked into her pretty face, the weight in his chest lightening. He squeezed her hand before slipping out the door.

⁕

Later that morning, Tara stood gazing out the window of Holly's office. A modern hotel rose in the background, the polished steel of its curved façade reflecting the sky. Below, sailboats dotted the bay like toys.

The penthouse view encompassed thousands of people—how would they feel when they knew what Tara knew? The pieces of the puzzle were fitting together, and the news wasn't good. It wouldn't be long before they had enough evidence to print the story.

Holly stared across her desk at Li Jing Wu, showing no interest in the papers the reporter had handed her. "The Kent Foundation is a charitable trust. We're not permitted to make political contributions."

Li Jing tapped her fingers on the desk. "Yet somehow, Foundation money ended up in the account for the mayor's re-election campaign."

Holly's assistant, Oliver, brought her the file on the donation in question. "Here's the email to the Arts Council about the wire transfer," he said. Holly glanced over the printout, then slid it to Li Jing.

Tara looked at Oliver, about twenty-five and slim with neat blond hair and a tailored suit. "Could Brooke have given you the wrong account number by mistake?"

Oliver paged through the folder with slender fingers. "The account number was different from the one we usually use. There's a hand-written note in the file with the new number—Ms. Genovese must have given it to me over the phone."

"You spoke to Ms. Genovese personally?" Holly rose. "Not her assistant?"

Oliver contracted the brow of his pale, narrow face. "I can't say for sure..." He looked around with wide eyes. "Did I deposit the money into the wrong account?"

Holly placed her hand on his shoulder. "It was the Arts Council's mistake."

Tara clenched her jaw. It had been no mistake. Brooke Genovese had diverted Arts Council funds into the mayor's campaign.

Li Jing left the office with Oliver to copy the file. Tara watched them go, then shut the door and turned to Holly. "I'm sorry about this."

"Don't be. It's your job." Holly approached and touched Tara's arm. "Thank you for coming to me with this."

Tara shook her head. "I hate to see your name associated with this scandal."

Holly tapped her foot on the stone tile. "If the mayor knew this was going on in his campaign..."

Tara looked out the window. Threads of clouds hung high in the sky. Her glance fell to a photo on the windowsill of Alex with his father. It must have been taken shortly before his father passed away, shortly before Tara had met Alex. She picked up the photo and caressed the frame with her fingertips. Alex looked so handsome, hair tousled in the sea breeze. Her breath caught in her throat.

She set the photo back down and turned to Holly. "I saw Alex yesterday."

Holly gazed at her intently.

Tara swallowed. "Ever since the shooting, he looks at me with desperation in his eyes. The divorce hurt him so much—I wanted to *free* him from pain."

A taut smile crept over Holly's lips. "Alex doesn't feel pain when he looks at you—he feels joy. Even if there's desperation in his eyes."

"I'm not strong enough to help him."

Holly knitted her brow. "Don't protect him from your grief. That's not what he wants—I don't think it's what you want either."

Tara's lips trembled and tears formed in the corners of her eyes. She sank into Holly's waiting arms. "I don't know what I want."

Holly stroked her hair. "Don't think so hard. Listen to your heart."

Tara's chest hollowed. Her heart wasn't talking. Her love was like a brook in winter, flowing beneath a layer of ice she couldn't break through. All she could do was wait for a thaw.

A knock on the door interrupted them, and Tara stepped back as Li Jing entered. "I've got everything I need. Are you ready?"

Tara nodded. She hugged Holly one last time before leaving.

On the way back to the newspaper office, Li Jing spoke excitedly. "It'll be my first front-page story! My dad won't believe it. He told me I'd have to wait *years*."

The young reporter's mood lifted Tara's spirits. As she assimilated the morning's events, her sorrow turned to anger. Brooke's crimes had threatened Holly— and Holly was family. Tara no longer feared revealing the truth.

∽✻∾

Later that morning, Alex returned from a client meeting to hear Karina banging her desk drawers closed. He stood in her doorway. "Something wrong?"

"The stupid prosecutor said the only time she could see me is over lunch. I was supposed to meet my sisters at Susanne's, but I guess that's out."

Alex suppressed a smile. "You see your sisters all the time."

"Yes, but if I'm not there, they'll talk about me behind my back. Or should I say, they'll talk about *us*."

Alex's breath stopped. Slowly, he nodded. Giving nothing away, he went to his office and called Dayne, inviting him to lunch at Susanne's.

At the restaurant, Alex requested a table near Lauren and Tara. He and Dayne followed the hostess. As they sat, Alex caught Tara's eye. She waved, then shielded her face with her menu. Alex looked away but his glance wandered back. When she looked up again, he met her gaze, and she smiled.

After Alex and Dayne ordered, Tara came over and pulled up a chair. She said to Dayne, "This is the place to be. You're here, the mayor's here..."

While she and Dayne chatted, she touched her hair and played with her necklace, all while studiously ignoring Alex. But he knew how her mind worked. She was *flirting* with him.

Hidden by the tablecloth, he slid his hand onto her knee. His body came to life at that simple touch, but she pushed his hand away before his mind could even process the rush of desire. Adrenaline sped his heartbeat. Had he misread the signs?

Tara continued to ignore him. She was *definitely* flirting. He moved his hand back to her knee, and this time, she let it linger a moment, sweeping her thumb across his fingers as she removed it.

He hid a grin. His heart felt too big for his chest. It was nothing, of course, just a simple touch that she could easily deny. But it could become something. It could be their new beginning.

In a placid voice, with no hint of the drama transpiring underneath the table, Tara asked Dayne, "Why's Jerry Silverstein having lunch with the mayor?"

An alarm buzzed in Alex's head. *Why's Tara asking that question?*

"They've been pretty tight lately." Dayne looked over at Jerry. "Maybe Silverstein's planning to challenge me in the next election."

"There's no official connection?"

Dayne scowled. "I thought you weren't a reporter anymore."

Tara shrugged. "Just curious."

Alex bit his cheek. *Curious my ass.*

The waiter brought the appetizers, and Tara went back to her table. Once she sat, Alex said to Dayne, "She's fishing. Could Silverstein and the mayor..."

"What?" Dayne stirred his clam chowder impatiently, steam rising.

"You tell me. Jerry's got connections—Brooke Genovese, for one."

Dayne narrowed his eyes. "He and Brooke split years ago."

"That's what he'd like his new wife to believe." Alex leaned forward. "At the Arts Council fundraiser at The Del last week, Brooke disappeared for half an hour—Mother looked everywhere. When Brooke reappeared...not one minute later, in walked Jerry."

Dayne's spoon clanged into his soup bowl. "He took his girlfriend to a hotel room, with his wife downstairs in the ballroom? He's got cojones."

Alex nodded. Throughout the meal, he glanced over at the mayor and Jerry. Several times, he caught Tara doing the same.

The mayor's demeanor seemed wrong—like he was uncomfortable, while Jerry was relaxed and in control. The mayor usually displayed more confidence than that.

As the mayor's party was leaving, Alex looked over at Tara. Excusing himself to Dayne, he headed to her table.

"Hey loser," Lauren greeted, eyes dancing.

He smirked at her, then pulled up a chair next to Tara. "I have some information for you."

Tara sat erect, then glanced at Lauren.

"I'll go say hi to Dayne." Lauren patted Alex's shoulder as she walked away.

Alex spoke in Tara's ear, repeating the story about the benefit at The Del. "It's not proof of anything…"

Leaning in, she whispered back, "Any idea how long it's been going on?"

Her breath on his cheek was like the fluttering of butterfly wings. He swallowed, working to keep his focus on the conversation rather than on the familiar scent of her perfume. "I haven't seen enough of Jerry lately to know."

She nodded and squeezed his hand. "Thank you."

Searching her eyes, he said, "I guess you can't tell me—"

"Nope. Sorry." With a sad smile, she added, "If I could tell anyone, I would tell you."

He stroked her hand, not wanting to let go. "I guess I should get back. Otherwise Dayne will try to pay the check."

He rose, and she followed suit. She said, "I'm glad we ran into each other."

"Me, too." He couldn't stop the grin that spread over his face.

Her lips parted, and she smacked his arm playfully. "Karina told you we'd be here, didn't she."

"It may have come up in conversation."

She arched her brows. "I *should* be mad at you."

"Then why aren't you?"

"I like a man who goes after what he wants. Unless it's in a creepy stalker sort of way."

"If I cross that line, let me know."

She brushed her fingers through her hair. "I can't picture you doing that. You've got too much class."

"You realize you're flirting."

"Am I?"

"It's just going to encourage me."

"Oh, dear. I suppose I'll have to pay the consequences."

His whole body heated. He wasn't sure what she wanted from him—maybe she wasn't sure, either.

Otherwise, she wouldn't be coy like this. Still, he had an opening, and he wouldn't let that slip away.

He breathed to slow the pounding in his chest. His mouth grew dry. "Look, um, the mayor invited me to some banquet thing tonight. Hoping to benefit from my good press, I guess, after what happened in the courtroom on Friday."

Tara smiled and squeezed his forearm.

He continued, "I hadn't thought about bringing someone, but since you're so interested in—whatever you're interested in..." He ran his palm over his fist. "We'd be doing each other a favor. I wouldn't look like a loser showing up alone, and you might get some useful information."

She poked his chest. "Are you asking me on a date?"

He raised his brow. "It's a business arrangement. Well, it's sort of a date." He glanced away. "It's whatever you want it to be."

She stepped in close. "Let's call it dinner."

⁓⟋⟍⁓

After showering that evening, Tara emerged from her bathroom to find Karina rooting through the closet.

"Here, wear this." Karina laid a black silk dress onto the bed.

Tara gritted her teeth. *Not again.* "I told you I'm wearing the Vera Wang. I ordered it just before I got pregnant and it's been hanging in a closet for two years. It deserves a night on the town."

Karina narrowed her eyes and tapped her foot.

"I'm not wearing it for Alex." Tara fought the glow of anger in her chest. "If the mayor's preoccupied with my cleavage, he'll forget I'm a reporter."

"You're a columnist."

Tara cast her eyes toward the ceiling. "Why are you against this?"

"Tonight means more to Alex than it does to you."

Tension gripped her temples and spread to her scalp. "You don't know what tonight means to me."

"Then why don't you tell me?"

Tara combed her wet hair. "Do we have to do this now? Alex is picking me up in twenty minutes."

"You're afraid to admit you're still in love with him."

"Kare, you've never loved a man the way I love Alex. You've never suffered the kind of loss I have. So don't tell me what I'm feeling."

"If you wear that dress, you'll be sending the wrong message."

The words twisted her gut. She couldn't deal with Karina's accusations—she had to get ready. "Alex knows it's not a date."

Karina stomped out.

⚜

Alex stood on the porch of Tara and Karina's house. He rang the bell, his stomach tense. Karina flung open the front door. Without speaking to him, she called up the stairs, "Tara, your date's here," and sat on the couch. Alex stood on the threshold a moment, staring into the open doorway, then entered.

Karina paged through a magazine. "I hope you're not expecting to get laid tonight."

He blinked. "I'm expecting to have dinner with my ex-wife."

"You're full of shit."

Hearing Tara's footfall, Alex looked toward the stairs. He drew his breath when he saw her. Upswept hair heightened the effect of the backless red halter dress. Beneath the beaded waist, the narrow tulle skirt draped almost to the floor. But Alex fixed his gaze on the curve of her shoulder.

She retrieved her wrap, and with a goodbye to Karina, he led her to the limousine. She belted herself in with a space between them, sitting half turned toward him. He pushed down his disappointment. Why was she keeping her distance? Was she as nervous as he was?

He tried to draw her out of her quiet mood. Hopped up on adrenaline, his words flowed easily. Before long, she was herself again, talking and laughing.

When they entered the banquet hall, cameras flashed. Alex had known there would be press. But he wasn't the guest of honor—just a last minute addition—

and he hadn't expected this attention. Yet Tara didn't falter. She straightened her posture and cracked her Miss America smile. Alex beamed.

She flitted among the guests, gathering information in the guise of gossip. Alex remembered the routine well from the early days of their marriage. Her frequent trips to the ladies' room were to write in the notebook hidden in her tiny sequined purse.

No one in the room could compete with Tara for beauty. When she smiled, her whole face glowed. Alex should have felt happy to have her on his arm. But her smiles weren't for him. She was working.

During the meal, she spent more time out of her seat than in it. Alex berated himself for feeling abandoned. But as she danced with the mayor, her head tilted to one side, the mayor's hand resting on her bare back, Alex's jealousy burned. She'd found one excuse after another not to dance with him. He now understood Karina's warning.

⁓⟊⟊⁓

Alex and Tara sat on her porch swing, crickets interrupting the stillness. The sky was black except for a purple glow rising from the city lights. Enveloped in darkness, Tara felt free—free of reporters, free of expectations. She filled her lungs with the cool, dry air. "I had a good time tonight."

Alex hunched over, his hands in his lap. "I wish I could say the same."

She fought the thickness in her throat, reminding herself that Alex wasn't rebuking her. "I'm sorry things didn't go the way you hoped."

"I had no right to hope."

"Was it really so awful?"

"Spending the evening constantly reminded that you don't love me?"

She fiddled with the clasp of her purse. "I never stopped loving you, Alex. I lost myself."

She wanted to offer him comfort but didn't trust her own will. Her desire yawned beneath a tissue of self-control. The briefest touch could trigger an onslaught of emotion.

Alex sat up. "You said we had a bad marriage—but for my life, I don't remember that. I remember we fought sometimes toward the end, and you said I was stifling you. But I tried to give you the space you needed."

"We were both damaged after the shooting. We added to each other's pain."

"We were grieving. You didn't give us the chance to find out what kind of marriage we'd have once we got past the pain."

"I'll never get past it." Tara gripped her purse tight, sorrow rising in her throat. "I'll never be that happy wife you want."

"I want *you*, Tara. For better or worse."

He rose, hesitating a moment before heading down the steps toward the waiting limousine.

Tara started after him, then realized it was pointless. The whole evening had been a sham. Alex wouldn't have asked her to dinner if he'd known she was investigating the D.A.'s office. She couldn't be honest about their relationship as long as she couldn't be honest about that.

∽෨ℛe∾

Alex, meanwhile, sat in the limo trying to make sense of the evening. Whenever he'd gotten close to Tara, she'd bristled—as if his touch were loathsome. Yet her looks had been inviting, her smile engaging, her words softly encouraging. He wondered what she'd started to say on the porch, before he'd taken the conversation in another direction. She'd had a good time. Perhaps the evening had gone better than he thought.

The next morning, Alex entered Dayne's office. Dayne held up a copy of *The Observer,* where a photo showed Alex and Tara looking cozy at the banquet. "What's this?"

"Beats the hell out of me." Alex closed and locked the door. "Guess who else was at the mayor's extravaganza." His voice was low but animated. "Jerry Silverstein."

"Lunch *and* dinner with the mayor? Tara's right. Something's up with those two."

Alex flopped into a chair. "Think he's grooming Jerry as his successor?"

Dayne rolled his pen between his hands. "When a guy like Silverstein goes into politics, he's a scandal waiting to happen. Why's he suddenly the mayor's golden boy?"

"Maybe he's got something the mayor wants."

"Or maybe he knows something the mayor doesn't want to get out."

Alex nodded. "That would explain Tara's interest."

Dayne rose. "When I ran for D.A., I promised to clean up this town. Maybe I should start with my own office."

10 Harder to Breathe

RIDAY MORNING, IN THE PARKING LOT OF *THE Observer*, Tara laid her head against the steering wheel. She was going to kill Evan. Squeeze his oversized, round head until it popped like a cherry tomato.

She stepped out of her silver Mercedes into a howling wind and forced the door shut with her hip. White crape myrtle blossoms swirled in the turbulent air and littered the ground.

She hurried into the lobby of the newspaper office and combed her fingers through her hair to straighten it. Evan hadn't warned her that he was printing the story about the corruption in the D.A.'s office in that morning's paper. Hadn't warned her that he was including her name as a contributor.

The paper had gotten a brief statement from Dayne before going to press, but she was sure the story had blindsided him. She had left a rambling voice mail on his cell phone that morning, apologizing, but she didn't expect him to call her back. He had probably deleted the message without listening to it.

Her throat tightened. Evan should never have put her in the position of having to choose between her job and her friend. She wasn't ready to face him yet, knowing he'd be gloating. This was the biggest story the paper had run since Evan had taken over as editor-in-chief.

To collect her thoughts, she sat in a chair near the reception desk and pulled the morning's paper out of her briefcase. The headline made her cringe: *Mayor Suspected in Campaign Fraud, D.A.'s Office Linked to Cover-up.*

She skimmed the article again, hoping it would lose its edge on a second reading. It didn't. Even though the article barely mentioned Dayne, accusations of corruption against the A.D.A. were bound to raise questions about how far the problem spread. She closed the paper and shook her head. This was a disaster. Everything she had dreaded since Evan first mentioned the story had come to life.

She rose and dragged herself into the bullpen. Heading toward her office, she stopped short. Behind her open door, Alex paced, the corded muscles of his neck straining against flushed skin.

Her heart dropped. She had known he would be angry, but she hadn't expected this. He looked up, and the cold fury in his eyes made her tremble. Drawing in her shoulders, she slinked toward him.

He pounded a copy of the newspaper onto her desk. "You set him up."

"Alex, no—"

"You used your friendship with Dayne to get a quote for a story that could destroy his career!"

Though cowering inside, Tara breathed and straightened her spine. "That quote distances Dayne from Jerry, and ties Jerry to the mayor. I made sure the article didn't implicate Dayne—"

"You can't run that headline without implicating him!"

"I had nothing to do with that headline." Tara set her computer bag on the floor with a hollow thump. "In case you didn't notice, we showed that your mother was innocent."

Alex leaned forward, hands resting on her desk. "So even though you screwed over my best friend, I should give you points because you didn't also screw over my mother." He stood upright, his features taut.

"My first obligation is to the truth."

"What *is* the truth, Tara? Dayne has more integrity than any man I know, yet your article casts doubt on that." He shook his head, his shoulders rigid, the light gone out in his eyes. "I don't know who you are anymore."

He strode toward the exit without looking back. She wanted to call after him, but her throat closed. He was right. She hadn't been honest with Dayne or with Alex.

She sank into her chair. Alex's anger hung in the air, a contrast to his normal control. When they were married, she had used sex to calm him, to ground him in the fertile earth of their love.

If she tried to seduce him now, how would he react? Would he want her anymore? It was a stupid thought, anyway. They were divorced. They didn't need to make up.

The thought filled her with despair.

She tried calling Dayne again but got no answer. She dialed Chantel, his wife. A low chuckle greeted her. "You sure stirred up trouble this time, didn't you."

"Does Dayne hate me?"

"No one hates you, sugar. Dayne just wants to kill you."

A lump formed in her throat. "So does Alex."

"Yeah, but if you showed up at his place naked, he'd forgive you quick enough."

She thrummed her fingertips against her forehead. "Don't tempt me."

"Are you that much of a people pleaser? You'd seduce your ex-husband just so he won't be mad at you?"

"You know me better than to ask that question. Of course I am."

"Now Tara, that man is in love with you. You better not sleep with him unless you want him back."

Tara stared out her window.

"*Do* you want him back?"

"I'm thinking."

"Listen to me. Alex isn't mad about the article. He's mad because the divorce did a number on his ego. And Dayne, he knew you were asking questions about Silverstein. It's not like this article blindsided him. He just didn't expect it to be this serious. Give him time to cool off."

Chantel's words didn't ease the heaviness in Tara's chest. *She* felt like the criminal, instead of Brooke and Jerry and the mayor. How could they bear the weight of their lies? She had exposed the truth, and guilt consumed her.

Tara was staring into space when Evan bounded through her doorway. "Jerry Silverstein resigned—can you believe it? Said he couldn't do his job while facing these allegations. But the mayor is defiant. Submitted a press release denying all charges and breaking ties with Genovese."

Tara looked up, the glee in his voice chafing her nerves. "Look at the puppet-master and all the lives he's destroyed."

Evan gaped, his eyes filling with confusion. He straightened his shoulders and glared. "Why aren't you happy? This is the biggest story of your career."

"Alex and I double-dated with Brooke and Jerry. They could go to jail because of this story."

"They could go to jail because they committed a felony or six." Evan tapped his foot. "A quarter million dollars in illegal campaign contributions—that's the difference between victory and defeat. How do you think his opponent feels? The mayor stole that job from her."

"You're right. Add one more name to the list of people we hurt today."

Evan flailed his arms. "How can you be angry with me?"

Tara jumped from her chair. "You named me as a contributor to the article. That wasn't part of the deal!"

"I gave you credit." Evan's slackening features showed his bewilderment.

Tara looked away. She didn't want to see his hurt expression.

Evan pulled the door shut. "I've earned your support, Tara. When you didn't want to work as a reporter anymore, I took a chance and made you a columnist. I gave you this office, even though people would think I was playing favorites. Maybe I was, because I know I can count on you. Right now, I need you to celebrate this story. We scooped the TV stations, we scooped the tabloid press...it's party time."

Tara stared out the window to the dusty street below. She knew Evan was right, but Dayne deserved her loyalty, too. He had rescued her from a rip current when she was twelve. He had scared off a boy who was stalking her when she was sixteen. The bond between them was stronger than DNA—and now Dayne felt betrayed, and she didn't know how to make him see her side.

Tara turned to find Evan glaring, his pain still evident in his eyes. She cringed. She was tired of people being mad at her.

"Fine. I'll play the part. Just don't expect me to be happy about it."

She led Evan out of her office. They went to congratulate Li Jing, who was discussing the article with a group of well-wishers. From the corner of her eye, Tara saw another group gathered in the break room, their expressions dark. She could imagine what they were saying—that Li Jing had stumbled into the story. But Tara knew better. Li Jing had positioned herself in the right place, probed beyond the obvious, and earned the big payoff.

Later that morning, the newsroom watched as Dayne appeared at a televised press conference, speaking eloquently on the responsibilities of public service. Tara smiled to see him rising to the occasion. People would remember that during the next election.

Dayne then announced that two days earlier he had launched an internal audit of the D.A.'s office.

Evan pulled Tara aside. He stood with his ankles crossed, gazing at the floor, absently rolling a pen from one hand to the other. "Strange, isn't it, that Dayne Emery began investigating right before the story broke."

Her eyes widened. "I had nothing to do with that! I asked him about Jerry and the mayor, to get a quote. He's a smart guy—he figured it out."

Evan, silent, did not meet her eyes.

Quivering, she said, "This shows that Dayne was concerned about the integrity of his office before the story broke. It doesn't hurt us, and it may save his reputation."

Evan looked at her, sorrow lurking beneath his rigid expression. "When it comes to business, I need to trust you're on my side."

"I've already proven that!"

He strolled away. Tara simmered.

୭∽ℛℯ෨

A little after five, Karina crept toward Alex's office. He looked up. "Stop hovering."

Entering, she closed his door. "I wish you weren't so angry."

He rose. "This is none of your business."

The tension in her shoulders crept into her neck. She crossed her arms. "Tara would never use her relationship with you to get a story."

"Don't defend her. I don't have time for it. I'm meeting Dayne to brainstorm what to do about this mess."

Alex closed his computer and packed his briefcase. She noticed the tan line where his wedding band had been. She brushed her fingers across his hand, but he pulled it away. He glared so hard that for a moment, she thought he might hit her.

"Stay out of this." He grabbed his briefcase and ushered her from his office. With fire in his steps, he marched out.

She leaned against the wall, trying to decipher him. His natural state was cold detachment—usually, it was hard to tell whether he was upset or simply lost in thought. But today, his studied calm had terrified her. His flashing eyes had betrayed his rage.

Spending time with Dayne would be good for both of them. They needed to cool down. Then maybe she could coax them out of their anger.

Karina went home to a quiet house. In the graying dusk, the lights were turned off, though Tara's car was in the driveway. Karina found Tara in the sunroom, curled up in the window seat and hugging a pillow. Karina sat beside her and put her arms around her.

"I knew this would happen." Tara's voice was thin. "Alex is ashamed of me, Dayne thinks I betrayed him, Evan doesn't trust me..."

"I think you're a hero," Karina said. "You uncovered the fraud at city hall—"

"Li Jing did that. I just helped."

"To make sure the article was fair to Dayne. And in the process, you also protected Holly. So why is Alex ashamed of you?"

"Things were improving between us, but now..." She stared out the window. "I'm not sure where we stand. I feel like the universe is sending me a message.

The last time I chose my job over my family, I got shot. Yet here I am, doing it again."

"You would never choose your job over your family." Karina squeezed her. "Dayne and I are on opposite sides every day in our jobs. It doesn't interfere with our friendship, and it doesn't have to interfere with yours."

"Sometimes I wonder whether I'm capable of making good decisions anymore."

"Of course you are. But sometimes, maybe you make decisions too fast and box yourself in..." Karina stroked Tara's arm. "If you spent more time considering your options, you might feel more secure with your choices, and avoid these doubts afterward. You'd have time to adjust emotionally to the consequences."

"In my head, I know I did the right thing. Dayne's an elected official—I can't treat him differently because of our personal relationship. And still, the guilt is tearing me apart."

"I'm sorry." Karina hugged her. "If it makes you feel better, I'm proud of you. You exposed corruption at the highest levels of local government. The A.D.A. obstructing justice? That's huge!"

"And the mayor." Tara said. "Don't forget about him."

Karina grinned. "The mayor has never argued a legal point against me while staring down my blouse."

Tara laughed through her tears. "So you're on more intimate terms with Jerry?"

"In his dreams." She stroked Tara's hair. "Give it time. Alex and Dayne will get over it."

Tara's voice tightened. "While Alex and I were married, he would never have sided with Dayne. I know this sounds crazy, but I wasn't prepared for how the divorce would change Alex's feelings for me. I'm not the most important person in his life anymore."

Karina scowled. "So what are you going to do about it? Mope around the house, or fight for your man?"

"He's not my man, Karina. After all the pain we've been through, maybe we've lost our capacity for kindness. He was awful to me this morning."

"He was awful to me all day long. That's Alex."

Tara stared out the window, and Karina's eyes followed. The sun was a sliver on the horizon. Tara said, "I don't know if I can open myself up to that kind of rejection again."

Karina exhaled. "Alex didn't reject you. You filed for divorce."

Tara drew up her legs, wrapping her arms around them and tightening into a ball. "I didn't know how else to make the pain go away. I'm not ready to invite it back in again."

Karina leaned back, resting her head in the corner. When Alex had first come back to town, she knew she'd get sucked into his messed-up relationship with Tara. But they didn't want her help. They were wallowing in self-pity, and damn proud of it.

Karina kissed Tara's forehead, then went into the kitchen. She heated up leftovers for dinner, since apparently Tara wasn't cooking. Waiting for the microwave to finish, Karina looked into the polished stone countertop at her reflection. Floating around it she imagined the faces of those she loved. She brushed her hand over the granite, sweeping the faces away, and looked hard at her own image. But she couldn't make it out. She couldn't see Karina.

11 *Addicted to Love*

ALEX BRUNCHED WITH HIS MOTHER AT THE BEACH house on Saturday. Outside, the wind stirred the sand, and the sea pummeled the shoreline. But the breakfast room was an oasis lined with windows overlooking the ocean. A fountain in the corner filled the room with music.

The fragrance of bergamot rose from Holly's tea. "Your letter to the editor in today's paper was persuasive," she said.

Alex stirred his coffee. "You could speak more strongly in Dayne's defense."

"I've said Dayne Emery is a man of integrity."

"Couldn't you say you're confident of his innocence? The man's my best friend."

"But he's not mine," she said. "We're not even on a first-name basis."

"You would be, if you'd ask him to call you Holly."

She picked up her knife with long, slender fingers and sliced her scone. "Darling, would you please pass the strawberry jam?"

The subject was closed. Alex admired his mother's aplomb, as exasperating as it was.

He stared at the white china, the pattern one his mother had chosen. Tara had hated its cool, even lines. Instead, she and Alex had bought service for twelve in a baroque style sprinkled with violets. Those dishes were packed away now.

A smile lit his mother's face. "I lunched with Tara yesterday. I told her to keep her head high—she made the honorable choice. If Dayne Emery had needed her to warn him about this story, he wouldn't be fit to be district attorney."

Alex met her glance but didn't respond.

His mother raised the stakes. "I got some insight into why Tara wanted the divorce."

Touché. He silently conceded defeat. "Please, enlighten me."

She took a dainty bite of her scone, then gazed out the window. The ocean churned, spilling itself onto the sand, then retreating. She sipped her tea.

"After your father's affair..." She broke off. A pelican swooped down and captured an unsuspecting fish. "I focused so hard on keeping the marriage together, I lost sight of my own needs. If I'd spent time apart from your father—if I'd given myself space to heal, the way Tara did—perhaps I could have worked through my pain, rather than turning distant."

Alex's jaw tightened.

She held his eyes. "Don't spend the rest of your life wishing you'd done things differently. Tara's your best hope for happiness—don't lose her."

"I already have. We're divorced."

"But if your love is strong—"

"Sometimes love isn't enough."

"And sometimes people are too stubborn to admit they're wrong." She slid her chair back, rising. "In that case, they deserve to be miserable."

∼⦇∽

Karina drove home from the grocery store that afternoon to find Lauren's Accord parked in front of the house. Lugging two canvas bags in each hand, Karina entered the kitchen. Lauren and Tara were huddled at the table. They sat up when they saw Karina. They greeted her affectionately, but she couldn't help feeling they'd changed the subject so she wouldn't overhear. They'd been doing it her whole life, but it hurt every time.

Tara rose and cupped her hand over Karina's shoulder. "I hope you don't mind. I'm going to Lauren's tonight."

Karina felt a wave of disappointment. "I thought we were going to the Saloon."

"I'm sorry...I'm not up to the crowd."

Lauren approached, saying to Karina, "You're welcome to join us. I borrowed some DVDs from the library."

"Thanks, but...I'll go to the Saloon by myself." Karina shrugged. "I'm bound to run into someone I know."

"Be careful," Tara said. "Get someone to walk you to your car when you leave."

Biting her lip, Karina unpacked the groceries. She stuffed a package of grape tomatoes into the refrigerator. When Lauren was around, Tara behaved as if Karina were an irresponsible teenager rather than a criminal lawyer. But Karina kept silent.

She went upstairs to shower, turning the water as hot as she could stand it. Rubbing exfoliating gel over her skin, she breathed the ginger scent. She told herself to stop feeling jealous that Tara was choosing Lauren over her. But that old wound never healed.

Karina slid into a white dress with a dainty floral pattern. The tight-fitting top flared to a flouncing skirt, the hemline at mid-thigh. It was her signature look, sexy yet innocent. She knew that men would notice her. But desire wasn't love. She had learned that lesson long ago.

An hour later, Karina entered Monterey Jack's and spotted Alex at the bar. She stopped short. Should she leave? But he saw her and smiled. Tentatively, she approached.

"Are you alone?" she asked.

He nodded, then swallowed his scotch. "You?"

"Thanks to Tara." Karina slid onto the barstool next to him. She ordered a cosmopolitan and watched Vinny make it. The crushed ice swooshed in the stainless steel shaker.

As the bartender slid the martini glass toward her, her mouth watered at the sweet-tart fragrance of the pink concoction. She sipped, then turned to Alex. Still unsure of his mood, she asked, "How'd it go with Dayne last night?"

"He's come up with some candidates for A.D.A. He's leaning toward Kimi Cho."

"She'd be a good fit." Karina relaxed. Alex's anger seemed gone. She bumped against him. "I heard you and Kimi had a thing."

"Briefly. A long time ago." He smiled and rotated his glass. "She was quite bendable."

Karina smiled. "I'm glad you're not mad at me anymore."

"I wasn't mad at you."

"No, you were mad at Tara, and you took it out on me."

"Sorry." He tickled Karina.

She squirmed. Warmth flowed through her like an alcoholic flush. But she knew her cocktail wasn't the cause.

She gazed at the stemware glimmering above the bar. "I don't like it when you're nice to me. Somehow, it means more coming from you."

"Because you know I'm sincere. I'm not just hoping you'll show me how bendable you are."

"Please. You're dying to see how bendable I am."

The bartender took their empty glasses, his sun-bronzed hands contrasting with his pale fingernails. He brought their refills, and Karina said to Alex, "I'd better slow down. I'm more tense than I realized."

"Something wrong?"

"Nothing you want to hear about." She looked away but felt his eyes watching her. "I can't believe Tara bailed on me. I'm her baby sister, so she thinks her plans with me don't count. See, aren't you glad you asked?"

Alex sipped his scotch. "No one should take you for granted."

"It's my own fault. I care too much. I set myself up for heartache."

Alex grinned. "You should be more like me."

She laughed. She tasted her drink, letting the cool liquid sit on her tongue before she swallowed. Her mind grew fuzzy, and the room took on a dreamlike quality. Alex alone seemed real. He made her feel appreciated and loved. Their mutual need was drawing them together, but she didn't care about the reasons. She wanted to feel good for a change.

When she finished her second drink, Alex ordered another round. She looked wistfully at her empty glass. "I've reached my limit."

"My driver can take you home."

She bit her lip. "That's tempting, but…"

"It's barely nine o'clock."

She tapped her fingernails on the bar. "Okay, but only if you dance with me. I need to work off some of these calories." She coaxed him onto the floor.

Alex was a good dancer, showing no signs of self-consciousness. When a slow song came on, he placed his hands at her waist. His touch turned her knees to liquid. She was afraid to meet his eyes.

When he pulled her close, she tried to slow her eager breath, but her head grew light.

Why did he affect her like this? *I'm not in love with Alex. I repeat, I'm not in love with Alex.* But damn, his body was hard, and his suit fit perfectly on his broad frame. He held her with a grip both confident and possessive, as if knowing she wouldn't flee, knowing for that dance at least, she was his.

She ventured a glance up at him. He smiled. She clasped her fingers behind his neck, brushing the tender flesh beneath his hairline.

A soft moan escaped her throat. She hoped the music covered it. In that moment, her fantasy was complete: Alex's arms were strong, his movements graceful. He didn't take his eyes off her. The hormones flowing through her body told her she was loved. Happy in the illusion, she laid her head on his shoulder.

"Careful." Alex pressed his hand to the small of her back. "We can't let the alcohol make us too comfortable."

"I'm safe with you."

"I could hurt you more than any man you've ever known. I could ruin your relationship with Tara."

Karina closed her eyes. She tried to play out in her mind the aftermath of sex with Alex, but her thoughts never made it past foreplay. All she could see was a figure wrapped in shadow who chased away her memories of the men who'd disappointed her.

∽◦§◦∽

Karina woke the next morning to the sound of Tara's knocking on her bedroom door. Tara peeked inside. "Are you getting up for church?"

Karina groaned and pulled the covers over her head. A few minutes later, she heard Tara drive off to teach her Sunday School class. Karina drifted back to sleep. When she woke again, it was after eleven.

After a quick shower, she went downstairs and drank a tall glass of water, hoping rehydration would quiet the mallet thumping in her head. It didn't.

She made a pot of strong coffee. Listening to it brew, she thought about Alex. What had happened in the limo during the ride home? The details were fuzzy, but she knew he had been a perfect gentleman. She was grateful.

She shouldn't have let the alcohol affect her that way. Fantasizing about Alex? When she had first met him, he seemed the personification of arrogance and privilege. Letting Tara wait on him, never lifting a pinky to help. Checking his phone rather than listening to Karina speak. Dismissing other people's opinions if he disagreed with them. She would need to draw on those memories whenever her misguided fantasies of Alex popped into her mind—and not the memories of his lips on hers, warm and urgent, that night at the beach house, or the tender feel of his arms around her on the dance floor the night before.

She poured the coffee, and the caffeine helped her headache some. Soon her family would arrive for Sunday dinner, a tradition after church each week. Tara was the head chef, and Karina the sous-chef. Lauren was relegated to salad duty.

The rumble of a car drew Karina's attention to the front window. Her father parked in front of the house, and Sean pulled in behind him. She stepped outside. "Where are Lauren and Tara?"

Sean took Nissa out of the baby seat. "Picking up your car at the Saloon."

Karina nodded. She vaguely remembered telling Tara the night before that Alex had brought her home.

Jack put his arm around Karina. "Feeling better?"

"A little."

"Maybe my bartenders need a refresher course on dram laws."

"It's not the bartender's fault," Karina said. "You know I can't hold my liquor."

"That doesn't keep you from trying, though." He kissed her temple.

Once inside, Karina brought a pitcher of iced tea and five glasses into the family room. Jack was in the easy chair playing with Nissa, and Sean was sitting on the couch watching the Padres game. Karina slumped beside Sean, saying, "Would you mind turning down the volume?"

"Sure." He turned it up instead.

"Sean!"

He smirked and turned down the television.

Nissa began to fuss, and Jack took the baby upstairs to change her. Once Jack was out of earshot, Sean said to Karina, "What happened at the Saloon? The last time you got drunk, it was because of Alex."

She looked away, annoyed by his discernment.

"You can talk to me," Sean said. "I can offer perspective your sisters can't."

Karina stared at the clawed feet of the coffee table. "Alex and I are dealing with it. We know what's at stake."

"You and Alex are recovering from a trauma. You've tapped a need inside each other. Don't underestimate that."

"You're making too much of this," she said. "The thing with Santos—I'm over it."

"Have you talked to a counselor?"

"I don't need counseling. I'm fine."

"You're binge drinking."

Anger exacerbated the throbbing in her temples. "Four drinks is not a binge."

"Yes, Karina, it is."

She stared at him with wide eyes. "That's a stupid rule."

Tara thrust open the front door with Lauren on her heels, laughing. Tara shot a glance at Karina. "Look who's up!"

Karina bounced against the back of the couch. "So I slept in—I didn't get home last night until two."

"Two-eighteen, to be exact." Tara turned to Lauren. "The quieter she tried to be, the louder she was."

Karina tensed. "Like you've never come home drunk, Tara."

"Never when I was driving."

"I would have stopped after the second drink if Alex hadn't offered to take me home."

Tara stared. "He offered you a ride so you could get drunk?"

"We were having a good time."

"How good a time?"

Karina jumped from the couch. "I didn't sleep with him, if that's what you mean."

Sean interrupted. "Do you want your father walking in on this conversation?"

Tara glared at Karina. "We'll discuss this later."

"There's nothing to discuss!"

Their father descended with Nissa. The pounding in Karina's head intensified.

"Everything okay?" her father asked.

Her throat tightened. "Dad, I'm sorry. I thought I was feeling better, but..." She kissed his cheek and went to her room. The white eyelet duvet looked warm and inviting. She closed the blinds and sank onto the bed, covering her head with her pillow.

Downstairs, the family room grew quiet. Tara's emotions raced around her brain, colliding in little sparks.

Lauren took Nissa from Jack. "Dad, I don't think Tara's up to cooking a big meal today. Maybe you could come home with Sean and me, and I could make my famous Trader Joe's mojito salmon."

Jack placed his hand on Tara's shoulder. "What do you think?"

Tara struggled against her tears. "Lauren's right. It's been a rough couple of days—I'm beat."

Jack hugged her. "Alex won't stay mad at you long. You protected Holly. He'll remember that after Dayne's troubles blow over."

Tara nodded absently and saw her family out. Then she tightened her jaw, blood rushing in her ears. It was one thing for Alex to accuse her of using her friends to get a story. It was another for him to retaliate by putting the moves on her sister.

She picked up the cordless phone, barely containing her anger until Alex's voice came on the line.

She blurted, "Thanks for bringing Karina home drunk last night."

"You're welcome."

Heat pulsed through her veins. "How many drinks did you buy her?"

"Three or four."

A hot column of pain and outrage surged from her gut to her chest. "Were you trying to get her into bed?"

"If that's what I wanted," he said, "I wouldn't have to get her drunk first."

Tara clicked off the phone and slammed it into the cradle.

Trembling, she closed her eyes. Fury shot through her veins, burning her fingers and toes. She stomped into Karina's room.

"We had an agreement."

"I remember." Karina lay curled in bed.

"I don't want you going out drinking with Alex anymore."

Karina hugged her pillow. "You're right. It's a bad idea."

"I hate what this is doing to us!" Tara's eyes scanned the wallpaper, thorny rosebuds pulsating against their cream-colored background. "Why is it so difficult for you to stay away from him?"

Karina sat up, her cheeks flushed. "Because every day I see how much pain he's in, and I want to fix it. But it's not me he wants, it's you. You're stringing him along while you make up your mind. Even though you know he's your soul mate. And every day, a little more of him dies inside. Show some compassion, Tara. Throw him a bone."

Tara gaped. "You're telling me to sleep with Alex so he'll stop sniffing around you?"

Karina's lips formed a wry smile. "It would be such a hardship."

Monday morning Tara stared at her computer screen, struggling to focus her thoughts. She sat forward and rubbed the back of her neck. A sip of cool water did little to revive her.

Alex's indifference to her on the phone the day before weighed on her. She wasn't sure why they were fighting. It wasn't about Karina, really, and it wasn't about Dayne. The night of the mayor's banquet, Alex had felt rejected all over again, and she had no words to express what was in her heart.

Burying the pain had meant burying the happy times, too. She struggled to access that feeling. Like the magic of the last vacation she and Alex had taken together, a resort in Waikiki overlooking Diamond Head. Breakfasts in bed feeding each other guava and passion fruit. Evenings kissing on the balcony while plumes of palm fronds fluttered against the apricot sky.

Could she experience happiness like that again, a love without fear?

She channeled her restlessness into her column. She wrote about men and women who dedicated their careers to public service and sacrificed their personal lives for the civic good. Her goal was to help the city recover from the scandal surrounding the mayor. But mainly, she realized with a weight in her heart, she was trying to coax Dayne out of his anger.

She crafted each phrase to evoke the proper tone—passionate, thoughtful, fair. She was reclaiming her voice: During her weeks advising Li Jing, she had submitted her column as a draft for Evan to polish. His harder edge had shone through.

After lunch, Evan bounded into her office, sliding a sheet onto her desk. "Here's the latest poll results."

Tara brightened. "Dayne's approval rating is up."

"But the mayor's is way down." Evan jingled his car keys. "I want to call for his resignation, but except for his sudden friendship with Jerry Silverstein, we still can't prove he knew about the illegal money or the cover-up."

Tara rubbed her fingers across the leather of her desk pad. "Li Jing will find something."

"You don't want to keep working on this story?"

"I need to concentrate on my column. Readers are complaining I've been biased lately—meaning you've been biased."

Evan fidgeted with her stapler. "Columnists are supposed to have opinions. You were relentless as a reporter—my dad wants you in national syndication five years from now. But you can't fall apart when Dayne Emery gets mad. Sometimes, you need to piss people off."

Tara sucked in her cheeks. She knew Evan was right. Maybe the tragedies in her life had made her soft. But that old hunger still lurked inside her, that impulse to fight for what she believed in. The time had come to reach down and yank it out of its hiding place.

Late one workday, heading toward his office, Alex found Karina standing at the copier with the doors and drawers flung open. She peered into the guts of the machine, gingerly poking the levers to avoid raising a puff of toner. She looked at him forlornly. "The machine keeps telling me to lift this flap, but I did that seventeen times already."

He squinted. Turning a knob, he released an accordion sheet of paper. The copier clicked and hummed.

She smiled. "You're my hero."

He squeezed her shoulder and returned to his office. With his door closed, he sat at his desk grasping a pen between his fingers, capping and uncapping it. He wasn't above enjoying the ego-stroking Karina offered.

But he was coming to rely on her, and it wasn't healthy. He needed a woman in his life, someone whose lies he could believe at least for a little while, until this constant ache for Tara left him.

A knock on Alex's door roused him from his thoughts. Sean entered without waiting for a response. Alex was glad for the interruption.

Alex paged through the psych report Sean handed him. "You didn't have to bring me that tonight."

"I wanted to finish it up."

Alex set down the report and looked at his watch. "It's after six. I can understand why *I* don't want to go home—but you have a beautiful wife and daughter waiting for you."

"I'm on my way out." Sean sat. "How about a round of golf this weekend?"

Alex smirked. "Give it up...you suck at golf."

"That's because I can't afford a country club membership, so I have to sponge off my friends." Sean leaned forward. "Come on, Alex. It's healthier than spending your Saturday at a bar drinking with your ex-sister-in-law."

"That happened *once*."

"You need to be careful. This thing between you and Karina..." Sean steepled his hands. "I'm not sure you realize the effect it's having on her."

"Karina's fine."

"She's not fine," Sean said. "Drinking too much, missing church—she's so wrapped up in your life, she can't see what she's doing to her own."

"She's a grown woman." Alex rose, annoyance bouncing around his chest. "Maybe you don't agree with her choices, or mine, but it's not your concern."

Sean stood and rested his palms on the desk. "This doesn't affect just you—it affects everyone around you. And if you can't manage to care that you're hurting Karina, then think what you're doing to Tara."

"Tara's not my problem anymore."

Sean glared. "Is this the man you want to be? After everything you've lost, you want to destroy your self-respect too?"

Sean shook his head, then turned and walked out. With simmering anger, Alex picked up Sean's report and read. Engrossed in facts, his emotions dissipated.

After work, Alex headed to Monterey Jack's. He ordered a scotch, then noticed a woman at the end of the bar eyeing his Dior wallet. She was pretty: early thirties, dark hair, violet eyes. Her full lips reminded him of Tara's.

He approached, and they ordered appetizers. Alex quickly assessed her: she had married too young, and now, newly divorced, was enjoying the power that came with independence. Her web design business was doing well if her Prada clutch was any indication.

As if watching himself from a distance, Alex was conscious of saying and doing all the right things. He was charming, attentive, witty. He was confident and kind. But when she invited him to her place, he declined. Even if he could enjoy the act—despite the self-loathing that always came with it—he couldn't bear the sickness in his gut that would last for days whenever he thought of how he'd allowed himself to be seduced the way his father had been seduced by that woman who'd tried to destroy their family. Alex would not allow himself to be weak the way his father had been weak. Better to spill his seed upon the ground.

12 Heat of the Moment

AUGUST WAS A SERIES OF UNIFORM DAYS, OF sunshine bouncing off stucco and asphalt. But the first week of September brought a chill that left the tourists shivering in their beachwear. On Labor Day, Sean fired up the grill, piling on marinated chicken breasts and portobello mushrooms. Tara helped Lauren in the kitchen, while Jack joined Sean outside. Karina tended little Nissa.

Karina noticed that the baby's dark hair had grown long enough to curl at the ends. Eleven months old, she had nearly mastered walking but struggled with stopping. She kept going until she reached a wall or a piece of furniture, like an old-fashioned windup toy.

The chatter in Karina's head quieted. Watching her niece, she experienced the world in all its vibrancy: the fragrance of mesquite chips, the plush of the carpet, the music of a laugh. Every moment counted. In another year—another month— Nissa would be a different person.

After dinner, Lauren wrapped up the leftovers while Karina loaded the dishwasher. Lauren said, "Tara's doing better, don't you think?"

Karina nodded. "She seems less afraid of her grief. But she's still as rigid as ever, and Alex is just as bad. Neither of them will admit they're wrong. At this rate, I don't know how they'll get back together."

"You think they're headed that way?" Lauren asked.

"Don't you?"

Lauren shrugged. "Hard to say."

Karina scrunched her brow. "Whenever Alex's name comes up, I can see it in her eyes. She still loves him."

"That's not the point, though, is it? Love alone won't make a marriage work." Lauren dried her hands. "Maybe you're seeing their relationship from Alex's perspective. What he wants may not be what she wants."

Lauren brushed her hand against Karina's shoulder. Karina stared at the stone floor, her stomach tense. She wondered whether Lauren was right.

That evening, on the way home, Karina sat in the passenger side of Tara's car, watching the city lights swim past. Karina said, "It's good to see Lauren and Sean so happy. I can't help being jealous—it's been a while since you or I have been on a date."

"I'm not convinced dating works." Tara turned the corner onto their street. "With Alex and me, it was spontaneous combustion. You can't create that. Either the spark is there or it's not."

"Do you think you can find the sort of love you had with Alex again?"

Tara sighed. "That kind of all-consuming love...it's exhausting. I'm not sure I have the energy."

"So you're giving up?"

Tara grew silent, then said, "I'm taking one day at a time."

Karina bit her lip. She wanted to shake Tara out of this complacency. Alex was slipping away from both of them. If he and Tara went their separate ways for good, he wouldn't want Karina in his life. He'd leave the public defenders' office, join a private firm, maybe do pro bono work. Sorrow welled in Karina's throat, choking her. She couldn't stop her tears.

"What's wrong?" Tara turned the car into their driveway.

"I want things to be the way they used to be," Karina said. "Back when we were happy."

Tara parked the car and stroked her sister's arm. Still, Karina sobbed. She felt powerless to heal the gaping wound in her family. When Alex and Tara divorced, Karina lost something precious, something she couldn't name, something that reassured her the world was essentially good. She needed to find it again.

The next morning, Karina rose from bed and shuddered against the chill. She looked out at the sliver of sun on the horizon. The gray sky felt more like dusk than dawn.

In the shower, the beads of her cinnamon body wash abraded her skin. Thoughts of Alex haunted her. She wasn't about to let him out of her life, even if Tara was. Maybe Karina's feelings for him were codependent and semi-incestuous, but they were real. She wouldn't give up his friendship without a fight.

Dressed for work, she entered the kitchen to find Tara searching the refrigerator. "We're out of milk," Tara said. "You didn't get some at the market yesterday?"

Karina slumped. "I forgot."

Tara emptied her coffee mug into the sink. "This day sucks already."

"Spare me the melodrama. Stop at Starbucks."

Tara rubbed her temples. "Sorry, I didn't mean to get emotional. Today is—"

"I know what today is." Tension rose in Karina's neck. "You and Alex aren't celebrating your anniversary because *you* ended the marriage, remember? If you want Alex, go get him. If not, stop moping and move on with your life."

Tara rinsed her coffee mug. "It's not that simple."

"What's complicated about it?" Karina slung her briefcase over her shoulder. "Make a damn choice. Alex deserves love in his life—if not with you, then with someone else."

Tara's lips parted. Karina grabbed her purse and left.

Karina tossed her purse and briefcase onto the passenger seat of her Miata. She drove to work careful of her speed, her foot too heavy. Searching for music on the radio, she found only the prattle of morning shows. She smacked the power button and listened to her thoughts instead.

She was fed up with Tara's self-pity. Men had always adored Tara, starting with their father. She was beautiful and sweet and kind to animals, like Cinderella in the Disney movie. She'd even married the handsome prince. It was every little girl's fantasy, and she'd thrown it away.

Karina, meanwhile, was twenty-seven years old without a man in her life, harboring a crush on her sister's ex, withering at the memory of his kiss. Alex knew how to touch a woman. Was it wrong for her to want—just once—to be with a man who didn't leave her wondering what the hell he was doing down there?

She pulled into the parking lot and breathed. In her office, she found Alex waiting, staring into a photo of Tara. He didn't look up when Karina entered.

"You know what I remember?" His fingers caressed the silver frame. "She wanted to get married in a church and I wanted to get married on the beach. She wanted a swanky affair and I wanted a quiet ceremony with family. Whenever we disagreed—it felt like the end of the world. But then we'd remember why we were getting married in the first place, and we'd compromise." He tapped on a tiny crack in the glass. "If you'd told me then we wouldn't make it to our fifth anniversary, I wouldn't have believed it."

Karina rested her hand on his arm.

"Today should be a different milestone for me," he said. "This is the day I stop looking back."

A smile snuck over Karina's lips. "Let's add an incentive. The first one who gets to a third date wins a hundred bucks."

He grinned. "You're on."

                    ✤

That afternoon, Tara left the office early, taking her laptop. On the way to her car, she called Lauren.

Tara entered her sister's yard through the gate. Lauren was sitting on a stone bench, grading papers while Nissa played at her feet. Behind them, spires of sunflowers waved their blooms above tangerine cannas and starry-eyed sedum. Lauren looked up and smiled. Tara sat next to her on the bench and stared at the clouds, trying to form them into shapes in her mind.

Karina's words from that morning percolated through Tara's memory. She rocked in place, waiting for her thoughts to settle, but they refused. Finally, she said to Lauren, "I feel like I'm camped at a crossroads, afraid to choose. I can't go backward—Alex and I aren't the same people anymore. But we were happy together, at least most of the time. If we could find a way to overcome the pain..."

Lauren took Tara's hands. "You'll feel the pain, with or without Alex."

Tara nodded. "I need to be sure. There's more at stake than my own happiness."

Lauren smoothed Tara's hair. "You tried moving forward without Alex. Think about the reasons you divorced him, and ask yourself if they're still relevant."

Tara watched the squirrels in the live oak tree chase each other through the branches. She didn't want to relive the pain of the divorce, but she was running out of time. Alex wouldn't wait forever.

She picked up Nissa and held her in her lap. Tara felt the wave of joy, then the wave of grief that always followed. But she didn't tense against it this time. She breathed through it until it passed. Closing her eyes, she basked in the warm sunshine. Shutting out pain meant shutting out happiness, too. It was time to make a decision before Alex made it for her, leaving her the rest of her life to regret it.

Around five, in his office, Alex got a call from Sean. "My meeting is running over," Sean said. "If you can hang around, I'll bring you that psych report when I'm finished."

"I'll be here." Alex hung up the phone, shaking his head. Sean was working late again.

Alex watched the second hand turn on the mahogany clock that had once been his grandfather's. Alex wanted to tell Sean to treasure every moment with his wife and daughter, because he could lose them in an instant—and through the endless sleepless nights that followed, he wouldn't once wish he'd worked harder. Alex's life on this day was no different than it had been before he met Tara, as if the past five years had never happened. Except now he knew what it meant to have everything and lose it.

Rubbing his temples, he wondered when his loneliness would subside. Then Karina burst into his office.

She swung the door shut. "What's with this cleaning crew—they have to start vacuuming right at five o'clock?"

An unbidden smile crept over his face. "Kare, you've been tense all day."

"I've been tense for months."

Rising, he massaged her neck, slowly working toward her shoulders. His hands glided across her silk blouse. Her muscles loosened under the pressure of his hands.

"That's good," she cooed.

"You like that?"

"Oh, yes, Alex."

"Tell me what else you like," he murmured in her ear.

Giggling, she turned to face him. "You're bad."

Clasping her palms, he held her gaze.

"I thought we agreed we wouldn't do this anymore," she said.

"We did," he replied. Her hair smelled of vanilla.

She pulled away. "I should go back to my office."

He watched her a moment, wanting to protest. She was right, of course. He sat at his desk, but she didn't move.

"Something I can do for you?" he asked.

"There's a whole list of things you can do for me." She perched atop his desk, next to his chair. "But I came here for a reason. The Santos case."

"You can't represent him. You're a witness." Alex watched her cross her legs. He tried not to notice the dimple of her knee. "Your need to help people is pathological."

Karina shrugged. "Lauren was the smart one, and Tara was the pretty one...so I was the helpful one."

"Your sisters aren't a ruler to measure yourself by."

Karina looked away, but he stood and lifted her face toward his. "You're beautiful," he said. "By any standard."

Karina's breath fluttered. He met her eyes, suddenly aware of the sunshine she wove into his darkest moments. Transfixed, he gazed at the pink round pearls resting along her throat.

"Alex," she warned, her voice a soft wind straining through the reeds.

He brushed his thumb against her cheek, and he felt her body tremble. An ache welled up from deep within and spread through every cell. Her sweet vulnerability called to him, demanding an answer.

Maybe this was how things were supposed to be. Maybe his whole life had been leading to this moment. He breathed her intoxicating scent, and she offered no resistance. He pressed his lips to hers.

She clutched his arms, her fingers kneading the cotton of his shirt. "We can't," she murmured.

"Can't we?" He pushed her hair aside and kissed her neck. Rushing waves of desire drowned his conscious thought. His lips caressed her ear, then her temple.

"We have to stop." A sob escaped her throat. "Don't force me to be the strong one."

He laid his cheek against her hair. His throat tightened. "Most of the time, I feel dead inside. But not when I'm with you."

"Don't say that," she pleaded. "Your heart's not free, but mine is. I can't afford to fall in love with you."

"You're the best thing in my life, Kare."

A knock came on the door, and he looked up as Sean entered.

"Alex, I—" Sean stiffened as his eyes shifted from Alex to Karina. Alex stepped back, and Karina hopped down from the desk.

Pale and trembling, she turned toward Sean. "It's not…This isn't…" She wrung her hands, then hurried from the room.

Sean shut the door, then tossed a report onto the desk. "What the hell is going on with you two?"

Alex paced, running his hand across his hair.

Sean crossed his arms. "Are you sleeping with her?"

"What? No."

Sean glared. "You're preying on her affection."

Alex slammed down his fist. "I would never hurt Karina."

"Then why was she crying?"

Alex straightened his desktop, aligning his stapler with his tape dispenser.

"She's in limbo," Sean said, "waiting for Tara's permission to get involved with you. But you're not in love with Karina. She's not a woman you could spend your life with."

"You don't know that."

"If Tara wanted to reconcile, you'd do it in a heartbeat."

Alex scrubbed his face with his hands. Sean was right—of course he was. What had Alex been thinking? Slowly regaining control of his emotions, he stared at the empty wall. "Karina knows we don't have a future together."

"She needs to hear those words from you. Her heart is telling her something different." Sean turned and walked out.

Alex's self-loathing rose again. He'd lost control, after he'd sworn to himself that it wouldn't happen again. Worse, he'd let his fevered mind believe that Karina could be an option for him.

How could he have succumbed to that impulse? If Karina had tried to seduce him, he could have resisted. Instead, she was sweet and ingenuous, and that drew him in.

It had to stop. Alex wouldn't make that mistake again. He was smarter than that.

∾◦ℳ◦∾

Karina sat at her desk, her throat raw and swollen. She tossed a damp tissue into the trash. It was bad enough she had let Alex kiss her, but now Sean suspected the worst. She fought the urge to go back to Alex's office. The comfort he offered was an illusion.

She thought about her last boyfriend, the one she'd been seeing when Tara got shot. He'd drifted out of her life soon after. Karina had been on a few dates since then, but nothing serious. No wonder she felt weak when Alex touched her. Eighteen months of self-imposed celibacy had left her vulnerable.

She drank the remains of her water bottle. She thought about some of the single men from church, but none interested her. Maybe Alex was too exciting by comparison. But even without the obvious complications, Karina knew that a fling with Alex would be disastrous. Still, that didn't keep her from wanting it.

She looked at the clock. It was almost six, and she wouldn't get any more work done that day. She slinked home, overwhelmed with shame and a persistent, carnal craving.

⌒⊙𝔐⊙⌒

Tara heard Karina's car enter the driveway. She hummed, sautéing the vegetables for dinner. Karina entered the house through the back door, and Tara noticed that Karina was empty-handed. "You forgot again, didn't you."

Karina jumped. "What?"

"The milk."

Karina's features fell. She took her car keys back out of her purse. "I'll get some right now."

"That's okay. I picked some up just in case."

"Of course you did, because I always let you down." Karina brushed back tears, but more followed. She dropped her purse onto the countertop. "I'm so sorry, Tara. I was awful to you this morning. Your relationship with Alex is none of my business."

Tara tapped a wooden spoon against the frying pan. "That's okay."

"It's not okay." Karina clutched her temples. "I've got to get that man off my mind!"

Tara clenched her jaw. She opened the oven, releasing the aroma of chicken with bitter orange sauce. She slid out a baking dish and plunked it onto the stovetop. "You need to start dating again."

Karina grew quiet. "Alex needs to start dating, too—to get *you* off his mind."

Fear clutched Tara's heart. "Am I on his mind?"

"Yes, but he's open to being with someone else."

"You think I've lost him."

Karina stared at the stone floor and shook her head. "You gave him up."

Tara winced. In her heart, Alex was her soul mate. No court could dissolve that bond. But to the world, the divorce decree was as final as death.

After dinner, Tara went to her room. Her head ached. Cloaked in darkness, she lay on her back and splayed her arms as if they were angel's wings. Her memories flowed like water over the earth at the dawn of creation, bearing the spark of life.

13 Crazy Little Thing Called Love

2003 (Five Years Earlier)

TARA STEPPED OUT OF THE LOBBY OF THE NEWSPAPER office, and the May sun warmed her face. In planters along the sidewalk, lemon mops of verbena cascaded beneath purple geraniums. A stream of traffic hummed by as she headed along 1st Avenue.

Passing the vibrant shops of Horton Plaza, she remembered needing to buy Karina's college graduation gift. Her sister had been hinting for a Gucci briefcase— but Tara was operating on a reporter's salary. A simple leather one would have to do.

She willed away the pang in her chest. She had to get over this jealousy. Karina had worked hard to get into law school. It wasn't as if Tara had wanted an advanced degree—three years out of college, she had the job she'd always dreamed of. That ought to be enough.

Her grandmother—her father's mother—had always called Tara the pretty one, apparently the consolation prize for not being as smart as her sisters. Not like she was *dumb*. She had graduated fifth in her high school class, but her sisters had both graduated first.

It wasn't as if they had escaped unscathed from those comparisons. Lauren had no idea how beautiful she was. At least since she'd started dating Sean, some of her insecurities had faded.

And Karina pushed herself harder than anyone Tara had ever seen. As much as Karina pretended to be a party girl, it was just a veneer. She'd spend an hour or two Friday night drinking and letting loose, then study all weekend. It helped that she was genuinely curious and loved being exposed to new ideas.

Tara's curiosity took a different form. Chasing down a juicy story, exploring it from all angles—that's what energized her. It wasn't just about getting the facts. She wanted to understand how people were affected, how different ideologies clashed. Issues were rarely as simple as one side or the other led you to believe.

Tara continued the short distance to the Hall of Justice. She'd convinced her boss to let her interview Dayne about his promotion to Assistant D.A. He had political ambitions, and she didn't see anything wrong with her using her job at the paper to help further them along. He was newsworthy now.

Entering a room of dark-suited lawyers, she felt underdressed in her white blouse and poplin skirt. But

she relaxed when she saw Dayne. His bright smile
welcomed her.

Alex stood at a window at the D.A.'s office, adjusting the
blinds to let in the light. Outside, the city bustled with
possibilities. Alex welcomed them. He was ready for a
change.

His mind should have been on the case he was
working, but he couldn't stop stewing over his date from
the night before. The way she'd launched herself at him
in the back of the limo was borderline assault. She
wasn't the first who had tried to seduce him with the
hope of getting pregnant. He'd had enough of vacuous
women who inhabited bars and knew the smell of
money.

The sound of laughter reached his ear. He turned
to see a young woman approaching Dayne. Her honey
hair bounced as she walked, brushing her shoulder. She
touched Dayne's arm and beamed with affection.
Watching the two head into Dayne's office, Alex craned
his neck and caught her eye. Before Dayne closed his
door, Alex had time to see her smile.

Alex accosted Dayne's secretary. She looked at
him over her bifocals and said the woman was Tara
Fields, a reporter. Alex went to his office and tapped his
pen on his desk, watching Dayne's door.

When Dayne and Tara emerged, Alex approached. He patted Dayne's shoulder, then turned to Tara. "Hope he didn't say anything to embarrass himself."

"Dayne's an old friend," she said. "I wouldn't write anything to embarrass him."

Alex looked at Dayne, waiting for him to introduce them, but Dayne ignored the hint. Instead, Tara did the honors, offering Alex her hand.

He squeezed it, her firm touch and soft skin sending a tingle through him. "Your name sounds familiar."

"Maybe you've seen my byline."

He stroked his chin, and the memory came flooding back. "You wrote that series on wildlife conservation."

Tara drew her breath. A pink blush rose in her cheeks, and her green eyes sparkled. "I can't believe you remembered that!"

The articles had been a study in persuasion—objective yet passionate. It was the passion that had led him to notice her name. He'd never have guessed she was so young—or so beautiful.

Don't stare, no matter how pretty she is. Stop it. Dude, you're still staring. "Can you join Dayne and me for lunch?"

She beamed, then a scowl crossed her face. "I've got a meeting. Rain check?"

"I'd like that," Alex said. Disappointment weighted his chest, but he welcomed the chance to get her number. He placed the business card she gave him in his wallet where it would be safe.

Stopping at the exit, she waved. Alex waved back, eyes following her out the door.

He turned to Dayne, words rushing like flood waters. "You know a woman like that and you never introduced me?"

Dayne crossed his arms. "Introduce Tara to a player like you?"

The man had a point. Not that Alex had set out to be a womanizer. Somehow he attracted the wrong type. Tara was different.

He leaned against the wall, feigning a wounded expression. "I could settle down if the right woman came along."

"Don't even think about it. If you hurt her—"

"Now why would I do that?"

The next evening, Tara sat on her bed, the memory of Alex's voice echoing through her head. Usually, a man calling so soon was a sign of over-eagerness—but Alex had been calm and confident, witty and self-deprecating. Thinking about him, she couldn't stop smiling.

Tall, dark, and handsome was her thing, and Alex had that going *on*. He wasn't a pretty boy, though—his face had character. Bright smile, dancing blue eyes—with what appeared to be a fit body underneath his beautifully tailored suit.

More important, he was smart and funny and seemed genuinely interested in her. In *her*, not just her looks. Like a man she could discuss anything with, from books to politics.

Her heart fluttered violently. Ugh, she had barely met the man, and already she was falling for him. Someone like that could seriously break her heart if she let him.

Breathing to still her excitement, she called Dayne. "What can you tell me about Alex? I Googled him, but all I got were pages of hits for *novelist* Alexander Kent."

"Forget about Alex. He's a player."

She startled, confusion rippling through her mind. Dayne disapproved? Or was he just being overprotective, as usual? "We have a date Friday night. Alex is taking me to the best restaurant in town."

"Tara…"

"I thought he was a friend of yours."

"He is," Dayne said, "but poison when it comes to women."

Heaviness gathered in her chest. "Why?"

"Let's just say he gets disillusioned easily."

Tara rubbed her temple. Dayne had already decided this was a bad idea. Whether that was a fair assessment or not, there would be no persuading him otherwise.

She pondered the situation a moment. "What does Chantel think of Alex?"

"She's crazy about him. But trust me, Tara, you don't want to date him."

"I'm pretty sure I *do* want to date him. I haven't been able to think about anything else since I met him."

Chantel was a shrewd judge of character, and her cop instincts rarely led her astray. If she liked Alex, that was a good sign. *One date can't hurt.*

Ending the call, Tara lay on her bed and stared at the ceiling. Dayne looked for the worst in people—an occupational hazard, she supposed. Her intuition told her Alex had potential. *Be cautious. Don't give your heart too fast.*

With a sinking feeling, she wondered if it was already too late.

⁓◈⁓

Friday night, Alex picked her up in his BMW. They headed down Pacific Highway to Harbor Drive, light from the setting sun sparkling on the bay. When they pulled into the parking lot at Susanne's Bistro, Tara laughed.

Alex braked, then searched her face. "What's wrong?"

"Best restaurant in town, huh?"

His eyes widened. "You don't like this place?"

"Dayne didn't tell you? My father owns it." She patted Alex's hand resting on the gearshift. "You're scoring points already."

Alex smiled.

Once they were seated, Alex ordered a bottle of old-vine zinfandel without looking at the wine list. Tara knew that his selection was neither trendy nor expensive, yet it was one of the finest in the house.

He turned to her, candlelight flickering in his eyes. "I wouldn't have minded if you'd wanted to go somewhere else."

"I'm not sorry you brought me here. Tonight is about getting to know you." She unfolded her napkin and placed it on her lap. "How long have you been friends with Dayne?"

"When I started at the D.A.'s office, he hounded me every day until I passed the bar. I hear you've known him forever."

"He used to babysit my sisters and me."

Alex opened his menu and pretended to scan the entrées. "What did Dayne tell you about me?"

"That your longest relationship with a woman lasted four months, and *she* was married."

"Separated. And I had nothing to do with that." His lips slanted into a natural smirk. Tara found the expression pleasing.

Her father approached. She whispered to Alex, "I should have warned you that if we ate here, my dad would spy on us."

Her father laid his hand on the back of her chair. She rose and embraced him. "Sweetheart," he said, "you give the world's best hugs."

He looked over at Alex, and Tara introduced them, saying, "Alex is a deputy D.A."

Jack smiled. "My youngest starts law school at Stanford this fall. I told her the world doesn't need more lawyers—"

"That's why you brag to everyone that Karina's going to law school," Tara said.

"At Stanford. Don't forget that part."

With a broad smile and a last appraising glance at Alex, Jack excused himself, walking off to make his rounds. It was a busy night, every table full, and the sound of clinking glasses punctuated the air. Tara's mouth watered as a waiter hurried by carrying her favorite entrée, grilled lobster with pineapple sauce. But she ordered the ahi salad.

After dinner, Alex drove them to the beach, where they walked hand-in-hand beneath the crescent moon. The breeze cooled Tara's face and the sand cushioned her feet. With the veil of night dimming her vision, her other senses deepened, capturing the rich tones in his voice. "Tell me about your mother," he said.

Tara bowed her head. She had mentioned her mother at dinner but hadn't gotten into the details. "She died when I was nineteen. Pancreatic cancer—it happened fast."

He stroked her fingers. "My father died three months ago. Heart attack on the golf course. Mother always said that game would be the death of him, but at least he died doing what he loved."

Tara laughed impulsively. "I'm sorry!"

"I shouldn't joke about it." A thread of moonlight glistened on the water. "I miss him."

She encircled Alex in her arms. He pressed his cheek to her hair, saying, "Your dad's right. You do give the world's best hugs."

A knot formed in her throat, and she laid her head against his shoulder. Oh, he *was* all hard muscle underneath his clothes. She breathed his spicy scent— not cologne, just soap and clean skin with base notes of sex pheromones that were doing weird things to her brain. Her heart beat faster.

Finding a cove cut into the rocky shore, they sat side-by-side sheltered from the breeze, their legs touching. It was comfortable and familiar without being overly intimate.

"Why didn't you listen to Dayne's warning about me?" Alex asked.

"I don't mind that you've dated a lot of women. Why stay in a relationship if there's no future in it?"

Alex grew quiet, drawing shapes in the sand. "I haven't had many relationships."

Tara listened to the ocean. "Why is that?"

"Because I'm difficult and demanding and...way too honest for my own good, especially on first dates."

She laughed. "I don't mind honesty. In fact, I prefer it."

"Your dad seems a straightforward guy. I'm glad you're close to your family."

"Are you close to your mom?"

He shifted his weight. "I'm all she's got left, and that scares her. She badly wants grandchildren. I keep telling her to be patient, but that's not one of her virtues—although she creates the impression it is. Everything in Mother's world is perfect. I'm the exception."

Tara bumped her shoulder against him. "Which of your parents do you take after?"

He shrugged. "Both, I guess. Mother went to law school before it was fashionable for women. Given her conservative upbringing, she showed a lot of courage."

"Her parents disapproved?"

Alex stared toward the sky. "She lost her mother when she was fourteen—horrific car crash. They were close, apparently. But my grandfather never supported Mother's choices. So she married my father and moved as far from Boston as she could."

"She's a rebel?"

He chuckled. "She'd rather change the world than rebel against it. When she was working in corporate law, she convinced her board of directors to divest of companies supporting apartheid in South Africa. They were one of the first corporations to do that."

"She must be a persuasive woman."

"Her strategy is simple—politely make a nuisance of herself until she wears people down."

Tara smiled, holding his hand. She wondered how Dayne could have been so wrong.

As the words subsided, Tara laid her head against Alex's shoulder, letting the music of the waves seep inside her. He draped his arm around her. The sky brightened, and a bronze sheen spread across the water. Soft bellies of clouds glowed with lemon and apricot.

"It's sunrise." Tara grinned. "And you haven't kissed me yet."

He cupped her cheek in his palm and met her gaze, then pressed his lips to hers. Her senses vibrated, the sound of the waves turning to a symphony. She leaned into him, savoring his touch, grasping his thickly muscled arms. Her desire rose, body aching for his strength. His mouth on hers was soft but insistent, and she moaned with the pleasure of it, a soft hum in her throat. He held her tenderly, kisses slowing, and gradually pulled away. An empty ache formed in her chest.

He massaged her hand. "This is the best date I've ever had."

Her stomach trembled. She wanted to trust his words, but could she? To lighten the mood, she teased, "Even though I didn't sleep with you?"

His eyes maintained their intensity. "Despite what Dayne told you, I've never used a woman unless she was using me. And I don't want you to think I'm using you now." He swept his thumb across her palm. "You're safe with me."

She touched his cheek, her breath shallow. "If that's a line, it's an awfully good one."

He lowered his head. "You proved my point. You don't trust me."

"Dayne wouldn't be friends with you if you weren't a good man."

"I'm not a good man, Tara."

Her stomach hollowed. Who in his life had convinced him of that? He was an officer of the court, and had treated her with absolute kindness. She lifted his chin, searching his eyes. "I'll decide that."

During the next two weeks, Alex and Tara spent every spare moment together. They roller-bladed in the park and went to concerts downtown, rented romantic comedies but then kissed on Tara's couch instead. Talking until the small hours of morning, they survived on caffeine and adrenaline. And every day, as Tara worried it was too good to be true, it got better.

Friday morning, Alex called to say he'd made special plans for the evening, but would only tell her to bring a bathing suit. When he picked her up for dinner, she asked, "Where are we going?"

"A place on Coronado."

They crossed the bridge and turned onto Orange Avenue, a boulevard blooming with roses. Palms sprang from the flat land, their fronds like dreadlocks. As the car neared the shore, Tara said, "There's that house I like so much."

Visible through the breaks between the tidy bungalows, a Spanish-style mansion in the distance overlooked the ocean. Plantings of cypress, agave, and Mexican sage softened the buff stucco and terra cotta roof. "I'd love to know what the inside looks like," Tara said.

Alex made the next turn. "We could drive up and see if they'll let us in."

She laughed. "We can't just knock on the door and ask to see the house."

He continued driving in the direction of the mansion, now in full view.

"Look, it's gated." She squirmed, the pitch of her voice rising. "Alex, I won't do this. I won't go in there with you."

He turned his BMW into the driveway and pushed a button on the rearview mirror. The front gate opened. "Good evening, Mr. Kent," the security guard greeted.

Warmth rose in Tara's cheeks. Alex watched her from the corner of his eye, but she refused to look at him. How could he humiliate her that way?

He continued toward the house and stopped at the front door. A crisply dressed man in a chauffeur's hat approached from the garage. Still, Tara kept silent, arms crossed, ire burning in her throat.

"We're here," Alex said.

"I told you, I'm not going into that house." Tears welled in her eyes. Why had he deceived her—was she a joke to him?

He drummed his hands on the steering wheel. "It'll embarrass me in front of the staff if I bring a date home, and she won't get out of the car."

"Good." The trees rustled in the breeze.

"Sweetheart, I'm sorry. I was teasing you." His voice pleaded, but she continued to look away, the silence thick. Finally, he said, "Do you want me to take you home?"

"No."

He touched her hand. "Will you come into the house?"

"No."

Alex gazed out the windshield. He stroked her fingers, and she didn't pull away. "We could sit by the ocean."

She nodded, throat still tight, but she didn't want to ruin the whole evening. Her shoulders relaxed as they got out of the car.

He led her behind the house. The flagstone patio stretched the full length of it, a hundred feet or more, on multiple levels. It was more beautiful than she had imagined. In the center, a low fountain gurgled and splashed, and urns of star jasmine fragranced the air. Flanking the staircases to the lawn, spirals of topiary cypress reached for the sky above white hawthorn and pink fairy roses.

This is what Heaven should look like.

Under the setting sun, the ocean turned purple. They sat on a wrought-iron bench with real redwood slats. He stared into the distance, his voice thin. "Tara, I didn't mean to upset you."

Despite the beauty of the setting, despair crawled over her. She watched the waves sputter against the rocks and sink in succession like dominoes. "Why would you hide this from me? Did you think I was some gold-digger?"

"Of course not." He turned to her, eyes intense and pleading. "I can't read people the way you can. My parents taught me to be cautious, especially about women. But Tara, you make me better than I am. That's why I brought you here tonight. I trust you."

Some of the heaviness lifted from her chest. "I don't like being mocked."

"I didn't mean it that way. I'm sorry I upset you."

She looked into his face, misery written on his features. The prickling in her stomach subsided. Feeling foolish, she reached out and clasped his hand. "I'm sorry. I overreacted."

He stared toward the crimson clouds, his brow taut. "I wanted tonight to be special."

"It is special." She kissed him. "I'm with you."

He smiled, and some of his earlier enthusiasm returned.

Inside, the house was furnished in light, beachy colors and a casual style—yet every adornment was a work of art, from the Persian rugs to the hand-carved moldings to the porcelain vases graced with blooms. "I could never have pictured this," she said. "It's beautiful, Alex. It feels like home."

⚬⚬⚬

After dinner, they relaxed in the hot tub secluded next to the pool. Moonlight sparkled on the water, its undulations lulling them into stillness. The breeze whispered through the cypress.

In the darkness, Alex might have thought he was dreaming. Everything about Tara had been perfect so far, even her anger earlier in the evening. She had cared less about his wealth than his honesty. He put his arm around her, caressing her soft skin.

She snuggled against him. "I could stay here forever."

"Sounds perfect." He kissed the top of her head. The stars seemed closer with Tara there. Throughout his twenties, dodging debutantes and opportunists, he had wondered if he could love, if he could trust. Tara was his answer.

He lowered his eyes toward her. She smiled, and he drew her close, meeting lips. With her body pressed to his, he ached for her yet cherished every moment of desire.

He ran his hand along her arm and kneaded her earlobe with his tongue. With eager fingers, he loosened her bikini top. "Tell me if I'm moving too fast."

Instead, Tara's lips molded to the curve of his neck and her hand slid down his back.

With his thumb, then his fingertips, he stroked the side of her breast. Lust burned heavy in his belly, but he ignored it as best he could, wanting to treat Tara like the treasure she was. He lost himself in the indulgence of her flesh, kissing her until he felt her warm tears.

He pulled back. "What is it? Did I do something wrong?"

She shook her head. "You've done everything right since I met you."

"Then why are you crying?"

"It doesn't matter."

"Of course it matters!"

Her hand on his chest seemed small. "If we do this," she said, her voice taut, "I'm afraid I'll never see you again."

"Oh, Tara." He held his breath. Sadness weighed on his shoulders. "I thought you trusted me."

"I do—"

"No, sweetheart, you don't." He combed his fingers through her hair. "Which means you're not ready."

"I am, Alex." She barraged him with soft, sweet kisses.

He stopped her, though it took all of his strength. He had never wanted a woman with such intensity—not just physically, but emotionally, spiritually, even intellectually. Tara was perfect for him, and he wouldn't let lust overpower his good sense. "I can't do this knowing you're wondering if you'll regret it."

"I won't regret it."

Rising, he offered his hand and helped her out of the hot tub. "It's late. I should take you home."

"Alex, no! I was being silly."

He wrapped her in a towel, swaddling her against the night chill. Though his chest was heavy, he couldn't help smiling at how adorable she looked, long hair damp and sticking to her face. "I handled this whole evening badly," he said. "You're overwhelmed—"

"I'm fine."

He pressed his finger to her lips. "You're shivering. Let's get dressed."

They went to their separate cabanas and changed into their clothes. Alex emerged first. He watched the water in the swimming pool ripple in the moonlight. The disappointment hanging over him was no match for his determination. He'd rather be overly cautious than careless with Tara's heart

The latch opened on Tara's door. Approaching, he laid his arm across her shoulders, drawing her into a long embrace. Then, he took out his car keys.

"You're making too much of this." Tara's voice was thick. "I want to stay."

He kissed her forehead. "We don't need to rush into anything."

He turned, and she followed. They walked to his car in silence, her tears glistening in the moonlight. He hung his head. "Tara, I'm not doing this to hurt you."

"I've ruined everything."

He took her hands. "Sweetheart, everything is fine."

"I don't want tonight to end like this."

"I'm not worried about tonight. I'm worried about tomorrow and every day after that."

With a ragged breath, she got into the car.

He drove her home and they stood at her front door, her body cradled in his arms, his fingers gliding through her hair. "Are you okay?" he asked.

She nodded.

"I'll see you tomorrow, then." He squeezed her hand. "I love you, Tara."

He kissed her goodnight, and she watched him drive off, sure she would never see him again.

The next morning, in the house she shared with Lauren, Tara woke to a knock on the bedroom door. Lauren entered carrying a vase of orchids. Tara's jaw dropped. "For me?"

"They're certainly not for me." Lauren placed the arrangement on the dresser. "Sean wouldn't spring for a bouquet like that. He'd need to take out a second mortgage."

She handed Tara the card, and Tara ripped it open. *You're the rare and precious flower I've searched for all my life.* Tara drew her knees up to her chest, warm with happiness.

Lauren reclined next to her sister. "Are you ready to talk about what happened last night?"

Tara's thoughts turned dreamy. "Alex and I were kissing in the hot tub...did I mention he's the best kisser?"

"Once or twice."

"Then I remembered Dayne saying Alex had never been in a committed relationship. I worried it was all about the chase—if I slept with Alex, I'd never see him again." She drew the covers up to her chin. "But when I started crying, he wouldn't go any further. He said I wasn't ready."

Lauren's lips parted. "That's so sweet!"

Tara traced the raised pattern of the bedspread with her fingertips. "I guess it is. But last night, it felt like he was rejecting me."

Lauren grinned. "Those orchids are definitely not a rejection."

Tara held the card to her heart. She got up and examined the flowers, white blooms with purple throats, their fragrance hinting of vanilla. She imagined Alex on the phone, waking some florist from sleep, insisting these flowers, no matter how impossible to procure, be delivered to the doorstep of his beloved by eight the following morning, whatever the cost. It pleased her to think of his demanding nature and his satisfaction once his plan had succeeded—a plan to reassure her, upon waking, that he adored her.

In truth, he'd probably had his butler arrange it, but she liked her version better.

∽❦∾

Tara showered, then ate a quick breakfast. Karina was coming over so the sisters could address Karina's wedding invitations. She arrived without makeup, her hair pulled into a ponytail.

"Rough night?" asked Tara.

"If you call tequila shooters at McGillicuddy's a rough night."

Lauren rolled her eyes.

Karina got an orange out of the refrigerator. "I took my last final yesterday. I was celebrating." She brushed a strand of hair off her cheek.

Tara grabbed Karina's left hand. "Where's your engagement ring?"

Karina gazed at the empty spot on her finger. "I gave it back to Tim. He asked me to choose between him and Stanford, and I chose Stanford."

Lauren gaped. "Excuse me?"

"Just because *he* didn't get into Stanford—because he was too busy drinking beer with his buddies to study for the LSATs—why should I go to my second choice school?"

Tara suppressed a laugh, but Lauren cried, "Karina, there's a wedding dress hanging in the closet upstairs! There are boxes of invitations on the dining room table!"

"How'd the invitations come out, anyway?" Karina went to look at them. "Ugh, pastel pink—what was I thinking?" She picked up the boxes, took them out back, and dumped them into the trash. Lauren continued to gape, but a strange sense of relief washed over Tara.

Karina re-entered the house. "Lauren, don't have an embolism. I've been having second thoughts for a while. I assumed it was cold feet, but when Tim gave me that ultimatum..." She sliced her orange in half. "He cares more about his immediate comfort than my future. I'm not saying he's a bad guy—it just wasn't right."

"Are you sure about this?" Tara asked gently.

"So sure." Karina sat at the kitchen table and ate the orange with a spoon, like a grapefruit. She said to Tara, "So when do I get to meet this Alex guy?"

"He's picking me up around two, if you want to hang around. We're going to the art museum."

Karina pointed her spoon at her sisters. "I dated Tim for three years, and he never once took me to an art museum."

Lauren squeezed Karina's shoulder. "Maybe you should think about this."

Karina shook her head. "Giving back that engagement ring was way too easy. I know worrying is your specialty, Lauren, but I did the right thing. Be happy for me."

∽◈∾

Promptly at two, the doorbell rang. Karina's stomach fluttered as Tara rushed out to the foyer. Karina turned to Lauren. "Is this guy as hot as Tara says he is?"

Lauren smirked. "Just wait." The sisters rose from the couch as Tara led Alex into the family room.

Karina drew her breath and forced herself not to gape. Though she wouldn't have called Alex handsome, he was tall and athletic with a pleasing face and a movie star smile. When he shook her hand, she noticed his smooth palms and manicured nails. Yet his grip was firm and the muscles of his forearm well defined.

Karina raised her brow. The man was...*yummy.* Like a brownie covered in ice cream and gooey hot fudge sauce. If you were into that sort of thing, which Karina definitely was not. From now on, she was only dating men who were blond and muscle-bound and a little bit stupid. In other words, the opposite of Tim.

Without taking her eyes off Alex, she said, "Tara, you're right, he's *fine.*"

Alex relaxed his stance. "Glad you approve."

"I didn't say I approve." Karina flipped her hair. "I don't impress that easily."

He smirked. "I understand you're headed to Stanford."

She couldn't help the flush of pride that rose in her chest. Her talents were a gift from God, but she'd had to work hard every day through seventeen years of schooling to get into one of the best law schools in the country. Yet Tim expected her to give that up for him? *Nope.*

"I got my law degree from Berkeley," Alex said. "Stanford was my backup school."

Her jaw dropped. Was she having a stroke? She must be, because Alex could *not* have just said that.

"Kare, he's kidding." Tara dragged him out the front door.

Karina turned to Lauren. "Son of a bitch!"

After church the following afternoon, the sisters cooked dinner in their father's cozy kitchen. Plants dotted the windowsills, and a slate countertop capped the green-painted cabinets. Chicken with rosemary scented the air.

Karina grabbed the biscuit mix from the cupboard. The unopened box was heavy in her hand. Her shoulders slumped, and a thread of sadness wove through her. Breaking her engagement was the right decision, she told herself for the fortieth time. Still, she felt excluded listening to her sisters talk about their dates the night before.

Lauren sprinkled the croutons on the salad. "Sean and I set a wedding date. May 12."

"Next year?" Tara cried. "How can you stand to wait? When I get engaged, I want to get married right away."

"That sounds hopeful." Lauren got out the dressing. "Are things better between you and Alex?"

A glow suffused Tara's face. "I'm adjusting. Friday night...I was overwhelmed. I thought Alex had lawyer money, not my-great-grandfather-founded-Continental-Railroad money."

Karina measured the biscuit mix and dumped it into a stainless steel bowl. "That's a big secret to keep."

"In a way, I'm grateful," Tara said. "Now I don't have to wonder whether his wealth affected my feelings for him."

Karina sucked in her cheeks, then said, "Rich men are as easy to love as poor ones. And easier to forgive."

Lauren squinted at Karina. "Jealous."

So. Not. Jealous.

Tara basted the chicken, eyes turned downward as she said to Karina, "Alex asked me to go away with him Memorial Day weekend. Do you mind if we take off after your graduation lunch? We don't have to leave right afterward—we just want to get to his cabin before nightfall."

Karina bit her cheek and stirred the batter. "That's fine." *Whatever.*

"You're upset."

Karina tossed the batter by spoonfuls onto a pan. "Just because you've known me my whole life, and you've known him for three weeks, why would I be upset that you want to bail on my graduation to have sex with him?"

Tara turned to Lauren, who grinned. Tara tugged Karina's hair. "I'd never miss an important day in your life. Alex and I can be flexible—if you decide you want to party 'til dawn, we'll wait until Sunday."

Karina scowled. She liked Alex less and less.

"Sweetheart, stop fidgeting." Alex squeezed Tara's hand as they rode the elevator to his mother's penthouse

Friday evening. He smiled at Tara, struck by how sophisticated she looked. Her lavender dress was elegant, her hair upswept, her jewelry understated. His mother would approve.

The butler showed them into the front parlor and poured them each a glass of wine. Then he went to get Holly. Tara sat upright on the couch, her knees clamped together. "At my father's house, I just barge in." Her gaze fell toward the Lladró figurine atop the coffee table, a bare-breasted mermaid with floating hair.

Holly entered wearing a cream-colored Chanel suit and antique pearls. She smiled as Alex introduced her to Tara. Holly's expression was serene, her tone even, but Alex wasn't fooled.

He paced, his eyes catching a bouquet of white lilacs. The day before, he had heard his mother ask the butler if the vase was sitting a few millimeters off center. Alex was accustomed to his mother's exacting standards, but he worried he had misjudged in exposing Tara to them this soon.

Tara's smile hid her nervousness as she answered Holly's questions. "My degree's from UCSD," Tara said. "I double-majored in journalism and political science."

"Alex tells me you work at *The Observer*."

Tara nodded. "I've been a reporter for three years."

"Then you know Evan McCade," Holly said. "Did Alex tell you that Evan's my godson?"

Tara gaped, covering her mouth with her hand.

Holly crossed her legs. "I'm not surprised. The two of them barely speak these days." She looked at Alex, but he didn't meet her glance.

She turned to Tara. "And what does your father do?"

"He owns a restaurant."

Holly's eyes sparkled. "Of course! You're Jack Fields' daughter—I should have seen the resemblance. I hired Jack's catering service last year, and now I won't use anyone else."

Tara beamed. Alex loved how her face lit up with pride whenever her father was mentioned.

Holly leaned toward Tara. "I understand your sister was accepted at Stanford." She sipped her wine.

"Oh, no, has he been bragging to customers?" A blush touched her cheeks. "I'm sorry."

Holly arched her brows. "I hope I'm more to Jack than a customer. I only bring it up because Alex's father went to Stanford. He was disappointed when Alex chose Berkeley."

Tara stared at Alex. "Is that why you told Karina that Stanford was your backup school?"

Holly gasped. "Alex, you didn't!"

Tara sat back. Alex followed her glance to the still-life on the opposite wall. Bright heads of sunflowers gazed in all directions, some spilling out of the cobalt pitcher onto a lemon-covered tabletop.

Tara bolted upright, her eyes wide. "Is that a Matisse?"

"My in-laws were collectors," Holly said.

Tara pressed her lips together. Alex could see her trying to contain her shock. Stupid of him—he should have warned her. With a little sigh, she said, "You have a lovely home, Ms. Carter-Kent."

"Thank you, darling, but please call me Holly."

Alex choked on his wine. Tara came and patted his back until his coughing subsided. His mother rarely asked anyone to call her by her first name, and never someone she'd just met. He looked at Tara, amazed and proud, thinking how he'd kiss her if his mother weren't in the room.

⚜

The following evening, Tara and Alex arrived at his cabin. From the driveway, a gravel path led to the sloping redwood building. She watched with a tickle in her stomach as he unlocked the front door.

Inside, a stone fireplace and wooden mantle gave the space a cozy feel. The great room opened to a kitchen updated with golden-brown granite and stainless steel appliances.

While he turned on the gas fireplace, she unpacked the groceries, surveying the sienna hills that stretched beyond the window. Vegetation grew in scattered clumps, the gray-green leaves reflecting the sun. The copper sky whispered the promise of day melting into night.

She sighed. "It feels like we're a hundred miles from civilization."

"Yet we have all the comforts of home." Alex opened the refrigerator. "Champagne, fresh fruit, caviar—" Suddenly the lamp in the refrigerator went out. He scowled, then tried switching on the overhead light. Nothing.

"Blackout," he said.

Her stomach tensed. "How will I cook dinner?"

He shrugged and gave her a crooked grin. "Guess we'll have to settle for champagne and caviar."

Tara nodded. Things could definitely be worse.

She devised a makeshift meal, and Alex found candles to stave off the darkness. They laid a blanket on the living room floor and sat in the light glowing from an iron candelabra.

Alex raised his glass. "To the power company, for ruining our plans."

"Here, here." She sipped her champagne, the bubbles vibrating on her tongue. "I hope you didn't mind staying late at Karina's party today."

"Of course not. I want your family to see me as part of your life now."

Happiness spread through Tara's body, even to her fingers and toes. "My dad likes that you're smart and ambitious—not some spoiled rich kid. He says you're worthy of being Holly's son."

Alex's eyes brightened. "I hope so."

She placed champagne glasses onto the heart-pine table, and they jingled. "Do you worry we're moving too fast?"

"What we have exists outside of time. We can waste our energy analyzing it, or we can enjoy it."

"Alex, you analyze everything."

"Not this." He slipped a strawberry between her lips. She licked the juice from his fingers.

His crystal-blue eyes followed her. His expression was open, with nothing hidden. All the things Dayne had told her rushed back, but they didn't scare her anymore.

She sighed. "You're the most perfect man."

A distant howl echoed through the canyon. "If you believe that, I'm bound to disappoint you."

"You could never disappoint me," she said.

"I'm trained in the art of persuasion. I know how to manipulate people."

"And I'm trained to spot a liar. I know you're not manipulating me." She leaned forward and brushed her finger against his chin. "You may dazzle people with your charm—and I admit, that's what first attracted me—but when we're alone like this, I see your heart. You can be brash and overbearing, but I admire that. You own who you are. You give me courage to be who I am, too."

He cupped her face in his hands, then kissed her hard. His happiness fused with hers, filling her heart almost to bursting. And in that moment, she knew.

This is what forever feels like.

Dusk turned to darkness, and the candles cast long shadows across the floor. Alex couldn't take his eyes off Tara. Goosebumps rose on her skin, so he turned up the fireplace and drew her close to warm her.

She unbuttoned his shirt, trailing her fingers along his chest. Then, she reclined on the blanket, lying flat and curling her arm over her head. Alex lay next to her, caressing her in this receptive pose.

His life until now had been a prelude. For the first time, he was living in present tense. His only thought was Tara, her skin fragrant with strawberries, her hair glistening with gold. He unfastened a single button of her cotton blouse, nuzzling her neck and breathing her sweet scent. Opening the next button revealed a hint of black lace. He brushed his lips against her flesh, the delicate fabric tickling his chin. Another button, and he resisted the temptation of her front-hook bra. Instead, he nibbled her earlobe.

"Alex," she murmured.

"Every inch of you is a work of art." His breathing slowed, and he found her mouth. She fumbled with his belt, but he grabbed her hand. "Tara, we've got all night. And I love kissing you."

"Can't you kiss me without pants on?" She suckled his neck hungrily, and he gave up arguing.

Candlelight flickered in shadow on the walls as they stripped off their clothes. The blanket smelled of clean cotton beneath them, and the thick rug formed a cushion. The fire brightened the hearth, chasing away the chill.

Tara pressed her nude body against him. His mind went blank a moment before he caught his breath. He ached for her, but couldn't let her think this was just physical for him. It was everything.

Her fingertips glided down his arm and she spoke in his ear. "Please, Alex."

"I thought we were taking this slow."

"Don't make me wait."

Her lips were on his, and he said between kisses, "You're not the submissive type, are you."

"Stop teasing."

"But this is the best part."

"Not quite." Tara took control.

Stars pulsed in front of his eyes as a deep hunger permeated every cell. "You're right, that's better."

She kissed him. "No talking."

With their bodies joined, he rolled on top of her. His eyes fixed on hers. Attuned to each murmur and movement she made, he watched the color rise in her cheek and listened to the rhythm of her breath until he felt her contractions and let the wave of pleasure roll over him. Breathing hard, he clung to her, and she began to laugh.

He smiled. "Not the reaction I was hoping for."

"I'm laughing because I'm happy."

He was happy, too—happier than he'd ever been, too happy for words. Language couldn't capture his joy.

He lifted her hand and pressed her palm to his lips. "All this time, I've been missing the most important part of me."

She met his eyes and gave him a smile that said everything.

They snuggled together beneath the blanket, her head against his chest. He kissed her fingertips, and her breathing slowed.

"My Alex," she murmured in a sleepy voice, "always."

14 Call Me

2008

WEDNESDAY MORNING, THE GRAY LIGHT OF DAWN crept through Tara's window. She rose, despairing of sleep. Memories of the five years since that night in the cabin replayed in her mind. Thinking of Alex now, a new sense of peace settled on her heart. She could remember the good times without the ache of what they had lost.

Combing her fingers through her hair, she walked to the window and gazed out. In the still air, clouds like smoke ascended from the hills. Slivers of sunlight broke the horizon. With silent hope, the world turned from black and white to color.

Tara went downstairs in her pajamas to make coffee. While it brewed, she opened her work laptop and checked her email. She was on her second cup when Karina joined her, dressed for work.

Karina hugged her. "Did you sleep at all?"

"A little. I emailed Evan that I'm working from home today."

Karina nodded. "Maybe Lauren could stop by at lunchtime to see how you're doing."

"I'm okay."

"You're not okay. You sobbed for two hours last night."

Tara breathed, a sense of calm washing over her. She had finally been able to let go. All the pent-up emotions over the loss of her marriage had surfaced, as if some blockage in her heart had cleared away. "Sorry about that. I didn't mean to keep you up."

"Keep me up? Tara, you're my sister. You don't have to apologize to me. I'm here for you, always. Nothing is more important to me than you are."

Tara nodded. She hated feeling dependent, but Karina wanted to help. If the situation were reversed, she'd want to help Karina, too. "Thanks for sitting up with me. I needed a good cry. I feel like I'm finally coming to terms with what happened with Alex and the baby, so I can move forward. I mean, I know it's a process, but I feel less stuck, you know?"

A shadow of sadness crossed Karina's features. She nodded and kissed Tara's forehead before heading off to work.

Karina arrived at the public defender's office with her mind in a jumble. If Tara was moving on, did she mean without Alex? Karina couldn't even bear to think about Alex—not after what had happened between them in his office the night before.

That kiss had been different from the first time. She couldn't say it was innocent. They both wanted it, even though they knew they shouldn't.

But Tara's sobs the night before had brought it home for Karina. Alex wasn't just Tara's ex—he was her soul mate. No matter what happened between Alex and Tara, he was off-limits to her forever. Their pheromone-driven behavior had to stop before it did any more damage.

She spotted him across the room and her body shrunk with the horror of what she had done. He caught her eye and followed her into her office, closing the door.

Her muscles turned rigid. "You can't be in here."

"Last night was my fault." His pallor gave his eyes a hollow look. "It won't happen again."

Karina nodded but said nothing, drained of emotion. She couldn't give him the comfort he so obviously needed. That wasn't her place. It never had been.

Alex said, "You remember yesterday morning, the bet we made?"

Karina's lips parted, a hollow feeling permeating her chest. "You mean about dating?"

"We agreed it would be good for both of us."

Karina kneaded her hands. She couldn't believe he was bringing this up so soon after the kiss. It wasn't like she had any claim on him, of course, and dating other people would help end their lingering attraction. It was the rational thing to do—so of course Alex would do it. No point letting their messy emotions get in the way. Or maybe she was alone in those feelings, a poor sap who had fallen for a man she could never, ever have. Maybe to Alex, she meant nothing at all.

He drummed his fingers on the desk. "Chantel says I should ask out Yvette Dupree...the tall brunette who works at the police department?"

"Sure. Yvette," she said mechanically. "She seems nice."

Alex grinned. "She seems fun, at least."

Karina examined her peach-painted nails. The dead feeling in her chest had spread to her gut. "Don't take her anywhere fancy. You don't want to give her the wrong idea."

He slid his hands into his pockets. "It bothers you?"

Please, God, let me get through this conversation without crying. "Okay, Mr. Egotistical, maybe a little. We never played this thing out, and now it's hanging there, unresolved."

"You know we're wrong for each other," he said as if addressing a jury. "We have different instincts, different goals. If we got involved, I'd only hurt you."

"I don't care if you hurt me." Hugging herself, she swallowed down the emotion that threatened to overrun her. "I wanted to make you happy, even for just a little while. But not at Tara's expense."

He looked away. "I never meant to use you."

"Alex, don't flatter yourself. This isn't about you. It's about me and my pathological need to help people, as you put it. If it weren't you, it would be someone else. So don't act like I'm the victim."

⁂

Tara sat on her couch with her computer on her lap. Her fingers tapped with the frenetic pace of a concert pianist, then lapsed into idleness. A smile lit her face. She set aside her computer and rose to make lunch, but a knock on the front door interrupted her.

She looked out the side lights and saw Lauren. Letting her in, Tara said, "You didn't have to come over."

Lauren cocooned Tara in her arms. "Karina said you were up all night crying."

"She exaggerates." Tara led Lauren to the sunroom. They sat on the window seat. "Last night, beneath the grief," Tara said, "I found the only truth I needed to know."

Lauren, her eyes acute, brushed the strands of hair away from Tara's face. Tara took Lauren's hand, seeking to reassure her. Tara knew that in her quiet way, Lauren worried about her as much as Karina did.

"After the shooting," Tara said, "when Alex reached out, I responded with rage. But I can't access those feelings anymore. I'm free." Through the window, Tara watched a butterfly alight on a purple coneflower, wings rising and falling in measured beats. "I've been in denial for so long—about Alex, about my grief. How could I not have seen it?"

"You didn't want to see it," Lauren said. "You wanted to work it out for yourself, in your own time."

Tara buried her face in Lauren's shoulder, feeling the heat of her own breath. "What have I done?"

"Nothing irrevocable." Lauren stroked Tara's hair as their mother had when they were little. Tara closed her eyes, longing for the security she had known as a child—the feeling she had found again with Alex.

They made themselves a quick lunch, chatting about Nissa, about Lauren's job—anything but Alex and next steps. Because Tara had no idea. Emotionally, she felt ready to move on. But in a practical sense, what did that even mean?

Lauren's lunch hour passed too quickly. At the door, Lauren looked one last time into Tara's face. Tara gave her a broad smile—and for the first time in months, it came from her heart.

The rest of the afternoon, Tara poured her thoughts into her column, watching the clock and wondering why the phone didn't ring. Around five, Karina called to say she was stopping at Fashion Valley after work. Tara made herself a simple dinner, her heart light. She still didn't know what the future held, but the past was losing its grip.

Karina came home carrying shopping bags. Tara watched her show off her new outfits—sheer, colorful things with short skirts and tight bodices. Tara said, "You know how you shouldn't go grocery shopping on an empty stomach, because you'll buy things you wouldn't otherwise? The same goes for clothes shopping when you haven't dated in six months."

"I need action."

"That dress will get you some," Tara said.

Karina smiled, looking so happy and pretty that Tara couldn't argue anymore.

Tara jumped when the phone rang. It was her father, whom she assured for the third time that everything was fine. After she hung up, Karina said, "Were you expecting someone else?"

Tara curled into a ball on the loveseat, sitting with her knees drawn up to her shoulders. "I left Alex four messages. He's not home, and he's not answering his cell—"

"He's on a date."

Tara bolted forward, clutching the cushion beneath her. Her stomach dropped. "He's seeing someone?"

"This is their first date."

"So they're not involved." Tara's heart formed a lump in her throat.

Karina shrugged. "I guess that depends on what happens after dinner."

Tara tapped her heels against the loveseat, breathing to slow the adrenaline pumping through her veins. "Do you know what restaurant they went to?"

"Why? Are you going to storm over there and interrupt them?"

Tara rose, possibilities playing out in her mind.

"Sorry, he didn't say." Karina grinned. "Too bad you didn't have a satellite tracking chip implanted behind his ear while you were married."

"This isn't a joke! What if he falls in love with this woman?"

"He won't fall in love with Yvette Dupree. He may sleep with her, but he won't fall in love with her."

Tara pursed her lips. She pulled her cell phone out of her pocket and sent Alex a text.

Call me.

If his phone was turned on, he wouldn't sleep with another woman. Not while Tara was on his mind.

The next morning at police headquarters, Alex marched toward the office of Lt. Chantel Emery, frustration fueling his steps. She looked up from a desk piled high with paperwork and grinned brightly. "How'd your date go?"

He entered and slammed the door. "When you told me Yvette had a thing for me, you could have warned me she's also fucking crazy."

"Is she?" Pleasure continued to shine in her gray eyes. "I did not know that."

"She brought handcuffs. Department issue."

Chantel threw back her head and laughed. "Sounds like a hell of an evening."

"A hell of a short one." He sank his forehead into his palm. "Every date I go on is a disaster. But Kare and I agreed the only way to end this dance is to see other people."

Chantel arched her brows. "End what dance?"

Fuck. The muscles in his jaw tightened. He didn't need another lecture about his relationship with Karina. Not that he *had* a relationship with Karina.

She rose and crossed her arms. She wasn't exactly tall, but after sixteen years on the force, she could look threatening if she wanted to—especially while wearing a shoulder holster underneath her dark suit jacket. Apparently, at that moment, she wanted to.

Alex said, "You know what a flirt Kare is."

"Karina's not a flirt. She gives people her undivided attention, and men *think* she's flirting."

Alex flattened his lips and looked away.

"Don't tell me you fell for that," Chantel said. "Why would you give Karina power over you?"

Irritation crawled up his neck. "She doesn't have power over me."

"No, of course not. And neither does Tara. That's why you can't have a good time on a date." Chantel tapped her foot. "What are you punishing yourself for?"

He scowled. "I'm not."

"Alex, it's no exaggeration to say you're one of the five most eligible men in San Diego. You've been divorced for over a year, yet in the past six months, you've been on *one* date—and you come here while I'm supposed to be working to tell me how badly it went. On top of that, you've got some flirtation thing going with your ex-wife's sister. If that's not self-sabotage, I don't know what is."

"It isn't—"

"I am *not* done talking. If you want Tara back, then get her back. If you want to move on, then move on. Don't stand here spinning your wheels and acting like last night was *my* fault. You could find a woman if you wanted one. So why don't you?"

"I gave Tara the best I have, and it wasn't enough." He shoved his hands into his pockets, a dismal sense of failure washing over him. "She thinks so little of me, she used me to get a story."

"Tara doesn't use people. You knew she was chasing down a story, right? And you offered to help."

He glared at her. "Dayne tell you that?"

She approached and patted his shoulder. "Remember who you are, Alex. You represented a U.S. senator and got a full acquittal. Don't let your ex-wife steal your confidence."

He jingled his keys in his pocket. His time in Washington seemed like another lifetime. "Tara's opinion used to mean everything to me. But things change. And I need to change with them." He smirked at her. "Just don't expect me to take any more dating advice from you."

⁓⊶⊷⁓

At noon, Karina entered the police station. Chantel had texted out of the blue that morning and asked her to lunch. The invitation had come right around the time Alex got back to his office. That was no coincidence—something was up. Chantel hadn't let on what, but Karina hoped it had to do with Alex's date, since he wasn't talking. He'd been in dark mood all day.

Chantel stood chatting with a young man, blond and nicely built—a detective, Karina guessed. Nearing, she slowed her pace. Her stomach did a backflip as she swept her gaze over the tall hunk of man muscle. *That's new.* She'd have remembered if she'd seen him before.

"There you are," Chantel greeted her. "Have you met Ryne Applegate? We used to work together at Western Division, but I got him transferred here as soon as he made detective."

"It's a pleasure." Ryne shook the hand Karina offered. "Chantel's been telling me about you."

A thrill rushed through her as his fingers brushed her palm. She tilted her head back and raised her eyes toward his. They were golden-brown with a soft expression. She fought the urge to smooth his curls.

Chantel checked her watch. "Sorry, Kare, I need to make a quick phone call before we go. Excuse me."

Karina watched after her as she closed the door to her office. The puzzle pieces fell into place—but if this was a setup, Karina wasn't complaining.

She turned back to Ryne. "What has she been telling you about me?"

"Just that she was having lunch with a friend from the public defender's office. She didn't mention that you were so beautiful."

Her heart jumped, and she twirled her hair. "That's very unprofessional, detective."

He grinned, revealing a dimple in the middle of his square chin. "Looking at you, I wouldn't have guessed you were a lawyer."

"What do lawyers look like?"

"Disillusioned?" he said with a shrug.

She leaned toward him, catching the faint scent of bergamot and grapefruit. "And most cops don't wear professionally pressed Ralph Lauren shirts."

He flattened his tie. "So I guess you and I work on opposite sides."

"We all work on the side of justice."

"That's one way to look at it." He raised his brows skeptically.

She planted her hands on her hips, challenging him. "How do you look at it?"

"We take the bad guys off the streets, and you put them back on."

"You uphold the law, and I uphold the Constitution." She poked a finger into his lapel. "Somebody's got to keep you guys in line."

Light from the window flickered across his face. His expression softened. "You really believe in what you do."

"You sound surprised." She stepped in closer. "I protect the citizens from tyranny. Why wouldn't I believe in what I do?"

He smiled. "You're good."

"I haven't even gotten to the good stuff yet." Karina fingered the dragonfly charm on her necklace.

He leaned in. "How do I get to see some of that?"

She took out a business card and wrote her home phone number on the back. She slid it into the breast pocket of his shirt. "Call me."

∽✵∾

Tara met Lauren for lunch in Little Italy, a neighborhood set atop a hillside overlooking the ocean. In the quiet family restaurant, garlic and basil sweetened the air. Tara smoothed her napkin. "I still haven't heard from Alex."

Lauren straightened her silverware. "The last time you called Alex, wasn't it to yell at him for getting Karina drunk?"

"Yes."

"And didn't you hang up on him?"

"Yes."

"So you can see why returning your call isn't on the top of his to-do list."

Tara tugged at the red-and-white checked tablecloth. He was making her wait to prove a point—it was a power play. And damn if it wasn't working. Sexy and unattainable worked for him.

"Maybe it's better if he doesn't call," Tara said. "He'll be mad when he sees tomorrow's newspaper."

Lauren raised her brow. "What did you do?"

She brushed her hair back from her face. "I wrote a column about politicians hiding behind their lawyers when they get into trouble. It's mainly about the mayor, ever since the paper proved he knew about the conspiracy." She unrolled her silverware, spreading the red napkin over her lap. "But I also laid into Senator Hartley. Even if her actions weren't illegal, they were irresponsible. She should apologize for her mistakes."

Lauren stirred her iced tea, the spoon clanging against the glass. "Are you sure you're not just mad because her lawyer hasn't called you back?"

Tara smiled. "Evan thinks my column needs a harder edge, so that's what I gave him."

Their entrées arrived. Lauren twisted her fork in her spaghetti. "I don't get it. Your strength is *resolving* conflict—why does Evan want you to create it?"

"Conflict sells newspapers."

"I thought he said your column has increased circulation."

"He did, but—"

"Then why does he want to change it? And why are you letting him?"

"He says I'm too soft."

"You confront the tough issues—but in a way that brings people together instead of tearing them apart. Does the media always have to be divisive?"

Tara clanged her fork against her plate of ravioli. "What am I supposed to do? Evan's my boss."

"But he's also your friend," Lauren said. "He needs to know the stress this is causing you. He's asking you to be someone you're not."

"It won't hurt to give him a little of what he wants, and see how people react."

"It goes against everything you believe in."

"Stop it."

Lauren grinned. "Am I making you uncomfortable—telling you things you don't want to hear, even though you know they're true?"

"Can't you play nice?"

"In this situation, nice isn't working for you."

"I'm keeping an open mind. Read my column tomorrow, *then* tell me what you think."

That evening, Tara was in the kitchen after dinner when a call came through on the landline. She rushed over and answered it breathlessly, heart beating a little faster at the sound of Alex's voice. She leaned against the wall and teased, "It took you long enough."

"I've been busy." A smile resonated in his tone.

Lightheaded, she inhaled deeply. "Can we get together and talk?"

"Sure." After a pause, he continued, "But I've got plans tonight. And I'm meeting Mother for dinner tomorrow night. How's Saturday?"

She rapped her knuckles against the wall behind her. Was he serious, or still playing games? If they were married, she'd call him on it, but she didn't have that right anymore. Swallowing her disappointment, she asked flatly, "You can't see me sooner?"

"I have a life," he said matter-of-factly.

"Fine." She clenched her toes, trembling inside. "Thanks for fitting me into your schedule."

"You're welcome."

She sank to the floor, chest aching.

His tone warmed. "Tara…"

"What?"

"I'm not blowing you off. I really do have plans."

She stared at the floor tiles, tears blurring her vision. "I understand."

"Do you?"

"Yes."

"Then I'll see you Saturday," he said.

She hung up the phone, then banged it into its cradle three times.

She marched into the family room, where Karina was sitting on the couch reviewing some case files. "Did Alex mention having plans tonight?" asked Tara. "His butler said this afternoon that Alex was free."

Karina pursed her lips. "You'll get that poor butler fired if you keep using him to check up on your ex-husband. Why don't you ambush Alex at his house again?"

"I don't want to piss him off." Tara sat on the couch, resting her chin in her hands. "He's already mad at me."

"He's not mad at you." Karina put down the files. "At the core of your relationship is one essential truth: Alex loved you, and he lost you, and he doesn't understand why."

"I divorced him because it was the only way to preserve our love."

Karina narrowed her brow. "That...doesn't make sense."

Tara's eyes traced the crown molding. "Our emotions were raw—we kept hurting each other. I was afraid if we stayed together, we'd destroy our relationship, and I didn't want to lose anything more."

"O-o-kay..." Karina crossed her arms. "That still doesn't make sense."

Tara tapped the toes of her shoes on the floor. "It seemed rational at the time."

Karina exhaled a thin stream of air. "You're more messed up than I thought."

"You have no idea."

Ryne Applegate stood in his kitchen, wiping the stainless steel cooktop until it shone in the muted light. Picking up a mug of coffee, he went into the family room, where Tony Bennett's voice crooned in the background. Ryne took Karina's business card from his pocket. He stared at her home phone number on the back, wondering if he could call without seeming anxious. His instincts told him Karina was not a woman to keep waiting.

She answered the phone with a voice that twittered like a catbird's. "I was hoping you'd call," she said.

He smiled. "I'm flattered."

"You should be."

Karina threw him off balance, but he liked the way it felt. He tried to recreate her features in his mind: large, dancing eyes; a heart-shaped mouth that curved into a sly but inviting smile; a narrow, sloping nose, like a kitten's. He wished the image were more vivid, wanting to remember everything about her.

He picked up a coffee table book, the cover a panoramic photo of the great pyramid at Giza. In the setting sun, it burned red against the sky. Ryne turned the smooth pages, listening to the music of Karina's voice. His eyes stopped on a photo of the Sphinx crouched in its bed of limestone, its eyes glancing heavenward, the union of earth and sky.

"Chantel tells me she's excited about working with you again," Karina said.

"You two talked about me?"

"Are you afraid she spilled your secrets?"

"I don't have secrets," Ryne said. "I'm a police officer—I need to set a good example."

"Then I'll presume you're innocent until proven guilty."

He leaned back in his red leather chair. "Maybe I could take you to lunch tomorrow and set the record straight."

"I'd like that."

He lurched forward, his stomach in his chest. Did lunch count as a date? He hadn't thought he was asking her on a date. But he hoped it was a date. He was already dying to kiss her.

15   We Belong

THE FOLLOWING MORNING TARA STOOD TREMBLING in her office, staring at that morning's *Observer*. Again, her eyes scanned her column, but her disbelief persisted. Her first thought was vandalism by someone in prepress. But the line was too clever—the words were targeted to wound. The attacker knew his victim.

Feeling numb, she barely reacted when Alex burst in, his eyes wild.

"Is this what it takes to sell newspapers?"

She straightened, collecting her emotions. "It's not what you think."

He threw his copy of the paper across the room, hitting the bookshelf with a thud.

Her body shrank. When he was like this, it was impossible to reason with him. "Please listen to me—"

"You said enough in your column." He pounded his palms on her desk. "Whatever you think of my personal ethics, have the decency to keep my clients out of it. The media lambasted Deb Hartley based on nothing more than allegations and innuendo, which I worked hard to disprove."

"Deborah Hartley is not some ingénue. If she didn't know what was going on in her campaign, she should have."

"This column had nothing to do with Deb. It's a personal vendetta against *me*. Are you on some power trip, publicly vilifying people who care about you?"

Evan strode in and knotted his arms. He stood face-to-face with Alex, his eyes like ice. "Do I have to call security?"

Alex loomed closer. "You publish any more garbage about my clients, and I'll sue you into bankruptcy." He left without looking back.

Tara wanted to run after him—but he was too angry to listen, and she was too angry to speak. Instead, she let her tears fall.

Evan said, "Don't worry, Legal reviewed that column before it went to press."

"You think *that's* what I'm upset about?" She struggled to form her thoughts into words. "The column I submitted didn't have Alex's name in it. You added it, in the most insulting context. How could you do that? He's my ex-husband!"

Evan smirked. "The operative word being *ex.*"

"The operative word being *husband*!" She grabbed a tissue to dry her eyes. "You twisted what I said about Senator Hartley's conduct into something derisive. You couldn't resist taking a swing at Alex."

"I wrote things you didn't have the courage to say."

"It's courageous to call a lawyer smug and self-interested? That's nothing but a tired cliché. Whenever Alex spoke to the press about Senator Hartley, he was passionate about her innocence. And with a sentence, you negated that."

"Please," Evan said, "Alex loved being in the spotlight."

"Your opinion is beside the point. This is not your column."

"No, but it's my newspaper to run."

She stepped back and looked at him with wide eyes. Her thoughts swimming, she closed her laptop computer. "You're asking me to choose between my job and the people I love. That's an easy choice. I quit."

⸙

Karina was in court most of the day, but late that afternoon, she got a call from Tara. Hearing the news, Karina sat at her desk, blood rushing from her face. She stared at a waterfall poster on her wall. "Tara, I understand you're upset, but isn't this extreme?"

"I can't be what Evan wants. I'll keep disappointing him."

"After what Evan did to your column, you're worried about disappointing *him*?" Outrage blossomed in Karina's chest. She adored Evan, but sometimes his impulses took him too far.

"We'll never agree," Tara said, the pitch of her voice rising. "Our friendship gets in the way of our professional relationship."

"Meaning you don't want to confront your friend about what a lousy boss he is."

Tara was silent a moment. "He's a good boss, most of the time. But he takes advantage of our friendship."

Karina picked up her stuffed penguin and squished its insides. "Then set some boundaries."

"If I knew how to do that, half my shoe wardrobe wouldn't be in your closet."

Karina fought back a laugh.

Once off the phone, she sat back and closed her eyes. This was classic Tara, opening the escape hatch instead of navigating a rough landing—forgetting she'd end up bruised either way. Karina clutched her forehead, wondering how she'd fix Tara's life this time.

Alex passed by her door. Karina threw a pen at him and said, "Tara quit her job thanks to you."

He stared blankly. "She...? But Tara loves her job."

"If you'd talked to her instead of attacking her, she could have explained what happened."

"I know what happened. She painted me as a self-serving, manipulative—" Alex paled, and his mouth fell open. "Evan changed her column."

"Ya think?" Karina said. "You jackass."

⌒⊃⟨⟩⊂⌒

Alex rushed out, calling Tara on his cell phone en route to the parking lot. Long shadows stretched across the ground as the sun sank toward the horizon, but the light was still bright.

Tara met him at her front door wearing a trembling smile. She let him inside and sank into his arms. He surged with relief.

The feel of her in his arms was bittersweet. He wanted to hold and cradle her, dry her tears with his kisses, coax a smile onto that beautiful face. But she wasn't his—not yet—maybe not ever.

He cupped her face in his hands. "Don't give up your job over this. I should have realized you didn't write those things about me."

"The column had my name on it. The whole city thinks I wrote those things about you." She rested her head on his shoulder. "But I'm too tired to be angry with Evan. I can't remember what happiness feels like anymore."

He led her to the couch. They sat, and he locked her hands in his. He watched her intently, aching for her, searching her eyes for what she needed. "How can I fix this?"

"I keep telling myself this is a positive thing. I've been working too hard. I need a fresh perspective." She ran her thumb across his palm. "But it's not fair to Karina. I've got a mortgage to consider—"

"I'll worry about the mortgage."

"Alex..."

Determination settled on his shoulders, calming him. This was a way he could make her life easier. "You wouldn't accept the divorce settlement. Let me do this for you."

Her eyes glistened. "It's not fair to offer when I'm too weak to argue."

He returned the smile she gave him, thumb brushing a tear from her cheek. Then, the swirl of memories loomed, the awful meetings across a conference table, lawyers by their side. He swallowed, heaviness gripping his chest. "I never understood why you didn't take that settlement."

"I didn't marry you for money. I married you for love."

He traced a pattern on the back of her hand, then realized it was a heart. His throat tightened. "What happened to us, Tara?"

She laid her other hand on top of his. "The fear inside me was so strong, there was no room for anything else." She sat back and hugged a pillow to her chest. "I was so cruel to you."

"You were healing."

She smiled. "You know me so well."

"I used to."

She let the pillow fall to her side. "You think I've changed?"

He shrugged. Had she? "In the past five months, I've seen you a handful of times, and we've spent most of them fighting."

"But the night of the mayor's banquet..." She leaned toward him. "It felt right, Alex. It felt like us."

The emotions of that night rushed back, and with everything else he was feeling, he almost broke down. "You didn't want me touching you."

"Because I knew if I got close, I'd end up spending the night. And I wasn't ready."

He stared, squeezing the arm of the couch. His throat closed, stopping his breath. "Why didn't you tell me that?"

She drew in her shoulders. "I was afraid you'd be mad when you saw the story about the mayor—"

"Damn it, Tara!" A frustrated laugh escaped his chest. "You treat every conflict like the end of the world. Do you think I'd let a *newspaper article* come between us?"

She took his left hand and massaged his ring finger. "You took off your wedding band."

"You took yours off a long time ago."

"But as long as you were wearing yours," she said, "I thought there was hope for us."

His muscles twitched. The world fell away, until there was only Tara, his Tara, the one he'd fallen in love with all those years ago, looking up at him with wide eyes. His voice came out a rough whisper. "Is there?"

"I'm not afraid anymore."

He held her hand in his, caressing her palm and forcing all thought from his mind. Warily, he met her eyes, and she raised her body toward him. He cradled her in his arms but didn't dare close the space between them.

Tara's lips brushed his, soft as velvet, and he lost himself in her touch. Their breath mingled, flowing from one into the other, and his heart filled his chest to aching. He kissed her hungrily, claiming her, devouring her, unable to get enough of her smooth skin, her silken hair, relearning the curves of her body—until panic settled on his brain and he pulled away.

He stared into space, listening to his heartbeat, trying to still his tumult of emotions. He breathed hard. "I'm finally learning to live without you. If we get caught up in the moment..."

"This isn't the work of a moment."

He sank his forehead into his hand. "I can't lose you twice."

"You never lost me, Alex. I lost myself. But now I've come home."

She rose onto her knees and straddled his lap. Wrapping her arms around his neck, she kissed his mouth, her body soft and eager. Dissolving into desire, he had neither the strength nor the inclination to resist her.

They hurried upstairs leaving a trail of clothes behind. Long rays of sunlight fell across the bed and her almond scented kisses tumbled over him. Lost in pure pleasure he melded into her flesh, clutching her against him, her murmurs singing in his ears. His fingers wove through her hair and his lungs filled with her perfume. He felt her breath on his shoulder, her tears on his cheek, her skin on his skin until the fire subsided, and warm embers burned in its place.

He brushed her hair away from her cheek, floating in her beauty. "There are no words."

She kissed his fingertips. "Now I remember what happiness feels like."

Giddy with joy, he drew her close. She pulled the covers over them and snuggled against his chest. Her eyes fell closed, and her breath grew deep and rhythmic. His body sated, his spirit free, he sank into heavy sleep.

⚭⧜⚮

Tara woke with a start to the ringing phone. She fumbled for it in the half light. Still drunk with slumber, she heard her father's voice say, "Is your sister around? She's not picking up on her cell."

Tara hesitated, her mind muddled. "I don't know. We fell asleep."

"Who's 'we'?"

She bit her cheeks. "Alex and me." She looked around. "What time is it?"

"It's seven o'clock."

"In the morning?"

"No, at night. Sweetheart, is Alex there? I thought maybe your sister knew where he went after work. He was supposed to meet his mother at the restaurant an hour ago."

"Oops." She giggled and turned to Alex. "Weren't you supposed to have dinner with your mother?"

"Shit!" He sat bolt upright and reached impatiently for the phone.

"Dad, can you put Holly on?"

Alex took the receiver from Tara. "Mother? Sorry...No, I'm not lying dead in a ditch somewhere... I promise I'll make it up to you. I'll buy you dinner another time."

Tara grinned.

Alex clicked off the phone. "I can't believe our parents caught us."

Tara laughed.

They put on some clothes and went to look for Karina, but could find no sign of her. Alex said, "Maybe she saw my car in the driveway—and my pants on the staircase—and decided to give us some privacy."

"Yay, privacy!" Tara said, and kissed him.

⸎

Karina sank back into Lauren's couch, letting it envelop her. The tracks of dried tears felt tight on her face. Lauren, sitting next to her, patted her leg. "I'm sorry, sweetie."

"Don't be sorry." Karina sat forward and sipped her tea, now tepid. "Tara deserves this. Just because I fell for my sister's ex, like an idiot..." She dropped her head to her chest. "Why did I let this happen?"

"Because you were on a dating moratorium, and Alex brought romance into your life. And without intending to, you responded to that."

Karina nodded. "I know I don't belong with Alex. I wanted him and Tara back together." Her voice cracked. "So why does it hurt like this?"

Lauren shrugged. "It's natural to feel rejected—"

"Alex didn't reject me. I rejected him. I could have had him if I wanted."

"For how long?" Lauren gave her a wry smile. "Alex is not your soul mate—he's just a guy you wanted to get naked with. Tara wants to have babies with him, to grow old with him. If you'd slept with Alex, you'd have jeopardized her whole future."

"You think I don't know that?"

"I think you *do* know it. That's why it never happened."

Karina pouted, and Lauren wrapped her arms around her sister's neck. Lauren said, "Wallowing in self-pity is fine, for now. But you've got to stop fantasizing about Alex. It's not healthy."

Karina knitted her brow. Her crush on Alex wasn't the problem. She'd had crushes on hotter men than him. But after everything she and Alex had been through together, she felt a deep connection to him. Would that mean anything to Alex, now that he was back with Tara? Had Karina been just a substitute? She wanted to think she meant more to Alex than that. The bond that had grown between them would stay with Karina forever. But she couldn't be sure Alex felt the same.

∽❦∾

To lift her spirits, Karina headed to Monterey Jack's. The prospect of music and company lifted the mist from her mind, and she wondered why she'd let herself get upset over a man she didn't want anyway. Alex was too rigid, too controlling. Karina knew she could never be happy with him.

In the dim light, through the crowd of fashionistas, suited businessmen, and tattooed grad students, she spotted her father standing next to Holly's tall bar table, a thick slab of granite topping a wrought iron base. "Are you two on a date?" she teased.

"Your father's keeping me company. My date stood me up."

"Apparently, Alex got a better offer." Jack's eyes danced. "What's going on with him and Tara?"

A knot formed in her throat, but like a trooper, she swallowed it down. "When I got home, there was a trail of clothes leading up the stairs, and the door to Tara's bedroom was shut."

"About damn time she gave him some nooky," Jack said. "A man can only go so long."

"Dad!"

"I have to agree." Holly swirled her martini. "Alex was overdue."

Karina shifted her gaze between them. "Have I stepped into some weird, parallel universe?"

"Darling, parents know about sex. That's how we got to be parents." Holly glanced at Jack, then continued, "This is exactly what Alex and Tara need to get their relationship back on track."

Jack nodded. "Never underestimate the power of a good roll in the hay."

Karina stared. After the trauma the two of them had been through, how could sex solve anything? "Shouldn't they...you know, talk out their problems first?"

Holly's face softened. "The lack of intimacy *was* the problem."

"After losing the baby...Tara closed her heart." Jack frowned. "Poor Alex never had a chance."

Holly patted Jack's hand. He went back to work, telling Karina to keep Holly company.

Karina watched her father walk away, her stomach churning. She'd never been alone with Holly before.

Holly's features softened. "You don't have to babysit me." Her eyes scanned the room. "Are you meeting someone?"

"No, but I'm looking to meet someone." Karina tilted her head, eyeing Holly. "You want to pick up guys with me?"

Holly laughed, then downed her drink. "Oh, what the hell."

Karina blinked. She hadn't expected that, but it might be fun. Maybe Holly would be the perfect wingman. She leaned back in her chair. "Have you ever picked up men at a bar before?"

Holly tilted her head. "I don't believe I have."

"Remember, no last names. You don't want some crazy Googling you."

The Saloon grew more crowded. Holly and Karina invited two gentlemen standing by the bar to join them at their table. As the foursome chatted, Karina detected something in Holly she'd never noticed before: Holly was nervous! Despite the poise that came from her aristocratic upbringing, Holly seemed uncomfortable around these strangers, watching them to get her bearings before speaking. Karina didn't mind taking the lead. If she made a fool of herself, people would think she was whimsical. Karina placed a reassuring hand on Holly's arm.

Sipping her second martini, Holly grew more easy. Her eyes brightened, and Karina perceived the warmth and humor hidden beneath Holly's reserve. Blood rushed to Karina's cheeks. How could she ever have thought Holly cold?

After the gentlemen had gone, Holly looked at her watch. "It's late."

Karina smiled. "We should do this again."

Holly tapped her fingers on the tabletop. "Let's make it lunch instead. Small talk with strangers isn't my forte."

"That one guy liked you—what was his name? Ronald, Donald..."

"Ronald Donald was not my type."

It surprised Karina to think of Holly as having a "type." Karina asked, "What sort of man do you like?"

Holly's eyes searched the bar. "Smart, successful...with gentle hands and a gentle heart."

Karina nodded. "I want someone who understands me. No one's understood me since..." Emotion choked her voice, catching her off guard.

Holly laid her hand on Karina's. "Your mother?"

Karina stared, wondering how Holly knew. Then, Karina remembered. "How old were you when you lost your mom?"

"Fourteen. You and I are more alike than you think." Holly sat back. "You remind me of her. She had the same curiosity, the same enthusiasm. My father accused her of saying the most preposterous things, but she'd argue she never knew if her ideas were any good unless she talked about them."

Karina's skin warmed. A memory teased her mind. She was floating through the air on a swing, her mother pushing her as high as she could go.

Karina looked at Holly. "I don't know why we never talked like this before."

"During most of Alex and Tara's marriage, you were away at law school."

Karina studied Holly's face. "You're a good listener. You don't judge me or tell me what to do, you just...listen."

"I enjoy listening to you."

Karina brightened, emotion squeezing her heart. "Would it be okay if I called you sometime, just to talk?"

Holly smiled. "I'd like that." She patted Karina's hand.

Holly went to the bar and paid the tab before leaving. Karina watched her, realizing that Holly and Alex were nothing alike, even though their behavior was similar. Alex was brusque. When he withdrew, it meant he was done with you. But Holly was quiet, thoughtful, like Lauren. Karina's spirits lifted at the prospect of getting to know Holly better.

Karina stretched her arms, wondering if she should go as well. Then, her eye caught Ryne Applegate ascending the staircase. A smile pressed into her cheeks. She admired the way he looked in black jeans and a slate gray button-down shirt woven to a rich sheen.

Karina walked over and greeted him. "What a coincidence," she said, "you showing up at my dad's club."

He grinned. "I admit it. I go after what I want."

"I'm flattered."

"You should be." He touched her arm, and she slipped her hand into his.

To escape the noise, Ryne and Karina took their drinks downstairs to the lounge set aside for guests waiting for a table. It was a dimly lit room secluded from the dining area. Karina could count on it to be empty at this time of night.

He rested his arm on the back of the overstuffed couch. "Tell me why you became a lawyer." His hand brushed her shoulder.

Leaning back, she flashed a smile. "I'm the youngest of three sisters. I learned to argue at an early age."

"Seriously."

She gazed up at him, warm in the light of his eyes. "Lauren likes telling people what to do, and Tara likes pleasing people, so they mesh well. But I like questioning things. Debate crystallizes our convictions."

"And you're passionate about your convictions."

Her eyes focused on the Berber carpet. "I was sixteen when my mom died of cancer—I learned early the value of compassion. Those who deserve love least are the ones who need it most."

"Like Miguel Santos?"

She pressed her fingertips into the couch. "Santos was in terrible pain. What kind of person would I be if I couldn't forgive him?"

His hand wrapped around hers. "In your job, you see the worst society has to offer. But you find goodness in people the rest of us have written off. You lift them up."

She tilted her head. "Do you really see us as being on opposite sides?"

"We're different pieces of a puzzle. Only when the parts fit together can you see the big picture."

Warmth rushed over her. "I like thinking of us that way."

He leaned closer and she stilled, like a fawn in tall grass. He drew toward her, and she submitted to his kiss, tingling at the softness of his lips. She wasn't ready to let go—her heart remained cautious—but his warmth, his scent of citrus and musk, filled her with a sense of peace, as if the future might somehow be okay.

He pulled back, breaking the kiss, and clasped her hands. "That was better than I expected. And I had high hopes."

Pleasure rippled through her. Her eyes surveyed the soft curve of his ear, the strong line of his jaw. Maybe this day didn't suck after all.

16   In Your Room

ALEX WOKE AT DAWN TO FIND HIMSELF IN HIS BED alone. At the window stood Tara, watching the sun's rays spread from behind the mountains to suffuse the sea with light. He walked up behind her, slipping his arms around her waist, happy but unsure. "No regrets?"

She rested against him, her back to his stomach, her hair tickling his chest. "I'm finally home." In the stillness, the only sound was the rising and falling of her breath, and it was enough.

He caressed her nude body, and his hand brushed the scar on her belly. She turned toward him. He touched the scar again, then knelt and kissed it, wrapping his arms around her waist.

Her fingers tunneled through his hair. "At first, I hated that scar. It was an ugly reminder of how we lost our daughter. But now it's become a precious reminder of how we loved her." Tara cupped his face in her hands. "The first time I felt her move, the first time we heard her heart beat...I don't want those memories tinged with sadness. She made every day magical."

He stood and kissed her. "For so long I've wanted to share this with you—"

"I was afraid to let the pain in. It was about survival, Alex, not my feelings for you."

With careful fingers, he caressed her cheek. "If you needed time away from me to heal, I accept that."

She laid her hands on his shoulders. The morning light turned her hair to gold. "I don't want us to be apart again. Ever."

"Then move back home."

She blinked, and her lips parted.

Shit. He'd said the words aloud before his conscious mind could stop them. He had to be more careful—he couldn't risk scaring her away. "I'm sorry. It's too soon."

Head tilting to one side, she tapped his chest with her fingertips. Her face was pensive but serene. "I'll think about it."

She smiled and led him back to bed. They crawled under the covers, and she slipped into quiet slumber. But his mind stirred with the chatter of the waves.

❧

Later that morning, Lauren stood in her kitchen cutting open a package of biscotti, releasing the scent of anise and cinnamon. Karina hummed, carrying mugs of coffee to the table. As they eased into the ladder-back chairs, Lauren said, "Tell me about Ryne."

Karina's face brightened. "His mom's a history teacher, and his dad's an airline pilot. He has a sister in Santa Barbara who's a stay-at-home mom, and his eyes sparkle when he talks about his niece and nephew. He double majored in criminology and public administration at San Diego State, and even though he loves working as a detective, I can see him rising through the ranks—"

"Kare, slow down." Lauren squeezed her sister's hand.

"He asked me to dinner tonight."

Lauren shook her head while her brain caught up. "Be careful. You're on the rebound."

Karina frowned. "I am?"

"Last night you showed up here in tears—"

"Please, I'm over Alex."

Lauren shook her head. Her brain couldn't keep up with Karina's, and how it constantly changed direction. "Kissing a cute boy doesn't make you over Alex."

"Ryne is a *man.*"

"That's a refreshing change."

Karina flopped her arms down onto the tabletop. "Why can't you be excited for me? Ryne's a cop—Chantel has known him for years. What's the worst that could happen?"

"He could break your heart."

"My heart's been broken before. I'll survive."

Lauren rested her chin on her hand, knowing this was an argument she couldn't win. Karina was like a child at a nuclear power plant, wanting to push all the buttons to see what would happen.

"You always put more into a relationship than you get back," Lauren said. "Pace yourself—you barely know this man."

"I know I like him."

Lauren massaged her temples.

Karina smiled. "Don't think about it so much. Uncertainty keeps life interesting."

"My life's interesting enough, thanks to you and Tara. Have you heard from her this morning?"

"No, and I'm dying to find out what happened yesterday." Karina clutched her cell phone. "Why hasn't she called?"

⁓❦⁓

Alex and Tara stood at their daughter's graveside, the sun chasing the mist from the earth. Tara knelt by the headstone. "The lilies are beautiful," she said, breathing the scent of pink petals speckled with nutmeg.

"It's the one thing I can do for her," Alex murmured, "making sure she has fresh flowers every day."

Tara brushed her hand along the cold marble. Her heart couldn't connect this plot of earth with the life that had grown inside her, stretching and tumbling, waking her with flutters and jabs.

Tara's first memory upon emerging from the coma was the stillness in her belly. She had known something was wrong, but she had not imagined that her daughter was already in the ground. Tara swallowed. "I hate that I missed her funeral."

Alex stooped beside her. "I was afraid to leave your side, even for an hour. But your dad said if I didn't go, I'd always regret it." Alex turned silent. "Your dad couldn't see how close we were to losing you."

The knot tightened in Tara's throat. Light filtered through the leaves of the pepper trees and trembled on the grass. Red berries littered the ground, their flesh cracked open to strew their seeds. Tara gazed up at the patches of sky visible through the weeping boughs. She kissed her fingertips and touched them to the name carved into the stone.

She and Alex walked to the car, the zoysia grass cushioning their feet. Overhead, goldfinches twittered. Tara stopped and turned, letting the ache flow through her, then softly ebb. Alex brushed his hand along her back.

They climbed into the car. Tara scanned the quiet land, feeling connected to the generations that had come before. She squeezed Alex's hand. "Let's go see your mother."

At the penthouse, Holly greeted them in the library, her smile a welcoming hug. The room was open, windows stretching almost to the ceiling. Bookshelves of pale maple housed literature ranging from medieval poetry to microeconomics. Clusters of daisies filled vases of Chinese porcelain.

Tara laid her head on Holly's shoulder, sinking into her protective arms. Her voice unsteady, Tara said, "I've missed having you as my mom."

Holly's grip tightened, until at last she ran her hand down Tara's back. "My love comes without conditions."

They sat on the white divan, conversation weaving through the gaps in their relationship. Holly radiated warmth and earnestness, and Tara felt at ease. They chatted like girlfriends, barely giving Alex a chance to speak. But his arm around Tara's waist, his fingers combing through her long hair, assured her of his constant presence.

Finally, Holly asked Tara, "Have you decided what to do about your job, after what Evan wrote in today's paper?"

Tara's eyes widened. "I haven't seen the paper."

Holly rose, bringing her the Focus section. "Evan printed a retraction, then re-ran yesterday's column just as you wrote it."

Tara scanned the page, drinking the words but barely comprehending them.

Alex read over her shoulder. "Evan's hated me since my G.I. Joe beat up his Ken doll—but he actually apologized to me."

"This..." Tara said, "I..."

"Evan must really want you back."

Alex's words added to her confusion. She tried to process the sudden change, her certainty eroding. She had made her decision, and she was happy with it—wasn't she? But Evan's apology changed everything.

Alex's touch reassured her. "You have a talent for finding common ground—make Evan see the value in that. If he wants controversy, he can write his own damn column."

Tara blinked, a flash of inspiration curving her lips upward. "You may be on to something."

⁓◦§◦⁓

After lunching with Lauren and Sean, Karina was gathering her purse to leave when Alex's car appeared in the driveway. A thrill of happiness pulsed through her.

She hurried out and squeezed her sister in a long embrace, feeling the lightness that had overtaken Tara's body. She said a little prayer of thanks that Tara was finally on her way to recovery. But Karina struggled to meet Alex's eye. Would things always be weird with him now?

Lauren and Karina whisked Tara upstairs to the nursery, leaving Alex to chat with Sean. The sisters sat on the braided rug with Nissa in Tara's lap. Tara was her normal, serene self, but now joy radiated from her.

"For so long I was afraid of my emotions," she said. "I worried that somehow I deserved what happened to me. Reconnecting with Alex...it's like reconnecting with myself."

Karina snuggled against her. "Even your shoulders are smiling."

"I never thought I'd feel this confident again. I trust myself." Tara stroked Nissa's hair. "I want to reassure Alex that this is real—that I'm back for keeps."

Karina sat hugging her knees, thinking of the Alex she'd come to know over the past five months...so different from the man she thought he was before. If only she could forget how it felt to kiss him.

Forcing herself to think of Ryne, the memories made her smile. She liked that he was pursuing her. Confidence was an aphrodisiac, and Ryne had it.

Karina tugged Tara's shirt sleeve. "Did Holly tell you she and I scoped out guys at the Saloon last night?"

Tara's eyebrows rose. "I thought you didn't like Holly."

"I completely misread her." Karina hung her head. "But I'll find a way to make it up to her. She's my new best friend."

"I thought Ryne was your new best friend," Lauren said.

Karina brightened. "He's got potential."

"Just don't rush in to anything," Tara added.

Karina narrowed her eyes. "Excuse me, but *I've* never slept with a man unless we'd dated for at least a month. Can you two say that?"

Lauren frowned. "Sean was an exception."

"Second date. You slut," Tara teased.

"I married him. That cancels it out."

Giggling, the sisters descended the stairs, Lauren carrying Nissa. They joined the men in the family room. Tara sat on the couch next to Alex, and Karina plunked down next to her. Alex draped his arm over Tara's shoulder.

Damn it. The flash of jealousy in Karina's belly pissed her off.

Lauren set her daughter on the floor and joined Sean on the loveseat. Nissa picked up the sippy cup from the coffee table and shook it, but it was empty. "Appa chu?" she said.

"You want some apple juice?" Sean turned to Lauren.

"She's already had four ounces today."

Sean smiled. "Water it is, then." He carried Nissa into the kitchen.

Karina watched after her niece. "What happens if she gets more than four ounces of juice?"

"Too much sugar could rot her teeth," Lauren said.

Karina grinned. "All three of them?"

"Kare, leave it alone," Tara said. "Lauren's just more disciplined than you."

"I'm not undisciplined!" Karina looked to Alex for support, but he wouldn't defend her against Tara.

"I didn't mean it like that." Tara squeezed Karina's hand. Karina smiled and squeezed it back.

"So while you were picking up guys at the Saloon last night," Tara said, "did Holly get any offers?"

"A few, but she turned them down."

Alex's eyes shifted between them. "Holly who?"

"Your mother?" Karina teased.

Alex flushed. "My mother doesn't pick up men in bars."

"They seem to like her."

He stared at Karina. "You think she wants to date?"

"She's been alone for five years," Karina said. "You think she hasn't dated in all that time?"

"She never mentioned anything."

Lauren grinned. "Maybe she was afraid you'd react like this."

"A woman in her situation..." Alex wrinkled his brow. "Men might see her as easy prey."

"Your mother's a big girl," Lauren said. "She can take care of herself."

"Or maybe she's tired of taking care of herself." With a wicked smile, Karina rose.

She joined Sean in the kitchen. Nissa stood at his feet drinking from her sippy cup. Karina poured a glass of iced tea to chill her emotions.

"Why am I so stupid?" Karina fumed, her voice low. "Alex made me feel like he wanted me more than any man had ever wanted me...when in fact, he wanted sex more than any man had ever wanted sex."

Sean laughed, but then protested, "Don't say that. He cares about you."

"That's the problem." Karina frowned. "Lauren and Tara think I can't make good choices, but a sophisticated man like Alex takes me seriously."

"Your sisters think it's their job to protect you."

Karina picked up a lemon from the fruit basket and rolled it on the countertop, wondering how different her life would have been if she'd been born first. "I guess we're stuck in those roles from childhood."

"It's deeper than that. You like shocking people. If you want your sisters to take you seriously, you need to tone it down."

She leaned her elbows on the countertop and rested her chin on her hand. "So when I'm dressing for my date tonight, I shouldn't put on my skimpiest outfit just to watch Tara's reaction?"

"What do you think?"

Karina knelt next to Nissa. "Your daddy spoils my fun."

As the afternoon waned, Alex and Tara entered her father's bungalow. Tara called out, but Jack didn't answer.

"Told you we should have phoned first," Alex said.

"He didn't pick up. But the door's unlocked, and the restaurant manager said he was here."

They stepped into the family room. Furniture constructed of dense tropical wood anchored whimsical accents: bronze monkeys, hand-woven baskets, chocolate-colored pottery. Above the couch hung a painting of a brown-skinned boy in a pale cotton tunic perched atop an elephant. Riding through tall grass, he wound toward a distant village, leaning toward home. But out of his sight lurked a tiger, watching.

Jack emerged from the back of the house, buttoning his shirt cuffs. "Isn't this a surprise!" He kissed Tara's forehead. "That's the way it should be—the two of you together, smiling like that. I knew you'd come to your senses."

They talked a few minutes before Jack apologized, saying he had to meet a client about a catering job. As Alex and Tara walked to their car, she said, "He seemed in a hurry to get rid of us. Do you think he had a woman in there?"

Alex laughed, but stopped abruptly when he spotted a white Jaguar parked behind the house.

Tara's eyes twinkled. "My father doesn't own a Jaguar."

Alex stood like stone. "No. But my mother does."

Tara squealed, then grabbed Alex's arm and dragged him to his car.

With the sun winking in the western sky, they drove to Tara's house. She looked through her bedroom closet, selecting clothes for church the next day. Alex stood with his hands in his pockets.

She bit her lip. "I know you think it's silly, packing clothes for a few days at a time, when I'm sleeping at your place..."

"Stop worrying what I think."

She eyed him uncertainly. "Buying this house with Karina helped me find my strength. Living with you, I felt dependent. You gave me so much, and I felt guilty whenever I denied you anything."

"We've talked about this. Sharing my wealth with you doesn't make me poorer."

"My mother raised me to be self-sufficient."

He squinted. "You can make a gourmet meal without opening a cookbook. I can't fry an egg without setting the kitchen on fire." He cupped her face. "I'm not trying to buy your love. I just want to make you happy."

She melted into his arms. "You do."

They went downstairs, and she started dinner. Karina entered from outside and dropped the mail onto the counter. "How was Dad?"

Alex scowled at Tara. She said, "Dad was busy." But she couldn't suppress a smile.

Karina's eyes widened. "You mean he was *getting busy*? With who?"

Tara laughed, and Alex glared.

Karina puzzled a moment, then gasped. "*That's* why he and Holly looked so cozy last night?"

Alex hung his head.

Karina flitted around the kitchen. "This is the best news!"

"Slow down," Tara said. "It's all speculation."

"And you're willing to leave it at that?"

Alex frowned. "I already know more than I want to."

Tara grinned at him. "I can't believe we caught our parents!"

~⚮~

That evening, Ryne took Karina to an upscale restaurant in Little Italy offering a view of the harbor. Sitting in a wooden booth carved with grape clusters, she gazed out at the rooftops dotting the slopes below. She watched the sun fade into the ocean, a kaleidoscope of golden light.

Ryne ordered a bottle of pinot grigio to complement their appetizer, a ceviche of green mussels and artichoke hearts. Karina admired his culinary fluency. "How did you develop such good taste?"

"Mom jokes that when she met Dad, he could pilot a 747 but couldn't make a grilled cheese sandwich. She forced me to learn my way around the kitchen."

"My mom tried to do that. She was an artist— food was her palette. But cooking has always been a chore to me."

"Some people express their love through cooking. You take care of people in other ways."

Heat rose in her cheeks. "Ryne..."

He entwined his fingers in hers. "I want to know everything about you."

She tilted her head. "A woman likes to maintain an air of mystery."

"You lost your mother as a teenager, you endured an assault by a desperate man—yet you believe passionately in the goodness of life. Where does that come from?"

"From my faith, I guess. I couldn't survive if I didn't believe bad things happen for a reason."

He gazed into the candlelight, the white-gold tip of the flame dancing about its blue center. "Yesterday, I went to a crime scene where two little kids had stumbled into a drug deal. The five-year-old was killed, and his eight-year-old brother may be paralyzed for life. What reason could there be for that?"

"I don't know," she murmured. Sadness rose from her core. "But I trust there is one."

"You believe a loving God would let hate and greed destroy two young lives."

"God isn't in the hate. God is in the healing."

He paused for breath. His brow wrinkled, and his eyes focused on her. "That's intense, Karina—and a little scary."

She smiled. "You think I'm scary?"

"You have powerful convictions. That can be intimidating."

"Maybe to someone who's not secure in his beliefs." She stroked the back of his hand. "But a strong, brave police detective like you—you're not threatened by me, are you?"

He smiled, and her insides fluttered.

After dinner, they walked to Amici Park, where cypress trees sheltered them from the sidewalk. In the light of the crescent moon, they stood beneath an arbor draped with bougainvillea. He took her in his arms. "I was nervous about tonight," he said, "but you made everything easy."

"That's because I like you."

"See, you did it again." He caressed her cheek. "I love your openness."

Her breath quickened. Her whole body quivered with desire. He was handsome and strong and smart...everything a man should be. She needed to be very careful. "It could be a verbal sleight-of-hand."

"Why? What secrets are you hiding?"

"You're a detective. You tell me."

"I'll need to conduct a thorough investigation." He pressed his lips to hers, and his hands slid down the arch of her back. Ignoring a twinge of conscience, she yielded to his kisses.

He smiled. "How'd I get so lucky? I hear you've been shooting down every guy who's asked you out lately."

"I wanted to focus on me for a while. The last few guys I dated..." She tilted her head. "Sometimes women expect men to know intuitively what we want. But there's a reason it's called *women's* intuition. Men don't have it. From now on, when I want something, I'm asking for it. And I won't feel guilty about that."

"You deserve to get what you want." He held her close, and his lips found hers. She sensed how much he wanted her, and she savored that desire, letting it fill the empty places in her heart.

17 So Emotional

SUNDAY MORNING, HOLLY AND JACK ENTERED THE breakfast room at her penthouse, dressed for church. They settled into their chairs, sunlight playing on the cranberry glassware and reflecting on the pale lemon walls. Plates of papaya topped with crème fraîche sat on the table.

Beside Holly's place setting was a phone message. She arched her brows as she read. "Karina invited me to Sunday dinner with your family."

Jack smiled. "I warned you if Alex saw your car yesterday, the jig was up."

Holly laid down the slip of paper. "Poor Alex. I didn't want him to find out that way."

Jack glanced at her as he stirred his coffee.

"When should I have told him?" she asked. "While he and Tara were going through their divorce? When he first moved back to San Diego?"

"Maybe when we first got involved?"

"Oh, that would have been lovely. 'Alex, I'm sleeping with your father-in-law. I don't know if it will amount to anything, but we're having a good time of it.'" She squeezed Jack's hand. "I'm glad the children know about us."

"Are you?"

Holly drew in her shoulders. "I worry things could go wrong. At least now, Karina realizes I'm not the enemy."

"I told you she'd like you once she got to know you."

Holly eyed the bone china sugar bowl. "I wasn't raised to be open the way you are. My family can trace its roots to the Mayflower—when I told my father that Matthew and I were engaged, he was *apoplectic*. Matthew wasn't even Ivy League. My father hadn't sent me to Radcliffe so I could marry a Stanford man."

Jack shook his head.

Holly lowered her teacup. "After my mother died, I used to imagine that some bohemian without a penny would show up claiming to be my real father. He'd whisk me off to a commune, where we'd milk goats and grow organic wheat. A childish fantasy, I suppose, but when I turned eighteen, I started living on my own terms."

"Which you've been doing ever since."

She knitted her brow. "Do you think that's wrong?"

Jack grinned. "You're a philanthropist, Holly. How could that be wrong?"

She watched him dig his spoon into his papaya. His hands were callused from working the earth, growing herbs for the restaurant in his garden. Yet his touch was as gentle as swaying fields of lavender.

In his arms she had found peace. Now, she contemplated the changes to come. She was relieved to be ending the secrecy. Yet she wondered what would happen to her hidden treasure once it was revealed.

❧

After church, while the duck roasted, Karina sat with her family, bored by the football game on television. She looked over at Lauren and Sean cuddling on the loveseat, Nissa dozing in Sean's lap. Alex and Tara were cooing at each other on the couch and ignoring all the issues between them. Jack sat next to them wearing a satisfied grin. He'd said nothing about Holly, but Karina was sure he knew about the invitation.

Karina crossed her legs and bounced her foot, contemplating her pathetic life. Then, she thought of Ryne. Having a hot boyfriend made her less pathetic—although he didn't really qualify as a boyfriend yet...

Karina's eyes caught sight of Holly's car pulling into the driveway. She smiled.

Alex shot to his feet and walked to the window. He turned to Karina, his eyes glinting like steel. "I told you to stay out of this."

Karina rearranged the sunflowers bunched in a vase on the coffee table. "Dad doesn't mind my inviting his girlfriend to dinner."

Lauren blinked. "His *what?*"

Karina met Holly at the door. Holly smiled, but her eyes looked apprehensive. Karina kissed her cheek. Holly turned to Alex and patted his shoulder. "Don't worry, darling. You'll get over it once the shock wears off."

At dinner, Alex vacillated between staring at his plate and stealing glances at his mother and Jack. She was as calm as ever, with only a faint smile to reveal the emotions lurking beneath her surface. Alex had thought he was the one person who could see through his mother's façade. Obviously, there were aspects of her life even he didn't know.

Alex turned when Nissa banged her fist on the tray of her high chair. She squealed, then stuffed bits of roast duck into her mouth. Her face and fingers gleamed with fat.

Sean cut up a few more pieces and put them on her plate.

"Don't give her too much," Lauren said. "She's never had duck before. I don't want to upset her little tummy."

"She has chicken all the time."

"It's not the same thing. It doesn't hurt to be cautious."

Sean shook his head.

Tara's eyes grew distant. Alex laid his hand on hers. "You okay?"

She breathed deeply. "I'm getting a migraine." She closed her eyes, her lashes coating with tears. Rising, she headed upstairs.

Karina gazed at Alex. "Aren't you going after her?"

"Later. She needs time alone."

Karina shook her head. Alex wondered for a moment if Karina was right. But when it came to Tara, he trusted his instincts.

After dinner, Alex went upstairs and found Tara sitting on her bed, staring into space. He closed the door and sat next to her. Putting his arm around her, he kissed her temple. "Feeling better?"

"I'm thinking about our future. My life's been on pause for so long—I want to put it on fast forward."

He smiled, unsure and apprehensive, but he knew how impatient Tara was. Once she made up her mind, she didn't like to wait. "Things happened fast the first time. How long had we known each other when we got married? Three months?"

"Almost four. But I'm not waiting that long this time." She brushed her lips along his collarbone.

Desire rushed through his body, turning him to flame. "Don't start something you can't finish."

"Who says I can't finish it?"

He kissed her mouth, then pulled away. "We should wait 'til we get home."

"I am home," she said.

He nodded, his stomach tightening.

She gazed downward. "I'm sorry."

He lifted her chin. "Don't be. Asking you to move in was an impulse. I shouldn't have brought it up so soon."

"I'm making you unhappy."

"Tara. You *are* my happiness. If you think otherwise, that's the fear talking. Don't listen to it. That's not who you are."

"Maybe it should be. Do you think Lauren would have chased down a story in a questionable part of town while she was seven months pregnant?"

"Lauren holds her breath every time Nissa takes a step. Even Lauren knows her fear isn't healthy."

Tears fell from Tara's eyes. "I can't stop blaming myself."

He pulled her against him, kissing the rim of her ear, clutching her thick locks of hair. He understood how she felt—he'd been riding that same roller coaster of self-reproach for far too long. "It's not your fault."

She sighed. "If it wasn't my fault, then it was out of my control. Letting go of the guilt means accepting that in some parts of my life, I'm powerless." She met his eyes. "You need to do that, too."

Heaviness settled in his chest. "How do we get there?"

She kissed him. "Together."

∽⦇§⦈∼

Downstairs in the kitchen, Karina and Lauren were cleaning up. Karina's stomach tied itself in knots, worrying about Tara. *She's got Alex now. He'll know what to do.* The thought gave her comfort while also filling her with despair.

She didn't want Alex. But she *did* want a man who loved her the way Alex loved Tara. Would she ever have that? Could Ryne be that man? Or would putting that kind of pressure on the relationship so soon break it before it had a chance to grow?

She had to stop jumping three steps ahead in every relationship, hoping for forever before she even learned his middle name. So far, Ryne seemed like a good guy, and she enjoyed his company. That should be enough for now.

Holly entered and looked around, wearing an ironic smile. "May I help?"

Lauren grinned. "Have you ever used a dishwasher?"

"Is that what this machine is called?" Holly asked.

Karina shook her head, wondering whether Holly was just joking or if she'd actually never seen a dishwasher in real life. "That's okay, it's a two-person job."

"You could put away the leftovers," Lauren suggested.

Holly scanned the platters covering the countertop. "How would one go about doing that?"

"I'll show you." Karina dried her hands. "You can do it Lauren's way, which is to organize the plastic containers according to which plate of leftovers will best fit into them. Or, you can do it my way, which is to grab the closest container and start filling it."

Holly smiled at Karina. "I prefer your method."

"No one appreciates my effort," Lauren complained.

"We appreciate it," Karina said. "We just don't want to imitate it."

After cleaning up, the women made their way from the kitchen to the family room. Holly and Karina joined Jack on the couch, while Lauren sat on the loveseat next to Sean. Lauren looked over at her father. "Do you think Tara's okay?"

"She keeps her sadness inside. Writing is how she lets it out."

"The survivor guilt is weighing on her," Holly murmured. "If she hadn't been pregnant, *her* body would have born the full impact of that bullet."

Jack nodded. "Her pregnancy saved her life."

Karina rose, hugging herself, shivering in the bright sunlight that streamed through the window.

Tara descended the stairs with Alex. Karina rushed over and embraced her. Tara kissed her sister's cheek. "Please don't worry about me," Tara said.

"I want you to be safe. Always."

"Says the woman who works with violent criminals."

Karina smiled. "I'm on their side, remember? And they're not all violent, and they're not even all criminals."

Alex smirked, but eyeing Tara, he said nothing.

Tara rubbed her temple. "I could use some caffeine. Who wants coffee?"

"I'll make the coffee," Jack said, rising. "You sit."

"No thanks, Daddy, I've had your coffee." Tara followed him into the kitchen.

Alex flopped onto the couch next to his mother. "Kare, when was the last time you represented someone who was innocent?"

"Justice is about more than guilt and innocence." Karina paced, emotion rising inside her. "Most people I represent were abused or hooked on drugs or never had anyone to set them on the right path. That doesn't make them criminals. It makes them lost. People like that are no threat to me."

Alex rose, eyes narrow. "Unless they turn desperate, like Miguel Santos."

Karina looked away, but Alex pressed on, "If you hope to survive in criminal law, you need to lose that naïve attitude."

"I'm not naïve, I'm optimistic. Ryne says I lift people up."

Alex laughed, a dry, heartless sound. "Cops *live* to put bad guys behind bars. If he said that to you, it was to get you into bed."

Karina's lips parted, shock crushing her chest. She ran out the front door and sank onto the porch swing, one hand clinging to the chain.

The swift change in Alex's treatment left her stunned. She clutched her stomach, nauseated, thinking how she had shown him the most tender parts of herself. And now...she was ridiculous to him?

Lauren crept outside and sat next to Karina, taking her hand, feet skimming the gray floor boards. Enveloped in silence, the sisters glided together like swans borne by the water. Beyond the banister, silver artemisia wove a brocade among purple asters and rosy heads of sedum. Honeybees gathered the nectar, whirring tirelessly to support the hive.

Karina's voice pushed through her taut throat. "All this time I thought Alex respected me. He told me that I was brilliant—that I was beautiful. But he was lying, hoping to get me into bed."

"Alex doesn't lie to women to get them into bed. The truth works just fine."

Karina thumped her shoulders back against the swing.

Lauren took her hand. "Maybe you *want* his affection to be a façade. You know you need to distance yourself from him, and that's easier to do if you tell yourself he doesn't care about you."

Karina closed her eyes. "I used to know exactly what I wanted. I can't remember anymore."

"You turned to Alex because something is missing from your life—it's time to figure out what that is."

Karina's mind shuffled back to the day when everything changed. Her body heaved at the memory of entering Tara's hospital room, wanting to flee rather than see Tara small and pale and still, a spider web of tubes attaching her to machines that kept her alive. The odor of disinfectant and body fluids caught in Karina's throat. Life became endless hours of watching and waiting and praying.

And miracles. The doctors were gentle and grave, never hinting at prognosis, talking of treatments and seeing what would happen. But Tara surpassed their hopes until the doctors wore faint smiles and walked with light steps. Little by little, Tara came back.

Still, Karina prayed. *Please God don't let me hope too much. Just let her be okay.*

Tara was more than okay. She was fine. She was splendid.

But she was different. She was quiet and earnest. Her eyes were dull, her mouth expressionless. Karina told herself it was the painkillers. And the grief. But the grief could be gotten over. Alex and Tara could have another baby. Not right away, of course, not until Tara healed...

Then, Tara started saying strange things. She didn't want to go home to the beach house, where the staff would hover over her. She wanted to stay with her father while she recovered. Alex didn't object. Then, once settled in Jack's guest room, she asked Alex not to visit so much. It was draining him. Alex was hurt and confused, but he complied. Then, she asked him to stop calling. She was fine, really. He didn't need to check up on her. Alex began to panic: she was slipping away from him. But she complained he was pressuring her, and she couldn't bear the stress. So Alex fought every urge inside him and gave her the space she said she needed.

And then she asked for a divorce.

Alex convinced the doctor to change Tara's medication. Yet Tara held firm. Karina could hear Tara's voice in the bedroom next to hers: *We're hurting each other, Alex. We bring out the worst in each other. If we stay together, we'll destroy our love. I couldn't bear that. I've lost so much already.*

Despite his skill at rational argument, Alex couldn't break through her bizarre tangle of emotions. It all made sense to her. And the more he tried to dissuade her, the more agitated she became. He worried she would have a relapse.

So he ignored every impulse inside him. He didn't fight the divorce.

Karina took it in stride. *Tara's crazy right now, it's the drugs. She'll get over it before the divorce is final. By then, Tara will be herself again. This isn't what she wants—she loves you, Alex. Give her time.*

Instead, Alex took a job in Washington.

Karina watched Alex pack his things from his desk at the D.A.'s office. *Have you lost your mind? This isn't right—Tara needs you.*

He said it was the only way. He loved Tara too much to stay away from her otherwise. She was pushing him away. So he left.

Karina couldn't contain her rage. *God damn Alex.* He and Tara had the perfect marriage, but at the first sign of trouble, he ran.

Alex Kent—brash, confident, cunning, devoted, and desperately in love with his wife—ran like a coward.

Karina clutched the arm of the swing, feeling the grain of the wood on her fingertips. She glanced at Lauren from the corner of her eye and said, "How could Alex leave? How could he give up on Tara?"

"Tara needed time in the dark because she was afraid of the light." Lauren gazed into the house through the window. "But look at her now—at the expression on her face, at the way she carries her body. She's surrounded by light, and it's all thanks to Alex. He gave her the freedom to find her way back to him."

Karina gazed at the starry blooms of sweet autumn clematis scrambling up the trellis. The afternoon sun cast its warmth into the earth. Karina breathed the scented air, clearing her head.

She remembered what she had said to Ryne the night before, that God was in the healing. It was easier to be philosophical when the bad things were happening to other people. Finally, though, Karina could see God's hand at work in Alex and Tara's lives. Yet she had no clue what God's plan was for her. Was Ryne her future? Karina didn't know. But she liked the way he made her feel.

Hours after her family had gone, Tara sat on her bedroom floor searching her closet for the mate to a pink Jimmy Choo slingback. She could feel Karina's stare piecing the back of her head.

"Have you had a brain transplant?" Karina asked. "You and Alex have been back together for two days."

"We can work on our relationship more effectively living under one roof."

"When you divorced Alex...you said that you confused your emotions with his, until you couldn't tell what you wanted anymore. Are you sure that's not what's happening now?"

Tara stood and faced Karina. "If I'm sleeping at his place, I'm living at his place. We may as well call it what it is."

Alex entered and raised up the handle of Tara's wheeled suitcase.

Karina glared at him. "I thought you were supposed to be the rational one."

"Stay out of this. Tara doesn't need your bullshit right now."

"I'm looking out for her best interest, unlike you," Karina said.

"Maybe you're not in a position to know what she needs."

Tara massaged her temples. "Will you stop talking like I'm not in the room? This isn't about what you two want, it's about what I want."

Lauren entered, and Tara gaped. She turned to Karina. "You called in reinforcements?"

"What choice did I have? You never listen to me." Karina stomped out.

Alex looked at Lauren, then at Tara. They stared at him in silence. He wheeled the suitcase into the hallway.

Tara shut the door, then sank onto the bed. "Know what my personal idea of hell is? Two lawyers arguing in my bedroom."

Lauren smiled and sat next to her. "You're sure you've thought this through?"

"I want to be happy again." Tara leaned her head on Lauren's shoulder. "This has been a good year for you. You've got a new daughter, a solid marriage, a fulfilling career—and meanwhile, I've struggled through every day. Now I feel like me again."

"The timing worries me."

"You'd worry no matter what."

Lauren nodded, protesting no further.

While Alex and Tara packed the luggage into their cars, Karina sat in the kitchen, where Lauren had corralled her. She sat with her arms crossed, glaring at Lauren. "Why aren't you more upset about this?"

"I've known Tara for thirty years, and not once have I seen her make a decision based on what someone else thought she should do."

"First she rushed through the divorce, now she's rushing through the reconciliation. It's not healthy."

Lauren rose and poured herself a glass of ice water, letting the condensation drip over her fingers. "You know what I miss? When I was away at grad school, I'd talk to you guys on the phone once or twice a week. We'd have nice little chats, and I didn't have to hear about every crisis in your lives."

Karina's eyes hardened.

Lauren set down her glass. She sat beside Karina and took her hands. "This is why you don't know what you want anymore. You're too focused on Tara. You helped her through the most difficult time of her life— but she's Alex's problem now. And if you push her to rethink her decision to move in with him, you'll confuse her. Uncertainty immobilizes Tara—she needs resolution. Let it go."

~◦§◦~

At twilight, Alex entered the bedroom at the beach house to find Tara standing at the window. He walked up behind her and slipped his arms around her waist, watching the waves sweep onto the shore. He suppressed the urge to fill the silence. Tara was processing, and she needed space for that. He was happy to give it to her. She had come back to him, and that was all that mattered.

She turned and pressed her hands to his chest. "Kare's right about one thing—we still have issues to work through."

His lips thinned. "That worries you?"

"I don't know if I'm strong enough. Sometimes with you I feel...meek."

The word made him smile. "Tara, you're as strong-willed as I am, and even more stubborn."

"That's the problem. When we argue, it steals my breath. I don't know how to please you without losing myself in the process."

He lifted her chin. "We don't have to agree on everything. But we'll never agree on anything unless you're willing to engage in a heated debate."

"You're better at that than I am. You do that for a living!"

"But you're better at finding common ground. If you stand firm, I'll back down."

"I don't like fighting with you." She sank her forehead into his shoulder.

He ran his hand down the length of her hair. "Nothing bad will happen because we disagree."

"Promise?"

He soothed her with persuasive kisses, and she stilled.

⁕

Karina sat across from Ryne in his kitchen, watching him finish the last slice of pizza. Spicy-red earthenware plates topped the black Formica table. A square pillar candle, scented with sandalwood, stood on a copper base.

Ryne picked up the nearly full bottle sitting in front of Karina. "You're not a beer drinker, are you."

She grinned. "Sorry."

"Why didn't you say so?" He got up and opened the refrigerator. "There's wine in here, and...I almost forgot—diet mango iced tea."

She smiled, and he handed her an iced tea. "I picked some up after you ordered one at lunch on Friday," he said.

"You're sweet."

"Don't tell anyone. It doesn't fit my tough guy image."

She stood and kissed him, tasting the cayenne pepper on his lips.

He washed the dishes while she dried and put them away. His cabinets were organized but not meticulous. She approved.

Once the dishes were done, Ryne took Karina's hand and led her into the family room. She scanned the golden yellow walls hung with framed 1940s movie posters and signed photographs of Nat King Cole and Sammy Davis Jr. The wood furniture gleamed in black enamel, and the sprawling entertainment system boasted the latest technology. The voice of Sarah Vaughn flowed from the speakers.

Ryne sat next to Karina on the red leather couch. "I'm glad you came over tonight. If you give me more notice next time, I'll cook for you instead of ordering pizza."

She reclined with her bare toes hidden beneath his thigh. "You could cook for me every night, now that Tara's moved out."

"I know you're worried about her. But I've read Tara's column—she's a smart, confident woman."

"Both my sisters are."

"You say that like you're not."

She drew up her shoulders to ease the tension in her neck. "Lately I've felt a hole in my life. I've got all this love inside me, and no one to give it to."

"Maybe that's why you have a history of dating men who seem damaged. You think your love will heal them. But Karina, men like that can only take. And like it or not, you're a high maintenance woman."

She smiled and leaned toward him. "Does that worry you?"

"I can handle it."

"You can handle *me?*"

He drew her close. "You should be handled often," he said in his best Clark Gable voice, "and by someone who knows how."

She giggled, feeling like a stupid teenager but not caring. Ryne's weight on her body awakened her desire. His arms around her chased away her worries, and his kisses made everything right.

18   Our Lips Are Sealed

EVAN SAT AT A STOPLIGHT MONDAY MORNING, HIS hybrid-electric car silent. To avoid his thoughts, he turned up the volume on his John Coltrane CD. It had been a gift from Tara. He wondered if it would be the last.

The light changed and he drove on, his eyes scanning the storefronts. He evaluated the fashions cloaking the skinny mannequins, the housewares gleaming among clouds of linens, the antiques elbowing each other for space. But they couldn't distract him long.

He arrived at the newspaper and pulled into his prime parking space—the one marked "Evan McCade, Editor-in-Chief." But that was a joke, and everyone knew it. His dad had given him that job only because his own interest in the newspaper business was waning. He was grooming Evan to take over the Print Media division of McCade Communications. But what did Evan know about running a newspaper? He had a flair for words and a nose for trends, but no leadership skills. He surrounded himself with a talented staff and left them to their jobs. Yet whenever he credited them with the newspaper's success, his dad praised Evan for his delegating skills. Evan couldn't understand it.

He relied on Tara to tell him what people needed. She'd say, "Renata's bored as a copywriter. If you don't promote her soon, she'll quit." Or, "The art department's struggling with that new software—show them you appreciate their effort." Tara watched Evan's back. Without her, he felt exposed.

He stepped inside the building. The percussion of fingers tapping on keyboards faded beneath the buzzing of his foolishness in his ears. His chest heavy, he gripped the knob to his office door and entered.

He blinked, then laughed gleefully. Sitting in his chair, feet perched atop his desk, was Tara.

"Here's the deal," she said. "I write my column, and you write a response. That way, we both get our say—but you don't put words into my mouth."

Evan smiled. "I love it...almost as much as I love those shoes!" He eyed her Kate Spades jealously. He had the build of a running back but the heart of a ballerina.

He followed Tara to her office and watched her unpack her belongings. "What's the subject of today's column?" he asked.

"How about sisters who interfere in your relationship when they don't know what they're talking about?"

"An evergreen topic." He narrowed his eyes. "Since when are you in a relationship?"

"Since I hooked up with Alex again." She set her wedding photo atop her desk.

"But...he was furious on Friday!"

"He was angry about what you wrote, not what I wrote."

The corners of Evan's mouth pinched inward. He looked sideways at the wedding photo, his chest tightening as he recalled his humiliation when Alex had chosen Dayne as his best man—Dayne, whom Alex had known for three years, when he'd known Evan his whole life.

Evan helped Tara settle into her office, arranging her *Wizard of Oz* figurines artfully on her desk. Her hair swayed as she moved. Heat rose in his cheeks. "Do you forgive me?"

She tilted her head, her eyes glistening. "Evan, I love you."

"My dad threatened to fire me if necessary to win you back."

She grinned. "That was sweet of him. But I'm not mad at you. I just wish you and Alex would end this feud."

"We're not feuding. We just don't like each other."

With a Mona Lisa smile, she slid a dog-eared copy of *Sin and Syntax* onto her bookshelf. She squeezed Evan's hand. "Thank you for apologizing to Alex."

"Don't scare me like that again. If there's a problem, talk to me."

⚭⚶⚭

Evan left her office, and Tara gathered ideas for her column. In that morning's paper was another article about the mayor denying he had any personal involvement with the illegal contributions accepted by his campaign—despite photos of him with the contributors, during a luxury vacation to Cabo at their expense.

Tara shook her head. She didn't condone what Brooke and Jerry had done, but at least they had the integrity to come clean once they were caught. The mayor seemed caught up in a narcissistic fantasy.

She was thinking about calling Sean, to get a psychologist's perspective, when Evan skipped back into her office.

"I just got word—Brooke Genovese is giving her statement this week. Li Jing is trying to get the details, but the mayor's arrest warrant could be issued by the weekend."

Tara raised her brows. "Will they offer him a deal?"

"Looks that way. Question is, will he take it, or risk a trial?"

Tara shook her head. "The mayor is so accustomed to power...I can't imagine him confessing to a crime and submitting to the punishment."

"It's like you wrote in your column last week. Sometimes, the only way to maintain your dignity is to admit you made a mistake and accept the consequences."

Brooke, Jerry, the mayor—all of them headed to prison. A tear formed in the corner of Tara's eye. She'd never been this close to a public scandal. It was personal to her.

She rubbed her hand across her stomach. Her body bore the scar of violent crime—the mayor's actions seemed innocuous by comparison. Yet on another level, she understood the far-ranging effects of his corruption. He had bought an election. Such crimes came with stiff penalties for a reason. She wanted to wave a magic wand and make it all go away. But justice had to be done.

❧

At the public defender's office, Karina opened her blinds. She glanced at the street below, the pedestrians dressed in summer colors, the cars weaving through avenues and cross-streets. The morning sun touched her face.

She was humming when Alex entered. "You're in a good mood," he said.

"I had another date with Ryne last night." She grinned. "And you owe me a hundred bucks—remember our wager?"

"How do I owe you a hundred bucks? Tara moved in with me—and you've only had two dates with Ryne."

"You didn't go *out* anywhere with Tara, so it doesn't count as a date." She folded her arms behind her back. "Plus, Ryne and I had lunch together on Friday, and I ran into him at the Saloon Friday night...That counts as two *half* dates."

He examined her features, then pulled out his wallet. He handed her the cash. "Third date...does that mean what I think it means?"

"None of your business."

Alex shook his head. "Be careful."

"I don't need your advice."

He wrinkled his brow but said nothing as he left her office.

Karina watched him go, her jaw tightening. She wouldn't let Alex ruin her good mood. A she checked her email, an instant message from Ryne popped up.

Miss you.

Happiness warmed her skin. *Free for lunch?*

Unless someone gets murdered.

She smiled. *Nothing like a homicide to ruin your plans.*

At noon, Ryne picked up Karina in his 1973 Corvette. The day was warm, but a breeze blew in from the shore. Ryne drove to a restaurant on the bay, a weathered gray building with an open-air bar. Karina emerged from the car, squinting against the light reflecting off the water. She started toward the restaurant, but Ryne walked around and opened the passenger door. He pressed down the manual lock.

"Oops, forgot again." Karina sucked in her cheeks, hoping he wasn't annoyed.

Ryne grinned and closed the car door. He ran his hand down her back and placed his arm around her waist. His touch sent electricity through her body.

They walked toward the restaurant. She eyed the cedar clapboards, the fading paint on the sign. "I must have driven by here a thousand times, but never stopped in."

"Sometimes the funkiest places have the best food."

She nodded, but a wave of uncertainty washed over her. Her shoulders tensed.

He halted. "Should we go somewhere else?"

"This is fine." Karina's gaze wandered to the boats moored at the docks.

"Kare, be honest."

"Really, the restaurant is fine. It's just..."

She bit her lip. She didn't want to have this conversation, but couldn't relax until she did. "Last night was a big step for me."

He squeezed her hands. "I hope you don't think I pressured you."

No, he hadn't pressured her. After eighteen months of celibacy, her body had turned to butter at his touch. She couldn't make herself feel sorry. Six-foot-two of naked policeman with diamond-cut abs was exactly what she had needed.

She tugged on his tie. "You were wonderful."

"If you want to slow down—"

"It's not that. I'm still processing it, but I've got no regrets."

He met her eyes and caressed her hair. "After eight years on the force, I know when someone's hiding something. Tell me what's wrong."

She scanned his features, admiring the way his blond curls fell onto his forehead. She bit her lip. "Are we a couple?"

"Of course we are." He massaged her hand. "I'm sorry. You shouldn't have had to ask that."

He drew her close, and she rested her head on his shoulder, feeling at ease. This was how dating should be. Ryne was a gentleman, and in his arms, she felt like the most desirable woman in the world.

She just hoped that rushing into bed hadn't jinxed it.

19   Pour Some Sugar on Me

TARA ARRIVED AT WORK THE FOLLOWING MONDAY TO find Evan waiting in her office. His face was pale. "I got a call from Li Jing," he said. "She's on the scene, but I can't get confirmation, they're trying to reach the son at college. The girlfriend—they took her away in an ambulance because she was hysterical. Li Jing heard her babbling before they sedated her...She found the body, the girlfriend did, I mean, so there's no doubt—"

"Breathe, Evan." Tara clutched his arm, panic washing over her. "Tell me what's going on."

"The mayor." He swallowed. "They're saying it was suicide."

She collapsed into her chair, her stomach twisting. Evan continued to ramble. Tara stared into space, her vision framed in black.

She remembered the mayor's expression when she'd danced with him at the banquet a few weeks earlier. He'd seemed confident and carefree. All these weeks of denial—had it just been a façade to cover his despair?

Tears blurred her sight. She should have done something, reached out to him somehow. She hadn't known the man well, but he was a human being, not just a news story. Could a kind word have made a difference?

Evan's cell phone rang. Tara watched him anxiously, hoping for good news, but the look on his face confirmed the worst. He hung up the phone and stood at her side, utterly still.

Tara rocked in her chair, hugging herself. Her eyes darted. Her shallow breaths didn't dispel the heaviness in her chest. "It's our fault. If we hadn't done that story—"

"The truth would have come out eventually." Evan pressed his hand to her arm. "We were just the instrument."

She nodded.

"Are you okay?" He scanned her face. "I could get you some tea..."

Her heart warmed. "You're sweet. But don't you have a newspaper to run?"

Slowly, Evan nodded and left her office.

Tara breathed, dispelling the tightness in her chest. She knew Evan was right. The mayor was the victim of his own bad choices. He had burdened her with sorrow so he could die as mayor, not a convicted felon. She cleared her head and started her column.

⁓ঌ৹

At noon, Lauren surprised her. Tara greeted her with a weak smile.

"Having a bad day?" Lauren asked. Tara nodded, and Lauren embraced her.

"He wasn't even fifty," Tara said, her anger rising. "After prison, he'd have had twenty good years left. Now, he'll never know his grandchildren, and they'll never know him."

Lauren coaxed her out onto the Embarcadero to split a sandwich. Glimpses of the harbor peeked between the buildings as they walked. Seagulls undulated above them, and the sun beamed.

The sisters sat on a shaded bench watching sailboats wobble on the bay. With overstated cheerfulness, Lauren said, "Karina seems to like this Ryne guy."

Tara smiled, knowing Lauren was trying to distract her. Tara said, "Every time I talk to Karina about him, she tells me how great he is, but she never talks about her feelings for him. I don't understand why she's being evasive. It's as if she's hiding something. Do you think she's sleeping with him?"

"She's been in an awfully good mood lately. Calmer, too."

"So why won't she confide in us?"

Sunlight filtered through the leaves. Lauren squinted. "Sean says that sometimes, Kare's afraid to tell us stuff, because we act like we don't trust her judgment."

Tara lurched forward. "She told *Sean* that?"

"Think about it this way. Would you take advice from Karina?"

"About shoes, maybe." Tara bristled at her own words. Was this how she treated Karina? She leaned back against the bench, exhaling slowly, letting her emotions settle. "When Kare insisted I was still hung up on Alex, I dismissed it. But she was right." Tara tossed bits of bread to the sparrows. "Do you trust Karina's judgment?"

"Her approach to life is different from mine. I make safe choices."

"Sometimes Kare acts without weighing the consequences."

Lauren smiled. "Which you never do."

"I weigh the consequences. But I have a higher tolerance for risk than you."

"Would you say Karina has a high tolerance for risk?"

Tara pursed her lips. "Karina has to tempt fate. It's a compulsion."

⁓⧉⁓

Holly sat in her office watching the clock. Oliver, her assistant, had turned on the radio to listen for updates about the mayor. But Holly wasn't thinking about that.

At two o'clock, she told Oliver she was leaving to meet the caterer about the menu for the upcoming Cancer Society benefit.

She entered Jack's bungalow. "What do you think about serving Thai food?" She kicked the door closed and unbuttoned his shirt.

Jack kissed her, pressing her against the wall. "Thai food's good."

"We could have spring rolls and rice noodles and entrees served in pineapples…"

"Sounds elegant." He unzipped her dress. "I'll get right on that."

His lips tickled her neck as he danced her to the bedroom. His breath in her ear sang of laughter and freedom and lust. She trilled her fingers through his hair at the nape of his neck, hair cut too long to be tidy. She closed her eyes, luxuriating in his touch. He played her like a virtuoso, evoking rich and beautiful tones until the rhythm of their bodies slowed and ended in a perfect pianissimo.

He bestowed serene kisses on her lips. "My arms belong around you." He gazed at her, his eyes unblinking, as if memorizing her features to sustain him through the hours and days without her.

She brushed her fingers against his cheek and admired his calm expression. "I wish the rest of my life were this simple. Reporters have been calling all day, asking for a statement. But I'm out of platitudes. Even when I spoke with the mayor's ex-wife this morning, I felt resigned. Isn't that awful?"

Jack lay against the pillow. "After the reports of graft in this morning's *Observer*...the mayor doesn't deserve more from you."

"I thought you liked him."

"He was good for business." He cupped his hand over her white shoulder. "But I don't want to talk about business."

She tasted his mouth, filling her lungs with his scent. His sweat cooled her skin, and she drew his crumpled sheets around her. This modest room with its sepia walls and bamboo furniture was her oasis. In these stolen hours, her life felt complete.

The following week, Karina lunched with Tara at the art museum café. The pavilion overlooked the sculpture garden and the blue-and-yellow tile dome of the Museum of Man. The bell tower chimed the half-hour.

Karina was excited when Tara had invited her to lunch. She worried the two were growing apart since Tara had moved out. She'd never forgive herself if the drama with Alex had damaged her relationship with her sister.

Looking at Karina sideways, Tara asked, "How are things with you and Ryne?"

Warmth rushed over her. "Ryne's great. He listens to me, and he asks my opinion..."

"And you like him?"

"Well yeah I like him. Have you seen him? What's not to like?"

Tara scowled. "I mean, do you have interests in common—like is he a Shakespeare fan, has he ever read Camus?"

What kind of question was that? Karina hadn't read Camus since her senior thesis for her bachelor's. "If I hold out for a hot guy who's interested in French existential literature, I will die alone."

"Fine." Tara arched her brows. "So tell me about the good stuff."

She grinned, tapping the toes of her shoes on the floor. "Let's just say, gee, he hits the spot!"

"See, I told you you had one." Tara emptied a packet of oyster crackers into her curried tomato bisque. "You're the most adventurous person I know—yet when it comes to sex, you're like a Victorian bride, waiting for the groom to show her the way."

Huh. Was that true? Karina shook her head, memories flooding back. "Can you imagine if I'd married Tim? He may have been an Eagle Scout, but he couldn't find a G-spot with a compass."

Tara smiled and stirred her soup.

"With Ryne, everything is easy," Karina said. "We're so different, yet he seems to understand me. He makes me feel special."

Tara bit her lip. "I know things have been difficult for you lately. I feel like I abandoned you, moving in with Alex suddenly…"

"I'm fine. I wanted you and Alex back together, remember?"

Tara nodded. "Sometimes you know what's best for me before I do. Even if I don't follow your advice, I do respect your opinion."

Karina stared, waiting for the punch line. Tara squeezed her hand instead.

She relaxed her shoulders, easing the tension stored there. "Let me ask you a question. Do you think I'm moving too fast with Ryne?"

"That depends. What do you think?"

"He's worth the risk."

Tara nodded. "So you close your eyes and take a leap of faith."

"Not the best strategy, huh?"

Tara shrugged. "I don't know, it's gotten you a law degree from Stanford, a job you love, a hot guy who treats you right…It seems to work for you."

She smiled but grew pensive. Was Tara right? Was her relationship with Ryne doomed to fail if they didn't share common interests?

Karina wouldn't let that happen.

Karina woke in Ryne's bed Saturday morning amid golden yellow sheets and down pillows. Sunshine peeked through the blinds, casting ridges of light onto Ryne's sleeping face. Karina felt peaceful watching him, the curls matted to his head, the stubble rising from his chin. She liked seeing him in the stillness, where there was no pretense. Ryne was a strong, good man—husband material. But for now, she was happy for his company, with no expectations.

He stirred, and she kissed him. He opened his eyes and jerked her body toward him. He was an exuberant lover, never tentative. His confidence left Karina feeling free.

They rose and showered, then went to make breakfast. As a cast-iron pan heated above the gas flame, they discussed plans for the weekend.

"There's a concert at Balboa Park this afternoon," Karina said, whipping the eggs, "and a new exhibit at the art museum."

Ryne chopped the red bell peppers for the omelet. "We can do that."

She grinned. "Why don't you sound excited?"

"Kare, I love being with you. It doesn't matter what we do."

"But it should be something we both enjoy. How do you usually spend your weekends?"

He shrugged. "Surfing, working on the Corvette—"

"You surf?"

"Since I was a toddler."

She gazed at him, a thought forming in her mind. "Maybe you could teach me."

He squinted. "The first time a wave hits, and messes up your hair—"

"I'm not like that. I'm adventurous."

"You're certainly not boring." He watched her a moment. "You really want to do this?"

She shrugged. "Why not? It could be fun."

A few hours later, beneath a crystalline sky, Karina wrested herself and her surfboard from the pummeling waves. She unzipped her wetsuit. "I suck at this!"

"It was your first lesson." Ryne sleeked his hair off his face. "You'll get better."

They stuffed their wetsuits into the mesh duffle bag. A lone egret flew by, searching for a fishing spot. It alighted, wading knee deep into the water, but soon moved on.

Ryne and Karina sat on a blanket to dry off in the heat of the sun. She asked him to put lotion on her back.

"How about on your front?"

She shook her head. "What is this fascination men have with breasts?"

He shrugged. "It's in our genetic code."

"But you could be more discreet about it." She ran her fingers through his damp curls. "Women know we've got what men want—it's to your advantage to act less interested. Men make sex so available, there's no challenge."

"You don't want a challenge—you throw a hissy fit if you don't get your own way."

"Excuse me, are we at the art museum right now?"

With a grudging smile, he conceded they were not.

That evening, they stayed in. After a dinner of chicken tostados, they snuggled on her couch and watched *Casa Blanca*. The ending didn't quite make her cry, but it did inspire some real-life kissing.

In bed Sunday morning, Ryne rolled toward Karina. She leaned into him as he threaded his fingers through her hair. His body beside her was an aphrodisiac, making her feel warm and languid. Unfortunately, she couldn't stay in bed all morning.

She turned toward the clock. It was after eight. "I need to get up soon."

He gripped her in his arms. "Can't you miss church this once? Your father will understand."

"He'll understand I skipped church because my new boyfriend talked me into having sex with him instead." With a kiss, she slid from underneath him.

He sulked. "I'll miss you."

"Come to church with me." She picked up a brush from the top of the dresser and ran it through her hair.

"I haven't been in years."

"Then it would do you good."

He wrinkled his brow, looking at her skeptically. "I went to Sunday school as a kid. I got all the religion I needed."

"The church is a community. We feed needy families and tutor underprivileged kids. And on the evenings of the full moon, we sacrifice a goat and dance naked at midnight."

"Funny."

"Church is part of my life. I want to share it with you."

He didn't respond.

She set down the hairbrush and approached the bed. "At least come to dinner afterward? It's at Holly's this week."

"Kare, I know your family is important to you. But dinner with Holly Carter-Kent? She's one of the most prominent women in San Diego. I wouldn't know which fork to use."

"It isn't a fancy dinner party. It's a family meal." She tickled him.

He grabbed her hands, sliding her down onto the bed. "If it were at your place, that would be different. But a big house surrounded by servants..."

Karina mussed his hair. "A big house with servants is awfully easy to get used to. Just ask Tara."

She headed into the bathroom, letting the warm water cascade over her skin. She understood if he needed more time. Dinner was a big step. But what did it say about a man if he were willing to share a bed with her, but not share a meal with her family?

She forced the thought from her mind. There was plenty of time—she'd keep working on him. Still, she missed him through the service, and especially at Holly's place, where everyone else was paired up.

So when the doorbell rang at one o'clock sharp, her heart jumped. Ryne presented Holly a bouquet of yellow roses and sat next to Karina at the table. She took his hand, her throat thickening. It was still early, but Ryne was starting to feel like The One.

20 You Keep Me Hangin' On

THE FOLLOWING SATURDAY, THE FIELDS FAMILY AND their close friends gathered at Jack's house, laden with gifts for Nissa's first birthday. In the kitchen, Karina and Ryne sat with Dayne and Chantel. The chandelier cast a dim light on the country oak table. Trouble, Jack's cocker spaniel, sniffed the floor at their feet.

Karina tapped her fingertips on the tabletop. "It was strange seeing Jerry Silverstein on TV last night, wearing a prison uniform."

Dayne nodded, jaw firm.

"Silverstein lucked out." Chantel speared a grape tomato with a cocktail toothpick and dipped it in ranch dressing. "He gave his statement before the mayor's suicide, so the deal stands."

"You're not upset the mayor's dead," Ryne said. "You're upset you didn't get to arrest him first."

"He lived a coward, and he died a coward."

Karina wished she could argue with that statement, but in her heart, she didn't disagree. She said, "He and Jerry jeopardized their freedom, their reputation, their self-respect—all for the sake of power and influence. If they'd had anything meaningful in their lives, the risk wouldn't have seemed worth it."

Dayne shook his head. "With his drinking and womanizing, Jerry's been trying to self-destruct for years."

Chantel nodded. "With everything he's seen as a prosecutor, maybe he decided there's no justice in this world. The more he got away with, the more he felt like life's a long journey with no destination—so you might as well enjoy the ride. This could be the best thing that ever happened to Silverstein. Maybe now he can find peace."

"But he's been disbarred!" Karina said. "What will he do?"

"What most people do when they're publicly disgraced." Chantel swirled her glass of Coke. "Get his own radio talk show."

Karina smiled. "Prison's an opportunity for him to re-evaluate his priorities. Everything happens for a reason. God has a plan for him."

Dayne sipped his beer. "I hope the media circus surrounding that case dies down soon."

"Then," Chantel said, patting his hand, "you can focus on the media circus surrounding the Pauling case."

Karina tensed and stole a glance at Ryne. His face was stoic. He was set to testify in the serial killer's trial in a few weeks. He turned quiet whenever the subject came up.

She looked at Dayne intently. "I hear Pauling's lawyer is trying to negotiate a deal. Think of the money you'd save the state if you accepted life without parole."

"This isn't about money," Dayne said. "It's about justice."

Karina pursed her lips.

Dayne scowled. "You got something against justice?"

"Society doesn't profit by taking lives." Karina rose, chair screeching against the floor. "Do you think I feel better because the man who shot Tara was killed by police? It doesn't bring my niece back, and it doesn't heal the wound in my family."

"It stops him from hurting anyone else," Ryne said. "It's closure, Kare. Knowing he's not a threat anymore."

Karina clasped her hands behind her back. "When society decides to end a life, it should be an act of compassion, never an act of vengeance."

"I agree with that," Dayne said. "I'm seeking justice for the victims. That's what the people of this county elected me to do."

Karina walked to the fridge and refilled her glass of mineral water. Her heart filled with sadness. She understood Dayne's point of view—but it hurt her that no one at the table understood hers.

The rest of the guests arrived. Ice cubes rattled, conversation hummed, laughter rippled through the air in sudden bursts. The group gathered in the living room to watch Nissa open her presents. Lauren and Sean admired the gifts, and Nissa sat on the floor feeding bits of tissue paper to Trouble. It was the highlight of her day.

Tara wandered outside to the small garden behind the house. The blooms of September were sparse but still colorful: blue salvia, golden sunflowers, the pink heads of 'Autumn Joy' sedum. Tara remembered how Lauren had helped their father plant these beds. That mutual love of the earth nourished the bond between father and daughter.

Tara wondered who her daughter would have taken after. During her pregnancy, Tara had imagined Susannah as precocious and talkative, analytical like Alex, but with surprising moments of empathy. Tara hadn't allowed herself to think about those dreams much since the shooting. But she wanted to think about them now, to mourn not only the baby she had lost, but also the toddler, the child, the adolescent, the young woman. All the things Susannah would never become. Tara felt, at last, that she could bear the magnitude of her grief.

The door behind her creaked open. She turned, and Alex approached. He took her hand. The last light faded, and cardinals chipped a parting chorus.

Tara sighed. "Watching Nissa open her gifts, I kept imagining..." She buried her face in his shoulder and held her eyes closed. "I hate that I can't fully enjoy days like this."

He stroked her cheek. "Give it time. It'll get easier."

"But it will never pass." She looked up at him.

He nodded. "The pain is part of us now."

She squeezed his hand. A frog wailed in the garden pond, then splashed into the water. The lavender dusk fell. He kissed her, his arms giving all the comfort she needed.

She didn't want to lose the pain, because that would mean losing the hold Susannah held on her heart. The only way forward was to embrace her new life, the new woman she had become.

⁓⚬∯⚬⁓

The guests soon departed, and the family cleaned up the house. Karina supervised as Sean and Alex loaded the gifts into the Jeep. The floodlight cast a yellow glow through the shadows.

"This stuff will never fit," Sean complained.

"Not if you're so meticulous," Karina said. She crammed the plush toys between his neat stacks of boxes.

"That works." Alex pushed in a collection of Baby Einstein videos. "And that's the last of it."

Karina stared up at the sky. The moon formed a halo in the clouds. She sat on the tailgate of the Jeep with Sean and Alex on either side of her. "This was a good day," she said, "well...except for Ryne being called to the station."

Alex grinned. "A public defender dating a cop. That makes sense."

Karina rubbed her arm. "Ryne and I have fun together. This morning, he gave me my second surfing lesson, and I actually stood up for two seconds."

Sean smirked. "If you wanted to surf, why didn't you ever ask me to teach you?"

"Because you're not my boyfriend," she teased.

"You don't want to surf," Sean said. "You want Ryne to think you two have something in common."

She scowled, tired of Sean's lectures. "I'm not pretending with Ryne. Learning from each other is part of the fun of dating."

Alex bumped against her shoulder. "If Ryne makes you happy—"

"He does. Except now I have to go home alone."

Alex shrugged. "You can come to the beach house and hang out with Tara and me."

"Thanks, but I'll wait for Ryne at his condo." She tilted her head. "Is that pathetic?"

"Yes," Sean said.

"Only if it means you have no life," Alex countered.

"It means he's important to me." Karina combed her fingers through her hair, contemplating the ways she might surprise him. The thought made her smile. "Wouldn't you like to come home and find a naked woman in your bed?"

Alex grinned. "Depends on the woman. If it were you, I'd be in trouble."

She punched his arm and grinned. Maybe things *wouldn't* be weird between them forever.

⁓◦ℰℓ◦⁓

Back inside the house, Jack took the last of the serving dishes into the kitchen. Lauren washed them in the hot, soapy water, and Tara dried them with a linen cloth. Jack watched their synchronous movements and listened to their hushed conversation, thinking he was the luckiest man in the world.

He headed to the makeshift nursery, where Holly was watching the baby sleep. He kissed Holly's cheek, then looked at Nissa. "There's nothing like it, is there."

"She's so peaceful and precious." Holly pouted. "I want one."

"Medical science can work miracles these days."

371

She smiled. "A grandchild will do. But Alex and Tara need time."

"And they should get married first."

Holly eyed him tenderly. "You really are old-fashioned, aren't you."

"If it's old-fashioned to believe in marriage, I guess I am."

"The rules have changed since we were young." Holly clutched the rail of the crib. "Now that divorce and illegitimacy don't carry the stigmas they once did, people are freer to make the right choices."

"They're also freer to make the wrong ones," Jack said. "Divorce is a quick fix—but do people end up happier?"

"I guess I'm old-fashioned, too. Despite everything Matthew and I went through, I never considered divorce." Her eyes grew distant. "I wonder, though, whether marriage limits us...whether devoting so much of ourselves to someone else keeps us from reaching our potential. The fact is, I put more into the marriage, and Matthew got more out. It was a losing proposition for me."

Jack frowned and drew his brow, his light mood leaving him.

Karina awoke the following morning with Ryne's warm body pressed to hers. He stroked her hair and said, "I'm glad you were here when I got home last night."

"Me too." She kissed him, unable to get enough of that firm body and those gentle hands. But the next moment, her stomach contracted, and she looked away.

He knitted his brow. "Did it bother you I had to leave the party early?"

"Your job is important. I'm proud of that."

"Then what's wrong?"

She looked at him intently, then sighed. "It's nothing."

His forefinger outlined her lips. "If you're upset, I want to know about it."

She ran her hand across the cotton blanket. "My stupid brothers-in-law were teasing me yesterday about a public defender dating a cop. They were joking around, but then I started thinking—"

"Don't listen to them." His teasing kisses distracted her. "We're good together."

"Yes, but we're so different."

"That's what keeps it interesting. It's okay to disagree, as long as we respect each other."

Karina sighed. She couldn't fault his logic, but Ryne was missing the point. On some level, they weren't connecting. She needed to verbalize what was bothering her, or eventually it would erupt, as it had with her previous boyfriends. She didn't want that to happen with Ryne.

"Yesterday," she said, her throat taut, "when we were talking about the Pauling case, I felt like you weren't really listening to me. My views about capital punishment aren't sentimental or naïve—I've been a victim of violent crime. I believe in justice. But I don't believe that focusing solely on punishment makes society safer."

Ryne squeezed her hand. "I know you have strong convictions. I don't mean to sound like I'm dismissing them."

Her skin warmed. "I'm making too much of this."

"Don't be afraid to be honest with me. I love you." He kissed her. "No holding back."

She nodded, hoping her eyes didn't reveal her sudden panic.

⁓◊⁓

At the beach house, Alex and Tara stood in the hallway staring at the closed door to the nursery. "Are you sure you want to do this?" he asked.

"It's time."

He opened the door, and she drew her breath. They went inside.

The jeweled chandelier cast a soft light. The crib stood in the corner, a mobile of goldfinches and indigo buntings fluttering over it. The layette set was scattered with purple and yellow hearts.

Alex clutched Tara's hand as her eyes surveyed the surroundings. Breathing deeply, she began to tremble. Alex held her as her body convulsed.

His blurred gaze fell on the crib that had stood empty for two years. He thought about the hours they had spent choosing the furniture, Alex worrying about the sturdiness of the construction, Tara about the friendliness of the design. They had settled on light cherry in a modern style, each detail reflecting the union of their minds. Alex had never put so much of his heart into any endeavor. For Tara, it had been all-consuming. Now, after the attention and care, they had only this furniture to show for it.

A wave of anger ceded to deep and enduring sadness. Electrical outlets, sharp corners, drawers of knives—these were hazards Alex could contain. A random bullet he could not.

His throat grew raw and his chest heavy. He kissed Tara's cheek, his tears mixing with hers. Her sobs quieted.

She clung to him. "Sometimes I dream the hospital made a terrible mistake, and she's really out there alive somewhere..."

"I have that dream, too." He buried his face in Tara's almond-scented hair, grateful beyond his considerable powers of expression that the chilling violence that had taken his daughter had not also taken his wife.

He kissed her fiercely until his terror yielded to tenderness. Tara's caresses wore away the edges of his grief. He thought about the miracle of her, about having her home again, about the promise of their new life.

She caressed the downy blanket hanging over the rocking chair. She looked around again. A ray of sunlight streamed across the floor.

"This room is full of happy memories," she said. "I don't want to lose them." She took his hand and led him out of the nursery. He started to close the door. "No," she said. "Leave it open."

21   Dirty Laundry

ON MONDAY, SEAN LUNCHED WITH ALEX AND Karina in Karina's office. Her desk, piled with manila folders, seemed in disarray. But whenever she needed a file, she could instantly pull it out of the stack.

Sean noticed Karina's escalating irritation with Alex, who sat fidgeting with his cell phone. Karina tossed a copy of *The Morning Star*, a daily tabloid newspaper, across her desk to Alex. "Why aren't you more upset about this?"

"No one believes that garbage." Alex slid the tomato out of his sandwich.

Karina speared the tomato and dropped it into her salad. "They're accusing your mother of tax fraud."

"My mother did not commit tax fraud. The mayor's campaign manager said as much in her deposition."

"But this paper twisted everything around. Now that your mother's being audited—"

"Millions of people are audited every year. Don't make a federal case of it."

"It's *already* a federal case." Karina crossed her arms. "You're not going to do anything? Threaten a libel suit?"

"I won't stoop to their level. Tara can set the record straight in her column." Alex checked the messages on his cell phone again.

"Excuse me, I'm talking to you," Karina said.

He looked up at her, then back at his phone. "I'm expecting an important call."

"Don't you know how rude that is?"

"Sorry you're not the center of my universe." His cell phone rang and he smiled. He left Karina's office.

She shook her head, then sat forward and picked up her Beanie Baby penguin, squeezing its middle.

Sean watched the sparkle dim in her eyes. "He's teasing you, Kare."

"I know." She set down the Beanie Baby.

Sean squinted. "Something else bothering you?"

She leaned back and stared at the ceiling. "Ryne said the *L* word yesterday."

Sean wrinkled his brow. "Lesbian?"

"No—"

"Las Vegas?"

"Sean!"

"Lilliputian?"

"Will you stop? He told me he loved me."

Sean adopted the requisite brotherly concern. "And that's a problem?"

"I didn't say it back."

He nodded. "How'd you smooth over the awkwardness?"

"With sex."

"Then relax." Sean clasped his hands together. "That's probably all he wanted anyway."

She threw a paperclip at him. "Maybe Ryne's talking about those happy feelings you have when you first start falling for someone. Should I lighten up and say it back?"

"You won't do him any favors by telling him you love him if you don't."

Panic rose in her eyes. "I don't want him to think I don't care about him."

Alex entered, closing his cell phone. "Sorry, that was Len Hartley."

Sean raised his brow. No wonder Alex had been so calm about his mother's audit.

Karina stood and hugged Alex. "Tell me everything will be okay."

"Everything will be fine." He patted her head. "What are we talking about?"

She explained her situation with Ryne, and Alex said, "Be honest. Tell Ryne it's something you don't take lightly."

"What do you care," Karina said, lips pouting. "You don't even like him."

"Of course I do," Alex said. "But I don't think anyone's good enough for you."

She smiled and stroked his tie. "You're sweet. Granted, I hate your guts ninety percent of the time, but the other ten percent..."

She gaped. "Wait. Len Hartley—as in, Secretary of the Treasury Llewellyn Hartley?"

Sean had wondered when Karina would figure that out.

Alex thrust his hands into his pockets. "Len said he'd make sure my mother's audit was handled fairly."

Sean smirked while Karina stared. Alex cast his eyes between them. "What? I kept his wife out of prison."

"You have the freaking IRS in your back pocket?" Karina stomped her foot. "It's so unfair Tara saw you first."

⁓◈⁓

In his office after lunch, Alex called Nick Spencer at his old law firm in Washington. "I understand Deb Hartley's got a book deal," Alex said, "and you're representing her."

"What kind of asshole calls a United States senator because his mom is being audited?"

"I didn't," Alex said. "Her aide transferred the call."

"Loser."

He put the phone on speaker and adjusted the blinds to let in more light. "If you're looking for a ghost writer for the book, my wife is a journalist—"

"Your wife? You mean Tara?"

"Her boss nominated her for an Oakes Award last year."

"And if you get her this job, maybe you can get back into her pants?"

Alex grinned. "Tara moved in with me a month ago."

Nick turned silent. "She has my condolences."

"Look, Tara would be a good fit with Deb—"

"The publisher's got someone in mind. Don't get me wrong, I'd love to meet the woman who took you back after she was smart enough to divorce you. But the writer we're signing has had two bestsellers. The publisher won't go with someone unproven."

Alex nodded. Hanging up the phone, he reflected on the path his life had taken. He missed the power he'd left behind in Washington. But being with Tara again, maybe starting a family...it was worth the tradeoff. Alex knew he wouldn't stay at the public defender's office forever. He'd have other opportunities to join a firm and work high-profile cases. But for now, he liked the stability of serving as a P.D.

In Washington, he had immersed himself in his work to block out his grief. But his quieter lifestyle in San Diego allowed him to deal with his emotions. Maybe he'd overreacted, calling Deb about the audit. But he wasn't about to let anyone hurt his family again.

∽◦§◦∼

After work, Lauren and Karina sat in Lauren's family room with Nissa at their feet surrounded by toys. Lauren glanced sideways at the pout on Karina's face. "I know that look," Lauren said. "It's the same one you gave me when we were little and you broke my china tea set."

Karina bit her lip. "I flirted with Alex today."

Lauren drooped against the seatback of the couch. "Sometimes I think if I cracked open your head, I'd find nothing inside but butterflies."

Karina sighed. "Ryne told me he loves me."

Lauren didn't suppress her laugh. "Interesting segue. Things are getting serious with Ryne—so you're flirting with Alex to sabotage the relationship."

"I don't want to sabotage the relationship! I'm pretty sure it's doomed anyway."

"Only in your world would your relationship be doomed because Ryne said he loves you."

"But I didn't say it back!"

"And how did he react?"

Karina tilted her head. "I'm not sure he noticed."

"Then what are you complaining about?" Lauren met her sister's eyes. "Name one thing in your life that makes you unhappy."

Karina scrunched her brow. "Nothing comes to mind."

"If you want to keep it that way, then stop flirting with Tara's husband."

"I was just playing." Karina slipped of her shoes, which were pinching her feet. "Besides, men like it when I flirt with them."

"Not all of them."

"It boosts their ego."

"Why would you want to boost Alex's ego?"

Karina nodded. "You've got a point."

Sean entered through the front door. He looked at Karina, then at Lauren. "Did Kare tell you her sob story about Ryne?"

Karina slid her shoes back on and stood. "I don't have to put up with this. I'm going home to get ready for my date."

Sean called after her, "Don't forget to take a condom in case Ryne tells you he loves you again." Karina slammed the door behind her.

⁓☙⁓

Dressed for her date, Karina walked to her car and stood in the driveway, wondering what to do about Ryne. In the mountains, wildfires burned. Smoke blurred the sky and mingled with the wisps of clouds, blanketing the horizon with a thick haze.

She drove down Goldfinch Street to Ryne's condo. He greeted her with a kiss. Lingering in his arms, she savored the tickle in her stomach. But she didn't feel a whirlwind sweeping her into destiny.

While he made dinner, she watched his movements. Animal attraction lurked beneath her surface. She loved that he cooked, that he enjoyed providing for her needs. Why weren't those feelings enough?

After the meal, they sat together on his couch. Karina drew in her shoulders and stared at the coffee table, the latest issue of *National Geographic* staring back.

Ryne took her hand. "Something wrong? You're quiet tonight. You're never quiet."

She fidgeted with her necklace. "No, it's good. Everything is fine between us."

He sat up, jaw tense. "Now I *know* something's wrong."

She bit her lip. "I feel like...maybe you and I are in different places in this relationship. I mean, I really care about you—"

"I care about you, too. But we haven't been together that long. We're still getting to know each other—"

"Then why are you rushing me?"

Ryne stared. "Wait. You think I'm rushing *you*?"

Karina met his eyes. "I like you a lot. But when I tell a man I love him, it doesn't mean I think he's hot, or he makes me feel squishy inside. It means I *love* him."

He blinked. "O-o-kay."

"I'm not there yet. So just...stop pressuring me."

He crossed his arms, his brow tight. "What did I miss?"

Karina hugged herself. "After you told me you loved me—"

"I did? When?"

"Sunday morning, while we were in bed—"

"Geez, Kare."

Her jaw dropped, and a chill rushed over her. "Oh, so if you said it in bed, you didn't mean it?"

"Of course I did." He took her hands. "But it was an impulse, not some major declaration. You make me feel like I don't have to hold back with you."

She stared into her lap. "Oh." Squeezing his hand, she looked up at him and smiled.

He kissed her, and his touch silenced the discordant music in her head. "When you kiss me," she said, "I feel like everything will be okay. I'm safe with you."

His eyes searched hers. "Maybe safe isn't what you want. You're the prototypical damsel in distress—you send this vibe you need protecting, so everyone will come running. But you don't want a man who caters to your whims. You want someone who won't let you manipulate him." He unbuttoned her blouse. "Now that

I'm on to you, things are going to change. No more fawning over you. If you want a challenge, you'll get it."

Karina's skin warmed. "You're so smart and strong."

He switched off the light and lowered her onto her back.

"Ryne—"

"Shh." He pressed his finger to her lips. "You think way too much."

His mouth wakened the flesh of her neck, and desire rose from her core. Her body submitted to his powerful hands, his expert touch. Shades of pink and gold pulsated behind her closed eyes. "Mm, Ryne," she murmured. "I love you." In that moment, in her heart, she meant it.

22 Holly Holy

ONE AFTERNOON THE FOLLOWING WEEK, JACK MET Holly at the penthouse. She greeted him with a kiss, then took off her earrings and led him to the bedroom, locking the door.

"Geez, Holly, we never talk anymore."

She unbuckled his belt. "I have to leave for a board meeting in an hour."

"Skip the meeting." He slid his lips along her throat.

"And let my brother-in-law name his idiot son CFO?"

"Holly!"

"Sorry. You steal my self-control."

They lay on the smooth white sheets, six-hundred thread count cotton. For this brief space of time, she was his, an angel captured in a jar. He listened to her whispers in his ear like the cooing of a dove until her body shuddered beneath him and he felt the release. But a longing remained in him that the physical act of love could not satisfy.

"Skip the meeting, Holly."

"I can't." She checked the clock.

"I miss you. How long has it been since we've spent a night together?"

"Things will settle down once the IRS investigation is over, and the benefit on Friday—"

"So I'm third on your list? Or is something else ahead of me, too?"

She paled. "I know I've been neglecting you. I'll do better, I promise."

"I'm sorry." He kissed her hair. "I don't want to waste our time together arguing."

Snuggling against him, she laid her head on his chest. "You're my sanctuary—my escape from the world."

"You've already caught the brass ring. You can get off the carousel whenever you want."

"My work is important."

"Of course it is," Jack said. "But you could promote Oliver, hire a new receptionist—take some of the burden off yourself."

"It's not a burden. My work gives me a sense of purpose."

A need rose inside him, one he'd been ignoring too long. He got up and dressed, sorrow filling his heart.

Holly drew the covers around her. "Jack, talk to me."

"How long are we going to do this—sneaking around like teenagers, hoping we don't get caught?"

She sat forward. "Is that what we're doing?"

"Isn't it?" The muscles in his face tightened.

She drew him down beside her. "We don't need permission. We can make our own rules." She enticed him with pixie kisses. "I love you. And I love what we have."

"What we have is sex." He pulled away. "And that's not enough for me anymore."

"Jack!" she called as he walked out. By the time she could don a robe and run after him, he was gone.

⌦✿⌫

Jack rattled around his bungalow that afternoon as light turned to shadow. He sank onto the couch. How had he had let two years slip by with Holly setting the terms?

He had thought that if Alex and Tara got back together, things would change. But nothing had changed. And Holly seemed to like it that way.

The sun's last rays glinted off a brass tiger on the end table. Jack grasped the statuette, feeling the cold metal. He'd always sensed Holly's animal nature lurking, unexpressed. It was part of what had drawn him to her. Maybe the secrecy of their relationship was part of the allure. But it wasn't worth the tradeoff.

Had he let sex overwhelm his judgment? He was old enough to know better. But then, so were those politicians who got caught sneaking around. Age didn't seem to make men smarter about sex. Maybe it made them stupider.

Jack didn't like feeling stupid—or worse, unprincipled. Holly might be happy in an affair with no future, but Jack wasn't. After two years, if Holly wasn't committed in the same way he was, it was time to end it.

He walked to the window and picked up a photo that sat on the sill. He and Susanne were smiling, surrounded by their girls. He'd never understood why God had taken Susanne, but he supposed God had His reasons. Jack didn't question that. He had thought that maybe Holly was his reward for having been a good father and a good Christian. But he didn't feel that way anymore.

⚜

In the blackness of evening, Holly went to Jack's house. He opened the door, the light dim behind him.

"I hate the way we left things." Holly entered and pushed the door closed.

Jack didn't take her into his arms as she expected. His eyes empty, he barely looked at her. "This isn't working anymore."

She struggled for breath, her thoughts swirling. "You know I love you."

"Whatever that means."

She hung her head and closed her eyes. She wondered how long his anger had been festering. Nausea welled in her stomach, the same sensation she'd felt when she'd learned of Matthew's affair, as if somehow, despite her efforts to give him what he needed, she'd failed. Her vision turned white, empty, as if she were disappearing. But too much was at stake for her to retreat now.

"Jack, talk to me," she said. "Tell me what's wrong."

"There's nothing to say. You and I want different things."

"I don't think that's true. Perhaps I haven't listened to you the way I should. But we're not so far apart we can't find our way back."

He met her eyes. "I can't keep playing by your rules. I need this to be a relationship—not a dirty secret."

"It *is* a relationship. But the timing couldn't be worse—"

"That's an excuse." Jack paced like a caged animal. "Maybe we're too different. Maybe that's what you've been trying to tell me, and I didn't want to hear it."

"Jack, no." Determination rose from inside her. "How can I fix this?"

His voice vibrated with a deep-seated anger. "I want to go on a date with you, Holly. In public. Like a normal couple."

She shrank at his tone, then processed his words. "You want to…"

Jack looked away, his shoulders slumped.

Her brow contracted. "We can do that."

"And not at some secluded place up the coast where no one knows us. I want to date you openly, even if people whisper behind our backs. I want them to know you're my woman."

Approaching, she said in his ear, "I'm proud to be your woman."

He looked at her, his brow wrinkled. With a tentative touch, he stroked her cheek. Then, he grasped her and kissed her with hard, breathless kisses.

Her blood flowed again, and she clutched his body to hers, unable to get close enough. The room saturated her vision with earthy color—moss and chestnut and goldenrod. She nestled her forehead against his neck. "All this time, you've been taking good care of me, and I've been neglecting you…Please don't be afraid to ask for what you want!"

"I want to show you off."

Her cheeks warmed. "A new exhibit is opening at the art museum tonight. We could stop by and surprise a few of my friends…"

"You're sure?"

"I have to face my fears eventually."

He nuzzled her hair. "What are you afraid of?"

"That the tabloids will say something awful that makes you feel small, and you'll resent me for it."

"No one can change my feelings for you."

A sparkle of doubt shimmered through her mind.

"Besides," he said, "I'm a self-made man. *SD Weekly* named me one of San Diego's most eligible bachelors. If some tabloid says you're slumming with me, screw 'em. I know who I am."

She traced the line of his jaw with her fingertips. Wrapped in his arms, she felt the strength of his love, and her apprehension stilled.

The next day, Tara strode into Evan's office and slid a copy of that morning's *Observer* onto his desk. On the society page was a picture of Jack and Holly at the exhibit opening.

Evan smiled. "If the lust in his eyes doesn't expose their relationship, his hand on her ass sure does."

"How could you print that?"

"The room was full of photographers. They couldn't have been *too* worried someone might snap a picture."

Tara shook her head. "All this time, she's been anxious about protecting her privacy, and her own godson turns against her."

Evan tossed a balled-up sheet of paper into the air. "I'd never print anything on the society page that could hurt Aunt Holly. She's become a minor celebrity— people have heard about the good work she's done, but now they're reading the lies in the *Star*...This story about her and your dad humanizes her."

"Alex is on the rampage."

"I'm not afraid of Alex."

"Are you going to be nice to him at the Cancer Society dinner on Saturday?"

"Now what would be the fun of that?"

She sat, staring into space. "How do you think people at the benefit will react to my dad?"

"He's been to these things before."

"But never as Holly's date. They may respond differently now he's penetrated their *sanctum sanctorum*."

Evan smirked. "Is that what he's done?"

Tara lurched forward, gaping. "No wonder Alex doesn't like you."

⁓ᔐᔑ⁓

Saturday evening in a hotel ballroom, Alex and Tara arrived at the Cancer Society benefit. Candles glowed on bronze pedestals, and a waterfall in the corner gurgled amid thick-leaved plants. The wait staff set out trays of steaming spring rolls.

Alex spotted his mother wearing her hostess face. Jack stood at her side, greeting acquaintances like old friends and strangers like new ones.

Alex approached his mother, his lips pressed thin. "Have you heard anything more from the IRS?"

"My accountant is handling it."

He bit his cheeks, troubled by her reticence. "You know there's nothing for you to worry about."

"Of course, darling. The paperwork is in order, and the IRS returned my files. So cheer up. I'm not going to jail."

Tara tugged his arm. She and Alex located their table, the red cloth topped with cream-colored porcelain and shimmering silver. He picked up a place card and frowned. "Of course. Mother seated us with Evan."

"You have to be nice to him," Tara said. "He and Michael just broke up. He feels self-conscious because he doesn't have a date."

"He'll feel more self-conscious if I'm nice to him."

Tara's eyes scanned the room. Then, she smiled. Alex followed her gaze to see Evan approaching, dressed in a royal blue suit. Probably Versace, if he knew Evan. Did the guy always have to draw attention to himself?

Evan joined them, sitting at the table. "The new assistant D.A. is here," he said to Tara. "What do you think of her?"

Tara shrugged. "I don't know much about her."

Evan raised his brows. "Alex does."

Alex tensed. The guy hadn't been there thirty seconds, and he was already causing trouble, judging from the expression on Tara's face.

"Did you date her?" she asked.

"For five minutes," Alex said.

Tara sulked a moment, then rubbed his arm. "She's the spokesperson for the Pauling trial. Maybe she'll tell me about their plans for the penalty phase."

"There hasn't been a verdict yet," Alex said.

"Please." Tara rose and disappeared into the crowd.

Alex blew a thin stream of air through his lips. He turned to Evan. "You *have* to stir things up."

"It's my specialty."

"Tara's not supposed to be working—she's supposed to be on a date with me."

"I can't help she likes me better than you." Evan rotated his glass of scotch. "So the Pauling jury—think they'll reach a verdict on Monday?"

Alex raised his own glass and sipped. "Maybe Tuesday. There's a lot of charges to deliberate."

"Dayne's pushing hard for the death penalty."

"I'm not a prosecutor anymore." Alex leaned toward him. "I'm not involved in Dayne's decisions."

"You two are still friends."

Alex narrowed his eyes. "You won't get a quote from me."

"I'm making conversation."

"You're full of shit."

Tara returned and whispered into Evan's ear. He clasped her arm and whispered back.

Alex scowled. "Are you two going to do this all night?"

Tara shot him a look. "I got a quote," she said to Evan, handing him a sheet of paper. He stuffed it into his breast pocket.

With a smile, she sat next to Alex. "All yours."

He continued to frown. Evan would be happy to monopolize all her time, just to show Alex he could. Yet she went along with his games.

She looked from Alex to Evan and back again. "I get tense just sitting here with you two. Can't you play nice?"

"Alex has never played nice," Evan said. "When we were six, he beat me over the head with a hockey stick for no reason."

"It was a tap," Alex said. "I was trying to play hockey, and you kept playing Ice Capades."

"And twenty-seven years later, you're still fighting over it," Tara said. "Maybe you should both be hit over the head with a hockey stick."

The wait staff brought dinner. Alex watched his mother and Jack approach the table. Dressed in a flowing white gown hemmed with gold, she could have been Athena presiding over her sisterhood. But then Jack's hand encircled hers, spoiling the illusion. She wasn't Athena, virgin goddess, but Gaia, earth mother.

Jack looked at Holly and smiled, cradling her hand like a pearl washed up on the sand. Had Alex's father ever looked at his mother that way? Alex couldn't remember. Images of his happy childhood, once so vivid, grew dim and cold. Alex wondered how much had been a lie.

∽❀∾

After the benefit, Holly slipped into a silk nightgown and combed her hair. Jack walked up behind her wearing a velour robe. Her heart warmed as he wrapped his arms around her waist.

"Tonight went well," she ventured.

He grinned. "If I didn't know better, I'd say your friends were happy for us."

Holly looked at his reflection in the mirror. That was no casual remark, and she knew it.

She was running out of excuses. The phantoms haunting her hadn't materialized. She and Jack had been met that evening not with sly stares, but with goodwill. Instead of introducing Jack to her world, she had entered his. She found it a welcoming place.

His expression turned serious, and he held her left hand. "I want to buy you an engagement ring."

Her cheeks warmed, and she looked away. After a long silence, she said, "I'm scared."

"You're thinking about what could go wrong, instead of how right we are together." Jack kissed her fingertips, then let her hand drop. "I don't know where we go from here, if you're unwilling to marry me."

"Jack..." She eyed the ceiling. "I'm not unwilling to marry you. But the situation is complicated. We both have considerable assets. This is a merger—we need to work out the details before we can discuss an engagement."

He crossed his arms. "Can't we discuss an engagement first, then work out the details?"

The simplicity of his argument dissatisfied her. She pouted but didn't protest. Turning to face him, she said in a small voice, "If we married...where would we live?"

Jack grinned. "You think I'd ask you to give up this penthouse to live in my three-bedroom bungalow?"

"Would you be comfortable here?"

"I don't know, Holly. It gets pretty annoying with all these servants waiting on me."

"You're making fun of me."

"Of course I'm making fun of you!" He drew her close, running his hand down her back. "Marriage to a wealthy, successful woman won't make me feel like less of a man. When I look at you, I see your heart."

She laid her head on his shoulder, joy gathering in her throat.

He tickled her neck with kisses. "You're not unwilling to marry me, huh? That's the most romantic thing anyone's ever said to me."

23 Can't Fight This Feeling

K ARINA AND RYNE SAT AT THE BAR AT MONTEREY
Jack's the following Saturday. The television
above the bar flashed an image of Wes Pauling,
the serial murderer. Karina shivered.

Pauling had been sentenced to death the day
before. Karina knew the trial had been difficult on Ryne,
though he hadn't talked much about it. She thought
about what a hard job he had. In the courtroom, the
evidence was neatly bagged and labeled. But Ryne had
witnessed the horrors firsthand, the blood pooling in the
grass.

Still, she could find no comfort in Pauling's
sentence. To punish killers by sinking to their level
diminished humanity. She wasn't sad for Wes Pauling.
She was sad for the State of California for making that
choice. She stared into her cosmopolitan, tightness
growing in her stomach.

Ryne knitted his brow. "Something wrong?"

She shrugged. "People cheered outside the courtroom when the Pauling verdict was handed down. But it's hard for me to find anything about that case to celebrate."

"I think a just sentence for a sadistic killer is worth celebrating."

With a swizzle stick, Karina mashed the pulp of the orange slice in her drink. "The death penalty seems...defeatist. Like, we don't know what to do with this person, so let's execute him and get it over with."

He squinted at her. "I think we know exactly what to do with him—that's why we're executing him."

"People serving life sentences have been known to get college degrees, to write beautiful poetry, to find the humanity inside themselves and share it with others. Maybe Wes Pauling is a lost cause...but if we execute him, we'll never know."

"He killed six people," Ryne said. "His last two victims were teenagers, in the wrong place at the wrong time, and he eviscerated them. When I got to that playground, I could smell blood a half a block away. So when the State of California makes sure he can never commit a crime like that again—yeah, I'll be happy about it."

Karina cast down her eyes. "I wish I could make you understand."

"Understand what? That I should feel sorry for Pauling because he grew up in poverty, because he was abused, because his mother was a drug addict? Most kids in that situation don't grow up to slice people open for the thrill of it."

"If Pauling can't be redeemed, then his crimes have no meaning."

"How can there be meaning in a random act of butchery?"

"Even a man like Pauling could have a spark of potential inside him."

"He forfeited his potential when he started killing people," Ryne said. "That's how it works—people who commit crimes forfeit their rights."

"Most felons aren't violent. Prison could be an opportunity to help them prepare for a better future, so that when they're released, they don't want to return to crime. If they believed in themselves and listened to their heart, they could build a meaningful life."

"Following their heart is what got them into trouble in the first place," Ryne said. "They need to follow the rules. Most of them don't share your ideals, Karina. They do what's expedient. And if that means reaching their goals by victimizing others, they're okay with that."

She swallowed her cosmopolitan, fighting the tightness in her throat. She was tired of arguing. "Maybe you're right."

Taking her hands, his expression softened. "I'm sorry. We shouldn't talk shop while we're on a date."

She nodded and motioned to the bartender for another drink.

Karina awoke Sunday morning in her own bed, Ryne at her side. She let him sleep while she showered. Downstairs, she made coffee. Gray light from the overcast sky filtered through the windows. The gurgling of the coffeemaker filled her ears.

She went to church alone, while Ryne stayed behind to start dinner. Karina couldn't focus on the sermon about Jesus and the lepers. Instead, she imagined how she would feel walking among the sick and exiled, touching their outstretched hands, restoring their health and wholeness. Then, she pictured Ryne as a Pharisee looking down on her, warning her the lepers were unclean.

When she arrived home with her family, the aroma of roasting lamb greeted her. Ryne had followed Tara's instructions to the letter, but the sisters chased him out of the kitchen. "No men allowed," insisted Tara.

Holly watched him go. "Karina, that man is dreamy."

Karina nodded. "He's strong when he should be strong, and he's gentle when he should be gentle..." Karina's throat closed, and tears dropped from her eyes. She grabbed a tissue.

Lauren's arm encircled her. "What's wrong?"

"No man's ever been as good to me as Ryne."

Tara opened the oven door and basted the lamb. "That's because you stay in bad relationships until they end of their own inertia."

The clanging of the oven racks vibrated in Karina's ears. At that moment, she knew.

She tried to put it out of her mind while she sat with Ryne at dinner. She tried while they snuggled on the loveseat watching the Chargers game with her family. She tried after her family had gone, when she and Ryne had the house to themselves, the smell of curry lingering in the air. But the knowledge wouldn't leave her.

Dusk settled, and Karina stood at the window watching the sun sink into the ocean. Her mind heard the whisper of the sea as it swallowed the last rays of light.

Ryne folded his arms around her, leaning his cheek against her hair.

Holding his hands tight, his warmth radiating into her, she breathed his scent until her heart ached, her knees almost buckling under the weight. She swallowed hard, forcing down the swelling in her throat so she could speak.

"Sometimes I feel like my life's a charade," she said. "The real me is watching the fake me pretend to be this confident woman—when I'm really a little girl struggling to be a whole person because I lost my mom before I finished growing up."

He brushed back the hair clinging to her wet cheek.

Her voice trembled. "I'm stuck at sixteen, shopping for clothes and talking on the phone and going out with boys. I'm trying to fill the hole in my heart, but I'm doing it all wrong."

He embraced her, but she pulled away. "I can't create love," she said. "As perfect as you are, you're not right for me, and the more I hold on, the more it'll hurt when you leave."

"Kare, I won't leave you." His eyes were wide and bright. "Where is this coming from?"

Filling her lungs with breath, she fought the tightening in her chest. "You're a good man. I wouldn't change you even if I could. But you want a world that's controlled, and I want a world that's uninhibited. The people you call criminals are the children of God, and I've dedicated my life to helping them find the potential inside themselves."

He clutched her hands. "Kare, I know your job is important to you—"

"It's not a job. It's who I am." Her stomach constricted. She pressed her palm to his cheek, examining the flecks of gold in his eyes. "I'm sorry. This relationship isn't right for me, and I have to get out before I get in deeper and don't know how to leave."

He jerked away. Pacing, he massaged his brow. "You're upset. The things I said last night...I know how sensitive you are..."

Sighing, she stared at the floor and drew an arc with her foot. "I keep trying to bridge this gulf between us."

"Karina—what gulf?"

"I don't know how to explain it..."

"You want to break up with me out of the blue, and I'm not entitled to know why?"

Her body trembled. "I try to picture us getting married and having kids, but I can't see it. I don't want to raise my children in an environment where following the rules is more important than following their heart."

He paled. "Please don't reduce what I said—"

"You and I want different things. Maybe if we tried really hard every day for the rest of our lives, we could make this relationship work. But love shouldn't be that hard."

"Kare, you're upset. You need some perspective."

She hung her head.

His arm slid around her waist and he kissed her temple. "I'm sorry—I was a jerk last night. If you need space to sort through this, I understand. But this isn't over. I'm not giving up."

When he left, the house was finally quiet. She closed her eyes and waited for the sobs to come.

24 It Must Have Been Love

KARINA SLEPT FITFULLY THAT NIGHT, RISING BEFORE dawn. She took a long shower to revive her muscles. The stream of water mixed with her tears. Draped in a bathrobe, her hair still wet, she gazed out her bedroom window. The city slumbered beneath the smoky haze blotting the sun. The day was warm, but she shivered.

Karina arrived at her office cloaked in thought. Walking past Alex, she barely acknowledged him. She unzipped her computer bag and took out her laptop. Struggling to align it in its docking station, she pounded it with her fist and swore aloud.

Alex appeared in her doorway, his brow furrowed. "Everything okay?"

"This computer is a piece of shit." Tears welled in her eyes. Alex stepped inside and closed the door.

"I'm not going to cry again." She picked up her Beanie Baby from her desk and flung it against the wall. "Ryne was the best boyfriend I ever had, and it wasn't enough. What the hell is wrong with me that I can't be happy?"

Alex scowled. "What happened?"

She slouched into her chair, then rotated from side to side. "He's not my soul mate."

Alex rescued the Beanie Baby from the floor and handed it to her. "I'm sorry."

Karina smoothed the plush with her fingertips. "Mom gave me this the day before she was diagnosed with cancer. It was the last innocent day of my life."

Alex squeezed her shoulder.

Karina wiggled the penguin's feet. She wondered if she was damaged somehow—if the hurt she bore from losing her mother kept her from giving her heart to a man. Karina said, "I'm tired of feeling like a scared little girl. My sisters are so much stronger than me—"

"Don't compare yourself to your sisters. You have strengths they don't."

"Name *one*."

"You never give up," Alex said. "You think the word *impossible* is a failure of the imagination."

"I gave up on Ryne."

"If you'd stayed with Ryne, you'd be giving up on yourself."

The light in Alex's eyes warmed her heart. She felt a smile nudge her lips. "You sound like Tara."

"She's a bad influence." He knelt down beside her. "If you need anything, you know where I am."

She nodded. Rising, he headed toward his office. She watched him go, and a lonely shadow fell over her.

Tara called Lauren after work. They went to visit Karina, sitting on either side of her on the porch swing. Through the creeping darkness, tree frogs wailed. Tara stroked Karina's hair, thinking how fragile she looked.

"Are you sure you're doing the right thing?" Tara asked.

"It would be so easy to stay with Ryne," Karina murmured, "but I'd be postponing the inevitable."

"If your gut is telling you it isn't right," Lauren said, "you've got to listen to that."

"I like him too much. When we disagree, unconsciously, I adapt to him because I don't want to fight. Afterward, I realize I'm compromising myself, and I can't keep doing that."

"And you shouldn't," Lauren said. "True love doesn't rein you in. It frees you."

Karina nodded. "Ryne is a panacea."

"I'm sorry." Lauren kissed her cheek.

Tara remained quiet, her stomach twisting. She thought about her relationship with Alex. Karina's words about compromising to avoid a fight hit a familiar note with Tara.

Since Tara had moved back in with Alex, their days had settled into the comfortable and familiar:

afternoon runs on the beach, sunset dinners on the terrace, long Saturday mornings in bed reconnecting after a chaotic week. But the comfortable and familiar hadn't kept them together the first time.

During the years of their marriage, Tara had internalized her anger and disappointments. A hundred small grievances had weakened her. The stress of the shooting had been more than she could bear.

The time apart from Alex had helped her find her confidence again. But now, she was back on the teeter-totter, balancing her needs and those of the relationship. She couldn't abdicate her power to Alex, as she had before. Alex wanted an equal partner, and he didn't respect weakness. Tara had to confront her fears.

On the way home, Tara stopped at her favorite independent bookstore. Forcing herself past the fiction section, she wandered among the shelves until she found self-help. She drew in her arms, worrying that someone might mistake her for a pathetic woman who couldn't handle her problems.

A few feet away, the cappuccino machine hummed. Tara glanced through titles like *Marriage for Morons* and *You Never Listen to Me*. She rolled her eyes. About to give up, she spotted a book called *I'm OK, You're Speaking Zulu Mandarin*. Smiling, she paged through it, engaged by its light tone and straightforward style.

She carried the book to the register, glad the cashier was no one she recognized. When she got home, she didn't mention her purchase to Alex. But after dinner, in the bedroom, she read.

The words opened a world to her, creating a language for things she'd always felt but couldn't express. She recognized how her indirect style conflicted with Alex's direct one: her gentle persuasion, well-suited to the dynamic of the family she grew up in, crumbled under a natural bulldozer like Alex.

She made her first attempt at applying the techniques when she approached Alex in the den. "I'm reading this book," she said. "It's given me some insight into how we can improve our communication. I'm hoping you'll read it too, and maybe we can try the exercises."

Alex eyed her suspiciously. He turned the book over, then thumbed through it. Finally, he asked, "Which of us speaks Zulu Mandarin?"

She breathed, reminding herself not to let his skepticism cool her enthusiasm. "I really think this could help us."

He laid the book atop the desk and drew her into his lap. Nuzzling her ear, he said, "I'll look at it."

"Thank you." She kissed him.

"What prompted this?"

"I want to make sure we're okay," she said. "I worry you've got some residual anger over the divorce."

He squeezed her hand. "Whatever anger I have isn't directed at you. And I won't waste my energy on the bastard whose last act on earth was shooting you and the baby. Karma has taken care of him."

⁂

At work Wednesday morning, Karina received a bouquet of yellow roses from Ryne. A lump formed in her throat. She hadn't returned his calls since Monday, and she was ignoring his emails. As good as he had been to her, he deserved better.

She called and thanked him for the flowers. "I think it's best if you don't contact me for a while," she said. "I miss you too much."

"Aren't we worth fighting for?"

The contracting in her chest warned her she was on the verge of breaking down. She took a deep breath. How could she make him understand? *Ryne* was worth fighting for. She wanted him in her life. But they couldn't be a couple.

She opened a container of multicolored paper clips and sprinkled them onto her desk pad, arranging them into shapes. "When I imagine this relationship five years from now, the knot in my stomach gets tighter. I ignored that feeling when I was with Tim—"

"You're comparing me to Tim now?"

"You make me doubt myself." She brushed her hair behind her ear. "I can't do this job unless I believe absolutely in the rightness of it. When you talk about those teenagers Pauling killed, it breaks my heart. I know what a violent crime does to a family—I saw what it did to mine. But I have a gift for bringing out the best in people, for helping them build a better life. It's my calling. And you make me feel like I'm wasting my time."

"Karina—"

"I know you don't mean to make me feel that way. It's the dynamic between us."

"But I admire what you do!"

"No. You admire me for doing it. You think that ninety-nine percent of my clients are a lost cause, and I'm Mother Theresa for helping them. But that's not how I see myself. I want to inspire my clients and empower them. Where you see a drug offender, I see a broken heart that's self-medicating to escape the pain. And maybe that's naïve, but I don't ever want to stop viewing the world that way."

"If I've been overbearing—"

"It's not you. It's us." She pinched her brow. "Please understand, it's tearing me apart to let you go. But it's what I have to do. If I stay with you, I'll lose myself. That's not a sacrifice I'm willing to make."

Silent for a moment, he sighed. "If you need time, I'll give you that. But this isn't over, Kare."

She was too tired to argue. Closing her eyes against the tears, she murmured her goodbye. She clicked off her cell phone and sat back in her chair, rubbing her temples. She didn't have time to cry. She had clients to think about—clients whose freedom depended on her.

At noon, at a sidewalk café, Karina discussed the situation with Holly. "Did I do the right thing?"

Suited pedestrians bustled past on their lunchtime errands. Holly rested her fork next to her Cobb salad. "That depends on what you want."

"I can't have a casual relationship with Ryne. I care about him too much. And I don't see how we can have a future together when our values are so different."

"So you're looking for a third option?"

Karina puckered her lips. "I should be able to close that door and move on. Tara's done it a dozen times—but I keep searching for another angle, another way..."

"Perhaps Tara's not the best role model when it comes to relationships."

Karina stared. She sat back, contemplating Holly's suggestion that anything about Tara could be found lacking.

Holly sipped her iced green tea. "It's natural to have second thoughts, Karina, especially about a decision that's left you unhappy."

"Even if it's the right decision?"

"If making the right decision were easy, no one would ever make a wrong one."

Karina scowled. Holly's gentle acceptance left her uncomfortable. Was Holly too accommodating, or was everyone else in Karina's life too rigid?

She smoothed her napkin. "I wasn't always like this. When I was in law school, I didn't have time for a relationship—I mean, I dated Keith for two years, but I knew we'd never get married, and that was fine. Where is this sense of urgency coming from?"

"Your needs were different then." Holly's eyes reflected the sky, their gray-green turning a soft blue. "I knew your father for years before we got involved. Only after I let go of my relationship with Matthew could I open my heart to someone else."

Karina stirred her Italian wedding soup. "I've never been madly in love. I want that. I'm ready."

⁓⊶⟡⊷⁓

Saturday morning, Tara sat with Alex on the terrace, where the butler had served breakfast. The salt air mingled with the aroma of her peppermint tea. Alex sipped his coffee.

Rallying her courage, she said, "You remember when we were doing that exercise from the book last night—and you said you wanted me to be honest with you, even if I thought it might hurt your feelings?"

He grinned. "Uh-oh."

"I don't want to go to Vail for Christmas with your Uncle Peter's family. I don't ski, and I hate the cold..."

"That's fine."

"Really?"

He scowled. "I'm not an ogre. Why are you afraid to tell me these things?"

Her eyes rested on the butter dish, a knife balancing across it. "Sometimes I feel like you do things just to make me happy. I don't want to influence you that way."

"You're supposed to influence me—you're my wife."

She shrank at the word, her cheeks warming. Silence hung between them. She struggled to respond.

He took her hand, caressing it with his thumb. "Tara, we're a team. Wherever we go, we go together."

That evening, Tara found Alex sitting on the bed, silhouetted in the apricot glow of the setting sun. Quietly, he stared into his hands.

She sat next to him, and he turned to her with anxious eyes. "I came across this today," he said. Between his fingers was her old engagement ring.

Her throat grew thick as she gazed at the cushion-cut diamond encircled with baguettes. Her heart tightened with longing. She extended her left hand, and he placed the ring on her finger.

Lips pressed to his, she leaned into him until he fell backward on the bed. She said, "The first time, we did things my way. Two hundred guests, a twenty-foot train...This time, let's do it your way. Just family and close friends on the beach at sunset."

"I thought a church wedding was important to you."

"God already sanctified our marriage. God didn't sanctify our divorce."

He her rolled onto her side, kissing her eyes, her cheek, her lips. "Whatever makes you happy."

"Alex...what makes you happy?"

"Marrying you on the beach at sunset, surrounded by family and friends, would make me very happy."

⁓◊⁓

The following week, Karina stood at her office window at lunchtime, staring at the graying sky. She had no appetite, though she hadn't eaten all day. Her head ached from lack of sleep.

Closing her eyes, she tried to shut out the loneliness. Alex wandered in and stood behind her, squeezing her shoulder. She refused to give in to her tears.

"I'm now older than Lauren was when she got engaged to Sean," Karina said. "Doesn't that suck?"

"Is this a contest?"

"If it is, I finished in last place." Her throat tightened. "It wasn't supposed to be like this. I grew up listening to stories about how Mom and Dad met in college, got married right after she graduated, had three babies before they turned thirty...And here I am with a string of failed relationships."

Alex stood next to her and gazed out the window. "I spent my twenties treating dating like a contact sport. It wasn't until my father died that I started thinking about settling down and having a family. And that's when I met Tara."

He stroked her hair and whispered in her ear, "You're a beautiful, intelligent woman. It'll happen when it happens. Stop worrying."

The corners of her mouth turned upward. She watched him stroll out of her office.

Sitting in her desk chair, she leaned her head back. Alex was a contradiction. Abrupt and unemotional most of the time, he kept his sweet, generous side hidden from the world. That part of him fascinated her. But she was tired of the crumbs of kindness he offered. She wanted a man who was nice to her all the time.

Her mind wandered to what Alex had said about meeting Tara when he was ready for a serious relationship. She sat upright, a memory bolting through her mind. Her mother had once told her the same thing—that you don't find the right person until you become the right person. Karina finally understood what that meant.

What would it would mean for her to become the right person? Ideas sprinted through her mind. She locked her office door and scribbled furiously on a legal pad.

No more rushing into a relationship, like with Ryne. No more making excuses when a man didn't treat her right. And he had to be a grownup, with a good job and a vision of the future. And damn it, she wanted an orgasm every time. Sex wasn't a charity event.

Karina's cheeks warmed. Had she really written that down—and at work? She locked the pad of paper in the secure compartment of her briefcase.

As she stowed her briefcase back in the corner, her stomach growled. Suddenly, she was famished. She went to the refrigerator in the break room to get her lunch.

⸛❦⸛

The following week after work, Tara met her sisters by the clock tower at Horton Plaza. Wearing happy smiles, the three entered the bridal salon to look at dresses. Tara had decided on white cotton for the wedding party. Looking through the samples, she chose a narrow shift for herself, while her sisters selected bridesmaids' dresses with a tailored bodice and full skirt.

The sisters left the salon to buy shoes and accessories. Overburdened with shopping bags, they slid into a booth at an ice cream parlor for a well-deserved break.

"Have you decided who to bring to the wedding?" Tara asked Karina.

Karina sighed. "Evan's coming stag, right? Maybe he can be my date."

"Things aren't that desperate," Tara said.

Karina stirred her strawberry sorbet. "I need to come up with a new strategy. Going on a dating hiatus didn't help me find the man of my dreams. I should try the opposite approach, and date as many men as possible. Even if the guy turns out to be a loser, he might have a hot friend!"

Lauren smiled. "It doesn't hurt to network."

"Can you recommend any cute guys?" Karina asked her.

"The single men I work with are over forty, unless you count my students," Lauren said. "I know lots of hot guys between the ages of eighteen and twenty-two."

"Your job does not suck." Karina licked her spoon.

Tara squeezed Karina's shoulder. "I meet new people all the time in my work. I can hook you up."

"I'd appreciate that."

Karina went to the restroom, and Tara turned to Lauren. "Do you think she's okay? She stopped dating for six months so she could focus on herself. Now, suddenly, she's obsessed with finding Mr. Right?"

Lauren shrugged. "When Karina pursues a goal, she channels all her energy into it. Now that her career's on track, she's focusing on her personal life."

"We should get her to lighten up and enjoy dating for a while, instead of looking for a serious relationship."

"Get Karina to lighten up? That's easier said than done."

Tara drew her brow, considering the irony of Lauren's words. Karina's carefree demeanor hid her serious nature. Tara felt guilty shopping for wedding clothes while Karina was going through a breakup. But if Tara waited for Karina's love life to settle, it could be ten years before Tara got married.

She savored the last spoonful of her chocolate ice cream. She had learned how tenuous happiness was. This time, she wouldn't let it slip away.

25 Cry

A S SUMMER FADED INTO FALL, RAINS QUENCHED THE
fires in the mountains. Soon, swaths of meadow
dotted the hills. The air regained its sweetness.
But as the weeks stretched on, the rains persisted,
drenching the earth.

Through the window of her limo, Holly watched
the gray clouds gather over the ocean. This streak of wet
weather didn't bode well for a wedding on the beach.
Bored in the rush hour traffic, she called Alex.

"Eight days," she said when he answered the
phone. "Are you nervous?"

"I'm ready," he said.

Holly smiled, wishing she could say the same.
She breathed to calm the fluttering in her stomach. "Can
I do anything to help?"

"Tara's got it under control."

"I'm sure she does."

Tara would have every detail planned, to make sure nothing went wrong. Still, what was a wedding without a few surprises?

"I hope you're not working too hard," Holly said.

"It's quiet here this afternoon. The women left for a bachelorette party at Susanne's Bistro."

"I'm on my way to the restaurant now. Is Karina with them?"

"She's the one who suggested Susanne's."

Holly ended the call as her car pulled into the parking lot. Before heading upstairs to Jack's office, she stepped into the dining room. She spotted Karina and went to say hello.

Holly brushed by a table piled with gift bags, goodies for the honeymoon peeking from beneath a haze of tissue paper. Heart-shaped balloons floated overhead, anchored to the centerpiece with silvery ribbons.

Karina rose and hugged Holly. Karina's cheeks were flushed, and her words flowed faster than normal. Holly offered her a ride home, but Karina said her father could drive her. With a satisfied nod, Holly squeezed Karina's hand, then headed upstairs.

She found Jack sitting at his desk in the small but comfortable office. The bookshelves behind him housed ledgers dating back to when he and Susanne had bought the business. Holly knew the early years had been lean ones. But now, this office contained the evidence of Jack's success. The furnishings were new and solid: cherry desk, brass lamps, a small couch striped with green and gold. On the wall hung a plaque from the Kiwanis Club and a letter from his congressman honoring Jack's work providing meals for needy families. Though a modest man, Jack treasured this recognition from his community.

He looked up and smiled. She stepped inside, closing the door behind her. Rising, Jack kissed her.

She rested her hands on his shoulders. "Karina seems to be enjoying the party with her friends."

"I'm glad. She's had it rough since she and Ryne split up." Jack's gaze rose to a portrait of his daughters on the beach as little girls, their white dresses fluttering in the breeze. "I want to see her married, with a couple of kids—is that so much to ask?"

"Be patient, darling. She's only been out of law school two years. Marriage and motherhood will come in time." Holly met his eyes. "You don't want your expectations to burden Karina. She needs your support."

He nodded.

"How late are you working tonight?" she asked.

"Unless someone calls in sick, I'll be home by seven."

She smiled. Her heart rose at the thought of an evening alone with him.

He stroked her cheek. "I promised I'd cut back my hours if you did. How's the new receptionist working out?"

"Oliver trained her well, and he seems to enjoy his new responsibilities." She smoothed Jack's collar. "All in all, this has been a happy arrangement."

His hands clasped hers. "You're not having second thoughts?"

"I feel like I'm jumping out of a plane and you're my parachute." A tickle rose in her stomach. Looking at him, a sense of completeness washed over her. She kissed him goodbye. "Come home soon."

Downstairs, through the window, Karina saw Holly step into her limo. Karina wished she'd accepted Holly's offer of a ride home. Then she would have had an excuse to leave.

She swallowed the last of her drink, then reached for the pitcher of martinis. Victoria, her boss, grabbed her hand. "Slow down, Fields."

Karina nodded, fighting her tears. She heard one of her coworkers mention Alex's name. The pounding in her head worsened. She couldn't believe Tara was doing this again, getting married so soon after Karina's breakup.

A blur of laughter and conversation closed in on her. She couldn't stay in this booth with these happy people. Rising, she said goodbye.

She started up the staircase toward her father's office, but didn't get far. Woozy, she descended, clutching the banister to overcome a decided pull to the left. Outside, the rain had stopped, at least temporarily. She sat on a bench in the cool breeze to call Sean.

"Hey, Kare," the voice answered.

She squinted. "Alex?"

"Ye-es."

"Why are you answering Sean's phone?"

"It's my phone."

"Oh. I meant to call Sean." She struggled to maintain her equanimity. "I need a ride."

"I'll be there in ten minutes."

"No, I'll call Sean—"

But Alex had hung up.

⁓⊶⊷⊶⁓

Alex sat in his limo, concerned by the tautness in Karina's voice. She'd been excited an hour before, when she and the others had left work for Susanne's. What had happened to upset her?

A light rain fell. Alex arrived at the restaurant to find Karina in her car, wet and shivering. Alex sent his chauffeur to the beach house, then got into Karina's Miata to drive her home.

He turned out of the parking lot. With the seat pushed back all the way, his legs just fit, but he had to slouch to get enough headroom.

"Why's it so cold in this car?" she complained.

Alex braked for a red light. "Because you cranked up the AC."

"I turned the temperature all the way up."

"No, you turned it all the way down." He adjusted her thermostat and simmered with frustration.

When they arrived at the house, Alex helped Karina inside. She was as pliant as a ragdoll.

"You take good care of me." She collapsed onto the couch.

He sat next to her. "How much did you drink?"

She looked at him, her eyes unfocused. "I played a little game. Every time someone said 'wedding,' I took a sip. They said 'wedding' a lot."

He glared, but she continued, "It's okay because I drink cosmos all the time and that's the same as a martini."

"Only if you replace the cranberry juice with more vodka."

She giggled.

"You need to sleep this off." He took her hand and raised her from the couch.

She stumbled as they headed for the stairs. He picked her up and carried her. "You're so romantic," she purred. "Like Red Butler."

"You mean Rhett Butler."

"Isn't that what I said?"

Reaching the bedroom, he lowered her onto her feet, and she sank onto the mattress. He removed her strappy black pumps and helped her under the covers.

She closed her eyes. "You're so good to me. I love you, Alex."

He stroked her hair, then left the room, closing the door behind him.

Downstairs, he sat on the couch. He should have anticipated this—Karina's neediness, her lack of boundaries. Why had he agreed to drive her home? He liked being the person she turned to, but it wasn't his place. Taking out his cell, he called Tara.

⁓ঞ⁓

An hour later, Lauren arrived to find Tara upstairs checking on Karina. They huddled outside Karina's bedroom. Tara looked pale.

Lauren hugged her. "Is she okay?"

"She's sick as a dog, but she'll survive."

Lauren shook her head. "She never binges like this unless she's upset. Obviously, she's more upset than we realized."

They headed into the bedroom. Karina was in the adjacent bath, sitting next to the toilet, her head in her hands. Lauren and Tara sat beside her.

Lauren massaged Karina's back. "What were you thinking?"

"That I'd feel better if I had another drink."

"Do you feel better?" Tara asked.

Lauren squeezed Karina's hand. "You need to find another way to deal with your sadness—and lay off the booze for a while."

"You guys are blowing this out of proportion."

"Alex said he found you in your car," Tara said.

"I didn't drive it. I sat in it to get out of the rain."

Tara trembled. "Do you know how much you scared us tonight?"

"Fine..." Karina clutched her forehead. "If you think it's a problem, I'll stop drinking."

"*You* need to recognize it's a problem!" Tara said.

Lauren sighed. "Tara, you're overloaded with wedding stress. Why don't you go home, take a hot bath, and get a good night's sleep. It'll give you perspective."

Tara didn't argue. Lauren watched her go, then listened to her footsteps descending the stairs. Pushing the bathroom door closed with her foot, Lauren said to Karina, "Tell me what's really going on with you."

Karina groaned.

"Why did you call Alex? This place isn't exactly on his way home."

"I meant to call Sean. I hit the wrong button on my phone."

Lauren scowled. "What upset you tonight? Ryne—or Alex?"

Karina groaned once more.

"I knew it!" Lauren said. "You're hung up on him again. If you're not in love with someone else, you're in love with Alex. He's your default."

Karina stared into space. "The whole time we were at the restaurant, I just kept thinking, if I'd pursued Alex, he would be with me now."

"You're picturing yourself in Tara's relationship with Alex. All *you* would have had with him is gratification. Get over it."

⸎

The following evening, in lieu of a bachelor party, Alex and Tara held a co-ed party at the beach house. When Karina arrived, Alex wouldn't look at her. She hugged herself, tilting her face downward. Light from the setting sun spilled through the windows and onto the pale wooden floors. Her throat taut, Karina reflected on her behavior the previous evening. She had to convince Alex to forgive her.

Her spirits rallied when Evan arrived. She went to greet him. "Finally, my date's here!"

"We may be pathetic losers," he said, "but at least we're pathetic losers together."

Lauren approached. "You guys make a cute couple." She squinted at Karina. "Maybe he could be your new default."

Karina smiled.

Alex wandered over and said hello to Evan. Still he didn't speak to Karina. Tears stung her eyes. She rushed to the powder room and breathed deeply, telling herself Alex would get over it. But she was afraid they weren't friends anymore.

Dabbing her eyes with a tissue, she reapplied her mascara. When she stepped out into the hallway, she spotted Alex alone in the den, looking at his Blackberry. She decided to take a chance.

Entering the den, she closed the door behind her. Alex looked up, his eyes wide. Karina said, "I'm sorry about what happened last night—"

"In one week," he said, his face red, "I'm marrying your sister. I've worked too hard to reach this point to let you screw it up for me! I don't know what's in that messed up head of yours, but you need to straighten it out. This is your problem. You will not make it mine."

Alex left the room, and Karina sank to the couch. She didn't think she deserved Alex's anger, when she'd helped him get Tara back in the first place. Emotion welled in Karina's throat. She was tired of wasting her effort on people who didn't appreciate her.

From beyond the door, she heard a little voice call. She stepped into the hallway and peeked into the nursery. Nissa was standing in the crib.

Warmth touched Karina's heart. She lifted the baby into her arms, nuzzling her delicate hair. She clutched Nissa's feet and said, "What happened to your socks? Your piggies are cold."

Karina spotted the socks on the floor, and she lowered the baby into the crib. Nissa squirmed as Karina put the socks back on her.

"All better." She stroked the baby's velvet cheek. The nightlight in the corner cast a soft glow. Nissa's lids drooped. Soon, her lashes pressed together into little smiles.

Karina watched the rise and fall of Nissa's belly as she slept. Deep peace settled over her. The tension of her struggles with Alex seeped out of her, and her shoulders relaxed. She had a hot date waiting for her—a hot, gay date, which was even better, because she could just have fun with no expectations about sex. She wouldn't let Alex ruin her night.

Karina sauntered into the living room. Evan grabbed her hand and led her to the hors d'oeuvres table. They filled a couple of snack plates with beef empanadas, curried cauliflower, and ginger-glazed prawns. A pineapple rum cake and petits éclairs sat waiting for dessert.

They sat together on the love seat, the indigo cushions dotted with pillows of seafoam and chartreuse. Karina looked at Evan's sharply handsome features, his glorious blue eyes. A tickle of lust fluttered in her belly. It was impossible to be close to a man like that and not feel *something*.

"How can a hotty like you be single?"

He pondered a moment. "I fall for the wrong guys and end up alone."

She thought of Ryne, and an ache settled in her chest. "Me too."

"When I first meet someone, I don't want to worry about what could go wrong. I want to enjoy the moment and see where it leads."

"Relationships are about taking chances," she said. "You can't know ahead of time whether it will work. You have to experience it. Sometimes you get hurt, but that's part of the process."

Evan speared a prawn with a toothpick. "Life is about having fun. I don't understand people like Alex who are so afraid to make a mistake, they can't enjoy themselves."

"It's not a mistake if you learn from it. It's a personal growth experience."

Evan nodded, but the corners of his mouth turned downward. "I think I've had enough of those for a while."

Karina squeezed his hand. They snuggled together, laughing and talking. She couldn't remember the last time she'd felt so comfortable and unselfconscious with a man. Was this how love was supposed to be? Had she put too much emphasis on attraction and not enough on friendship?

No wonder Alex made her so miserable. They were too different to feel this kind of ease between them. Yes, they were friends, but they could never be friends like this. She had to stop wishing for something she couldn't have.

She leaned into Evan and stuck a fork into the last of her empanada. "Here, I've had enough. You finish it." He took a bite and washed it down with a pale ale.

Evan took the plate from her and set it on the coffee table. He took her hands. "You cheered me up. I haven't had a date this fun since...I don't remember when."

Karina agreed.

Alex approached wearing a smirk. "If you two want some privacy, there's a spare bedroom down the hall."

She looked up at him and squinted. "You're jealous because I like Evan."

"You're not his type." Alex strolled away.

Karina smiled to herself. Apparently, Alex had forgiven her, even if he wouldn't admit it. She turned back to Evan. His eyes sparkled as they talked. He seemed to enjoy listening to her, even though he didn't care what was underneath her clothes. Karina couldn't picture Evan as her new default, but she could see him becoming a good friend.

26 Do That to Me One More Time

BRIDESMAID GOWN IN HAND, WHITE PURSE HANGING off her elbow, Karina looked around her family room to make sure she hadn't forgotten anything. Shoes, jewelry, and wedding gift were waiting in the car. She breathed, then set the security alarm. Stepping onto the porch, she pulled the locked door closed.

It was really happening. Alex and Tara were getting married in six hours.

Walking to the car, Karina inhaled the morning freshness. Above her, sunbeams trimmed the clouds. She pressed her hand to her heart. This day would be a new start for her family.

She met her sisters at a spa to relax before the ceremony. Karina lay on the massage table, lavender oil scenting her skin, the masseuse's hands working her muscles. Nearby, her sisters chatted while cucumber masks replenished their faces. Karina felt a twinge of sadness. Her sisters belonged to a different club than

Karina—the club of married women—and she hadn't earned the right to join.

She had gotten her wish: Alex and Tara were happy. And Karina was alone. Not that being alone was bad, necessarily. Focusing on herself, she could figure out what she needed. Plus, she'd gone on a few dates since the breakup with Ryne. They weren't good dates, but at least she was out there.

Now, with a better idea of what she wanted, she wouldn't settle for Mr. Good Enough. Even if he took her breath away like Alex did.

Damn it. He's marrying your sister today. Get. Over. It.

⁕

After leaving the salon, Karina followed her sisters to the beach house. White bows decorated the gate, and paper lanterns lined the driveway. Tall cages of white doves flanked the entry.

Karina shook her head. Birds should be free.

Inside, the staff was busy, the maids polishing every surface. The butler carried a floral arrangement into the foyer. From the kitchen came the sound of the caterers clanging the silverware.

She joined her sisters in the master bedroom to dress. Tara wandered through the suite in pursuit of nothing, her voice high-pitched and wavering. Karina tried not to smile. While the hairdresser worked on Tara,

Karina and Lauren changed into their white cotton dresses. The tailored bodice flared into a pleated skirt.

Holly entered carrying plumeria leis and placed them one by one onto the bed. Karina picked hers up, fingertips brushing the creamy white petals kissed with buttercup. She fluttered as she put it on, breathing the perfume. The flowers and her simple white dress made her feel like a child again.

"Here's the tuberose lei for the mother of the groom," Lauren said, placing it around Holly's neck. "I ordered it especially for you."

Holly smiled. She looked chic in her sleeveless white linen dress with a jewel neckline and straight skirt.

Karina kissed Holly's cheek. "You could be a bride yourself."

Once dressed, they found the bouquets laid out on the dining room table. Purple lisianthus added color to the white orchids and lilies.

They headed out to the beach where the photographer waited. In the waning hours of day, sunlight banded the sky with gold. The sound of the surf rushed in Karina's ears. She smiled until her cheeks hurt, obeying the photographer as he posed her like Gumby. "Relax," the photographer said. "Tara, pretend you're happy!" Tara laughed, and he snapped the picture.

The guests arrived, and Tara felt a surge of excitement. She and her sisters stepped out of the camera's sights. Tara waved at Evan, who was joking with Chantel. At the edge of the lawn, her father and Holly spoke with Evan's parents.

The photographer summoned the groomsmen. Alex stood tall in his starched white shirt and pressed white pants, flanked by Sean and Dayne. He met Tara's eyes, and her stomach fluttered.

The photographer called Tara over to pose with Alex. He stood beside her with his arm around her waist and murmured in her ear, "Is it time to kiss the bride yet?"

"You'll smudge my lipstick," she whispered back.

"I'll do more than that."

"Behave," she scolded.

Finally, the photographer called Holly and Jack. He took some portraits of the parents with the bride and groom, then a few of Holly and Jack together. Tara could see Alex growing restless.

With an hour of daylight left, they got into place for the ceremony. Tara smoothed the skirt of her knee-length white shift. She held her breath. Her heart quivered as her father walked her to the flower-strewn arbor and the waiting groom.

Taking her vows, she spoke serenely, her heart full, her voice certain. Alex, his expression solemn, seemed absorbed in the ritual. But when Reverend Freeborn announced the holy union, Alex gazed at her with eyes radiating happiness. His tender kiss lingered, and her head grew light.

Their family and friends surrounded them, offering hugs and good wishes. When the commotion died down, Jack said, "While you're here, Pastor, how about you hitch Holly and me?"

The wedding party laughed, and Reverend Freeborn went along with the joke. "Have you got a marriage license?"

Jack checked his pockets, then pulled out a sheet of paper, which he handed to the minister. "I do."

Tara sputtered. She covered her mouth as warmth rose in her breast. Karina squealed, and Lauren's blank expression turned to a grin. Alex gave his mother a wry half-smile, which she returned. The guests' stares yielded to laughter. Tara flung her arms around her father's neck and he met her eyes. Their joy reflected in each other's features.

∽

In the waning light, the moon rose. Karina watched her family head to the house for the reception. She wandered over to Evan, who stood on a rocky outcropping that jutted into the ocean, his phone pressed to his ear. When he ended the call, he showed Karina a picture on his phone of Holly and Jack exchanging their vows.

"A nice exclusive," Karina said.

Evan smiled. "Can you believe they got married?"

"I'd never have expected a surprise like that from my dad," Karina said. "But there's an alchemy between him and Holly... together, they're different from the sum of their parts."

"You're okay with it? Their getting married?"

"Of course—why wouldn't I be?"

"You seem quiet."

Slowly, she nodded. "If you'd asked me six months ago what I wanted most in the world, I'd have said I wanted Alex and Tara back together. And now..." Karina's throat grew tight. "I see how happy Tara is, and I want that to be me. Isn't that awful?"

Evan scuffed the sole of his shoe against the rock. "It isn't awful to want what Alex and Tara have. Everyone wants that."

"But I've got to make better choices, instead of just letting things happen. I want someone who's made for me, like Alex is made for Tara." Palm trees bowed to the breeze. "And to find that, I need to set boundaries."

Evan raised his brow. "What's the fun of that?"

"It's a tradeoff, I guess, between fun and happiness. And I choose happiness."

Evan laid his hand on her shoulder and drew her close. Arm in arm, they ambled toward the house. She thought about how hard it had been living alone since Tara moved out. It was time for Karina to find a healthy way to fill the emptiness in her heart.

Inside, they found the living room thick with tropical plants: birds of paradise, pink heart-shaped anthuriums, dangling yellow-slippered heliconias tipped with purple. Leafy garlands draped tables set with *kalua* pork and grilled ahi marinated in *liliko'i* sauce.

Alex and Tara approached. "There you are!" Tara grabbed Karina's arm. "You missed it—I threw the bouquet. Nissa caught it."

"Very funny—then what's that in your hand?"

Tara shrugged. "Maybe we should forget the formalities. I could just *give* you the bouquet."

"I do appear to be the only single woman here."

Evan's phone beeped, and he checked the text message. He smiled at Karina. "The photo made it in."

"Evan McCade, working when he should be partying," Alex said. "I've never seen that before."

Evan nodded. "Running a newspaper is hard."

"That's what managing editors are for," said Tara.

"You're right. I can't keep letting work interfere in my social life," Evan said. "As if I had a social life."

"You need to get back out there," Tara said. "You've lost your zing."

Evan turned to Alex. "Why is it that I'm always nice to people, and you're always mean—yet you're married to the most beautiful girl in the world, and I'm still single?"

Alex scowled. "Nice is your problem. You're generous to a fault, and people take advantage of you."

Evan looked from Tara to Karina. "Am I...hallucinating? Did Alex accidentally say something nice about me?"

Alex hung his head. "Don't do this now."

"He did—Alex said something nice about me!" Evan headed to the bar, strutting like a jazz dancer.

Karina said to Tara, "I think he found his zing."

Holly and Jack approached, and Holly put her arm around Karina. "Are you all right?"

Karina embraced her. "I'm so happy for you."

"But you don't look happy," Holly said.

Karina ran her fingers over her lei, feeling the smooth petals, releasing the heady fragrance. "Something's missing from my life. I've never lived alone before—maybe I should get a cat."

Holly touched Karina's arm. "That's a wonderful idea."

"Be sure to get one at the shelter," Tara said, "so you know it's healthy. Not like those strays you used to bring home."

Karina shook her head. "How will I survive while you're on your honeymoon?" she teased. "I'll have no one to tell me what to do."

"You're forgetting about Lauren," Alex said.

Karina looked at Holly. "Why does everyone pick on me?"

"Darling, don't listen to them. You're perfect the way you are."

Karina turned to her father. "I like my new mom."

Jack grinned. "I like her too." He drew Holly into his arms and kissed her, raising a little blush on her cheeks. The two of them looked as giddy as teenagers. A deep sense of joy tugged on Karina's heart. Her father deserved this after so many years alone, and Holly, too.

Tara asked, "Where are you two going on *your* honeymoon?"

"We don't have a choice," Holly said. "You're taking the jet, so we're going with you."

"I don't think so," Alex said.

"Not the same island," Jack said, "just the same area."

Tara turned to her father. "You know where we're going? All Alex would tell me is to pack a swimsuit."

"Sorry, I'm sworn to secrecy," Jack said.

⌒◦◦⌒

The following afternoon, Tara rushed to the window of the honeymoon suite. "Diamond Head!" She gazed at the glistening crater walls that rose over the sea. On the horizon, the sun hung sleepily in the indigo sky.

Alex walked up behind her and wrapped his arms around her waist. "See, I know your favorite place on earth."

"I love this view. And I love this room!" She skipped into the bedroom. A gauzy white canopy topped

443

the carved mahogany bedposts, softening the massive frame. She plunked onto the mattress and spread her hands across the duvet.

Alex sat next to her. "This bed was lucky for us last time." His eyes were wide, apprehensive.

Tara squeezed his hand. "Susannah was conceived here," she said, a hope in her heart.

He kissed her deeply, and they reclined against the pillows. "Do you want to rest up from the trip?" he asked.

She stroked his cheek. "I want to make a baby, in this bed, with my wonderful husband. Again."

⚜

Jack and Holly lay in a chaise on the balcony of their hotel suite in Maui. Seabirds flew in sweeping arcs over the waves. The islands of Lanai and Molokai rose in the distance, luring clouds from the heavens to adorn their peaks. Jack brushed Holly's hair away from her face, and she smiled.

Jack was glad his girls had accepted the marriage. He and Holly had discussed how Tara might react. In the end, they thought Tara would be happy no matter what. And Alex—well, it was hard on him to see another man take his father's place. Jack and Holly agreed a surprise wedding would be easier on him. Lauren would be miffed about the secrecy, but she'd get over it. And Karina...the last thing Karina needed was hearing more people talk about wedding plans. Besides, Karina liked drama and romance. She'd chosen a difficult path, going into criminal law. Holly could give her a sense of calm.

Jack watched a blue-eyed dove fly off toward the water. A dolphin arched in the shallow sea. Jack turned to Holly, breathing air perfumed with ginger. "I could get used to this," he said, "the two of us here alone in paradise, with no interruptions..."

She caressed his cheek. "We can come back anytime."

"Do you know how long it's been since I've taken a week's vacation?"

"I understand. You're worried about your baby. But the manager will call if anything happens at the restaurant."

He smiled. "You're saying I should enjoy a life of leisure."

"I'm saying you can do whatever you want."

"All I wanted was to marry you." He kissed her. "How about you—what do *you* want?"

Holly didn't blink. "Grandchildren."

27 Love Is a Battlefield

THE CHILL OF LATE FALL DESCENDED ON THE CITY. Liquid amber trees teased the sky with burgundy, and ginkgo biloba leaves shone like gold coins. Sudden showers broke from the clouds.

Karina leaned back in her desk chair at work, unable to focus. Beyond her door, ladders and drop-cloths dotted the carpet. The smell of fresh paint hung in the air. Karina's eyes skimmed the men dressed in white, their arms strong from manual labor. They were a refreshing break from the dark-suited lawyers she saw all day.

Her glance wandered to one of the painters. He was in his mid-twenties, she guessed, with heavy brows and dark eyes. He seemed quiet and earnest, mind focused on his task, hands moving with easy strokes. Karina imagined how it would feel to be close to him. A man like that wouldn't be a talker, she thought. He'd find other ways to make his intentions known.

She slumped her shoulders. Sometimes celibacy felt like an unnatural state. She was in her prime childbearing years—when an attractive man brushed against her, for a split second, she couldn't think straight. It didn't seem right to constantly suppress those feelings. But what were her other choices? Love, which she didn't have, and casual sex, which she didn't believe in. She was stuck.

A knock interrupted her thoughts. Ryne stepped inside her office, his eyes bright. "I read in the paper about your dad and Holly—congratulations."

Smiling, she rose and shut the door.

"How was the wedding?" he asked.

She took his hands. "I missed you."

He drew her close. She settled into his arms, closing her eyes to shut out the memory of yellow sheets and down pillows and the rich, smooth contralto of Sarah Vaughn.

His fingertips brushed her hair before he released her. "Let's stop being so hard on ourselves. Even if we don't work as a couple, we can be friends."

She fought the desire to kiss him. "I don't think either of us wants *friendship* right now."

"We'll start slow. I'll call you for lunch sometime."

"I guess lunch wouldn't hurt." She tensed. "But no sex—I mean it."

"I didn't know restaurants offered that option." He squeezed her hand before leaving. She was taking a risk, but her stomach fluttered with possibilities.

⁓⊸∮∿⊸

The following week, back from her honeymoon, Tara sat on Karina's couch after work, holding a black-and-white stripy kitten. "How cute!" Tara said. The pads of the kitten's feet tickled her hand.

Karina took the kitten and nuzzled her. "And she loves attention—don't you, Sparkles?" Karina set her on the floor and waved a fishing-rod toy. The kitten scampered and tumbled, chasing the lure.

Despite Karina's animation, Tara thought she looked pale, as if she weren't sleeping. With tension in her stomach, Tara wondered whether the wedding was to blame.

Karina looked at her and smiled. "Hawaii was good for you. You're so tan and relaxed."

Tara touched Karina's arm. "Are you doing better?"

Karina looked away and scratched the kitten's ear. "It's nice not coming home to an empty house."

Tara put her arm around Karina. "You were so supportive while Alex and I were apart...Let me help you."

"I'm getting through it. I'm dating again, even though no one so far compares to Alex."

Tara blinked. "You mean Ryne."

"No, I mean Alex. You married the ideal man. You're a tough act to follow."

Karina grinned, but Tara scowled. Karina stared at her shoes.

Tara realized, with some annoyance, that they were actually *her* shoes—her pink Jimmy Choo slingbacks that she thought she'd lost the mate to—but she let it pass. There was no point wasting one of Karina's rare quiet moods by fighting over footwear.

Karina looked up, her eyes distant. "I thought that when you got back together with Alex, I'd feel whole again. But things will never be like they were before the shooting. Every loss teaches us how fragile life is."

"But loss also teaches us how precious life is," Tara said. "It makes the joy more vivid."

Karina squeezed Tara's hand. Tara smiled, nurturing the small hope growing inside her.

⁓᷇ℬ᷈⁓

Alex sat in his office on Thursday, massaging his brow. Karina read to him from her notes on a case. Despite the closed door, paint fumes and construction noise filled the air. The back of his neck clenched into a knot.

Karina broke off in mid-sentence. "Are you okay?"

"Migraine." He pinched the bridge of his nose.

"That's it—I'm driving you home."

"I'm okay."

"Don't be a hero. Victoria said that during the construction, we can work at home when we're not in court. We can do this just as easily at the beach house." Karina closed his blinds and turned off the light. She went to get him an energy drink from the break room.

The throbbing in his head reduced his thoughts to vague sense impressions. The intermittent hammering registered as orange pulses, the odor of fresh paint as white swirls. In the center was a dark ball of pain.

Karina returned and placed two tablets in his hand. She opened the energy drink with a pop. He downed the pills, chasing them with the soft drink. It was tart and syrupy.

Alex followed Karina to her car. He adjusted the passenger seat to make room for his long legs. Despite his sunglasses, the reflections from the water blinded him as they crossed the Coronado Bridge. When they entered the house, the butler greeted them with peppermint tea. Alex wondered when Karina had called to let the butler know they were coming.

She settled into the den. "You go lie down," she ordered Alex, "until the Advil kicks in."

"We've got work to do. The trial's next week."

She pressed her hands to her hips. "Go. Lie. Down."

In the bedroom, he changed out of his suit. He drew the curtains and lay on the bed. The caffeine left him too wound up to sleep, but it helped the pain. After twenty minutes, he rose, the throbbing reduced to a dull ache.

He entered the den. Karina scowled. "What are you doing up?"

"I'm better."

Her eyes scanned his face. "Okay, here's what I've got." She stood and handed him some papers.

Sitting at his desk chair, he skimmed through them. "That's a lot of precedent. Is it all relevant?"

She rolled her eyes, then looked around. "Is the room too bright for you?"

"You don't have to mother me." Warmth settled in his stomach, and he got to work.

Later, toward the end of the work day, Karina gazed out the western-facing windows of the den. The sun cast long shadows across the police reports she had spread out on the coffee table. She rolled her head to loosen the muscles in her neck. Bach's *Brandenburg Concertos* played on the stereo.

From her spot on the couch, Karina glanced toward Alex at the desk, crafting the opening statement for the trial. She admired the acuteness of his expression and the grace of his hand as his pen flowed across the page.

She sighed and closed her eyes, trying to fantasize about that actor from *Grey's Anatomy*. But his anatomy failed to excite her.

Alex's pen stopped. Her stomach tickled with apprehension as he sat beside her, showing her his notes. She forced her mind to focus on his opening statement, and smiled her approval. "We may have a shot at winning this case."

He grinned. "Tara should be home soon. You could stay for dinner—"

"I need to go feed the cat." She gathered the papers from her lap and stacked them on the coffee table. "I'll leave you my notes."

She rose, and he did likewise. She avoided his eyes.

A scowl broke over his face. "Something wrong?"

"I just need to go."

"You seem upset." He laid his hand on her arm.

She pulled away. "Please don't." She swallowed hard. "I know you're back with Tara, and everything's changed for you. But it hasn't been that long since the last time you kissed me, and it's not as easy for me to forget."

He blinked. "You're kidding, right?"

"Unfortunately, no."

"Kare, that wasn't us. We're not the same people."

"Maybe you're not the same person. Nothing's changed for me. Except now you're married to my sister again, and these feelings are so wrong...And before your giant ego gets any bigger, this isn't about you. I've been on lots of dates lately, and there's been some kissing but nothing more. All that sexual energy has to land somewhere, and you're it. Sorry."

"Why me?"

She combed her fingers through her hair. "When you're close to me, those memories rush back. You talk about it as if it weren't real, but there was a connection between us. You cared about me, Alex. That night in your office...I can still feel how much you wanted me."

Alex's jaw set hard. "I lost control, I admit that. But what happened between us is in the past. It needs to stay—" He broke off, suddenly pale.

Karina spun and her heart froze. She wondered how much Tara had overheard.

Tara looked into their startled faces. She grabbed the door jamb, her legs turning to liquid. Throat tightened and thoughts raced. The wrenching in her chest stole her breath.

Alex and Karina's words replayed in her mind. Clearly, there had been more between them than a single kiss. Fear gripped her, a fear she'd tried to deny, that Alex had harbored deep feelings for Karina. What had they kept from her? How long had it gone on?

She looked at him and forced sound from her lips. "What happened in your office?"

He rushed toward her. "I never slept with her."

"But you wanted to."

He scrubbed his face with his hands. "We were divorced, Tara."

She bristled at the thought of her husband with her sister, as if millipedes were crawling on her skin. Her gaze shifted from one to the other. Unmoved by their shattered expressions, her arms grew cold.

"Put this into perspective," he urged. "Kare and I flirted—admittedly, a bad idea. We kissed a couple of times. But it was no more serious than that."

"Is that supposed to be comforting?" Ire rose in her chest. "It's one thing to be drawn together after a trauma...but in your office at work? How sleazy is that!"

Karina opened her mouth to speak, but Tara said, "Don't you dare act offended. You don't have the right."

Karina reached out her hands. "Listen to me—"

"I'm done listening to you, you husband-stealing slut! How many times did I tell you to stay away from him?"

Karina pinched her palm. "I'm so sorry."

"I don't care how sorry you are. Get out of this house."

With heavy movements, Karina started to leave, but Tara said, "On second thought, I'll go."

She headed into the hallway, but Karina grabbed her arm. "Don't do this," Karina pleaded. "If you want to be mad at someone, be mad at me. Don't hurt Alex."

Tara broke away, too angry to speak. She rushed to the bedroom.

Alex followed. "We need to talk about this."

"I can't even think about it. It makes me ill." She threw a suitcase onto the bed.

His voice shook. "You can't leave me over something that happened while we were apart!"

"I need space to come to terms with this." She flung her clothes into the suitcase.

He pressed the heel of his hand to his forehead. "It's in the past. It has nothing to do with you and me."

"Nothing to do with me? You tried to seduce my sister!"

"Is this your answer to everything?" he asked. "I make one mistake—"

"I can't talk about this now."

"When would be good for you? How long will you shut me out this time?"

"Once again," Tara said, "you make me feel guilty for my emotions. I don't care about your reasons or excuses. I have a right to feel angry, and that's what I'm going to feel."

Alex reached for her. "Tara, I love you."

"Please don't."

"Tell me what I can do—"

"Let me pack in peace."

Silent, he watched her, then turned and left. She locked the door behind him. Opening her briefcase, she pulled out a pregnancy test. She placed it in her lingerie drawer, then sank to the floor and wept.

∽◦◈◦∾

Later that evening, Tara curled up on Lauren's couch, hugging a pillow to her body. Her throat ached. She tried to breathe a lungful of air, but her chest was tight, unforgiving.

Lauren, her features soft, stroked Tara's hair. "You and Alex have gotten through much worse than this."

Tara tossed the pillow aside. "That's not the issue. Alex wouldn't have pursued Karina if she hadn't been in his face every day, shaking her little...ugh! No wonder he couldn't keep his hands off her."

"But you're not worried something might happen between them now?"

"I'm not jealous of Karina." Tara massaged her palms. "It's...possessiveness. Like when we were little, and she played with my Barbies even though she had her own. So *what* if I divorced Alex—that didn't mean she could have him."

Lauren smiled.

"I know," Tara said. "But it's a visceral response."

"Can you try to get beyond that?"

Tara crossed her arms, anger simmering in her gut. "What was Karina thinking?"

"Karina can't bear to see another living thing in pain. This time, that impulse was misplaced. But nothing serious happened between her and Alex. Karina could never betray you like that."

"It feels like she *did* betray me." Tara leaned her head back and stared at the ceiling. "I know she didn't have some diabolical plan to seduce Alex. But why couldn't she stay away from him?"

"He was her brother-in-law for three years. That connection didn't die because you divorced him. Maybe you don't think it was Karina's place to help Alex heal, but she did."

"I don't mind her being friends with him—but friends don't usually end up kissing."

"Sometimes they do, especially if they're both single and lonely...and sometimes, it has nothing to do with sex. Karina made Alex feel good about himself. She tended the wound in his heart until you were ready to take over."

"She had no business getting in the middle of my relationship with him."

"At the time, you didn't have a relationship with him. Maybe in your mind you did, but in actuality..."

"Why are you being rational?"

Lauren hugged her. "I know this hurts you. Try not to blow it out of proportion. They kissed a couple of times, and they shouldn't have done that. But Tara, they didn't do it to *you*. After you lost the baby, Karina put aside her own grief to be strong for you, and Alex offered her comfort."

Tara hugged the pillow again. "How could he kiss my sister? I understand he was lonely...But Karina? Out of all the women in San Diego? He wanted to hurt me."

Lauren shrugged. "You broke his heart, Tara. If he can forgive that, can't you forgive him for kissing your sister?"

Tara closed her eyes. Rage surged through her blood. She didn't like the way it felt. A few hours earlier, she'd been full of hope. She wanted that feeling back.

It was unfair to think Alex should have been loyal to her after the divorce. Karina, though, was another story.

Tara sighed. "Do you think Karina's in love with Alex?"

"I think she was lonely, and he was convenient," Lauren said. "Plus, he saved her life."

Tara nodded. "That probably had something to do with it."

Her chest swelled with pride. Alex was a bona fide hero. How lucky was she to be married to that man?

Before going to bed that night in Lauren and Sean's spare room, Tara called Alex. Her stomach fluttered. She said, "I'm not mad at you anymore."

"Then come home."

She ached at the desperation in his voice. "I need to sort through this."

"I'll sleep in the guest room—please, Tara."

"Sweetheart..." She drew the covers around her, enveloped by their warmth. "It's only for a day or two. If I come home now, I'll end up focusing on your emotions when I need to focus on my own."

"We just got married. You can't leave me again."

She tapped her fingertips to her forehead. "I'm not leaving you."

"Just come home. I'll do anything."

"Alex..." She broke off, her heart aching. He sounded so forlorn. But she had to stand firm and think of her own needs, too. "I can't talk to you when you're like this. You don't listen. Be patient, we'll work this out."

"Tara—"

"You said you'd do anything. I need you to stop pressuring me."

She listened to the silence on the other end of the line. Finally, he said, "Okay."

"I have to go now."

"Can't we talk for a while?" he asked. "I hate being alone."

"Maybe Karina could keep you company." Tara smiled to herself.

"I thought you weren't mad anymore."

"Apparently I was wrong." She tugged at the hem of her pajama top. "But I love you—I'm not wrong about that."

Once off the phone, she took a yellow legal pad from her briefcase and drew a line down the middle of the sheet. At the top of one side, she wrote, *10 things I hate about Karina.* Beneath that, she wrote, *She always takes my things,* then threw her pen across the room. She breathed to calm herself, then got up and retrieved the pen. She sat on the bed again.

She labeled the top of the second column, *10 things I love about Karina.* She didn't want to write anything at first, but the exercise was pointless if she couldn't be fair. So she made a list:

Makes me laugh.

Helps me take myself less seriously.

Would do anything for me.

Loves me more than life.

Tara closed her eyes. A memory stirred.

Soon after they lost their mother, Tara had noticed Karina wearing their mother's charm bracelet every day. Tara discovered that Karina kept other pieces of their mother's jewelry in a little velvet bag in her purse. Karina wore them sometimes, but mostly she just kept them with her. Eventually, the pieces made their way back into their mother's jewelry box. When the sisters were ready to split the jewelry between them, Karina hadn't asked for more than her share.

Tara lifted her hand from the legal pad and pressed it to her heart. Ever since the shooting, Karina had wanted to keep a piece of Tara with her. It wasn't Tara's shoes that Karina wanted. It was Tara.

Alex and Karina were bonded by their shared wound: those days in the hospital, those days Tara couldn't remember, when she was in a coma so her body could heal—and her family was suffering a terror she could only imagine. It was humbling to think how they loved her, how their internal scars were as permanent as her external one. She touched her belly and thought about the baby she'd lost. Then, she thought about new beginnings.

She allowed herself to picture Alex cradling their child in his arms. The image awakened a buried longing, one which at last she could bear. Turning off the lamp, she slid under the covers and floated into sleep.

At dawn the next morning, Karina stood in the shower, letting cool water trickle over her. It dripped from her hair onto her shoulders and down her back until she shivered. But Tara's words from the previous day burned hot in her brain.

Karina replayed the scene, still stunned by Tara's anger. She turned off the water. Her head ached.

Wrapping a towel around her, she wondered if she should call Tara. She decided against it, afraid of making things worse for Alex. But she had to do something.

As she dressed, ideas sprinted through her mind, every one of them bad. She shook her head. Hadn't she had good judgment once? What the hell happened?

She arrived at work just as Alex did. "I don't want to talk to you," he said as she approached.

Following him into his office, she closed the door. "Alex, I'm sorry. I know you're angry—"

He banged down his briefcase. "What were you thinking? It was ancient history."

"It was three *months* ago."

"Karina, this isn't a game. It's my marriage."

"It isn't a game to me, either. Tara's my sister. I was the one who looked after her while you were in Washington nursing your wounded pride. Don't act like you've got more at stake than I do."

"Things between Tara and me were fine—and now, thanks to you, she moved out."

"Don't be melodramatic. She didn't move out."

Alex paced, his features set hard.

Karina crossed her arms. "Would you feel better if you hit me?"

"Don't tempt me."

Karina smiled. "You know it's not that bad. Tara will get over this."

He continued to glare.

She stared at the carpet, pressing the toes of her shoes into the fibers. Her throat tightened, as if her world were shrinking and all the things she cared about were collapsing into a catastrophic void.

"Alex, I love you and Tara. I'd never do anything to hurt you. Please forgive me."

Alex looked away. Karina blinked back her tears, then headed for the door. But the next instant, she turned.

"You know what? I'm not taking the blame for this," she said. "You initiated that kiss—both of them, in fact. So don't stand there all stoic and judgmental while I pour out my heart. You're in this as deep as I am."

Alex flattened his lips.

"Admit it," Karina said, "part of you is relieved this is in the open. The secret was hanging between the three of us."

Alex's gaze fell to the desk. "It was a kiss."

"I know! Yet everyone acts like we did this terrible thing. Tara divorced you—she took a vow before God, and she broke it. And what did we do? We developed these natural feelings, which we struggled against and eventually overcame." Karina hugged herself. "Well, mostly overcame."

She grew silent. The ticking of the desk clock filled the air.

"Those feelings were misplaced," Alex said.

Karina nodded. "You never had romantic feelings for me, did you."

He rubbed his knuckles together. "I didn't mean to use you."

"We both knew there was no future in the relationship. But I *did* have romantic feelings for you, and they've gotten tangled with my other emotions. Sometimes it's hard to separate them." She held her eyes closed. "I can't keep hurting Tara like this."

He twisted his wedding band. "Why does she always run away?"

"That's her thing. Lauren bottles up her emotions, I throw a hissy fit, and Tara runs away." Karina squeezed his arm. "Just remind her she's safe with you, and she'll come running back."

⚬◦✵◦⚬

At lunchtime, Tara looked up from her desk to see Alex standing in her doorway. Her palms warmed, and she smiled. He looked handsome in his shirtsleeves and blue tie that matched his eyes. But he was pale and his eyes drooped with fatigue.

Closing the door, he knelt in front of her. "Tell me how to fix this." He laid his head in her lap and wrapped his arms around her waist.

She brushed her fingers through his dark curls. "I just need time to sort through it."

"What should I have done differently?" His voice wavered. "Should I have told you when we first got back together? Should I have told you when it first happened?"

"You didn't do anything wrong."

"Then why are you punishing me?"

She knelt beside him, meeting his eyes. "I'm not doing this to hurt you."

He clutched her body, pressing his head against her shoulder. His yearning flowed inside her. She brushed her lips against his cheek, and his mouth found hers. Trembling with the pleasure of his kisses, she felt foolish at letting her insecurities cause him pain. She yielded to his touch, but he broke away.

"I'm sorry." He sat with his knees pulled up to his chest and his fists against his forehead. "I don't mean to pressure you. Whatever you need—"

"What I need is you." She covered him with kisses, happiness rising in her chest. "I made a choice to move forward with you. What happened during the divorce isn't part of our relationship."

"I shouldn't have let it happen."

She touched her fingers to his lips, silencing him. "You don't owe me an apology, or an explanation. You're my husband and I love you. That's what matters."

He gripped her arms, desperation in his eyes. "I don't want this building up inside you and coming out later."

"It won't. I'm dealing with it."

He brushed her hair back from her face. "You're my life, Tara. You know that."

She nodded. "Forever."

Alex and Tara picked up her things at Lauren's that evening, then returned to the beach house. Their footsteps echoed on the foyer's marble floor. Alex thrust his hands into his pockets, prepared to give Tara as much space as she needed. "Where do we go from here?"

She wrapped her arms around his neck. "How about the bedroom?" Pressing her lips to his, she led him to the master suite, lifting the heaviness from his chest.

"I could change into something lacy," she enticed, opening her lingerie drawer, "or something silky—"

"What's that?" He peered into the drawer, his arms around her waist. Excitement rose in his stomach.

She stood motionless. "That's a pregnancy test."

"When did you buy it?"

"Yesterday, after work. But I didn't want to find out the results while we were fighting."

He squeezed her hands, struggling to temper the hope inside him. "Could you take it now?"

"Now is good." Her eyes turned distant, and her lips formed a pout. "I'll be disappointed if it's negative."

"We haven't been trying long."

She nodded. "I should relax and let nature take its course."

"In five minutes, we can know if nature's already taken its course."

She smiled and headed into the bathroom. He paced until she returned with the tester stashed discreetly back in its package.

"What's it say?" he asked.

"Nothing yet. It takes a few minutes."

She put down the package and kissed him seductively. He tasted her greedily, his body aching for the comfort of her touch, but his mind stayed focused.

"Is it time?" he asked.

She took the tester back out of the package, and they looked at it together. "There's a blue line," Alex said.

"That's the control line—it means I took the test right."

"There's a wrong way to pee on a stick?" he joked. Then, he squinted. "I see a pink line, too."

She gazed at the tester, and her breath stilled. "It's faint, but it's there."

"What does that mean?"

Sliding the tester back into the box, she looked up at him. "I'm pregnant."

Blind with joy, he hugged her and lifted her off the floor. A squeal escaped her. He ravaged her mouth with deep, needy kisses and danced her to the bed. Pulling her down on top of him, he rolled her onto her side and looked into her serene face. "You *are* happy, aren't you?"

"Of course—I'm ecstatic!"

"And you're okay about last night?"

She poked his chest with her forefinger. "I'll never be okay about what happened between you and Karina. But I know how irresistible you are, so I can't blame her." The hurt in her eyes belied her teasing smile.

"Seriously, we need to put this behind us." He trailed kisses across her forehead and rubbed her belly. "We're having a baby. Everything else is small by comparison."

Tara nodded, and he held her close, her body pliant to his touch.

∝ℒ∝

Tara invited Karina to the beach house Saturday morning. The December day was warm, and Tara waited on the front portico, the breeze fluttering the white peasant top she wore over sky-blue Capri pants. She watched Karina drive up. Tara headed toward the beach with Karina following. As they walked on the sand, Karina said, "Okay, let me have it."

Tara smiled. "You sound as if you're going to your execution."

"That might be preferable."

"I don't want to yell at you." Tara's eyes lighted on the prickly mounds of false cypress separating the lawn from the beach. "But I don't understand how you could risk our relationship for the sake of someone you had no future with."

Karina slid her hands into her pockets. "The first time Alex and I kissed, I didn't know what was happening until it happened."

"Yet you kept flirting with him."

"I've always flirted with Alex," Karina said. "The difference was, this time, he flirted back. When we realized the situation was getting dicey, we stopped. Until that day..." Karina sighed. "Alex was lost, and I wanted to ease his pain."

"That's no reason to sleep with someone."

"I didn't sleep with him! We never even got to second base."

Tara's jaw tightened, but she didn't reply.

Karina brushed the windblown hair off her face. "I've never experienced the kind of love you and Alex have—"

"You won't find it by getting involved with men who are unavailable to you. Or by sabotaging good relationships because you're pining for someone you can't have."

"Are you talking about Ryne?"

"You were so hung up on Alex, you couldn't see the potential in that relationship."

Karina halted. "Ryne is wrong for me. My feelings for Alex have nothing to do with it."

"You say that like you still have feelings for him."

"For Ryne?"

"No, for Alex."

Karina's eyes scanned the sky. "He's an attractive man. It's hard not to notice."

"Hello!" Tara knocked on Karina's head. "He's my husband!"

"Okay, calm yourself!"

"Those feelings are incredibly unhealthy."

Karina folded her arms. "You don't know what I'm feeling. Since you moved out, I've been drifting. Alex gives me clarity. He's confident even when he's completely wrong, and sometimes I need that kind of certainty in my life."

Tara giggled, then shook her head. "You two are a pair."

"Alex and I work well together. I want to cultivate that."

"As long as that's all it is."

"Of course that's all it is."

Tara skirted the pebbles dotting the damp sand. It bugged her that Alex and Karina had a relationship that didn't involve her. Yet she could hardly ask either of them to quit their job. She hugged herself, rubbing her arms. Then, her expression cleared. "I want my Jimmy Choo's back."

Karina stopped and stared. "What?"

"The pink slingbacks," Tara said. "I left them behind when I moved out because I could only find one shoe. But they're mine, Karina."

"You never wear pink."

"That's beside the point."

Karina squinted. "I think it *is* the point."

"Even if I never wear them, they're still mine."

Karina traced shapes in the sand with her toes. "Could I buy them from you?"

"Sure. You can have them for half-price because they're used. Three hundred bucks."

"Three hundred—!" Karina pursed her lips. "Fine. I'll write you a check."

Sunshine warmed Tara's cheek. The wind calmed. She took Karina's hand, and they walked toward the house.

28 The Reason

T HE FOLLOWING SATURDAY, KARINA STOOD IN THE
men's department at Macy's, a paisley tie hung
over her hand. Swirls of purple glowed against
an amber background. She walked up to Ryne and laid
the tie across the shirt he was thinking of buying.
"Perfect," she said.

Ryne looked at the Oxford shirt, lilac cotton
woven to a rich sheen. "You're sure this color isn't too
much?"

Karina imagined how Ryne would look in the
ensemble, his blond hair contrasting with the purple.
She remembered how it felt to run her fingers through
his soft curls. She breathed to ease the tightness in her
chest.

She brushed her fingertips against the dress shirt.
"Color says a man is confident."

"Or gay."

She crossed her arms. "No woman who kisses you
will think you're gay."

"It's a first date," he said. "I doubt there will be any kissing."

"That's not very optimistic."

"I prefer to take things slow."

"Funny," Karina said, "I don't remember that." She bit her lip, thinking about their first night together—they would have done it right there on the couch if the need for a condom hadn't driven them upstairs.

He nodded. "We rushed into things, and that was a mistake."

She crinkled her forehead. Reaching out to him, she took his hand and caressed his palm. "I don't think it was a mistake. Before you, the sum total of my experience was Tim the Immature, followed by Keith the Amateur, and finally, Greg the Premature. You showed me what a relationship should be."

He smiled. She loved putting that grin on his face, but every word she'd said was true. During her long celibacy after Tara was shot, Karina had missed sex, but she hadn't thought back longingly on any of her past partners. But now, lying in bed at night alone, she was conscious of missing Ryne.

He squeezed her hand. With the shirt and tie slung over his arm, he led her to the checkout counter. "How did your date go last night?" he asked.

"It was fine. Well, boring. He took me to a sports bar."

"I hope the chicken wings were good."

Karina chuckled. "It's not his fault. He doesn't know my mother trained at the Cordon Bleu in Paris."

The cash register clicked, totaling Ryne's purchase.

He and Karina stepped outside. The day was overcast and humid, unusual for San Diego. "So listen to us, talking about our dates," Karina said. "Is that a sign of growth, or are we in denial?"

"Probably both." He looked around. "Can we make a quick stop at the bookstore? My niece's first communion is coming up, and I want to get her something special."

Karina beamed. "I love shopping for little girls."

"I thought you would."

The bookstore was bright and open, the ceiling over the escalators stretching high above the second floor. Irish folk music murmured through the speakers. The smell of coffee and nutmeg spiced the air.

They headed upstairs to the children's section. Ryne spotted a book on Noah's ark and showed it to Karina. "Do people really believe in this?"

"Some do."

"It defies logic."

"That's the power of faith."

He shook his head. "But you don't believe in it."

Karina thought for a moment, as if constructing a closing argument. "I believe the Bible is poetic rather than literal." She picked up a story Bible and read, *"God said let there be light, and there was light. And God saw that the light was good.* Can you imagine a more beautiful description of the Big Bang than that?"

Ryne took the Bible from her hand and paged through it. "These illustrations are nice," he said, "and I like the language. Clear and simple."

"I had a book like that when I was little. I used to read a story from it every night before bed. I must have read through it six or eight times before I outgrew it."

"So you think this is a good choice?"

"She'll love it."

He nodded. "You would know better than me."

Karina's stomach sank. She grabbed his hand, desperate to reach him. "Ryne, the story of Noah's ark isn't a lie—it's a parable. The important part is the blessing at the end, the covenant between God and humanity. At least...that's the way I read it. But the Bible means different things to different people. If the concept of God you grew up with doesn't work for you, then open your heart to something deeper."

He looked away. "I wish I had your certainty."

"Then stop questioning, and start listening." She brushed her hand along his arm. "God is at work in our lives, even if we can't see it. You came into my life for a reason. We fell in love for a reason. It was is our destiny."

He put his arm around her, kissing her temple. "That I can believe."

∾◦§◦∾

The butler showed Karina into the den at Alex's beach house. Despite the darkness outside, the room was brightly lit by a Moroccan-style chandelier made of polished bronze and art glass in shades of red and gold. Karina never tired of looking at it.

Alex, dressed in jeans and a black polo shirt, rose from his seat at the desk. The butler withdrew. Karina was so accustomed to seeing Alex in a suit that his casual look drew her attention to his physique. She bristled at the sight of his muscular arms. Now that Tara was pregnant, romantic thoughts of Alex made Karina feel creepy.

She handed him a folder. "You left this in my office. I thought you might need it over the weekend."

"Thanks." Alex laid the folder on his desk.

"Is Tara here?"

"She's at a journalism association meeting."

Karina rolled her eyes. "Sounds exciting."

"She seems to enjoy it."

Karina scanned Alex's steely eyes and the firm set of his jaw. "Are you mad at me?"

"Not at all." His features remained unchanged.

"Okay, then." Karina stepped toward the door. "Tell Tara I said hi."

"I'd rather she didn't know you were here."

Karina turned and stared. What the hell was he talking about?

"It's nothing personal," he said. "I see no reason to risk upsetting Tara."

Karina scowled. She knew his fight with Tara had scared him, but it was crazy to think he and Karina should avoid being alone together. "You don't think Tara will be upset if you hide things from her?"

"You came here as a coworker. So this has nothing to do with Tara."

Karina shook her head. "You can't compartmentalize our relationship, Alex. We're not just coworkers. You're my brother-in-law."

Alex straightened the books stacked on his desk. "I think it's best we maintain a professional distance."

Anger rose in Karina's chest. "So now that you're married to Tara again, I'm an inconvenience to you."

He met her eyes. "You said yourself that given our history, it might be difficult for us to disassociate those inappropriate impulses—"

"Stop the lawyer-speak and talk to me like a human being."

"The last time we were here alone together, you started rehashing the past—and Tara walked *out* on me."

"She was gone one night. She's not suspicious of us. But she will be, if we keep secrets from her."

Alex massaged his temples. "Whatever."

Karina crossed her arms. "You think I'm still hung up on you."

"It's understandable if—"

"Oh no. I'm not listening to you analyze my feelings when you can't even admit your own."

"I was never in love with you."

Pain twisted in her chest. He excelled at using honesty as a weapon.

"And you think I was in love with you? No, Alex. When I looked at you, I could see the gaping hole in your heart, and I wanted to fill it up. But I'm done being used by men like you."

"Do *not* lump me in with those losers you date."

Her eyes widened. He was actually taking offense, as if he had the right. "What makes you any different? You never thought about what I needed. You *used* me to get to my sister."

He pursed his lips and looked away.

Karina shut the door with a heavy thud. She held back her ire to keep her voice down. "I've been jealous of Tara my whole life, and when you and I got involved, you fed every insecurity I had about her. I was the less gorgeous, less saintly, less loveable version of her, but still acceptable for a good lay. And if you squinted just right, you would see Tara instead of me when you fucked me."

His eyes darkened. "I won't dignify that with a response."

"Please, you love the sound of your own voice as much as any litigator. If you could deny it, you would."

He paced, combing his fingers through the hair on the back of his head. Karina could see anger in him, but something more as well. As if he were at war with himself, trying to decide whether it was worse if he'd used her, or if he'd had real feelings for her. Poor Alex, finally having to deal with the truth about himself and Karina. The truth she had been struggling with for five months.

And as she watched him, she could finally see how their relationship might have played out—if she weren't Tara's sister, and she'd been free to hook up with him that first night they kissed. The heat would have faded once she realized how his need for control prevented him from expressing, or even acknowledging, his emotions. She'd have tired of him quickly and been left with anger and frustration. And he'd have found comfort in Tara's arms. They'd be in the exact same place they were now.

Alex rubbed his palms together. "I didn't use you." His voice was aloof, almost clinical. "I was in love with Tara when I met you—there was never a chance for you and me. But while Tara and I were apart, you were the only woman who made me forget about her for five minutes. When I kissed you, I wasn't thinking about Tara. I was thinking about you."

His words hit Karina like a punch to the stomach. She'd ached to hear them for so long, but now she didn't want them. She didn't want Alex. He was Tara's. And Tara was welcome to him.

He looked out the window. Karina could see the struggle still etched in his features. Some other emotion was needling at him. She approached and laid an encouraging hand on his shoulder.

"I lost control with you," he murmured. "That's never happened before."

"Maybe that's why you don't let me get close. You're afraid that if you admit your feelings, you'll lose control again. But nothing could happen between us now."

The muscles in his face grew rigid.

Karina squeezed his arm. "You may be your father's son, but you're not a cheater."

Alex rubbed his fists together. In a barely audible voice, he asked, "How can you be sure?"

"Because I know you." She grasped his hands. "You let down your guard with me because I was safe. You knew I'd never betray Tara with you. But you also knew that you didn't have to pretend with me. We've seen each other at our worst, at our most raw. That bond will never go away."

Alex nodded. "That doesn't explain the sexual attraction."

Karina rolled her eyes. "Don't overanalyze it, Alex. I'm hot, and you were horny. Plus, you were single, which you aren't now. You wouldn't cheat on Tara."

"People do things under stress they wouldn't do otherwise."

"You and I didn't sleep together—even though we both wanted to—and we fought the attraction for a good three months before we even kissed again. I'd say that's commendable. Even if Tara thinks I'm a husband-stealing slut."

"She was angry."

"Are you angry?" Karina asked. "Because of what Tara overheard?"

He crossed the room. He picked up the folder she had brought him, tapping the corner on his desk. "I ignored the tension between you and me, hoping it would go away. Even though I knew it wouldn't be that simple for you."

She watched him, surprised by his honesty. He felt guilty for hurting her. All this time he'd been so stoic while his emotions had been churning underneath.

Warmth gathered in her chest. "I'm better now."

"I'm glad." He looked at her with sudden intensity. "I will always care about you. You know that, right?"

Karina swallowed hard, blinking back tears. She hugged him. He wrapped his arms around her and laid his cheek against her head.

"This is how we were meant to be," she said. "Good friends."

Alex held her a moment longer, then pulled back and smiled.

With his arm slung across her shoulder, he walked her to the front door. They had gotten as far as the foyer when Tara entered. Alex let his arm fall.

Karina beamed, scanning Tara's figure for a baby bump she knew wasn't there yet.

Tara hugged Karina. "I thought I saw your car."

Karina kissed her cheek. "How are you feeling?"

"You know me—I never feel healthier than when I'm pregnant. Except that I crash around nine o'clock."

Karina rubbed Tara's belly. "Hi, baby."

"It's not a baby. It's an embryo."

Karina snuggled against her sister. "I wish I could hold it."

"It's the size of a peanut."

Karina rested her head on Tara's shoulder.

Tara stroked Karina's hair. She said to Alex, "I can't believe you told her I was pregnant this early."

Alex smiled. "She finagled it out of me."

"I took one look at that big, stupid grin on his face, and I knew," Karina said.

"You mean like the one he's wearing now?" Tara asked.

Karina let go of Tara and went to hug Alex. "I love seeing you so happy."

"Thank you." His eyes sparkled.

Karina kissed Alex, then followed suit with Tara. Karina opened the front door and said, "Goodbye, baby!"

"Embryo!" Tara called.

Karina pulled the door closed, then danced to the driveway. She looked up at the inky sky and the brilliant starlight, breathing the chill air. And she realized, with a thickening in her throat, that this was what she wanted.

She crept down the path behind the garage and onto the smooth grass of the putting green. Looking down the shoreline toward the Hotel del Coronado, she watched its white lights glitter. She remembered Tara's birthday party, just seven months earlier, and how everything then had seemed wrong.

The pain of losing Susannah would never leave her family. But through the loss, love had endured. Her family had been tempered by tragedy, and now they were stronger. Karina was stronger. She felt more confident than she had since her law school graduation.

Closing her eyes, she listened to the ocean. Hope filled her heart. Though still single, she was never alone.

She ambled back to her car. Sliding a CD of *The Nutcracker* into the player, she hummed along to "The Dance of the Sugarplum Fairies." One day soon, her own fairytale would come true.

THE END

More Books by Andrea Hershey

Read more of Karina's story in *Wild Flower Fields*, available in December 2018. Visit Andrea's website at www.AndreaHershey.com and sign up for her fan list to learn more about new releases, special offers, and exclusive content.

About the Author

Andrea Hershey is a women's fiction author in Raleigh, North Carolina who writes happily-ever-after stories about romantic love and family dynamics. When she's not reading or writing, she enjoys gardening, scuba diving, and hiking active volcanoes with her husband.

www.ingramcontent.com/pod-product-compliance
Lightning Source LLC
Chambersburg PA
CBHW070827260626
47170CB00007B/2290